Eventual Beginnings
Stories Short and Longer

by

Joe
DeRouen

SMALL THINGS PRESS

SmallThingsPress.com

Visit Joe's website at www.JoeDeRouen.com

Find Joe on Facebook at www.Facebook.com/jderouenwriter

Connect with Joe on Bluesky via @joederouen

First Printing: June 2025

ISBN 978-1-7374975-1-6

Cover art by Getpremades.com

Author photo by Sunny Skaggs, SunnySkaggsPhotography.com

Editing by Jason Malandro

Proofreading by Andee DeRouen, Rebecca Jones, Jessica Walters, and Brittani Morrison

FIRST EDITION

Printed in the USA

✳ ✳ ✳

Small Things Press | www.SmallThingsPress.com

For Rebecca Jones and Jessica Walters, my sisters from different misters (and, in Jessica's case, a different mother as well.)

Novels by Joe DeRouen

The Small Things Trilogy:
Small Things
Threads
A Pattern of Shadows

The Small Things Trilogy Omnibus

Memories of a Ghost
Leap Year

Short Story Collections by Joe DeRouen

Odds and Endings: Fiction Short and Otherwise
Eventual Beginnings: Stories Short and Longer

Anthology Appearances

May the Fourth: A Collection of Stories Across Time and Space
The Cat, the Crow, and the Cauldron: A Halloween Anthology
Klarissa Dreams Redux
LegionPress: An Anthology of Speculative Fiction
House of Haunts
Hospital of Haunts

Acknowledgements

Thank you to everyone who contributed to helping make this collection happen, including (always first and foremost) my wife Andee and our son Fletcher, as well as Michael Neill, Jessica Walters, Robin Raven, Jenny Elliott, Rebecca Jones, and Brittani Morrison.

Special thanks go to both past and present members of my Patreon, including Angela Barnes, Shannon Brown, Kim Cameron, Cassie Cook-Ward, Bert Edens, Kris Milstead, Sarah Liberman, Krystle Poirier, Hannah Roberts, and Tamara Sipes.

Special thanks also go to the following people, whose suggestions via my Patreon and other arenas helped inspire some of the stories in this collection: Andee and Fletcher DeRouen (Hidden Rooms), Michael Neill (Alternate Life and The Magical Book), Jessica Walters (FORB1DD3N FRU1T), Elizabeth Lieberman (The Urn), Angela Barnes (What If), Rebecca Jones (A Match Made in…Somewhere), Meredith Wells (Haunted), Annie Sturdivant (Forks), Chris Greenberg (Online Undead), Cassie Cook-Ward (Next Time is Now), and Irene Knouff (Tom Cat).

Extra special thanks to Lisa Lauenberg, Tasha DeRouen, my photographer Sunny Skaggs, and my editor Jason Malandro.

Eventual Beginnings

Stories Short and Longer

Table of Contents

Preface

Way back in September of 2018, I started a Patreon page. To inspire people to subscribe, I decided to hold drawings from my subscriber pool. Whatever name I drew, that person would get to suggest what sort of short story they wanted me to write for that month. They could be as vague or as specific as they chose. Twelve of these sixteen stories were inspired by their suggestions. I definitely got more than I bargained for!

Rogers, Arkansas, December 4th, 2024

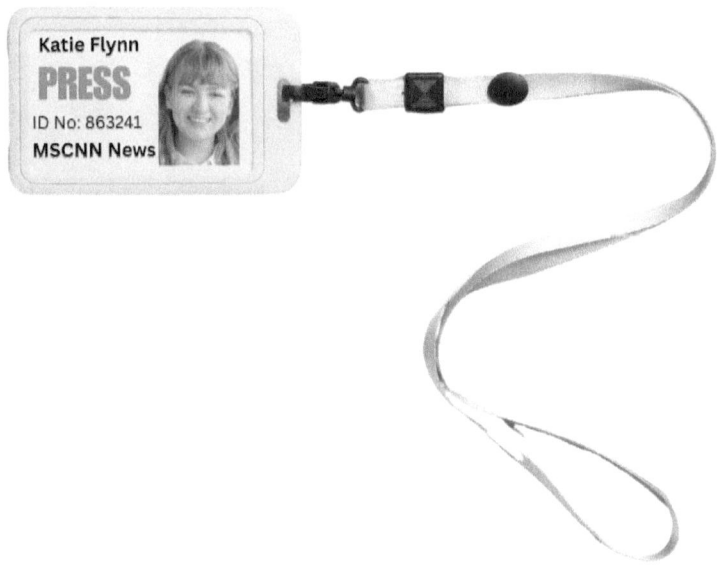

Connections

Justy Friedman was in her bedroom, getting ready for her first day back at high school after Thanksgiving break, when it started. One moment she was slipping into a cute little blue skirt she'd bought specifically for today, and the next she was rolling around on the floor, screaming at the top of her lungs.

The room had gone completely black, and someone was on top of her, straddling her, their hands on her face. She couldn't catch her breath. She tried desperately to push away the hands, but they wouldn't stop. Now the hands were wrapping around her throat, squeezing, choking the life out of her, and she couldn't even see her assailant.

"Justy?" asked a far-off voice, "are you okay?"

She reached out, grabbing at whoever was on top of her, digging her fingernails into their cheeks, and for just a second, she could breathe again. Then a fist punched her jaw, and she felt a tooth dislodge as her mouth filled with blood. The hands were around her throat again, squeezing harder, and she felt like she might pass out.

"Justine, you're scaring me," said the voice. "I'm going to call 911."

She blinked. The hands were gone, and she could breathe again. She opened her eyes, heart pounding, as she stared up into the face of her mother. "Mom…what happened?"

Regina Friedman's face looked as white as a sheet. She held her phone in one hand, a finger from her other hand hovering over the screen.

"I was hoping you might tell me that," Justy's mother said, letting her hands drop to her side. "What's going on? You scared me half to death."

Justy had no idea what was going on. All she could remember was an overwhelming feeling of dread, and hands clamping down around her throat. Her neck no longer hurt, and her jaw seemed fine. She shuddered as her mother helped her to her feet.

"I think I had a bad dream," Justy said, as she finished putting on her skirt.

Her mother raised an eyebrow. "Half-dressed? Justy, are you having...problems again?"

Justy had been overweight for most of her life. At thirteen, fed up with being picked on and bullied at school, she'd begun to diet. Dieting had turned into an obsession. By fourteen, she was 5'4" tall and weighed 78 pounds. She was terrified of eating, dizzy all the time, and having heart palpitations.

She'd fainted in the bathroom one night, and her mother found her and called an ambulance. She'd woken in the ER, attached to a saline IV, diagnosed with anorexia. What followed was months of treatments and therapy. She was now nearly eighteen years old and weighed in at a healthy 127 pounds, which was perfectly normal for her height and build.

That was over four years ago, and even though she'd done it for all the wrong reasons, the dieting worked. She'd gotten skinny and had become one of the most popular girls in high school. No one made fun of her anymore, and boys were always falling all over themselves for her attention.

"I'm fine, Mom," she said, looking her mother in the eyes. "I promise. I'm eating normally. I haven't lost weight. It really was just a bad dream."

"If you say so." She pulled Justy into a hug, and then kissed her forehead before letting her go. "Now finish getting ready. You don't want to be late for your first day back at school."

After her mother left the room, Justy tried to remember the vision, the nightmare, or whatever the hell it had been. All she could recall was the terror she felt, almost like she was dying, and those hands wrapped around her throat, squeezing the life out of her.

She sat back on her bed, eyes scanning her surroundings. Her school-issued Chromebook was on her desk, just where she'd left it. Her Chappell Roan poster was on the wall across from her bed, and her collection of Build-a-Bear plushies sat atop her dresser.

Samantha, the half-Siamese/half-tabby cat she'd been gifted on her tenth birthday, wandered into the room. Justy scooped the cat up into her arms, hugging her, not really caring if her clothes ended up covered in cat hair.

"There's my good girl," she whispered to the cat. "You'd never let anything bad happen to me, would you?"

She let the cat hop down on the bed beside her. Maybe she really did fall back asleep and the whole thing truly was just a bad dream, exactly like she'd told her mother. That made the most sense. Besides, she had more important things to worry about today.

Kissing Samantha's head, she rose from the bed and walked into the bathroom that adjoined her bedroom. She stared at herself in the mirror, and for a moment felt like someone else. She shook her head and ran a brush through her long blonde hair, quickly put on makeup, and then made her way downstairs for breakfast.

Justy sat in the cafeteria with Ashlie Bowman, Chrissie Stewart, Tegan Statlander, and Mikayla Danvers, eating lunch and talking about their college plans. They went to the Arkansas Academy of Fine Arts, a charter high school in Rogers, Arkansas, and were in their senior year. They were all planning to go to the University of Arkansas in Fayetteville next year, just a thirty minute or so drive from Rogers. Justy couldn't wait.

"Oh, God," said Ashlie, looking over Justy's shoulder, "here comes fatty."

Justy glanced at the new kid, Emmet. He wasn't that fat, not really, but he was definitely overweight. She didn't enjoy making fun of him, especially given her history, but if it kept her in the popular crowd, she'd do it anyway. What other choice did she have?

Ashlie was the de facto leader of their little clique, and for whatever reason had taken an immediate dislike of Emmet, which unfortunately meant the other four had to follow her lead or risk being ostracized.

"Don't let him get too close," said Justy, in a stage whisper, "or he'll run you over like a tank."

They all giggled, while Emmet stared at the floor and kept walking. Just like she used to do at her old school when the kids made fun of her weight.

This was wrong. In her mind's eye, she saw herself getting up from the table, walking over to Emmet, and apologizing for her words, maybe even giving him a hug.

She shook her head. She couldn't do that. She'd be the laughingstock of the entire school. Instead, she simply watched with a pit in her stomach as Emmet walked as far across the lunchroom from them as possible and took a seat by himself at an empty table.

"Why're you watching old thunder thighs?" asked Tegan, cocking her eyebrow at Justy. "Do you wanna bang him or something?"

All the girls laughed, and Justy's face turned crimson. "No thanks," she said, rolling her eyes. "I was just wondering why he transferred here halfway through his senior year, that's all."

"Probably because all the kids at his other school made fun of him or something," said Chrissie. "Though why he thought it'd be any different here is anyone's guess. He really needs to get his head out of his ass and work on losing some of that blubber."

They all laughed, but inside Justy felt like crying. This is the sort of thing the kids said about her at her old school, throughout grade school and junior high.

Enrolling at AAFA for Justy's Freshman year of high school after winning her battle with anorexia was her mother's idea, her way of giving Justy a fresh start, and she hadn't missed her old school at all with one exception: her best friend Matilda.

She and Matilda had stayed in contact throughout that first year of high school but eventually lost touch. She'd thought about emailing, texting, or calling her many times but felt embarrassed that it had been so long and so she never followed through. The longer time went, the harder it was to make contact.

Justy listlessly picked at her lunch of chicken nuggets and French fries, waiting for lunch hour to be over, while her friends talked about what they'd done over the Thanksgiving break. After this morning and the encounter with Emmet at the start of lunch, she didn't have much of an appetite for food or conversation.

"So, Justy…how was your Thanksgiving?" Mikayla asked, concern in her eyes.

"Oh, it was fine," Justy said. "We went to visit my grandma in Dallas, ate turkey and cranberry sauce and stuff, just like we always do. Same old, same old."

Mercifully, the bell rang, cutting the conversation short. Justy said goodbye to her friends and headed to her AP Government and Politics class.

She really needed to go to the bathroom. She should have gone after lunch but had been distracted. Mrs. Green was talking about something that happened a zillion years ago, when Jimmy Carter was president, and she hated to be interrupted, but Justy did not want to pee in the middle of the classroom, so she raised her hand.

"Yes, Justy?" asked Mrs. Green, with a long sigh. "What do you need?"

"I'm sorry, Mrs. Green, but I really need to go to the bathroom."

"You really *need* to learn to take your bathroom breaks before class and not during."

Justy remained silent, staring defiantly at Mrs. Green. Finally the teacher sighed again, made a shooing motion with her hand, and that was all the permission Justy needed. She hopped away from her desk and raced for the door.

She'd miss some things about AAFA once high school was over, she thought as she walked down the hallway and towards the bathrooms, but one thing she wouldn't miss was Mrs. Green. She was definitely ready for college and the freedoms that would entail.

And there was Emmet Sapp, walking towards her. She quickly pivoted away from him, ignoring her aching bladder, and pretended she was doing something at someone's random locker while waiting for him to pass.

She still felt awful for that thing she'd said about him being a tank, just like she always felt awful insulting him or any of the other, non-popular kids in school, but what was she supposed to do? She hated the thought of going back to being one of the kids who was made fun of like she'd made fun of Emmet, but was being one of the assholes really any better? Was being popular that important to her?

Now Emmet was at his locker. Good. She quickly darted past him and made her way into the girl's bathroom. The bathroom was empty, so she had her choice of stalls, which was always nice. She hated the one on the far-right end. The toilet seat was all janky, and had been that way since last year, which made for an all-around uncomfortable experience.

She let herself into the middle of the five stalls and sat down to relieve her bladder and check TikTok on her phone. One moment she was looking through some #BookTok videos, and the next she was somewhere else entirely.

She found herself in a dark room, lying on a bed. Someone was on top of her again, just like this morning, their hands squeezing, wrapped around her neck, and she couldn't move, couldn't breathe, could barely even think.

She tried to call for help, tried to move, but her arms were pinned to her side. Her vision darkened, darker even than the room she was in, and she felt herself begin to lose consciousness.

2

Emmet Sapp wasn't having a good day. First it was those stupid girls at lunch making fun of him, and now he couldn't find his homework for his AP English class. He searched through his backpack, hoping he'd simply misplaced it, but it just wasn't there.

"I'll give you until the end of the day to turn it in," said Mrs. Crowder, not unkindly, "but if I don't have it by then, it'll be counted as late."

"Yes, ma'am," he mumbled, not meeting the teacher's eyes.

"You're such a dumbass," whispered Nick Sebastian, from the seat behind him, as soon as the teacher was out of earshot. "Can't even keep track of your homework."

Nick Sebastian, not coincidentally Justy Friedman's boyfriend, had been bullying him ever since the first day he'd stepped foot inside this stupid charter school less than a month ago. Emmet ignored him when he could, and walked away when he couldn't, but it was almost becoming more than he could take.

He wondered what Nick would do if he turned around right now and punched him in the nose. But, no, he couldn't do that. He'd be the one who got into trouble and his parents would never let him hear the end of it.

He would be so happy when high school was over and done with. He hated this school even more than he'd hated Rogers West. At least there, he'd had Tildie. Until a month and a half ago, that is, when she'd left him and everyone who loved her behind.

Which is how Emmet had wound up transferring to the Arkansas Academy of Fine Arts High School halfway through his senior year. He absolutely refused to continue going to Rogers West after Tildie left. It was either transfer to another school or drop out, and there was no way in hell his parents would allow him to drop out. AAFA had an opening, and so they quickly enrolled him here.

Had that been a mistake? He wasn't that into the arts, and the bullies here somehow seemed more vicious than the ones he'd already known. But what was done was done. He just needed to put his head down and push through this final year of high school as best he could, and then he could tackle whatever came next.

He couldn't stop thinking about his missing essay. Had it fallen out of his backpack and into his locker somewhere? He raised his hand and asked if he could go look for it, and thankfully Mrs. Crowder said yes.

Emmet quickly left English class and made a beeline for his locker. Class would be over in just a few minutes, so he needed to hurry. He needed to find his essay on the writings of Stephen King. He'd spent weeks working on that thing, and the thought of not getting credit for it really pissed him off.

He searched his locker from top to bottom and back again, but the essay was nowhere to be found. He distinctly remembered putting it in his backpack this morning. If it wasn't in his backpack or his locker, where could it be?

He was slowly walking back towards his English class, feeling defeated, when he noticed something on the floor. It was the first page of his essay. What the hell? He picked up the paper. It looked exactly like it had this morning before he put it in his backpack, other than the fact that it was missing the other nine pages and the staple that had once held the pages together.

And there was the second page, about five feet down the hallway. He knelt to pick it up and then saw yet another page just a few feet away from that one. He followed the trail, down the hallway and around the corner, and before long had collected nine of the ten pages of his essay.

The trail, however, ended at the girl's bathroom, and there was no way in hell he was going inside to look for that last page. If someone caught him, he'd never live it down.

This had to be a prank. There's no way the essay just somehow fell out of his backpack and then dispersed itself down the hallway, ending at the door into the girl's bathroom.

He could see it now. He'd open the door, go inside, and someone would be there with their phone, taking pictures of him, posting them all over social media. Look, the big, fat tub of lard went into the girl's bathroom! This prank was so predictable.

But how had they gotten into his locker?

He heard a noise from within the walls of the bathroom, causing him to jump back. It sounded like a grunt, or maybe even a stifled scream. Was that how they intended to lure him into the bathroom?

"Help me," yelled a voice from inside, followed by another grunt.

Emmet looked around. The halls were empty. This was so obviously a set up. Just another way to humiliate him. He almost walked away from the prank, but then had a thought: what if it wasn't a prank after all? What if someone inside the bathroom really did need help? Could he live with himself if he walked away?

The bell rang, startling him. He almost sprinted for the door to Mrs. Crowder's room, which was just down the hallway, but instead spun in a slow circle, trying to make up his mind before the hallways filled with his fellow classmates.

"Screw it," he muttered, taking one last look around before pushing open the door.

The bathroom was empty, save for the last page of his essay on the floor in the middle of the room. Attached to it was the missing staple. Snatching the paper from the floor, he quickly surveyed the area. All but one of the five doors to the bathroom stalls stood open. He turned to leave.

"Get off me," a voice cried out from that one closed stall.

Without even thinking, he spun back around, ran to the stall, and yanked the door open. Justy Friedman was there, rolling around on the floor, clutching at her throat, her eyes scrunched shut and her cheeks covered in tears.

He dropped to his knees beside her, taking her hands in his. If this were a prank, it was an exceptionally good one, because the girl looked like she was scared out of her mind.

"It's okay, Justy," he said, pulling her up to a sitting position. "You're okay. Are you okay?"

Justy's eyes sprung open and she looked terrified. Her cheeks were red, like someone had slapped her. She scooted away from him, her back up against the toilet. "Where am I?"

"You're in the bathroom," Emmet said. "What happened?"

"I don't know," she whispered, her blue eyes wide and filled with tears. "Someone was choking me. At least I think they were. I don't understand what's happening to me."

"Maybe you fell asleep somehow and had a bad dream?"

Confusion danced through her eyes. "But it felt so real. What's going on?"

"I have no idea, but it isn't good. Do you want me to walk you to the school nurse?"

"No," she said. "They'll just call my mom, who already thinks I'm a freak."

Emmet stared into her eyes. Why was he here, helping this girl who at lunch had called him a 'tank' and made fun of him? He shook his head.

Just because she'd been awful to him, didn't mean he had to return the favor.

Sighing, he helped her to her feet, surprised when she hugged him. He tensed for a second before returning the hug.

"It's going to be okay," he said awkwardly, patting her back.

"I've been such a bitch to you," said Justy, almost as if reading his mind, "and you helped me anyway. How'd you even know I was in here?"

"I heard you yelling from out in the hallway. No one else was in here when I opened the door. I'd been out there searching for my English essay that I somehow lost and found one of the pages in the hallway. I kept walking down the hall and finding more pages. It was so strange. I found the second to the last one right outside the door to the girl's bathroom, and then I heard you scream. I came in and the last page was lying in the middle of the floor. As soon as I grabbed it, I heard you yelling again from inside the bathroom stall."

She stared at him with wide eyes. "That's weird. I was out in the hallway like five minutes ago and didn't see any papers. I don't understand what's going on."

"Me either," he admitted.

"What was I yelling?"

He closed his eyes for a second to think. "Well, before I came in, I'm pretty sure it was 'help me.' It was hard to hear from out in the hallway. And then once I was in here, I think it was something like 'get off of me.' But when I opened the door, you were the only one in there."

They heard voices in the hallway, coming closer, and then the sound of the door opening. Shit. If he were caught in the girl's bathroom, he'd never live it down.

"Quick, in here," whispered Justy, pulling Emmet into the stall with her and closing the door.

Emmet crouched on top of the toilet so no one would see his feet while Justy stood in front of him, her long blonde hair so close to his face that it tickled his nose. She did smell nice, he thought, then chastised himself for thinking such things while hiding in the girl's bathroom with a girl he barely knew.

"The first day back is always the hardest," said a girl's voice from outside the stall, "the day just seems to go on and on forever."

"Tell me about it," said another girl.

A moment later the sink turned on and he could hear one of them washing their hands and, a moment after that, the sound of the door closing shut. They waited a few seconds longer before Justy opened the door and stepped out into the bathroom, allowing Emmet to hop off the toilet.

"We're probably going to be late for our classes," said Justy, with a half-smile. "What do you say we just bail on the rest of the day, maybe go somewhere and talk? I have to figure out what's wrong with me before it's too late."

So now they were friends? He almost responded with something about him being a tank and afraid he might accidentally run her down but bit his tongue. This girl had been nothing but mean to him since he started at this school, so why should he help her now?

The second bell rang, which meant they were officially late for their classes. Emmett sighed. He might as well just go with it. He'd deal with the consequences of skipping school later.

"Okay," he finally said, "I don't know why I'm agreeing to this, but I need to drop off my essay at Mrs. Crowder's room before I do anything else."

"That's fair," she said, smiling. "Meet me out in the parking lot. Do you have a car?"

"I don't," he admitted.

"Well, lucky for us, I do. But you'll be driving, if that's okay. I'd hate to be behind the wheel and have another seizure, or whatever the hell that was."

He couldn't argue with that.

3

Kevin Haj leaned back in his desk chair, eyes closed, trying to make sense of what was happening to him. He should be preparing lesson plans for next week's algebra classes—that's what he usually did during his break period, when he wasn't grading papers—but he just couldn't concentrate, not with the way he was feeling today.

Like most people, he'd suffered small bouts of anxiety before, even a full-blown depression once, in his early twenties, but nothing like this, and for no fathomable reason as far as he could tell. All day, he'd been jumping at shadows. Every little noise startled him and set his heart to racing.

Miss Kirby said hello to him in the hallway a few minutes ago and he'd literally jumped. She'd laughed and apologized for startling him, which somehow made him feel even more panicky.

He shook his head. He'd been teaching for nearly fifteen years. Teaching was almost second nature to him at this point, or at least it had been before early this morning, when he'd awoke in a panic over some dream he couldn't even remember. Now he couldn't even write a damned lesson plan to save his life.

A knock reverberated through the classroom and Kevin jumped, his arm hitting a stack of papers, causing them to go flying. His heart pounded hard against his ribcage as he stared across the room, eyes wide, wondering who might be at the door and what they wanted.

What in the living hell was wrong with him?

He took a deep breath and counted to ten before calling out, "Who's there?"

A pause, and then, "It's just me, Lela. Um, Lela Kirby. May I come in?"

He stood up on shaking legs, supporting himself with a hand on his desk. He took three more deep breaths and then walked across the room, unlocking and opening the door.

"You seem a little…off today," said Lela, concern in her eyes. "I just came by to check on you. Are you doing okay?"

He forced a smile. "I'm okay. I just haven't been getting enough sleep lately."

That much was true, at least insofar as last night was concerned. Once he'd woken from that stupid dream at around four in the morning, he'd never been able to fall back asleep.

"First day back at school is always tiring anyway," Lela said. "Hopefully you'll be able to get better sleep tonight."

He looked at her, about to say something, when the room began to shift. Lela Kirby was gone, transformed into a younger, brown-haired woman, maybe a teenager.

She looked into his eyes and mouthed the words "help me" as tears began to cascade down her cheeks.

There were bruises around her throat, and blood dripped from her mouth. She almost looked familiar, like someone he knew or maybe had seen a few times somewhere, perhaps at Wal-Mart or the coffee shop he liked to go to after school or something. He blinked and the woman vanished, replaced once again by Lela Kirby.

"Kevin, are you okay? You look like you've seen a ghost."

"I think maybe I have," he muttered, as much to himself as to her.

"What do you mean?"

He sighed and glanced at the clock hanging on his wall above the dry erase board. He had a little less than 45 minutes before his next class started.

"I had a bad dream last night," he said, the words tumbling out in a rush, "and I've felt off ever since."

"About what? I mean, if you don't mind me asking."

"That's the thing, I don't really remember. I woke up scared for my life and I've felt panicky ever since. It just doesn't make any sense. I've had bad dreams before, but they usually don't affect me like this, especially not if I can't even remember them."

"Brains are weird sometimes," she said. "I know that better than most."

He remembered then that Ms. Kirby taught psychology. "Do you...do you think I'm mentally ill?"

"Mr. Haj, we're all a little 'mentally ill,'" she said, laughing. "I'm a little OCD, for example, not to mention ADHD to the hilt. In your case, however, I think you probably just need a good night's sleep."

"I haven't told you everything. Just now...when you came in here, after you came in, actually...for a second you changed, and I thought you were...I thought you were someone else."

"What do you mean, I changed? Who did you think I was?"

"You just looked...different somehow, but also strangely familiar. This person I saw...she was young, maybe a few inches shorter than you, wearing a blue top with a yellow butterfly on it, I think, and a matching skirt. Long brown hair, wearing blue glasses."

He didn't say anything about the blood, or the bruises around the poor woman's throat. Lela was probably around 5'6" tall and had dark brown eyes and short red hair. She looked nothing like this mysterious woman he'd imagined.

"And you thought I was her?"

He shook his head. "No. I don't know how to describe it. It was like you vanished for a moment and she appeared, if that makes any sense at all. I know I sound crazy."

"Well, maybe a little," she said, smiling. "But probably no more so than anyone. Like I said, brains are weird, but…wait a second, you said she was wearing blue glasses, right?"

Kevin nodded. "Yes, blue glasses."

"What shade of blue?"

He closed his eyes for a second, trying to picture the woman he thought he'd seen. "Light blue, I think. Like sky blue. They were very bright. Why?"

Her eyes grew wide. "Long brown hair in a bubble ponytail?"

"What's a bubble ponytail?"

"You know, several hair ties spaced down her ponytail to create the appearance of bubbles."

"I've never heard of that, but her hair did kind of look like that, now that you mention it. Do you know her?"

"Is she okay?"

"What do you mean, 'is she okay?' As far as I know, she doesn't actually exist." He remembered the bruises on her neck, the blood dripping out of her mouth. She definitely didn't look okay. But how could Lela know any of that?

She slowly backed away from him. "Never mind, just a silly question. I really need to get back to my classroom."

"No, wait. Please." He snaked a hand around her wrist. "Do you know this person?"

"Of course I do," Lela snapped, as she pulled away from him, "and so do you!"

She turned around and stomped out of the classroom.

4

Justy stood in the student parking lot, crouched down beside her blue Hyundai Venue, wondering how much longer it was going to be before Emmett showed up. She glanced at her phone. It was nearly 3:00. Where was Emmett?

"I'm here," he said from behind her, making her jump. "Sorry, I didn't mean to startle you."

"It's okay," she said, her heart beating heavy in her chest. "Did you turn in your essay?"

She'd never really looked at Emmett before. He was tall, had green eyes, and brown hair. Sure, he was overweight, but so what? It was definitely better to be overweight than anorexic. To top that off, he was handsome, smart, and he'd possibly even saved her life.

"I did. Now if we're going, let's get out of here before anyone sees us. Especially Nick. He might get the wrong idea and be even more of an asshole to me than he already is."

Nick Sebastian? Justy laughed. "We're not together. I dated him for like three seconds. He really is an asshole. You really need to pay better attention, Emmett. Now, let's go!"

She tossed her keys to Emmett and circled around to the passenger side of her car, then climbed in and put on her seatbelt. It felt strange letting someone else drive her Venue, but it was better than getting into a wreck because she had another seizure.

"Nice car," Emmett said as he started the engine.

"Thanks. Do you know where Lake Atalanta is?"

Lake Atalanta was a big lake at the edge of town. It had a playground, a swimming pool, pavilions, fishing piers, and, most importantly, a lot of walking and biking trails. She could think of no better place to walk and talk than Lake Atalanta.

"Of course I do," he said, a tone of annoyance in his voice. "I've lived in Northwest Arkansas all my life. I may be fat, but I'm not stupid."

She sighed. "Emmett...I'm so sorry for making fun of you. I never really wanted to, and if I could take it all back, I would, in a heartbeat. I just needed to fit in, and that was the easiest way. And saying that out loud, I know what a bitch I sound like. Again, I apologize."

Emmett didn't say anything as he backed out of her assigned parking spot, drove through the school parking lot, and turned left on Aldridge Road.

"Emmett?"

"It's just...you and your friends have tortured me since the moment I stepped foot inside this stupid school, you called me all sorts of shitty names, and now you expect me to help you?"

"Well, you are helping me, aren't you?"

"You're right. Maybe I am a stupid, fat piece of shit after all."

She felt like crying. She'd hurt this boy so badly, simply to make herself popular. It wasn't right. "You're not a stupid, fat piece of shit, and I was a complete and total bitch for saying you were. It was stupid and selfish of me. But I can't change the past. All I can do is try to be a better person going forward. So here we are."

"Here we are," he agreed, with a sigh. "Okay, at least I got that out of my system. I'm just...tomorrow when we're at school, are you going to do it all over again?"

She imagined being in the lunchroom, sitting with her friends, watching Emmett as he walked by their table. If Ashlie and the others made fun of him, would Justy join them? No, never again. She was done living her life that way.

"Not in a million years. I promise. I'm done being mean to you."

"And what about the other kids you girls make fun of? Allison Moxley, Joel DuBois, Harley Schmidt—"

"No more, ever," she said, interrupting him. "Justy the bitch is no more. Deal?"

He laughed. "Okay, it's a deal. I forgive you."

"Thank you," she whispered, "even if I don't deserve it."

"Hey, look," Emmett said, as he pulled her car into the parking lot. "We're already here. So what now?"

"Now we walk the trails," she said, opening the car door. "I figure that's a safe place to talk, and if I have another...seizure, you can just roll me into the lake and be done with me."

"I'd never do that."

"I know. We're friends now."

He stared at her. "You know, I think we just might be."

They walked through the park in silence, past the playground, ducks and geese looking for food, the gardens, and an old man with a scraggly beard fishing off the pier. It was a little windy, causing orange fall leaves to blow across the grass.

Justy loved Lake Atalanta. She remembered coming here for swimming lessons as a little girl with Matilda, which made her miss her former best friend all the more. She really needed to get over that feeling of guilt and reach out to her.

This had always been their favorite time of year. The temperatures were finally getting cooler, something that was all too brief in Arkansas, and there almost seemed to be a sort of magic in the air as everyone prepared for Christmas.

They were on the trail now, the one that led around the lake, with nature all around them. It was startlingly beautiful.

"So what do you think started these seizures or whatever they are?" Emmett asked, breaking the silence.

Justy shrugged. "I have no idea whatsoever. I was getting dressed for school this morning and the next thing I knew, my mom was in my room with me, about to call 911. She said I was rolling around on the floor, screaming."

"Just like in the bathroom at school."

"Pretty much, yeah. I don't remember much of it, just that it felt like someone was choking me, trying to kill me."

"Fuck."

Justy smiled. "Yeah, fuck. It was scary. Mom…well, she asked if I was having problems eating again."

"Eating?"

Justy took a deep breath. She didn't like talking about this, but she figured he deserved to know just who he'd gotten involved with. "When I was younger, I had anorexia. I stopped eating and got way too skinny and was sick all the time."

Emmett stared at her with his eyebrows raised in an unasked question.

"But that's not what happened, I promise," she said quickly. "I eat plenty. I'm healthy. I don't know what's happening, but it isn't that. Anyway, I told her I must have fallen back asleep and had a bad dream, but who falls asleep while getting dressed for school? It was so weird. So scary."

"It sounds like it."

They kept walking, past a giant oak tree and a pair of squirrels climbing its branches. It was quiet out here, the occasional whistle of a bird or the croak of a frog notwithstanding.

"And then it happened again in the bathroom, and that's where you came in."

"I hope it doesn't happen a third time."

"Yeah, me too. I have a feeling I might not wake up next time."

They walked in silence for a minute or two, before Emmett finally said, "One thing that's been bugging me, though…"

"What?" she prompted, when his words trailed off.

"I don't understand how my essay got all loose like that. It was almost like it led me to you, which is why at first I thought it was a prank."

"I promise you; I didn't steal your essay."

"I know. It's just weird."

They walked further down the trail, and Justy zipped up her red hoodie. The air felt crisp, which she loved, but it was getting a little cold as it got later in the afternoon.

She glanced over at Emmett. He seemed smart and funny; someone she'd enjoy being friends with. She hoped he really could get past her making fun of him and vowed to herself once again to stop joining her "friends" in their mockery.

"I'm going to get in so much trouble for skipping school," Emmett said, interrupting her thoughts.

"Yeah, same. But isn't it worth it? I think it is. It's so beautiful out here. So peaceful. I used to come here a lot with my friend Matilda when we were little. We even learned to swim at the pool."

Emmett stopped walking and stared at her.

"What?" she asked.

"You had a friend named Matilda?"

"I did, but we sort of lost contact when I switched to AAFA for high school. We stayed in touch for a little while, but…well, you know how that goes."

"Where did you go to school before switching to AAFA?"

"I did Kindergarten through eighth grade at Rogers West. Why?"

"I went to Rogers West High School until a month or so ago. We moved here from Fayetteville three years ago, so I didn't go to Rogers West junior high or grade school."

"I would have remembered you if you had," she said, smiling.

"Was your friend's last name Harper?"

She felt the hairs on her arms prickle. "How did you…do you know Matilda?"

"She called herself Tildie in high school."

"Tildie, huh? I like it. How is she? We haven't talked in a long time, and—" she stopped talking midsentence as anger clouded his face. "What?"

"You know exactly what. You never knew Tildie. This was all just some big prank after all, and I fell for it like the dumbass I am."

"What are you talking about?" she asked, her heart suddenly beating staccato in her chest. "Nothing about today was a prank, and Matilda was my best friend."

"Bullshit! She'd never be friends with someone like you."

He turned away from her and started walking back the way they'd come. She turned and ran to him, grabbing his shoulder. He shrugged her off and kept walking.

"What's wrong? I don't understand!"

"You can tell all your friends how you tricked this big, fat tub of lard."

She grabbed his wrist, and he spun to meet her eyes. For a minute she thought he might hit her and shrunk away from him.

"I'm not tricking you! Matilda really was my best friend. I don't understand what's going on."

He pulled away again. "Tildie has been missing for a month and a half! No one knows what happened to her. Are you happy now? I hope this was worth it."

She stared after him as he retreated, then fell to her knees, tears clouding her vision. Matilda was missing? How could this be happening? She began to shake, and felt invisible hands close around her throat, choking her, and a voice she'd never heard before said he was sorry but there was no other choice. She screamed as she collapsed to the ground, the world around her once again going dark.

✳✳✳

Emmett was pissed. It had all been a stupid trick and he'd fallen for it, even going so far as to believe he and this girl could be friends. He stormed off, then realized Justy's car keys were still in his pocket.

He nearly hurled them into the woods but stopped as he heard Justy screaming from behind him. His first instinct was to turn around and rush back to her, but he quelled that. She could walk home for all he cared.

She screamed again and then fell silent. He balled his fist so hard that one of the keys dug hard into his palm, drawing blood. Cursing, he turned around. He'd give her the stupid keys back and that was the last time he'd ever look at her lying bitch face again.

He hurried back up the trail, stopping short when he noticed Justy writhing around in the dirt, just like he'd found her in the girl's bathroom an hour earlier.

"Oh, stop," he spat. "I'm not going to fall for that again. I just came back to give you your keys."

She didn't stop. Her cheeks were covered in tears, and her hands were waving in the air, almost like she was fighting off some invisible assailant. He rolled his eyes and walked over to her, intending to drop the keys to the ground and be done with it, when he noticed her face turning blue.

"Oh, shit," he said, eyes wide.

He stared at her, all his anger replaced by fear. He knelt to the ground, reaching for her, but something unseen, something invisible, blocked his hands for just a moment as she gasped for air.

And then it was gone, and he took her in his arms, pulling her to him, as she sucked in deep, greedy breaths of air. She gasped, her eyes fluttering opening to stare at him, her lips trembling.

"I'm so sorry," Emmett said, his hands rubbing her back. "I thought…but you did know her, didn't you? You weren't lying. You did know Tildie. And when I tried to grab you, I felt…something was there, almost like invisible arms, holding you down."

Had he imagined that?

"I told you so," she rasped, burying her head into his shoulder. "And whatever it is, it's trying to kill me."

They drove mostly in silence, Emmet's left hand on the wheel and his other hand holding Justy's. Neither of them understood what was going on, but he'd be damned if he were going to abandon her to whatever was trying to kill her.

If he hadn't turned around to give her back her keys, she might be dead. That thought turned his stomach sour. He had a very hard time trusting people. He always had, really, ever since Grandpa Roy, but it had gotten much worse since Tildie vanished.

But he could trust Justy. He knew that beyond a shadow of a doubt now, and he needed to be there for her, needed to let her know she could trust him, too.

They were on Walnut Street, not far from the Cambridge Park development where he lived. Cambridge Park was right next to Whispering Timbers, where Justy lived, which was a strange coincidence. Could he really believe in coincidences anymore after Tildie? Rogers wasn't a small city, what were the odds of them both living that close to each other?

He glanced at the clock on the dashboard. It was almost six. They'd both texted their parents as they'd walked back to Justy's car, apologizing for skipping school and promising to explain later.

"Thank you for coming back for me," Justy said for probably the ninth or tenth time since they left Lake Atalanta.

"I should never have left in the first place. I'm sorry for the shit I said, and I'll never abandon you again," he said, meaning it. "We just need to get this—all this, what's happening to you and Tildie's disappearance—figured out, and the only way we're going to do that is by working together."

Emmet felt a strange connection to Justy that he couldn't quite understand let alone explain. He just knew—*knew*—he could trust her. He hoped he wasn't wrong, but that inexplicable feeling told him that he was right. He'd never been one to trust his gut, to listen to his instincts, but maybe this one time his gut was actually right.

"My hero," she said, smiling.

They turned right on North 34th Street, and, a few minutes later, left on Olive. Justy had offered to drop him off at his house, but he didn't want her to have to drive, even if it was only six blocks from his house on Sunset to hers on Mallard. He could walk, and truth be told the exercise wouldn't hurt him one bit.

As soon as they turned on 36th Street to enter the Cambridge Park neighborhood, she asked him to pull over.

"We should exchange numbers," she said, gesturing for his phone.

He handed his phone to her.

"You play Stardew Valley too, huh? I love that game."

"Me, too," he said, surprised. "The new update is fun."

Maybe they had more in common than either one of them realized, their connection to Tildie notwithstanding.

She entered her phone number into his phone, and his into hers, and then texted him her email address for good measure.

"There," she said, giving him back his phone. "Now, home James!"

He laughed and drove her home.

5

Tuesday

Emmet woke up around six, a full hour before his alarm would normally go off. He instructed his Alexa to cancel today's alarm and then rolled out of bed. He'd had a rough night sleeping so figured he may as well get up and get ready for the day.

Last night had been a shit show with his parents. In the end, he'd blamed Nick Sebastian, claiming Nick had stolen his essay and scattered it up and down the school hallways. Emmet had been so frustrated that he'd abandoned school all together after recovering and turning in the essay and walked off to a park to sulk.

His parents felt awful for him, of course, which made him feel even worse about lying to them, but he knew there was no way they were going to believe the truth. Hell, he barely believed it himself.

His father offered to call the school and demand that Nick Sebastian be punished for stealing his son's essay, but Emmet insisted that would only make things worse for him. In the end, his parents had thankfully decided to let it go on the condition that he'd tell them immediately if anything like that ever happened again.

Emmet stifled a yawn. He and Justy had stayed up until just past two in the morning texting, trying to figure out what was going on and getting to know each other a little better. They'd spent at least half of that time trying to figure out what might have happened to Tildie but were no closer to the truth than they had been when he drove her home.

Her interaction with her mother (her father wasn't in the picture, it seemed) had gone about as well as his with his parents, according to Justy. She'd made up some excuse and, thankfully, her mother had bought it.

His phone beeped. It was a text from Justy. He was surprised that she was up as early as he was.

Justy: *Yo, Em. You up?*

Emmet: *I just woke up and please don't call me that.*

Justy: *Sorry, EMMET.*

Emmet: *No problem, Juicy.*

Justy: *Ha. Okay, I get your point. Emmet. Better?*

Emmet: *Much better. Why're you up so early?*

Justy: *Bad dreams. You know, being strangled and all. No fun, would not recommend. 0 stars.*

Emmet: *I'm sorry. That sucks.*

Justy: *So…why are you up? Did you also have bad dreams?*

Emmet: *No, I just didn't sleep well.*

Justy: *I'm sorry to drag you into all of this.*

Emmet: *You didn't, I walked into it willingly. And we are gonna figure this out.*

Justy: *I sure hope so.*

✳✳✳

They chatted for a little while longer and then it was time to get ready for school. Justy was already dreading seeing Ashlie and the other girls, but promised herself she wouldn't give in and join them in making fun of Emmet or anyone else. She was done with that shit. Besides, she needed to focus all her energy on figuring out what was happening to her with these seizures, before it was too late.

She was a little nervous about driving to school today, given her seizures, so once again she asked Emmet to drive her car, and once again he accepted. This was becoming a habit, she thought, and she was strangely okay with that. The more she got to know Emmet, the more she liked him and wanted to spend time with him.

Justy hugged her mother goodbye and headed out the door. Her new friend Emmet was waiting for her by the mailbox. She used the key fob to remotely unlock the doors, tossed the keys to him, and then climbed into the passenger seat. A few seconds later he got into the car and then they were off, driving to school.

"What would your mother think?" Emmet asked as they backed out of the driveway.

"She probably wouldn't be very happy, but what she doesn't know won't hurt her, as the old saying goes."

"Works for me."

She relaxed as Emmet drove them to school, hoping with everything in her that the seizures were gone, while at the same time having the nagging feeling they were only just beginning.

✳✳✳

Kevin Haj sat on the couch in the living room of his apartment on Olive Street and 45th Street, across from Detective Amy Thompson. She had shown up at his door right before he would normally leave for school, saying the police had received an anonymous tip that he might be involved in the disappearance of Matilda Harper, a senior at Rogers West who had gone missing in mid-October.

Which was ludicrous, of course. He imagined it was a disgruntled student playing a prank on him. He glanced at the clock on the living room wall. He had called the school and told them he'd be late, saying he was having car trouble because he certainly couldn't admit he was being interrogated by the police about a missing student if he wanted to keep his job.

He hoped the interrogation didn't take much longer. He was already behind on grading papers and lesson plans, and the thought of getting behind on the lessons themselves gave him anxiety.

"And you're sure you don't know anything about this missing girl?" asked Detective Amy Thompson, holding up a photo of Harper.

"I do not," he said, for what felt like the tenth time. "I know who she is, of course. Everyone does. We had posters up all over the school for a while. Some are still up. It's awful, and I hope she comes home, but I didn't know her personally. She wasn't in any of my classes, at least as far as I can remember."

"That you can remember?"

"Well, I've been teaching at the school for almost fifteen years now, and it's a big school with a lot of students. I've seen a lot of faces."

She nodded. "Miss Harper had an after-school job working at Bliss Café in downtown Rogers. Do you ever go there?"

Kevin went still. He went there all the time, usually after school. He flashed back to yesterday afternoon, during his conversation with Lela Kirby, and in an instant knew she was the source of the "anonymous tip," because Matilda Harper was the girl he'd described seeing to her.

"Now that you say she worked at Bliss, I do remember her," he said slowly. "I didn't recognize her at first, not without the apron she wore at the coffee shop, but I do now. I didn't even know she went to our school. How could I not have known that?"

"You tell me, Mr. Haj. How could you not have known that?"

"It's not like I spent a lot of time with her," he said, defensively. "I just saw her at Bliss now and then and that's it. And I'm still pretty sure I never had her in any of my classes."

"Did you ever have any interactions with her at the coffee shop?"

"Several," he admitted. "She was a barista there."

He almost always ordered a venti vanilla-cinnamon latte, and if she got his order, she'd draw a little "pi" symbol in the foam. He thought it was cute, and it only now occurred to him that she'd done it because she knew he was a math teacher. He felt stupid for not realizing that sooner.

"That's right, she was."

"But she said her name was Matty, not Matilda…oh, Matty must be short for Matilda."

The detective nodded again. "She also used the name Tildie. Did you have any interactions with her outside of the coffee shop?"

"What? No, of course not," he said, a little too quickly.

But that wasn't quite true. The truth was, he'd seen her outside Bliss a couple of months ago, on a Saturday, which was probably right before her disappearance.

It had been a long Saturday spent at home grading papers and writing lesson plans, and Kevin couldn't wait to just relax inside Bliss with a nice latte and maybe play Candy Crush or one of the other games he had on his phone. He parked his car and walked across the street, reaching the door just as he noticed a young woman on the little green bench in front of the café, crying into her hands.

"Are you okay?" Kevin asked, without even thinking.

She looked up, startled. It was Matty, his favorite barista, the one with the bright blue glasses who always brought him his coffee with the "pi" symbol in the foam.

"Oh, yeah, I'm okay," she said, smiling, though the tears covering her cheeks said she was most definitely not okay.

"Are you sure? I know we don't really know each other, but if you want to talk, I'm more than happy to listen."

She brushed a hand through her long, brown hair, staring at him for a second, as if she were deciding whether or not she could trust him. She smiled, apparently coming to a decision.

"Yeah, I think I would like to talk a little. Thanks. I'm just having some problems with my…well, with the guy I'm seeing. And on top of that, my stomach hurts."

Kevin took a seat beside her on the bench. "Well, both of those things suck. I'm sorry. What kind of problems are you having with your boyfriend, if I might ask?"

She put her hand on her stomach and groaned. "Sorry."

"That's okay. Eat something bad?"

"Something like that. Anyway, yeah, my…boyfriend, we're just having a difference of opinion, that's all. He wants me to take a step I'm just not ready to take, and I want to do something that he's absolutely against but that I know in my heart is the right move for me. It'll all get resolved, I guess, one way or the other."

"I sure hope so. How long have you been dating?"

"Oh, not long at all. Just for a few months," she said, and then took a deep breath. "It's just that I think—"

Matty's phone beeped, interrupting her. She looked down at her phone and sighed.

"Is everything okay?"

"Just the boss, reminding me my break's over and that we're short-handed today. I'd better get back inside."

"Are you sure you're okay?"

"I will be," she said, surprising him with a quick, awkward hug. "Sorry, I know we're not really friends or anything, but I really appreciate you listening to me."

"I'm always happy to listen," said Kevin, "and you're welcome."

He followed Matty inside the coffee shop and ordered a venti vanilla-cinnamon latte, already thinking about sitting at the table he liked, sipping his drink, and playing Candy Crush.

"Are you listening to me?" asked Detective Thompson, bringing him back to the present.

"Oh, sorry, what did you say?"

She stared at him, irritation written all over her face. "I said, can you think of any reason why this anonymous tip would suggest you had anything to do with Matilda Harper's disappearance?"

"Honestly? Not really," he lied. "She was fine the last time I saw her at the café."

But not yesterday, when I saw her in a vision, he almost said. The same vision he'd described to Lela Kirby, minus a few important details like her throat being bruised and blood dripping from her mouth. No wonder she'd contacted the police. Clearly she'd recognized Matty from his description.

"Okay, Mr. Haj," said the detective, rising from the couch. "I'll let you get on with your day. If you can think of anything, anything at all, that might help us find Matilda Harper, please give me a call, but between you and me, I'm pretty sure she ran away with her boyfriend."

She handed him a Rogers Police Department business card with her name and phone number printed on it.

"Okay, thanks. I'll definitely call if I think of anything else," he promised, then walked the detective to the door and watched her leave.

As soon as Thompson was gone, Kevin collapsed onto the couch again. What had happened to Matty? When he asked about her at Bliss after not seeing her for two weeks, he'd been told by one of the other baristas that he thought Matty quit. He should have pressed further but, as a 37-year-old man, he felt more than a little creepy seeking out information about a young barista.

Kevin closed his eyes, remembering the vision he'd had yesterday of Matty with bruises around her neck. Were these visions real? Was Matty injured and trapped somewhere? He refused to even consider the possibility that she might be dead.

Sighing, he forced himself off the couch. He'd already missed an hour of school, and the clock was ticking. He walked out the front door, locking it behind him, hopped in his car, and headed to school.

6

Justy sat in the lunchroom with Ashlie, Tegan, Chrissie, and Mikayla, just like she did pretty much every lunch hour, but something felt off today. Were these girls ever really her friends? Certainly none of them were the sort of friend she'd had in Matilda, nor the kind of friend she felt Emmet could be. She definitely couldn't imagine any of them, other than maybe Mikayla, saving her in the school bathroom or on a trail at Lake Atalanta.

Hopefully, however, she'd never again need to be saved in the bathroom nor at the lake or anywhere else. She was halfway through the school day and had yet to have a seizure or feel invisible hands around her neck. Maybe whatever was going on had ended, but somehow she couldn't quite make herself believe that.

The connection between her and Emmet—Matilda Harper—was confusing. What were the odds that they had both considered her their best friend at different points in their life, and was it just a coincidence that they both knew Matilda in the first place, or was there something else at play? And where was Justy's former best friend anyway? Had she really run away? There were a lot of questions and precious few answers.

The first thing she'd done after talking to her mother last night was Google Matilda's name. There had been several missing person alerts, but beyond that, nothing.

"You're quiet today," Mikalya said, interrupting her thoughts.

"What? Oh, sorry, I'm just tired. Stayed up way too late last night."

"Doing what?" asked Ashlie. "Parker, maybe?"

Justy laughed. "Hardly."

She'd dated Parker Andrews for a few weeks back in September, but just like Nick, it hadn't worked out. Parker was nicer than Nick, but there just wasn't anything there. All he seemed interested in was getting under her clothes and she just wasn't ready for that yet. Not with him, not with anybody.

"Hey, look, it's old fatty," said Ashlie, as Emmet walked into the lunchroom.

Chrissie, Mikayla, and Tegan laughed, while Justy just wanted to scream. She'd been dreading this moment, but after yesterday there was

no way she was going to allow this to keep happening, let alone participate.

"Can we just not today?" asked Justy, under her breath.

All four of her friends stared at her like she'd said something ob-
scene, and she felt warmth rise in her cheeks. She couldn't believe she'd
gone along with this for as long as she had, especially after she'd been
bullied into anorexia at Rogers West junior high.

"What do you mean?" Ashlie asked.

"I mean, let's just lay off Emmet. He doesn't deserve the bullshit
we've been putting him through."

Emmet walked by their table, risking a glance at her. Justy smiled at
him, which caused Chrissie to laugh.

"This is some kind of joke, right?" said Ashlie as soon as Emmet
passed their table, settling at an empty table at the edge of the lunchroom. "Make old fatty think you like him and then, bam, crush his hopes
and dreams of finally getting the hot girl. Right, Justy?"

"Okay, that makes sense," Teagan said.

Mikayla added: "Hell, maybe he'll kill himself and his fat ass will
never spoil our appetite again."

Justy glared at her. "You really think suicide is a joke? What the hell,
Mik? That's low, even for you."

Mikayla flinched, but the other girls just laughed.

"Oh, come on," said Ashlie, anger flashing in her eyes, "you've said
just as bad, or worse. This has to be a joke, right?"

She had said just as bad or worse, and the thought made her feel like
she was going to throw up. It was now or never, and it really wasn't that
hard of a decision. It should never have been that hard of a decision, and
Justy was ashamed that she'd let this go on for as long as she had.

"No, girls," she said, standing up from her spot between Ashlie and
Tegan, "I'm just done with this. I'm done with being a bitch, and I'm
done with all of you."

"Are you going to let her get away with that?" asked Ashlie. "Mikayla, do something."

"Yeah, Mikayla," said Tegan, elbowing her arm. "Don't let her get away with that shit."

Justy turned away from them. It seemed like the whole lunchroom was staring at her as she picked up her tray of spaghetti and meat balls from the table she'd shared with her so-called "friends" for the last four years and walked over to Emmet's table and sat down across from him.

"You didn't have to do that, you know," he whispered, smiling, "but I'm glad you did."

"Me, too."

They ate in silence for a moment, him with his ham and cheese sandwich and potato chips he'd brought from home, and her with her now-cold spaghetti.

"Do you have any more ideas about what might have happened to Tildie?"

Justy shrugged. "None whatsoever. Like you, I scoured the internet looking for information, but other than the missing person alerts there's not much out there at all."

She felt guilty for not knowing her former best friend had been missing for the last month and a half. If only she'd reached out to Matilda, had done a better job of keeping in touch, maybe Matilda would still be safely at home.

If only, if only, if only.

"I messaged her sister. They're pretty close, so maybe she knows something."

"Corrie? I remember her. She's just a few years older than Matilda…Tildie…right?"

Emmet nodded. "She's in college now, U of A. I think a sophomore or junior."

"I wish I'd been better at keeping in touch with Tildie."

"One thing I didn't tell you," Emmet said, "is that she'd been different for the last few months or so. Not bad, just…different. Kind of secretive, if that makes sense. And the day she disappeared…we were supposed to meet at this place in downtown Rogers where she worked part-time after school, only she never showed. I thought she'd ditched me, and didn't find out until later that she'd never even showed up for work.

"If I'd reached out to her parents or something instead of feeling sorry for myself, maybe…maybe she'd still be here."

Justy's heart broke hearing the regret and self-recrimination in Emmet's voice. She knew exactly how he felt. She hadn't even known Tildie had a job. She reached out to take Emmet's hand. "None of this is your fault. And we're gonna find her. I know we will."

"So you abandoned us to hold hands with this loser?" said Mikayla, suddenly looming over their table. "What's wrong with you, Justy?"

"Mik, what part of 'I'm done' did you not understand?" Justy asked, staring at her former friend. "Leave us alone."

"Leave 'us' alone? Are you freaking kidding me? How is this fat piece of shit suddenly more important than us? Than *me*, your best friend?"

Justy watched as Emmet's face turned red and he pulled his hand from hers and looked away. This was the final straw. She stood up, grabbed her tray, and dumped the half-eaten spaghetti and meatballs over Mikayla's head. She stared at Justy, eyes wide, as if she couldn't believe what Justy had just done.

"You were never my best friend," Justy said, realizing it was true the moment it came from her mouth. "We just used each other to be popular and bully people to make Ashlie happy."

"You bitch!" screamed Mikaya, spaghetti sauce dripping down her face, as she slapped Justy hard in the face.

The lights of the lunchroom seemed to go dark, and then Justy was lying on her back somewhere, on a bed in a room she didn't recognize. Someone straddled her, their hands on her throat, squeezing hard.

"This is all your fault, Justy," echoed a man's voice through the room, as she struggled to breathe. "If you had just listened to me, none of this would have had to happen. This is all your fault!"

She scratched and clawed at the unseen face of the man holding her down, to no avail. She tried to yell, tried to buck him off her, but she couldn't move, couldn't breathe, could barely even think.

Justy had so many questions and precious few answers. Who was this man? What was happening to her? Was she dying?

And then everything went black.

7

Corrie Harper was livid. Her little sister Tildie had been missing for almost a month and a half, and the police had all but given up on her, saying everything pointed to her running away from home.

The night Tildie disappeared, she'd supposedly sent their mother a single text:

I'm in love with a boy from out of state and I know you wouldn't approve, so I'm leaving Arkansas. I love you, but please don't come looking for me. I'll be living my best life.

It was all bullshit. There was no way her sister had sent that message. She hadn't even been dating anyone, as far as Corrie knew, and they told each other pretty much everything. She sure as hell didn't run off with some rando.

Tildie's phone had gone silent after that message and 43 days later it had yet to show up on any network, despite her parents continuing to pay for the service.

The most maddening thing was her parents seemed to agree with the police. They claimed their youngest daughter had been acting "suspicious," which fell in line with the text she'd supposedly sent.

Due to Corrie's insistence, her parents had pushed the police to keep investigating, and so they'd tried but failed to track her phone. They said she must have thrown it away or destroyed it and purchased a new one, but she knew her sister wouldn't have done that. Tildie was a bit of a hoarder and didn't throw anything away, ever, so she couldn't imagine her throwing away her phone. Neither the cops nor her parents would listen to her, however. It was frustrating.

Corrie was in her third year of college at the University of Arkansas, studying political science, and ever since her little sister went missing her grades had bottomed out. She couldn't think about anything but Tildie. Her parents had urged her to just have faith that Tildie would come back eventually, but Corrie couldn't do that, couldn't just let it go and *wait*.

She'd driven to Rogers from her dorm in Fayetteville one afternoon a few weeks ago, to put up posters all over town pleading for help in finding her missing sister. The only phone calls she'd received so far had been prank calls. It was infuriating, not to mention depressing.

"Aren't you going to be late for your philosophy class?" asked Anna Macfadden, Corrie's roommate.

Corrie looked at the time on her phone. The class started at four, and it was 3:56. Oh well. She'd already missed so many classes, what could one more hurt?

"I don't think I'm going," she said, running her fingers through her short, brown hair. "I'm not feeling too great."

"Corrie…I know you're upset about your sister, but—"

"Upset? Of course I'm upset," Corrie yelled, turning to glare at Anna. "Wouldn't you be upset if your sister went missing?"

"I don't have a sister."

Corrie rolled her eyes. "Your brother, then, or your best friend, or whoever. She just up and vanished. What am I supposed to do?"

"Go to your classes. Get your degree. Don't you think she'd want you to go on living?"

"Jesus Christ, Anna, you say that like she's dead."

Anna stared at her for a moment before looking away. "I hope she's not."

"Yeah, me too."

Her phone beeped. Corrie glanced down to see she'd just received a text, but there was no number telling her who it had come from. It was blank. She clicked on the message.

It was just the numbers "9383." She tried to respond, but her Android phone went black. It was rebooting. When the phone came back up, the message had vanished.

She needed to have her phone checked. The same thing happened twice yesterday, but those numbers had been "36" and "308." It was very strange.

"Are you okay?" asked Anna.

"Yeah, my phone's just acting up. It's only about a year old, so I'm not sure what's going on with it."

"You still have time to go to your class, you know. If you hurry, you probably won't be even ten minutes late."

She knew Anna was right. She'd done all she could do. Shrugging to herself, she grabbed her backpack and headed out the door.

Corrie was almost at her class when her phone beeped again. Not a text this time, but a message through Facebook Messenger. She clicked it open. It was Tildie's best friend from Rogers West High School, Emmet.

Hi Corrie, the message began, *I'm sorry to bother you, but have you heard anything more about Tildie?*

Emmet had blown up her phone when Tildie first went missing, but she hadn't heard anything from him for the last week or so. He seemed heartbroken, and she'd assumed he'd simply given up. She was glad to see that wasn't the case.

I haven't, she replied, *and I'm super frustrated. No one seems to be taking this seriously except for us. I don't think she even had a boyfriend, so that text was pure bullshit.*

This was all stuff they'd said to each other before, ad nauseam, but it did help to have someone to talk to. He'd even helped her put up those missing person flyers a few weeks back.

She checked Messenger, but he still hadn't seen her response. She stood outside the door to her class, debating whether or not to go inside, when her phone beeped.

Corrie half-expected it to be Emmet, finally texting her back. Instead, it was another message from nowhere, this time with nine numbers. Her phone was going nuts. She started to put her phone back into her purse but instead stared at the phone in shock, finally understanding.

She quickly wrote the number down just as the phone rebooted. She looked at the other numbers, which she'd also written down on a notepad she carried, and they all made sense.

"Screw philosophy class," she muttered under her breath as she turned around and made a beeline for the student parking lot. Less than ten minutes later she was in her car, driving towards Rogers, to once again search for her missing sister.

✳✳✳

Emmet sat in the emergency waiting room at Mercy Hospital, along with Justy's mom. Justy had collapsed to the floor of the school cafeteria the moment Mikayla slapped her. Try as they might, no one could wake her. Someone had run to get Mrs. Meriweather, the school nurse, who had in turn called an ambulance.

"I just don't understand what's happening," said Mrs. Friedman, tears rolling down her cheeks, for at least the third time in the last five minutes. "Justy had…eating problems a few years ago, so I thought for sure this was related, but you said she's been eating normally?"

"She told me about her anorexia," Emmet said. "I see Justy probably every day at lunch, and she always finishes off her food. She ate about half her spaghetti today, before…before the incident with Mikayla Danvers."

Mikayla had been dragged off to the principal's office kicking and screaming by two of the lunchroom monitors while everyone else watched in shock.

"That little bitch needs to be expelled," said Mrs. Friedman, under her breath.

Emmet wasn't sure what to think. He'd seen Mikayla slap Justy, and there was no way that slap had been hard enough to knock her out. He was almost certain Justy had another seizure but wasn't sure how much to tell Mrs. Friedman. After all, he'd only known her for about five minutes.

He was still trying to piece together all the weird things going on but couldn't help thinking they had to be related. The trail of pages from his essay leading right to Justy, her seizures, her living just down the road from him, and the fact that at one point they'd both considered Tildie their best friend.

Was there a connection between Tildie's disappearance and Justy's seizures? What were the chances of all this happening at the same time and *not* being connected? Emmet knew there were no such things as magic or ghosts or any of that, but…what if there were?

What if even now Tildie were being held hostage in some dungeon by an insane wizard and she'd happened upon his spell book and managed to get off a few spells before getting caught, spells she used to contact her closest friends?

He almost laughed at himself. That's what he got for reading too many fantasy novels and playing too much Dungeons and Dragons. More than likely Tildie really had run off with some out of towner like her parents claimed and was doing just fine.

He had a hard time believing that, though, because wouldn't she have told him? Perhaps they weren't as close as Emmet had thought. That thought hurt almost as much as the thought that she'd run off with some dumb guy Emmet had never even met.

"Mrs. Friedman?" said a girl's voice. It was Mikayla, her shirt still stained with spaghetti sauce.

"What are you doing here?" snarled Mrs. Friedman, leaping out of her chair. "You did this. You may have killed my daughter."

"What? No! I just slapped her. I feel horrible that I did that, but she poured spaghetti on my head, and I was mad, and Ashlie…well, she told me to slap her unless she immediately apologized. I should never have slapped her, but I know I didn't hit her hard enough to kill her."

Mrs. Friedman started to say something, but Emmet found himself interrupting her against his better judgement, saying, "She's right, Mrs. Friedman. Mikayla was being a total…jerk, but it was just a slap."

Mikayla turned to Emmet, her eyes wide open in surprise. She mouthed the words, *thank you*, and he nodded.

"Oh, how do you know?" yelled Mrs. Friedman, turning to face Emmet. "You've been Justy's friend for, what, five minutes?"

"I know about the seizure she had yesterday morning," he said quietly. "And you probably don't know this, but she had another one on the trail at Lake Atalanta. That's where we were when we skipped school."

"Oh, God. Why didn't she tell me? It must be anorexia again. What else could it be?"

"I didn't even know Justy had anorexia," whispered Mikayla.

"She doesn't anymore," Emmet said.

Justy's mom started to respond just as a tall, redheaded nurse walked into the waiting room. "Mrs. Friedman, your daughter is awake now and appears to be doing fine. We've moved her to a room. Would you like to see her?"

"Thank God she's okay," Mrs. Friedman said. "And yes, I'd love to see my daughter."

"Can I come?" asked Mikayla. "I need to apologize."

"No! And before you ask, Emmet, you can't either. Not unless she asks for you, and maybe not even then. I don't trust either one of you."

Emmet watched in frustration as the nurse escorted Justy's mother down the hallway and out of sight.

8

Justy found herself lying in darkness, surrounded by the earthy smells of dirt, grass, and wood. The moon shone down from above, illuminating a figure dressed all in black standing above her, holding a shovel.

She tried to ask the mysterious person in black where she was and what she was doing here, but the words wouldn't come, nor could she move her arms or legs. What was happening to her? The last thing she remembered was pouring her spaghetti on Mikayla's head in the lunchroom, and her former friend slapping her.

What had happened after that, how had she wound up outside in the woods, and who was the person in black? She tried once again to speak, and then simply to grunt, but nothing would come out.

"I'm sorry it had to come to this, Justy," said a man's voice, "but you just wouldn't listen. Why couldn't you have fucking listened?"

She gasped, sucking in greedy gulps of air, and opened her eyes. She was no longer in a forest but instead lying in a bed in a small room that smelled of antiseptics. Soft jazz music played in the background.

Justy's vision was blurry, but blinking brought everything into focus. She looked around the room. She was in a hospital bed, and the television on the wall was turned to a channel labeled as "Smooth Jazz." She was dressed in a white hospital gown, and a large machine monitored her vital signs.

What had happened to her? She remembered getting mad at Mikayla and dumping her half-eaten spaghetti over the girl's head, and then Mikayla slapping her, and then…nothing after that. Had she been knocked unconscious by the slap? That didn't seem possible. Had she fallen and hit her head? Her head didn't hurt, so she didn't think that was it, but who knows?

A nurse walked into the room, smiled, and said, "Oh, you're awake! Thank goodness."

The nurse asked her a million questions (or so it felt like) and then left to retrieve Justy's mother, who was apparently waiting outside.

"Oh, Justy!" exclaimed her mother as she walked through the door, rushing to the bed, taking her in her arms. "I was so worried. Do they know what happened to you?"

"If they do, the nurse didn't tell me. Mom, how did I get here? The last thing I remember was getting into a fight in the lunchroom and Mikayla slapping me."

"That little bitch knocked you unconscious!" yelled her mother. "I'm sorry. I'm just so angry."

"I don't think it was her fault. I don't think she even hit me that hard."

"That's what Emmet said, but I have a hard time believing that."

Emmet! He must be out of his mind with worry. "When did you talk to Emmet?"

"Just a little while ago," she said. "He and Mikayla are in the waiting room, but I'm not letting either one of them see you until I get some answers. For starters, why didn't you tell me about your seizure at Lake Atalanta? Emmet told me about that as well."

She could understand why Emmet had come, and why he told her mother about the seizure, but why was Mikayla here? She couldn't imagine her friend–scratch that, her former friend–coming to the hospital, especially after they'd yelled at each other like that. There was only one way to find out.

"I want to see them."

"No, Justine, not until you answer my question. Why didn't you tell me about your seizure at the lake?"

"I didn't tell you because I didn't want to worry you," she said, "and I didn't want you to think I have anorexia again, because I don't. Now can I see my friends?"

"No. They aren't your friends. One of them almost killed you."

"A stupid slap isn't the thing that's going to kill me, Mom," said Justy, laughing.

"What is, then? What's wrong with you? This Emmet didn't get you involved with drugs, did he?"

"No! Never. It's…do you remember Matilda?"

"Of course I remember Matilda. You two were as thick as thieves up until you switched schools. How is any of this about Matilda?"

Up until you made me switch schools, she wanted to say, but she knew that wasn't fair, nor entirely accurate. She could have pushed back against it if she'd really wanted to, but she didn't. She'd wanted a fresh start for herself as much as her mother had wanted one for her.

"I'll tell you everything if you'll let me see Emmet and Mikayla. Please?"

"No. You'll tell me now, or you're grounded for life."

"I'll be eighteen in just under three months, Mom. You're not grounding me for life. Now let me see them. After that, I'll answer all your questions."

Her mother looked like she wanted to scream. "Fine. I'm not letting Mikayla near you, but I'll allow Emmet five minutes."

"Mom…both of them, please, and for as long as it takes. And then I'll tell you everything. I promise. Deal?"

Her mother looked like she might explode. She'd had anger issues ever since Justy's father abandoned them five years ago, but she'd been better lately. Had all that progress been lost?

Justy watched as her mother swallowed an angry retort, took a deep breath, and finally said "fine" before walking out of the hospital room and slamming the door behind her.

✳✳✳

"Justy had anorexia?" Mikayla asked, and Emmet nodded.

They were both sitting in the corner of the waiting room, away from everyone else waiting to see a family member or a friend, talking about Justy.

"She did, but that isn't the point. She's been over it for like three years now. She said it was over before she even came to AAFA. These seizures have nothing to do with anorexia."

"But then what's causing them?"

"Well, you slapping her in the face probably didn't help," Emmet said, immediately regretting his words when Mikayla flinched. "Sorry."

"No, you're right," she said, staring down at the floor, "I deserved that. I'm sorry I did it, and I'm sorry for all the shit I said about you. I was just trying to be cool. I didn't really mean any of it, I just did it because Ashlie told me to. I know that's no excuse, but it's the truth."

Emmet wondered if anyone ever really meant anything they said anymore, or if it was all for show, simply to improve their social status and make themselves feel better about their own inadequacies. He guessed in the end it didn't really matter.

"Look, we both care about Justy, right?"

Mikayla nodded. "I really do."

"Then we need to make sure she's okay, and we need to find out what's causing these seizures."

"But wouldn't that be up to the doctors? We're just high schoolers. What can we do?"

"We can find Tildie."

Mikayla looked confused. "Who or what is 'Tildie?'"

"It's a 'who,' and she's someone who's very important to Justy and me. Back when Justy knew her, she went by her full name of Matilda."

"Okay, that's great and all, but how can finding her help with Justy's seizures?"

That was the hard part. Emmet had no idea if it could, but he had a hunch he was onto something. But could he trust a girl who less than three hours ago was calling him names? Then again, he trusted Justy, who only yesterday had called him a tank.

"I'll tell you, but first I need to make sure I can trust you. Tell me something you wouldn't want getting out, something no one else knows."

"And if I do, you'll tell me what's going on?"

Emmet nodded. "I will."

"Okay, well…let me think. Oh, I know. I kind of, like, had a crush on Mr. Petermann last year. He's the history teacher and a real nerd. Into all sorts of video games, reads comic books, plays D&D, etcetera. But he's also really cute, and really nice. Anyway, I think he picked up on it because he started avoiding me, which I guess was actually pretty smart of him, come to think of it. Please don't tell anyone. I'd never live it down."

Emmet thought that was as good of a secret as any. Something about her confession, though, made him think of something else, some niggling memory, but before he could grasp hold of the thought, Justy's mother appeared back in the waiting room.

"Okay, you two, for some reason my daughter wants to see the both of you," she said, looking exasperated. "She's in room 118."

Emmet looked at Mikayla, who nodded and then followed him out of the waiting room and down the hall.

"Are you still going to tell me what's going on with this Tildie person and Justy's seizures?"

"I will, but first let's talk to Justy."

"What am I going to say to her?" asked Mikayla, her voice quivering.

"How about the truth? That you're sorry for slapping her?"

Mikayla smiled. "That's definitely a good start. Thanks, Emmet."

And then they were outside room 118. Emmet took a deep breath, unsure about what he might find waiting for him, then slowly pushed open the door and walked inside, followed by Mikayla.

Justy was sitting in bed, using the remote control for the television to flip channels. She turned off the TV when they entered the room, smiling at them.

"I wasn't sure Mom was actually going to let you guys see me," she said, "but I'm glad she did. We really need to talk."

"I'm so sorry," said Mikayla, tears streaming down her face, as she pushed past Emmet and rushed to the hospital bed. "I'm sorry for slapping you, for the things I said...for everything."

"For what it's worth, she also apologized to me," added Emmet. "And I think she meant it."

"I did. I do. I told Ashlie, Tegan, and Chrissie I was done. I don't want to be...I *can't* be that person anymore, and...I want to help you find your friend."

"It's okay, Mik. I'm sorry for dumping my lunch on your head." Justy patted Mikayla's shoulder and then turned her head towards Emmet. "You guys really talked, didn't you?"

"We did," admitted Emmet. "When your mother wasn't busy yelling at us. She thinks I got you involved with drugs or something."

Justy rolled her eyes. "She means well, I just…I really scared her yesterday morning, when I had the seizure. It brought back bad memories of my anorexia."

"You never told me about that," said Mikayla, her eyes still clouded with tears. "I guess it was before you came to Arkansas Academy of Fine Arts, right?"

"Yep," said Justy. "It happened when I was at Rogers West. Back when Matilda and I were friends."

"Emmet was just about to tell me about her when your mom showed back up," Mikayla said. "Why didn't you stay friends?"

"It's…complicated. We did stay friends, for a little while at least, but eventually we just sort of lost touch. At least that's what I tell myself. But I think it was my fault. I was really embarrassed about the whole anorexia thing, and I just kind of…pulled away, I guess. I didn't realize that until just now. I wish I'd handled things differently, and now it might be too late."

"What do you mean?" asked Emmet, though he had a feeling he knew exactly what she meant.

"When I was asleep, I had a dream or a vision or whatever the hell it was. I think these seizures are trying to tell me something. In the vision, some guy was standing over me, holding a shovel. I couldn't move or even speak. I think we were in the woods. He kept saying things like, 'I'm sorry I have to do this, Justy.' At least that's what I thought he said."

"Thought he said?" asked Mikayla. "Then what did he really say?"

"I think he really said—"

"Tildie," interrupted Emmet, a pit forming in his stomach, as Justy nodded. "Both of the names end in a 'Y' sound."

"Yeah. Exactly. I'm not used to the name 'Tildie,' so I think that's why I heard it as my name."

"Which means what, though?" asked Mikayla.

"I honestly don't know. If she's dead…could she be contacting me from the afterlife? As insane as that sounds."

"Don't say that!" yelled Emmet, his face turning red. "She can't be dead, she just can't."

"I'm sorry, Em," said Justy, reaching out to take his hand, but he pulled away.

Tildie couldn't be dead. He refused to even consider the possibility that she might be dead. They'd been friends for nearly four years, ever since they first met in their freshman year of high school. She was the best friend he'd ever had, and he couldn't imagine living the rest of his life without her.

But why would she run away and not tell him where she was going, or at least say goodbye? And if she were dead…that meant that text Tildie's sister had showed him that was supposedly from Tildie was a lie, and someone had more than likely sent it from her phone to cover up her murder.

Who on earth could hate Tildie enough to murder her?

"Are you okay, Emmet?" asked Mikayla.

"Emmet?" Justy asked, raising an eyebrow.

He wasn't okay and wasn't sure if he could ever be okay again. Without another word, Emmet ran out of the hospital room, down the halls, through the waiting room and past a startled Mrs. Friedman and into the hospital parking lot.

Panting, out of breath, he nearly stumbled to his knees. What was his life without Tildie? If she were dead, could he really go on living? He thought back to the day they first met, when she changed his life forever...

Emmet was having an awful day until she showed up. This was his first day as a freshman in high school, and he had to start it at an entirely different place, Rogers West. His father, a sales rep for a huge drug company, had taken a promotion last year that required him to drive to Rogers from Fayetteville every morning, a thirty-minute trip under the best of circumstances.

Six months into the new position Emmet's father had enough commuting, and they sold their house in Fayetteville and bought a new one in Rogers. It was a nice house, bigger and better than the old one, but Emmet missed Fayetteville. He missed his friends, what few friends he had.

He wasn't a popular kid, had never been a popular kid, but he'd known most of the kids he went to school with since kindergarten and had gotten used to them, even if they weren't always nice.

"Hey, my name's Tildie," she said out of the blue, during the third hour study hall, startling him, "what's yours?"

She'd been sitting right behind him.

"I'm Emmet Sapp," he said, turning around, amazed that a girl as pretty as Tildie had deigned to talk to him.

"Hi, Emmet Sapp."

"Hi, Tildie with the unknown last name."

She laughed. "I'm Tildie Harper. Nice to meet you, Emmet Sapp."

"Nice to meet you, too, Tildie Harper."

And that's how their friendship began. They'd quickly learned they had a lot of things in common, including their love of gaming, science fiction and fantasy novels, comic books from Anomaly Studios, and Dungeons and Dragons. They'd even formed their own D&D group, playing every week with three other nerds from high school.

Emmet had a crush on Tildie from the very beginning but quickly got over it when he realized she wasn't looking for a boyfriend. It was probably better that way, anyway. In addition to becoming his best friend, she slowly became the sister he never had.

How was he expected to live without his sister?

He wasn't sure he could.

9

Corrie Harper drove her little green Honda Civic down Interstate 49 North, listening to Jax's *I Choose Violence* at full volume, wondering just what she'd find when she reached her destination.

Take exit 2 towards Promenade Boulevard, for 0.4 miles, said Google Maps through her phone. She took the exit.

For a while a few years ago, she and Tildie had really gotten into Geocaching, travelling all over Northwest Arkansas to find hidden messages and little prizes. It'd been fun and only ended when Corrie went off to college in Fayetteville.

She couldn't believe it had taken her so long to figure out the numbers that kept appearing on her phone were GPS coordinates.

36.3089383, -94.1832605

She'd looked up the coordinates on her phone and was surprised to realize it led to Mercy Hospital in Rogers. Could her sister be there? Or was it just some asshole who knew about her old hobby pranking her? Could anyone really be that cruel?

She turned off Google Maps. She knew how to get to Mercy from here. A few minutes later, she pulled her car into the huge hospital parking lot and drove towards the emergency room. She figured that was as good a place to start as any.

As she turned the corner, someone in a dark blue hoodie darted out in front of her car. She slammed on her brakes, swerving to avoid hitting them, and then she saw the person tumbling to the ground. She quickly shifted her car into park and opened the door, leaping out onto the pavement, dropping to her knees beside him.

It was a young man with brown hair, probably in his late teens or very early twenties. He was holding his hip but otherwise seemed unharmed. Her heart felt like it was beating a mile a minute.

"Are you okay? What were you doing, jumping out in front of me like that? Did I hit you? I could have killed you!"

"You didn't hit me; I tripped trying to get out of the way. I'm sorry I didn't see your car," he said, his eyes filled with tears as he looked up at her. "I was just...Corrie?"

She stared at him. It was Emmet! She'd almost killed her missing sister's best friend. "Emmet? What are you doing here?"

"Justy's in the hospital, and I—?"

"Justy?" she asked, cutting him off. "Tildie's old friend? That Justy?"

"Yeah, that Justy."

"But how do you even know her? And why is she in the hospital?"

A loud honk rang though the parking lot before Emmet could answer. A black SUV, apparently not happy that Corrie's car was blocking some of the parking spaces.

"Can you walk?" asked Corrie, and Emmet nodded, taking her offered hand and pulling himself to his feet.

The SUV honked again, louder this time. Corrie had to resist the temptation to flip off the driver.

"Thanks. I really am okay. Just landed on my hip."

"Get in," she said, already walking around to the driver's side of her vehicle. "Let's get out of this asshole's way, and then I think we really need to talk."

✳✳✳

Emmet could hardly believe Corrie was here. But *why* was she here? Had she known he'd be here? He had so many questions.

"Okay, what's going on?" Corrie asked, staring at him.

"Well, like I said, Justy's in the hospital and—"

"You already said that. I mean…why did my phone bring me here? You didn't have anything to do with that, did you?"

Emmet stared at her. What was she talking about?

She told him a story about GPS coordinates that led her from Fayetteville here to the Mercy Hospital in Rogers.

"Okay, that's really weird," he said, when she was finished. "But what's even weirder is what's been happening with Justy."

He explained about Justy's seizures, his missing essay, everything. When he was done they both sat in silence for a few minutes.

"You think she's dead, don't you?" she finally asked, tears welling up in her eyes.

"I don't want to think that, but…yeah, I do, and I don't know if I can live with that, but it's the only thing that even remotely makes any sense whatsoever."

She reached out her hand, and he gratefully squeezed it. "When you ran out of the hospital, you…were you going to kill yourself, Emmet?"

He looked at the floor of the car, the dashboard, anything to avoid her eyes. "I was seriously considering it, but probably not by jumping in front of a car."

"Oh, Emmet," she said, pulling him into a hug, and then they were both sobbing into each other's shoulders.

"I know, it was a stupid idea," he said, once the tears had lessened. "I also know Tildie wouldn't want that for me, but...I just don't know how I can live without her. I don't know if I even *want* to live without her. The last month and a half have been bad enough, but losing my best friend forever? I just...don't think I can handle that."

"You're right about one thing," she said, grabbing his chin and forcing him to look at her. "Tildie would not want that for you. Not for anyone. But especially not for you."

And then they were crying again.

"Maybe she isn't dead," Emmet said after a while. "It's stupid to give up before we know anything for certain, and besides...whoever hurt her has got to pay."

"Truth. The question is, how do we find him? And how do we find Tildie?"

A knock reverberated through the car, startling them both. Emmet looked up to see Mikayla knocking on the window beside him. She looked angry.

Corrie rolled down the window. "And who are you?"

"That's Mikayla. She's Justy's friend."

"I'm your friend now, too, dickwad," said Mikayla, "and as your new friend, I have to tell you that what you just did, running out of her hospital room like that, really sucked. Justy is worried sick about you. What the fuck, Em?"

Apparently, the "Em" nickname had stuck. Truth be told, it was growing on him.

"I just...the thought of losing Tildie was more than I could take, okay? This is Tildie's sister, by the way."

Mikayla shifted her gaze to Corrie. "Hi, Tildie's sister. How'd you get here?"

"Corrie. Her name is Corrie Harper. And it's a long story."

"Hi, Mikayla," Corrie said, with a slight smile. "Do you think Justy is up for any more visitors? I really think we all need to sit down and have a talk."

10

Justy sat up in her hospital bed, vacillating between worry and rage. How dare Emmet abandon her like that? Was he okay? She missed him, while at the same time being pissed at him. It was confusing, infuriating, and probably a bunch of other adjectives she couldn't even name at the moment.

Mikayla had been out looking for him for a good ten minutes. She wanted to text her to ask if she'd had any luck finding him yet, but of course Mikayla had forgotten her phone on one of the hospital room chairs, so she'd never see the text.

Maybe she'd been wrong about Mikayla not really being her friend, after all. Maybe they'd been more similar than she realized, both of them doing bad things in order to avoid bad things being done to them. It was a sobering thought. If she were going to forgive herself, couldn't she also forgive Mikayla?

Justy's mom had come marching into her room shortly after Mik left, demanding answers, but when she tried to give them her mother just rolled her eyes. She hadn't believed any of it and had immediately accused Justy of coming up with "this outlandish story" to cover for something else, more than likely drug use or anorexia.

When Justy insisted the story was true and that she truly believed Matilda was communicating with her, possibly from the afterlife, her mother threw up her hands and stormed out of the room, saying she couldn't listen to her lies anymore and had to get back to work, and how she'd better not leave the hospital, or else.

Was Matilda truly dead and reaching out to her from beyond the grave? She didn't want to believe that, but nothing else made sense. Hell, that barely made sense. Were ghosts even real? She wished Emmet were here to talk to about all this.

She'd really only known him for two days, but he'd already become her closest friend. She couldn't believe she'd ever been so mean to him, made fun of him and called him fat. No wonder he'd run out on her. He probably still didn't trust her, and why should he? She'd been an absolute bitch to him ever since he'd shown up at AAFA several weeks ago, and two days of being nice hardly made up for that.

The door opened and there was Emmet. She jumped out of bed, ran over to him, and threw herself into his arms, hugging him for all she was worth. He hugged her back and she thought she was going to cry.

"I'm so sorry for leaving," he said, a choke in his voice. "I won't do it again, I promise."

"You'd better not," she said, holding back tears. "I need you."

"I need you, too," he whispered into her ear.

"Are you two gonna make out, or what?" said Mikayla's voice, laughing.

Embarrassed, Justy looked up to see Mikayla walking towards them from the door with someone else behind her, a girl who looked vaguely familiar. She blinked. Was that who she thought it was?

"Corrie?"

"The one and only," said Corrie Harper, Matilda's sister.

She released Emmet from her arms and took a step back. "What in the heck are you doing here?"

Corrie shrugged. "My phone magically gave me the GPS coordinates for the hospital. When I got here, I almost ran over Emmet."

She stared at her. "What? Almost ran over him?"

"She did say 'almost,'" said Emmet, with a half-smile. "Don't worry, I'm okay."

"Who sent you the GPS coordinates for the hospital? And why?"

"No clue. That's why I said 'magically.' And I don't know why, but I'm thinking it must've been to see you guys."

"That's what we need to talk about," said Emmet. "Corrie's magical GPS coordinates, and about a zillion other things. Where's your mom anyway? When she wasn't in the waiting room, we figured she might be in here."

"She got mad at me and left. She's still convinced I have anorexia or am taking drugs or something and am making all this shit up to hide it."

She wasn't mad at her mother, not really, but Justy was incredibly frustrated with her. Still, it might be better if her mother didn't get involved. It might be safer that way, at least for her.

Corrie suddenly looked down at her phone. "Oh, shit."

"What?" asked Emmet and Justy in unison.

"I just got two more GPS coordinates texts. The full thing this time, but in pieces like the one leading here."

"What's it for?" asked Mikayla.

"No clue. Quick, write this down, before my phone does the magical rebooting shit." She rattled off some numbers, which Emmet hurriedly entered into his phone.

"Okay, I put it into Google maps…here we go…Okay, this is weird. It's the Bliss Café, where Tildie worked."

"Matilda…Tildie worked at Bliss?" asked Justy, chills travelling down her spine. She'd been to Bliss a few times but never saw her former friend.

Had Matilda avoided her, or had her shift simply not lined up with Justy's visits? If they had run into each other there, maybe things would have been different. Maybe they would have reconnected. Maybe Matilda would still be alive.

"Yeah, she worked there for almost a year," said Emmet. "I thought I told you that, but I guess I didn't."

"You just said she worked part-time somewhere in downtown Rogers. I should have asked. I had no idea. I was a terrible friend."

Emmet started to say something, but Corrie cut him off. "If you were a terrible friend, Justy, then I was an absolutely awful sister. Apparently I had no idea what was going on in her life. If I hadn't been so wrapped up in college, then maybe—"

"Just stop," yelled Mikayla. "Both of you…and, hell, you too, Emmet. I didn't know Tildie, but I'm pretty sure she wouldn't want you guys beating yourself up over the past. All we can do—yeah, I said 'we,' because I'm in this now, too—is move forward and figure out what happened to Tildie and what we can do about it."

Mik was right. They could wallow in their feelings later. Now was the time to act, to do something, anything, and hopefully find Matilda.

Mik…was this the same girl who just a few hours ago had slapped her because she'd stopped bullying Emmet? Had this crisis brought out the best in her? Did it really matter?

She walked over and hugged a surprised Mikayla.

"What was that for?" asked Mikayla, eyes wide.

"Because you're absolutely right, and I think you just made up for that slap."

"She is right," agreed Emmet, while Corrie nodded.

"I'm not sure I can ever make up for that slap, but thanks."

"So who wants to take a trip to Bliss?" asked Corrie.

"Well, I'm not supposed to leave the hospital until I've been discharged," Justy said, making a decision. "But…fuck it, let's go. What are they going to do anyway, kick me out of the hospital?"

After slipping out of the hospital, Justy, Emmet, Corrie, and Mikayla all piled into Corrie's green Honda Civic, with Emmet sitting up by Corrie and her and Mikayla in back, and headed for Bliss Café.

11

Kevin Haj sat at a table near the back of the Bliss Café, trying to figure out what was happening to him. Was he schizophrenic? Google seemed to think so, at least according to everything that came up on the search engine, but he wasn't sure that was the case. Sure, he saw hallucinations, but…what if they weren't actually hallucinations? What if Matty really was in trouble and somehow psychically reaching out to him for help? What if…what if she were dead and had become a spirit?

Then again, isn't that what a crazy person might think?

He'd seen her again this afternoon, right before school let out. A student had come up to turn in a paper and for a moment she was Matty, bleeding from the mouth, begging him for help. His eyes had gone wide, and he'd jumped back, bumping his chair into the wall, startling the hell out of that poor student.

Taking a slow sip of his latte, Kevin looked around the café. There were two posters up asking for information on Matilda Harper, one by the entrance and one by the cashier. He'd seen the posters before, of course, but he'd never realized it was Matty. How could he not have known that? Had he really paid that little attention?

He watched as four teenagers entered the coffee shop. There were three girls and a boy. The boy he recognized as Emmet Sapp, someone who'd been in one of his math classes but abruptly left the school a month or so ago.

He'd wondered at the time why Sapp had left, especially in the middle of his senior year, but had assumed he must have moved.

Apparently he'd been wrong about that, just like he'd been wrong about so many other things lately.

Sapp and the three girls went up to the counter to place their orders, then paused to look at Matty's "missing" poster. Did they know her? He didn't recognize any of the girls, but that didn't mean anything. There were a lot of kids at Rogers West.

As they turned to walk through the café proper, one of the three girls began to change. Her long blonde hair turned brown in an instant, and blood began to seep out of her mouth. No! This couldn't be happening again, not now, not here, not in the middle of a crowded café.

He pinched himself hard on his left hand, trying to snap his brain out of whatever psychotic state it was going through, to no avail. Black bruises formed around the young woman's throat in an instant, and tears rolled down her cheeks. She mouthed the words, *help me*, as a huge bruise formed around her left eye.

He knew, now. He knew this was definitely Matty, and that she needed his help. He also knew, beyond a shadow of a doubt, that it was the boyfriend she'd mentioned that fateful day a month and a half ago who had done these terrible, awful things to her, who had beaten and bloodied her, and maybe done even worse. He didn't know how he knew, he just knew.

But what could he do? He had already failed her once, damn it, he wouldn't fail her again. He *couldn't* fail her again. He pushed himself up from his chair and began walking towards the group of teenagers, ready to do whatever he had to do to save Matilda Harper.

✳✳✳

Emmet hadn't been to Bliss Café for at least a month and a half, right before Tildie vanished. He remembered many times coming here in his father's car when her shift was about to end and hanging out for an hour or so before he drove her home. He desperately missed those times, but knew they were probably gone for good.

"You okay, Em?" asked Justy, elbowing him in the side.

"Just missing Tildie. We spent a lot of time together here."

"Let's order some drinks," Corrie said, "and then I guess just hang out and see what happens."

Emmet nodded in agreement. They'd spent fifteen minutes wandering around outside and investigating the parking lot but hadn't seen anything out of the ordinary. If there were anything here that might aid them in their search for their missing friend, it was probably inside the café.

"Order whatever you want, my treat," said Corrie.

Mikayla ordered a salted caramel and white chocolate breve, Justy ordered a coconut mocha, Corrie ordered a caramel and vanilla breve, and Emmet just asked for a bottle of water.

"Not a big coffee fan," he said, when Corrie raised her eyebrows at him.

"I'm glad they've kept the posters up," said Corrie.

Mikayla stared at the poster. "I always wondered about her, who she was, and all that. I know I didn't know her, but I hope you guys know I'll do whatever I can to help you find her."

"We do know," Justy said, smiling, "and I think I can speak for everyone when I say thank you for that."

Emmet nodded in agreement before opening his bottle of water and drinking nearly half of it in one huge gulp. "Let's go sit down and talk all of this through again. Maybe we can finally figure something out."

He began walking towards an empty table when he noticed Mr. Haj, one of Rogers West's math teachers, sitting near the back of the café. Haj was staring at Justy with huge eyes, and he looked almost terrified.

Could he be the person who'd hurt Tildie? Was he the reason Corrie's GPS had brought them here? He'd always seemed nice, but did that really mean anything anymore?

And then Haj was on his feet, running towards Justy, arms outstretched. "Matty," he yelled, "are you okay? What happened to you?"

"What the hell, dude?" Justy said, stepping back. "Who's Matty?"

Emmet instinctively leaped in front of Justy, hoping to protect her. He'd already failed Tildie, there was no way in hell he was going to let anything bad happen to Justy.

Haj reached them in a second, then blinked, looking lost. He peered around Emmet, shaking his head. "You're not Matty. I'm so sorry. I don't know why I thought you were her. You don't look anything like her."

"Who in the heck is Matty?" asked Justy, her eyes big.

It took Emmet a few seconds, but then he remembered that Tildie had made a point of calling herself Matty while at the café. When he asked her why, she said she wanted to keep her work life separate from her school and personal life, that she'd read somewhere that adopting a different variation of your name while at work helped to do that.

"That's what Tildie called herself at work," said Corrie, apparently having had the same discussion with her sister. She turned towards Haj. "Now, tell us who you are, mister, before we call the cops."

Everyone in the café was staring at them.

"That's Mr. Haj, a math teacher from Rogers West," Emmet said.

Corrie stared at Haj. "I remember now. I had you my senior year."

"You know Matty?" Haj asked, looking at Corrie. "Is she okay? Do you know where she is?"

"Is there a problem here?" asked a young woman with a name badge that read 'Hi, I'm Keelin, asst. manager at Bliss Café.' She probably wasn't much older than Emmet.

Corrie stared at the woman for a heartbeat or two before saying, "No, there's no problem here. Just a case of mistaken identity, that's all."

"Is that true?" asked Keelin, and everyone, including Mr. Haj, nodded. "Okay, then. Just try to keep it down, okay?"

The moment the assistant manager walked away Corrie took Haj's arm and led him back to his table, then sat down beside him. Justy and

Mikayla sat down opposite of them, and Emmet grabbed a chair from an empty table and pulled it over for himself.

"Let me guess," said Corrie, looking at Haj. "When you saw her, her hair was brown, and she was bleeding from the mouth. Right?"

Haj looked stunned. "Yes, that's right. How…how did you know that?"

Justy stared at Corrie. "Yeah, how did you know that?"

"Because for a second, right after he ran over, that's how you looked to me, too. It was…terrifying. You practically morphed into my sister right before my eyes."

Mikayla, who up until now had been silent, whispered, "Samesies."

Emmet couldn't believe it. Apparently Mikayla and Mr. Haj were experiencing visions of Tildie, but so far all he'd seen is his essay scattered around the school floor. If Tildie were dead—and it almost made him scream to even think that—why wasn't she reaching out to him?

Haj's eyes filled with tears. "I've been seeing her for two days now. Bleeding from the mouth and looking so scared. It's been awful, and I still don't understand it, but the fact that you two also saw it…means maybe I'm not going crazy. Or we all are, I have no idea."

"So, Mr. Haj," said Corrie, "let's start at the beginning, all right? How are you connected to my sister?"

They sat and listened as the math teacher explained how he'd never had Tildie in any of his classes and only knew her as a barista, but that she'd always made special lattes for him with a foam "pi" symbol and that he'd talked to her a few days before she disappeared, when she seemed very upset, listening to her complain about her boyfriend.

"I didn't even know she had a boyfriend," said Corrie, when he was done. "Why didn't she tell me she had a boyfriend?"

"Probably for the same reason she didn't tell me she had a boyfriend," said Emmet, a little too loudly. "She didn't trust me. Apparently she trusted a fucking teacher who didn't even know she went to his school over me. No offense, Mr. Haj, but seriously."

Corrie sighed. "Emmet…I know for a fact she trusted you. She loved you like a brother. She talked about you all the time. She told me about the Dungeons and Dragons campaign you made for her, about the comics you both read, the movies you saw, about all the shit you two did together. You were her best friend. She loved you. No, scratch that. She *loves* you, present tense. I'm not ready to give up on Tildie just yet, and neither should you."

Emmet was about to respond, to ask why, if she loved him, had she not confided in him, when Haj said, "I think she told me specifically because I didn't really know her. She needed someone to talk to and I just happened to be there, in the right place at the right time, so to speak. She was upset and needed to vent. I remember her being hesitant to mention her boyfriend, and she didn't really say much about him other than they were having a disagreement."

That was all well and good, but why wasn't he having any visions? Why had Mikayla, who never even met Tildie, had a vision when he hadn't? None of it made sense. Justy reached out to squeeze his fingers, and he almost pulled away. Instead, he took a deep breath and squeezed her fingers back in return.

None of this mattered right now. He could deal with his hurt feelings later. What really mattered, the only thing that really mattered, was find ing Tildie.

"Thanks, Juicy," he whispered, and she smiled.

"Look at you two, holding hands already," said Mikayla. "I wonder what Tildie's gonna think when she finds out her best friend from junior high is hooking up with her current best friend?"

Justy blushed and quickly pulled back her hand, stifling a little laugh.

Mr. Haj cleared his throat. "So what are we going to do about this? The detective said I should call her if I learned anything new. Do you think I should call her?"

"Do you think she's going to believe any of this?" asked Corrie.

"Well...probably not."

"Well, then, let's not call her."

Now it was their turn to tell Haj about Justy's seizures, about Corrie's GPS, and everything they'd learned. Haj sat there silently when they were done, looking overwhelmed.

"Wow," he finally said. "Just...wow."

"No kidding," said Emmet.

"And then I wound up in the hospital, and...oh, shit," yelped Justy, staring down at her phone.

"What's wrong?" asked Emmet.

"My mom's blowing up my phone. She found out I left the hospital and she's threatening to call 911 and report me missing. I have to call her. I'm gonna go outside. I'll be back."

Justy stood up from the table, and Emmet surprised himself by following her lead. Justy stared at him, raising her eyebrows.

"This feels like it's getting weirder and weirder, maybe even dangerous, and I'm not letting you out of my sight. That goes for all of you." He turned to look at Corrie, Mikayla, and Haj. "From now on, none of us are ever alone unless there's absolutely no alternative. Got it?"

A slow smile crept over Justy's face. "Got it."

"From everything you've told me, I'd tend to agree," said Haj.

Mikayla nodded in agreement, and Corrie said, "Got it."

Justy reached out to take his hand, and together they walked outside so she could call her mother.

12

Wednesday

Justy woke up feeling confused. She'd been dreaming of the time she and Matilda went to Silver Dollar City for Justy's birthday, back in fourth grade, before Justy's father abandoned her and her mother for some woman he'd met on Matchstick. Before she'd felt the need to lose weight, so she'd stop being bullied and ended up developing anorexia. Before she herself became a bully.

Before, before, before.

Things definitely hadn't been perfect "before," but they'd been better. Hadn't they? Matilda had been her bestie, that much was true, and her father had still been around, but things were far from perfect. Mom and Dad fought constantly, and even back then she'd been bullied.

As her mother's favorite singer Billy Joel once sang, "the good old days weren't always good, and tomorrow's not as bad as it seems."

Last night had been a shit show. Justy's mother screamed at her for what felt like hours (though, remembering it now, was probably closer to fifteen minutes) about leaving the hospital without permission and scaring the absolute shit out of her. She'd grounded Justy for a month and forced her to stay home from school today, "just in case" the seizures started again. At first she'd been insistent on taking her back to the hospital, but at least Justy had been able to argue her way out of that.

Her hospital tests had all come back negative. Her blood results were perfectly normal, and the x-rays and CT scans they'd done showed absolutely nothing out of the ordinary. The doctors couldn't explain her seizures, and yet her mother wouldn't believe her story and kept insisting she must have relapsed into anorexia. It was absolutely infuriating.

Mom was at work now, however, and wouldn't be home until after six, so what she didn't know wouldn't hurt her. After hearing Justy's half of the conversation with her mother, Emmet had offered to pretend to be sick today so he could stay home as well, and they could continue investigating Matilda's disappearance together.

She'd gladly taken him up on the offer. Mr. Haj wasn't able to get out of going to Rogers West, however, and Mikayla had tried to get out of going to AAFA, but according to the text Mik sent this morning her parents wouldn't have it, so she was stuck with Ashlie, Chrissie, and Tegan for now.

Corrie, however, had no such obstacles other than an 8:30 am physics class she didn't feel she could skip, and thought she could show up to Justy's house around 10:30 or so.

Mikayla and Mr. Haj had pledged to meet up with them after school, and to stay in touch throughout the day via a chat Corrie had started in Signal, a private messaging app she'd told them about and made them all download and install on their phones.

Samantha jumped up on the bed, startling her. The cat meowed and rubbed against Justy's hand.

"Who's the good girl?" she whispered to Samantha, stroking her silky fur.

Samantha purred, moving closer to Justy. She impulsively hugged the cat, nuzzling her face into Samantha's fur. Oh, how Matilda had adored Samantha. Because her father was allergic to both cats and dogs, Matilda never had any pets, but she loved Samantha as if she were her own.

Justy felt tears rolling down her cheeks. She'd missed out on over three years of Matilda's—Tildie's—friendship, because she was too scared to reach out to her. It couldn't be over now, could it, just when she realized what she'd been missing? If Tildie were dead, she wasn't sure she could survive the loss.

Her phone beeped. She reluctantly let Samantha go, wiped away her tears, and looked at the message she'd just received. It was from Emmet. She clicked open the text, a smile forming unbidden on her lips.

Emmet: *Yo, Juicy. You up?*

She giggled. Apparently she had a new nickname now. She guessed that's what she got for calling him "Em."

Justy: *I just woke up and please don't call me that.*

Emmet: *Haven't we been through this before?*

Justy: *I think we have. Maybe we're pulling a Groundhog Day?*

Her mother's favorite film was this ancient comedy starring Bill Murray called *Groundhog Day*, about a man who kept living the same day over and over again. She'd finally got Justy to watch it last year, and surprisingly Justy loved it. She and her mother had taken to calling repeating behaviors "pulling a *Groundhog Day*." She wondered if Emmet would get the reference. She thought he just might.

Emmet: *Ha. I love that movie.*

Justy: *Yeah, same. But please, no more Juicy, okay?*

Emmet: *Lol. I'll do my best, as long as you lay off the Em stuff.*

Justy: *No promises, but I'll try.* ☺

Emmet: *So…what are your ideas for today? I claimed to have a stomachache, and they let me stay home. I think they were a little suspicious, though, so I doubt I'll get away with it tomorrow.*

Justy: *Then I guess we need to make today count. Wanna come over?*

Emmet: *I thought you'd never ask.*

Justy quickly got ready, slipping into a pair of blue jeans and a light blue top and doing her makeup. She looked cute. She shook her head. What was wrong with her? Why was she trying to look cute? Emmet, the guy she'd treated horribly until just three days ago, was her friend, not her boyfriend. She wasn't interested in him that way. Was she?

And even if she was, she seriously doubted he felt the same way, not after the way she'd treated him. She started to change into something a little less cute when the doorbell rang. Well, damn. Cute it was, then. She shook her head at her own silliness and answered the door.

"Hey," he said, staring at her as he stood in the doorway.

"Hey yourself," she said, stepping back.

He didn't come in, and instead just stood on the doorstep in silence.

"What, are you a vampire or something? Come on in."

He laughed, then stepped over the threshold. "Sorry. I'm weird sometimes, I guess."

"You guess?" She laughed. "You're weird all the time, but that's okay. So am I. We make a good team."

She led him into the living room, sitting on the large brown couch occupying the southernmost wall. She patted the couch beside her, and he sat down, as far away from her as possible.

"So...do you have any ideas? About Tildie, I mean."

"Not really," she admitted. "You?"

"Nope. I stayed up half the night thinking about it, and I still don't know what to do. If she really is dead—God, it hurts to even say that out loud—all we can do is wait for her to make contact with us again. Well, not 'us.' With you or Corrie or Mr. Haj, or hell, even with Mikayla now, I guess."

He was still hurt about being left out, and she guessed she couldn't blame him. She had some ideas about that but wasn't sure how to broach them without hurting his feelings, so she just blurted it out.

"Emmet...you close yourself off, sometimes. And I get it, especially after how I treated you."

Emmet sighed. "It wasn't just you. It's been everyone, my whole life. Even my grandfather. I've tried to lose weight, tried not to be such a nerd, but...I'm just me, I guess, and nobody likes me."

"Tildie likes you. I like you."

"Well, maybe you do now, but if I hadn't come into the bathroom and found you, would you?"

"Probably not," she admitted, with a frown, "but that would have been on me, not you, and I wouldn't know what I was missing. If I'd ever taken the time to get to know you, I know I would have liked you, even if you hadn't saved my stupid ass."

They sat in silence for a moment before Emmet finally spoke. "Your ass isn't stupid, and neither is the rest of you."

Justy laughed. "Well, I sure was stupid to treat you the way I did, to treat anyone that way, and I really am sorry, and I hope you believe that."

"I do," he said softly.

She stared at him. He really was a good person. Sweet, funny, kind…and actually pretty cute, now that she thought about it. How had she not seen that before?

She scooted across the couch and leaned towards him, almost without thinking about it, wanting nothing more than to kiss him. Their lips touched only briefly before Emmet pulled back, eyes wide, and said, "What are you doing?"

"Oh my God, I'm so sorry," she said, embarrassed. "I just…I read something wrong, I guess, and…Well, fuck."

He was staring at her. He closed his eyes for a second, then quickly opened them. "You didn't read anything wrong," he said quietly, his words all coming out in a rush. "I really like you, probably more than I should, and I wanted to kiss you, but I didn't think you'd ever want that, and it's just super hard for me to admit that, to open myself up."

"Like I said earlier."

"Yeah, well, you were right. Everything always feels like a trick, something to humiliate and embarrass me. Last year, at Rogers West, a girl…her name was Alyson…she pretended to like me. She asked me to go to a school dance. I'd never gone to a dance, but I went to this one, for some stupid reason, and it was all a scam. Her friends all laughed at me. It was…absolutely awful."

"I'm so sorry, Emmet. I had no idea."

She felt like her heart was breaking for him. Who could do something so cruel? Then she remembered with a start that Ashlie had done something similar to a boy earlier this year, and they'd all laughed at him. She felt so ashamed.

"So what happened after that?" she finally asked.

"Tildie kicked her ass the next day and then got suspended from school for a week. She said it was worth it, though."

Justy laughed, feeling the tension break a little. "That's our Tildie."

"I just don't understand why you'd want to kiss me. Why anyone would. You're beautiful, and I'm just…well, I'm just me."

Emmet normally kept up an emotional shield of sorts, and he was letting it down now, just for her.

"That's kind of the point. You *are* you. You're smart, funny, kind, and cute." He started to protest, and she gently put her forefinger up against his mouth. "Shh. You *are* cute, even if you don't think you are, even if you can't see it yourself. You have beautiful green eyes, a terrific smile, and…you saved my fucking life, twice. How many people would do that?"

"But I'm fat."

She sighed. "No, you're not. I mean, yeah, you're a little overweight, but you're not fat, I never should have said you were, and even if you were, so what? Since when is anyone perfect anyway? I'm not! I hate that I ever made you feel 'less than,' because I think…well, I think you're just perfect…for me."

Emmet stared at her for a heartbeat or two, seemingly coming to a decision. "I do want to kiss you. I'm sorry I freaked out. I've…well, I've never kissed a girl before. Do you think we could try again?"

"Absolutely," she whispered, leaning forward, eyes closed, feeling her lips meet his.

They were able to enjoy the kiss for ten whole seconds before the alarm went off on her phone, startling them both.

"Shit! I forgot about the alarm," she said, as she rushed to turn it off.

She'd agreed to send her mother a photo of herself standing by the analog clock hanging on the living room wall every hour on the hour to prove she hadn't left the house. That was the only way her mother would agree to allow her to stay home instead of checking her back into the hospital. It was humiliating.

She quickly got up off the couch and darted over to the clock, snapped a selfie beside it, and then sent it to her mother. The only response she got was a thumbs up emoji.

"There are ways around that, though," Emmet said, after she explained the deal she'd made with her mother.

"Like what? She insisted I include the time stamp on the pics, so I couldn't change the clock and take a bunch of photos all at once."

"I just might know a way…"

Emmet changed the time on her phone to an hour in the future, then gave the phone back to Justy and changed the time on the analog clock. As soon as she took the selfie, he went through all the steps again, up until they had photos for every hour of the day until 6:00 pm, when Regina Friedman would arrive home. He then downloaded an automatic text sender from Google Play Store and set it up to send the text with the appropriate photos hourly. He even set up the 2:00 photo to be sent a minute later, along with a text that read, "Sorry, I was in the bathroom," because they didn't want it to be perfectly timed every time lest she get suspicious.

"You're a genius," said Justy, beaming at him, as she cancelled the hourly alarms on her phone.

"I'm no genius, just a tech nerd," he said, smiling.

"Lucky for us," Justy said, wrapping her arms around his neck, "I like tech nerds."

He wrapped his arms around her waist, and they began to kiss. This felt right. It felt good. The kiss deepened, and a few seconds later a knock on the front door reverberated through the house, making them both jump.

Emmet looked startled and then they both burst out laughing. "That must be Corrie. We really need to work on our timing."

Justy said, "We can definitely work on that later," and then gave him a quick peck on the lips before running over to the door.

She gazed out the peephole. Yep, it was Corrie. She opened the door and Corrie came inside.

"Hi guys," she said, walking into the house like she was treading through quicksand.

Corrie looked exhausted, like she hadn't slept all night. She was dressed in the same pair of black slacks and white blouse she'd been wearing yesterday, and her hair looked tangled.

"Are you doing okay?" asked Justy, immediately regretting it.

"What do you think?" Corrie barked out.

"She was just concerned," said Emmet, joining them in the middle of the living room "We both are. As much as we both love Tildie…she's your sister. I know this is hurting you, a lot."

Corrie looked like she was about to cry. "I know it's hurting you, too. I'm sorry for getting snippy. I love you both for doing what you can to try to find her, more than I can say." Her words came out in a rush. "I'm just…wiped out, I guess. Took forever to fall asleep and then less than two hours later an awful dream about that asshole strangling my little sister woke me up, and I wasn't able to go back to sleep again."

"You're having the dreams now, too, huh?" asked Emmet. "I'm sorry. That had to be scary."

"The good news is that I had a little time to think, lying in bed unable to sleep. Emmet…sometimes, you close yourself off."

A laugh burst out of his mouth. "No shit, Sherlock. That's what everyone," he said, turning to look at Justy, "has been telling me lately."

"It's not an insult," Corrie said, reaching out to take Emmet's hand, and Justy nodded in agreement. "I know some of the shit you went through in school, Emmet. I don't blame you one bit. But what if the fact that you close yourself off so much is the reason Tildie can't get through to you?"

Emmet stared at her, open mouthed. That was exactly where Justy's thoughts had been going. He kept himself so guarded, the most this supernatural force had been able to do had been to scatter his essay across the hall.

"I never thought about it that way," Emmet said, "but I guess it does make sense."

"These last few years…you've probably been closer to her than anyone, including me. It hurts me to admit that, but it's true. If you were to open up, just a little, enough to let her in, maybe she could reach you."

"I think she's right," Justy said, chiming in. She reached out to take Emmet's other hand, turning towards him. "I mean, don't you think it's worth a try?"

13

Emmet lay on Justy's bed in her room, eyes closed, trying to reach Tildie's spirit or whatever was sending all these visions, but it wasn't working. He'd been here for over thirty minutes now, and nothing. Justy sat with him for the whole time, holding his hand.

"Why isn't this working?" asked Emmet.

"Probably because you're not really relaxed," Justy said. "Maybe we need to try some soft background music again or something."

"Or we could try my idea," said Corrie, waving a little brown box filled with mushroom edibles at him.

Emmet wanted no part of Corrie's drugged up gummies. He'd never once tried 'shrooms, weed, or any sort of recreational drug, and didn't want to start now. Hell, he'd never even tasted alcohol. The mere thought of feeling out of control made him queasy.

His grandfather—his father's father—had been a raging, out of control, violent alcoholic. He'd died when Emmet was just eleven, but he had a lot of bad memories of the man, including watching him hit his grandmother. The thought of being under the influence, of effectively being out of control, had always terrified him. Grandpa Roy had done some awful things while under the influence of alcohol, and he could never allow himself to follow in that nasty old man's footsteps.

"I said no," Emmet yelled, opening his eyes, releasing Justy's hand, and sitting up in bed. "I'm not doing that shit."

"Then this may never work," countered Corrie. "I just don't get why you won't even try a little bit."

"I already told you why."

"Emmet," said Justy, reaching out to take his hand again, "you are *not* your grandfather. You're nothing like that horrible man. You're a good guy, and you want to help your best friend, and if giving up a little control is the only way to help her...shouldn't you maybe at least try?"

Emmet felt like crying. He knew she was right. Corrie had been here for a little over two hours, and nothing had changed. They'd tried meditation, they'd tried soft jazz, they'd tried progressive muscle relaxation, and they'd tried a bunch of other things Corrie had seen on TikTok, but nothing worked. If this were the only way for him to reach Tildie, shouldn't he at least try? Wasn't she worth at least that much to him?

Of course she was. When he thought about it that way, there was no doubt that he should do this. They had to find out if Tildie were alive or dead, and who that mysterious man was in Justy's visions.

"Okay," he finally said, in a whisper, "I'll do it."

The mushroom gummies, she'd told them, were designed specifically to relax you and open up your mind to the spirit world. They were also highly illegal. She'd purchased them from a dealer on campus this morning specifically with this in mind.

Justy squeezed his hand again. "It'll be fine. I'll be here with you, and so will Corrie. It's all going to be okay."

"Give it to me before I change my mind," he said, reaching his free hand out towards Corrie.

She handed him two little orange squares covered in sugar, which was not at all what he'd been expecting. He wasn't exactly sure what he'd been expecting, but it wasn't this. He popped the first one in his mouth and began to chew. It was actually pretty tasty, not far off from a regular piece of candy. He ate the second one much more quickly.

"Okay, now what?" he asked as soon as he'd swallowed both squares.

"Now you lie back down again and relax. I'll guide you through this," said Corrie. "Justy is here, too. You're safe. Everything is gonna be okay."

Emmet laid down, closed his eyes, and tried to relax. Justy's fingers stroked his hand, which was comforting. Never in a million years did he think he'd end up kissing and holding hands with Justy Friedman, the most beautiful girl in school, who just a few days earlier had called him a tank. It was a weird, wonderful world.

"Okay, Emmet, slowly inhale through your nose for four seconds, hold your breath for seven seconds, and then exhale through your mouth for eight seconds. Yeah, just like that. Very good.

"Now keep breathing like that, and I want you to clench your shoulder muscles for just a second and then relax them. Just let go. Okay, now your biceps. There we go, now relax. Now your butt muscles…your thighs…your knees…your feet…let all the tension go. You're relaxed, you're safe, and you're with people who care about you. Keep breathing 4-7-8 style."

He was starting to feel a little relaxed, probably more relaxed than he'd felt since Tildie went missing. Maybe more relaxed than he'd ever felt before in his whole life. The edibles must be working. He tried to block out everything but Corrie's voice and the feel of Justy's fingertips, while following the breathing instructions.

"You're safe, you're protected, and you're relaxed. Good. Keep breathing in four, hold for seven, and out for eight. You can feel yourself opening up to the universe. A pink light envelops you, protecting you from anything bad, but letting good things inside. Letting Tildie inside.

"Now think of her, Emmet, think of Tildie, and all the good times you two had together. Think about your friendship, and know that she loves you, and she misses you, and she wants to see you. Keep breathing 4-7-8, and now just let yourself go, breathe normally, and let her inside."

Emmet was no longer lying on the bed in Justy's house. Instead, he found himself in a wooded area. It was dark, but he was safe, surrounded by a pink, glowing light. He heard voices. He turned around to see a man dressed in jeans and a dark hoodie dragging Tildie by one wrist. Her eyes were covered with a blindfold, while her hands were tied together with a white cord of some sort. Her face was beaten and bruised, and she was screaming.

Emmet tried to move closer, to save Tildie, somehow, but the pink bubble seemed to keep him rooted to the ground. The man's face was mostly obscured by the hood of his jacket, but Emmet thought he saw an errant strand of thick blond hair sticking out to the side.

"No one can hear you way out here," said the man, in a taunting voice. "If you would have listened to me, none of this would have had to happen."

"You're sick. I don't know what I was thinking, ever letting myself get involved with you. You're just a predator. It was wrong!"

"Oh no, babe," he said, "it was right until you fucked it all up. I loved you, and you loved me. I still love you."

"I never loved you, and you sure as hell never loved me! You just used me for sex. That's all you cared about! Taking the virginity of a seventeen-year-old girl!"

The man stopped dragging Tildie and turned to face her. "You're wrong about all of that. I did love you and I do love you. I fell in love with you the first day I saw you. If you'd been on birth control, and if that fucking condom hadn't broken, we'd still be happy."

She kicked at his crotch, but he easily avoided her foot and then backhanded her across the face. Crying out loud, she fell to the ground in a sobbing, quivering heap.

"Get up."

"You wouldn't let me get an abortion!"

He grabbed her by the arm and hauled her to her feet. "You're carrying my child, Tildie. Now that he exists, I won't allow you to get rid of him. But once he's born—yes, it'll be a boy, we both know that—you'll be free to go, and you'll never see me again."

"Bullshit! I know you're going to kill me."

"Tildie...I'd never kill you or anyone. Not unless I was forced."

"My parents will find me! Corrie will find me!" She coughed, then began sobbing. "Emmet will find me, and then he'll kill you!"

The man laughed. "That lazy, fat piece of shit won't do anything."

Emmet wanted nothing more but to destroy this mystery man, to rip him into shreds and put him into the ground forever. He pushed against the bubble again and moved just a little closer, but then the man dragged her deeper into the woods, further away from him.

"Help me! Please! Somebody, anybody, help me!" she screamed, but the man just laughed.

"No one can hear you way out here."

She suddenly pulled away from him, darting back the way they'd come. He quickly caught up to her, however, and grabbed her by the hair. She gasped as she stumbled back into him.

"You're slower than you used to be, Tildie. After you have the baby, you really need to work on that. Why, I remember a time when—"

"Leave me alone!"

"You know I can't do that," he said, once again dragging her by the wrist.

"If you don't let me go…I'll…I'll kill the baby. I will! You're going to kill me anyway."

"Don't be stupid. If you kill my son, I really will kill you. And then I'll go after Corrie. Yes, I remember Corrie. I always liked her, but you better believe I'll kill her, and then I'll kill fat ass Emmet Sapp, and then I'll kill your stupid, gullible parents. They'll all be dead, because of you."

Tildie screamed, "Fuck you, you psycho," at the top of her lungs, kept screaming until she was coughing again, and her captor, her assailant, just kept laughing.

"I won't hurt Corrie or Emmet as long as my son is born alive and safe. I won't hurt your parents, either, I won't hurt anyone, and I'll let you go once the baby is safe and sound. Do we have a deal?"

Tildie screamed at him again, yanking against his grasp, but it was useless. She wasn't going anywhere, and even if she could get away, where would she go? She was in the middle of some giant woodland. She'd never find her way out by herself.

"Okay," she finally whispered, defeated. "Don't hurt anyone, and I'll do what you say."

"That's my girl," he said, once again guiding her through the woods.

Emmet floated along after them as they walked in silence. Eventually they came to a solid black storage shed. He slipped the blindfold from Tildie's eyes, and she edged backwards, but the man dragged her towards the shed.

"Bought this at Lowe's last weekend," he said. "Put it together, and then spray painted it black. This is where you'll be living until you have my baby. There's a sleeping bag in there as well as a good supply of water and some food. It's metal with no windows, so you can't get out."

"What the fuck is wrong with you?" she rasped.

The man in the hoodie laughed. "I've also double reinforced everything and installed extra locks on the door. You'll be safe in there. There are a few bottles of pre-natal vitamins in a Wal-Mart bag in there. Make sure to read the instructions on the bottle and take them when you're supposed to. I want you to stay healthy.

"I also brought a bunch of books so you shouldn't get too bored, and some extra clothing. There's also a battery-powered lamp in the shed, not visible from outside so don't get any cute ideas. I'll come by a couple times a week to check on you and bring you more food."

"You're sick," Tildie whispered. "Sick and twisted. How long have you been planning this?"

"Ever since you told me you wanted to tell your parents about us and the baby and get an abortion. Now let's get you inside."

Emmet's eyes snapped open just as the man drug Tildie into the shed and closed the door behind them.

He sat up from the bed.

"Are you okay?" asked Justy, still holding his hand.

"I saw everything," Emmet whispered, tears in his eyes. "I know what happened."

"But how?" Corrie asked. "Your eyes were only closed for maybe a minute at most."

Emmet shook his head. Did he really see everything he thought he saw, or was it simply the drugs? It seemed so real, but if it all happened in less than a minute...

"I don't know. What if it was just the drugs?" Emmet asked, looking up at Corrie. "What if those mushroom gummies made me hallucinate?"

"It wasn't the drugs, Emmet," Corrie said.

"But how do you know?"

"Because I know. Okay? It wasn't the drugs."

"Yeah, how do you know?" asked Justy.

"Because…they weren't really mushrooms."

Emmet stared at her. "What?"

"Just what I said. They were regular candy. Something called War-head Cubes that I picked up at Wal-Mart on the way here. I took two out of the bag and put them in that little cardboard box.

"Look, I don't even know a dealer. I made the whole thing up. I thought maybe if you relaxed, you could connect with her, and it looks like I was right."

"Are you serious?" asked Justy. "You lied to Emmet? To both of us?"

"It worked, didn't it?"

"Still. You had no right to do that."

Emmet laughed despite himself. Apparently, it did work. That, and the muscle relaxation and meditation bits. But it had taken the thought of losing control—of having that control taken from him—to really open himself up.

He didn't like being lied to, but it had definitely worked.

"It's okay. The important thing is, I think…I think, if we're lucky, Tildie might still be alive. We need to find her as soon as we can, before it's too late."

"But how?" Justy asked, after he explained his vision. "If she's alive, how is she doing all this? And…that doesn't gel with what I saw. He was standing over me…over her…with a shovel. There was no black shed. How is that possible?"

Emmet shrugged. "No clue, but I know what I saw. Also…she's pregnant."

"Pregnant?" Corrie exclaimed. "What the actual fuck?"

"Are you sure?" asked Justy, eyes wide.

"Oh yeah, I'm sure. Whoever her mysterious 'boyfriend' was, he knocked her up."

"Okay," said Corrie, "can you start at the beginning and tell us everything you saw?"

Emmet told them everything he'd seen. One thing stuck out; what Tildie had said about her captor taking the virginity of a seventeen-year-old girl. That had to mean he was older than she was, maybe in a position of authority over her. Maybe one of the managers or assistant managers at Bliss Café, or even a teacher at Rogers West.

"And he said he knew *me*?" asked Corrie. "Are you sure he said that?"

"I'm positive. He seemed to know me, too. It almost has to be a teacher at Rogers West, now that I think about it, because who else would know us both?"

He suddenly remembered Mikayla telling him about her crush on one of the teachers at Arkansas Arts Academy of Fine Arts. That wasn't unusual, to be sure, but a teacher taking advantage of the crush…it had certainly happened before, though he'd never heard of it happening at AAFA or Rogers West. Not that that meant it hadn't happened at one of those schools, of course.

"I wish Mr. Haj were here," Justy said. "Maybe he'd have some ideas."

"I hate to say this," said Corrie, "but could he be playing us? Maybe he's the one who kidnapped Tildie, after all."

"No, it's not him, but I'm glad you said that. It made me remember something. In the vision, I saw the kidnapper's hair. It was blond. Mr. Haj has black hair. Plus, I'm pretty sure he's gay, so he probably wouldn't be knocking up any seventeen-year-old girls."

"We should ask him to snoop around at the school," Justy said. "If whoever did this to Tildie is someone there, maybe he can find them."

Emmet and Corrie agreed, and so Emmet sent a message to their Signal chat encapsulating everything they'd learned.

I hope you're wrong about that, Mr. Haj responded, *but I'll snoop around and see what I can find out. Also, I'll be done with school at four. Do you think we can meet at my place around 4:30? It seems safer than the Bliss Café.*

Sounds good. Where do you live? Corrie texted back after discussing it with Emmet and Justy.

He texted back an address not too far from them, in a fancy apartment setup called "The Junction in Rogers." They agreed to meet at 4:30.

I'll be there, too, said Mikayla, through Signal. *It hasn't been a fun day at school. I'll tell you all about it later. Looking forward to seeing you guys.*

14

Kevin Haj sat in his classroom on the second floor of Rogers West, re-reading Emmet's description of his vision. This whole thing was crazy, and the craziest thing was thinking that one of his fellow teachers might be involved in Matilda Harper's disappearance. He didn't want to believe it, but what if it were true?

"Mr. Haj?" said one of the students, Quinn Simonson, as she walked up to his desk. "May I go to the bathroom?"

"Sure," he said, watching as she walked out of the room.

It was nearly two in the afternoon, and this was his last class of the day. The next period was his free period. All the students were studying for a quiz on Friday, however, so he didn't have a lot to do at the moment and didn't need to wait until his free period to do a little research. He typed in the school's URL on his laptop and clicked on the faculty listings.

It was a big school. In addition to a huge staff that had four assistant principals, there were over 200 teachers. Approximately half of them were men. Thankfully, he didn't have to go through each and every one, at least to start. He'd concentrate on the teachers.

He called up Matilda Harper's class schedule and made a note of the faculty who had taught her senior year. Of those twelve teachers, five were men. Of those five male teachers, only two were blond. John Gillespie, who taught English, and Trent Barnes, who, like himself, taught math. He knew both of these men pretty well, and had briefly dated Barnes, who was definitely gay, so that left only Gillespie.

He clicked on Gillespie's bio. The man was 53 years old, had taught at Rogers West for 28 years, was married, and had three children. He couldn't imagine Gillespie doing anything like Emmet had described, but maybe the image he presented was merely a façade. Who could say for certain?

The bell rang just a few minutes after Quinn finally returned to her seat from the bathroom, and the students were dismissed. He was about to check to see if Gillispie had a free period this hour when Lela Kirby walked into his room.

"Kevin," she said, "I really need to apologize to you."

"For calling the police on me?" he said, standing up from his desk.

Thanks to Miss Kirby, he'd been interrogated by Detective Amy Thompson for almost an hour. He'd been livid that she could think such a thing of him at the time, but looking back on it, he sort of understood.

"Yes, for that." She sighed, a frown on her face. "I figured you'd know it was me. I don't know what I was thinking. You just described Tildie Harper so perfectly. Anyway, the detective called me this morning and told me the lead didn't pan out, and I feel awful for even thinking you could do such a thing. I hope you can find it in your heart to forgive me."

Her words came out in a rush, and he suspected she'd been rehearsing them ever since she got the call from Detective Thompson. His anger softened a little. If he had been in her shoes, he could even see himself thinking the same thing and acting accordingly.

"I was pretty upset," he said, feeling bad when he watched her flinch at his words, "but in hindsight, I understand why you thought what you did. I probably came off pretty crazy."

"Maybe a little," said Kirby, a hint of a smile tugging on her lips. "But, still. I know you're a good man, Kevin, and I really am sorry."

"I accept your apology. However, you might once again think I'm nuts when I tell you what's going on."

"You still trust me?"

He thought about it for a second and realized that he did. As teachers, their first priority should always be their students. She had followed that model to a T. He couldn't really fault her for that.

"I do," he said. "Do you have time to sit down and talk?"

"This is my free period, and I know it's yours, too. I looked it up. That's why I showed up when I did. So, yeah, let's talk."

He told her everything that had been going on, including Emmet's vision. When he was done, tears were running down her cheeks.

"I teach psychology, as you know," she said, "and my first inclination should probably be to think you're all crazy, but…I don't. Things happen all the time that we don't understand. I've probably never told you— I don't tell this to a lot of people—but my mother died when I fourteen. She was in a car wreck at 2:17 in the afternoon, on a Tuesday.

"I was sitting in biology class at Bentonville High School, taking a quiz, and…I knew. I just knew. I hadn't even been thinking about my mom, but suddenly she was all I could think about. I knew she was gone. I panicked and ran out of the room without even asking. Ran to my locker, got out my phone, and called my mom. She didn't answer, of course, and so I kept calling, getting ever more panicky.

"Eventually a man answered her phone, a paramedic named Steve Walters. I'll never forget his name. He sounded so sad. He told me what happened, that my mother had been in a car wreck and died instantly. That she'd probably not even felt any pain."

"Jesus, Lela, I'm so sorry," he said, when she stopped talking. "I had no idea. How awful."

"It was horrible, but I knew what happened the instant it happened. They told me later that the accident took place exactly at 2:17, based on traffic surveillance footage and GPS information from the car. How did I know that?"

"I don't know," he admitted, "but maybe there are things we'll just never understand."

"Yeah, exactly," she said, sniffling. She reached out to take his hand. "I should have been more open when you shared that was happening with me, but instead I freaked out and called the police. But if you can believe what happened with me and my mother, I think I can believe you all had visions about Tildie."

"Thank you. And you know what? Ever since I met up with the kids at Bliss, I haven't had any visions at all. It's like I fulfilled my part and didn't need the visions anymore."

"Thank goodness for small favors," she said.

"And now I need to start investigating John Gillispie. I still can't believe he had anything to do with this, but Gillispie's the only person who fits what Emmet Sapp saw."

"Mr. Gillispie has really bad arthritis in his hands. I don't think he could put together a shed, let alone reinforce it and add new locks."

"Shit. You're right. I didn't even think about that."

Perhaps Emmet was wrong about it being a teacher, or at least a teacher from Rogers West. Kevin looked through all the teachers who would have had access to Tildie, and the only two who fit the bill had been ruled out, because of one being gay and the other having bad arthritis. He shared this with Lela, who shook her head.

"I agree that neither Mr. Gillispie nor Mr. Barnes has anything to do with this, but I think your search parameters need to be expanded a little. It's unlikely that any of the office staff would be involved, because they'd have very limited access to Tildie, but what about the teaching-adjacent staff? P.E. coaches, for example."

He couldn't believe he hadn't thought of that, that he's been so egotistical to think of just those who taught academic subjects as "teachers." Their suspect being an athletic teacher made a lot of sense, especially with the man in Emmet's vision talking about how Tildie used to move faster.

He quickly scanned Tildie's record again and saw only one possibility: the track team. She'd run track ever since her freshman year. Jared Cole, who taught P.E., was one of the track coaches. He was 28 years old, and blond.

He searched a bit further back to when Tildie's sister Corrie had been at Rogers West. Corrie was three years older than Tildie, and according to Cole's bio, he had started at Rogers West five years ago, after moving here from Tulsa, Oklahoma, so he may well have known Corrie. Scrolling down Corrie's records, he learned that she'd also taken track. Yes! Of everyone at the school, Cole made the most sense.

"Lela, you were right," he said, when he finished his searches, "I should have considered the rest of the staff. It almost has to be Cole."

"Should we call the police?" she asked.

"I don't think so, at least not yet. It's all circumstantial, and if we told them about the visions they'd just laugh at us."

"That's probably true. So what should we do?"

"I'm meeting Corrie Harper, Emmet Sapp, and the others I told you about at my apartment at 4:30. Can you come?"

"Sure, I can come. I'll help however I can. I just need to let my girlfriend know I'll be a little late getting home. Where do you live?"

He told her his address and apartment number, and she entered the information into her phone. They also exchanged phone numbers. In just a little over an hour school would let out for the day, and hopefully they could all work together to find Matilda Harper.

Kevin looked at Cole's schedule. He was doing PE right now, and had track practice after school, from 4-5. He thought about going down to the gym to snap a photo of him to show to Emmet, but realized he was once again making things more difficult than they had to be when Lela pointed out that he could simply download Cole's bio photo.

"We have to be strategic about this," Lela said. "We don't want to give him any reason to run. If he does, we may never find Matilda."

"You're right," said Kevin. "We have to be careful, and we need to make 100% sure it's him before we do anything. I don't want to accuse an innocent man."

"It all adds up, though. But yeah, we have to make sure. In the meantime, I need to go get a few things done for tomorrow and call my girlfriend. I'll meet you at your place at 4:30, right?"

"Yes, 4:30. Sounds good. See you then."

She gave him a hug and left the classroom. He watched her go, thinking how thankful he was for her. They weren't friends, exactly, but then again Kevin didn't really have a lot of friends. He'd always remained aloof, rarely to his benefit.

Maybe he should work on that.

15

Justy, Emmet, Corrie, and Mikayla all sat in Corrie's car, parked in front of the Junction in Rogers apartments, waiting for Mr. Haj. Mikayla had showed up less than ten minutes ago and joined Justy in the back seat.

"So, yeah, Ashlie was a real bitch today," Mik said, "and Tegan and Chrissie weren't much better. Ashlie said it was either them or you two."

"Well? Don't keep us in suspense," said Emmet. "Who did you choose?"

Mikayla started to respond, but Justy cut her off. "She chose us."

"Yeah, dummy," said Mikayla, with a smile. "You guys are my friends. I'm not sure Ashlie, Chrissie, and Tegan were ever really my friends, not for real. I let them turn me into a person I no longer want to be."

"I know that feeling," Justy said.

"It's hard when you're in high school," added Corrie. "We all want to fit in, because we usually feel like we don't."

"Exactly," Justy said.

"And sometimes we make bad choices in order to fit in," added Corrie. "And sometimes…every once in a while…we'll make the right choice. I know I don't know you very well, Mikayla, but it sounds like today you made the right choice."

Mikayla looked like she was about to cry. "Thank you."

Justy, sitting beside Mikayla, hugged her. She felt bad she had ever lumped Mik in with Ashlie and her minions. Hell, two days ago (had it really only been two days?) she had also been a part of Ashlie's bitch brigade. They'd both changed, and for the better.

"So you really think Tildie is alive?" asked Mik.

"We do," Justy said.

"I really hope she is alive, but if she is…how're we getting these visions?"

"No clue," Emmet said. "As far as I know, Tildie was never psychic, and if she were, she'd probably be a little more clear in her messages."

"Hey, there he is," said Corrie, pointing out the car window.

They watched as Mr. Haj got out of his car, turned to look behind him, and gestured for someone in a silverish Ford Flex to pull in opposite him. Then he walked over to the Flex and waited until the driver, a woman with red hair, got out.

"Okay, it looks like he brought a friend."

They got out of the car and walked up to Mr. Haj and the woman he'd brought with him.

"Who's this?" asked Justy, gesturing at Haj's companion.

"Hey, guys. This is—"

"Miss Kirby," Emmet said, cutting him off. "Psychology, right?"

She nodded. "Lela Kirby, at your service. You were in one of my classes last year, if I remember correctly."

"She knows everything," said Mr. Haj, "and she helped me figure out who we think probably has Tildie."

Justy felt the world fall out from under her for a second. Could Tildie really be alive? She realized just now that she'd refused to let herself completely believe that, because she didn't want to be even more devastated when they finally found her corpse. But what if Tildie really wasn't dead? She might have a second chance with her former best friend, after all.

"Maybe we should go inside," said Corrie, looking around the parking lot as another car pulled in.

Mr. Haj nodded and said, "Good idea. Follow me."

Justy knew these apartments were relatively new, having been built just a few years ago, and they looked really nice. Mr. Haj lived on the second floor. He led them up the stairs and unlocked the door to his apartment, gesturing for them to come inside.

The living room was filled with bookcases holding all sorts of books on one side, and a long gray couch on the other. Paintings of various landscapes filled the walls, along with a huge flat-screen television. It was a nice setup, though it kind of looked like a display out of an Ikea or something. Like he lived here, on the surface, but had never really settled in.

"Have a seat," Haj said, as he and Miss Kirby wandered off to another room.

Justy grabbed Emmet's hand and led him to the left side of the couch, and everyone else followed suit. Haj and Kirby appeared again a few seconds later, carrying two dining room chairs. Mr. Haj sat down on one, while Miss Kirby took the other.

"Jared Cole, huh?" asked Emmet, after Mr. Haj and Miss Kirby explained what they'd learned. "I remember him. Sometimes I'd go hang out on the bleachers while Tildie was practicing track after school. He always seemed a little skeevy to me. I said that once to Tildie and she… Oh shit!"

"What?" asked Justy.

"She got really upset, said I had no right to say that, and just kind of seemed distant after that. We didn't talk as much. That was like…maybe a month before she vanished? Yeah, probably about a month. I remember wondering if she had a crush on him or something. It almost *has* to be him!"

"Here's a photo of him," said Haj, showing them a picture of a blond man on his phone. "Does he look at all like who you saw in the vision?"

"It's really hard to tell, since it was dark, and he was wearing a hoodie. But the hair definitely matches."

"I remember him," said Corrie. "He was a pretty good track coach, all things considered, but beyond that…yeah, skeevy seems to be a good word for him. I always got weird vibes from him, like he was constantly staring at my ass or something, though he never tried anything inappropriate with me."

"Okay," said Miss Kirby, "we've established he's 'skeevy,' which I can't disagree with, but what are our next steps? We have absolutely no evidence that ties him to Tildie's disappearance."

"One thing we didn't mention in the Signal chat," said Corrie slowly, "is that she's apparently pregnant, so Cole must be the father."

"Holy shit," said Haj, his eyes growing large, "it all makes sense now. When we talked at Bliss Café, she looked kind of queasy and said her stomach hurt. She kept touching her stomach. I just assumed she'd eaten something bad."

"My best friend is pregnant with her first child," Miss Kirby said, "and she said she had stomach cramps in her first few weeks of pregnancy and always felt a little like she was going to throw up, so that does makes sense. Once we find her they could certainly do genetic testing to prove he was the father, but how do we figure out where she is in the first place?"

"Maybe we don't have to," said Justy. "Assuming Tildie's still alive—and I have to believe she is—then he must go see her from time to time, in that horrible shed Emmet saw."

"In my vision, he said he'd see her a couple times a week," Emmet said, "to bring food."

"And presumably make sure she hasn't escaped," added Mr. Haj. "We could start following him, see where he goes."

"But what if he's already gone for this week?" asked Justy. "How long can we afford to wait? And how do we know exactly when he'd go so we could follow him?"

"I think I might have an idea," Mikayla said excitedly. "Like, what if we can do something to scare him, to make him think he has to go check on her, like, right now? Immediately?"

"Mikayla, that's a great idea," said Emmet, his eyes lighting up. "I know just the thing that'll scare the shit out of him."

Mikayla and Emmet high-fived each other, grinning, and then Emmet explained his plan. They all agreed it was the best course of action, but there were still a few things that needed to be worked out.

"But how do we do that?" Justy asked when he finished talking. "None of us are students at the school, so there's no way we could get close enough to him." She turned to Mr. Haj and Miss Kirby. "One of you would have to do it, and you'll have to make it believable."

"I can do it," Mr. Haj said. "I let Matilda down once before, by not realizing who she was. Maybe I can make up for that now."

"I'll help any way I can," said Miss Kirby. "Just tell me what you need."

Together they mapped out the plan, and then it was time to go. It was 5:40, and Justy needed to get home before six. As Justy got off the couch, however, another seizure took her, causing her to stumble backwards, falling into Emmet's arms.

She was someplace else entirely now, surrounded by nothing but darkness. She could hear someone crying, sobbing, and in an instant knew it must be Tildie. But she still couldn't see anything. It was so frustrating.

"Find her," whispered a young woman's voice in her ear, and then she was opening her eyes, staring up at Emmet and Corrie.

"She's awake," Emmet said, a quiver in his voice. "Justy, are you okay?"

She was lying on the gray couch. She pushed herself into a sitting position, blinked, and said, "I think so."

"What did you see this time?" Mik asked.

"I...I don't really know. I guess I didn't really see anything, because it was pitch black. I heard someone crying, and then a voice whispered, 'find her' in my ear. I didn't recognize the voice, so it definitely wasn't Tildie."

Her words came out in an excited rush. She was almost certain the sobbing was Tildie, which had to mean Tildie was alive. But who was the spirit giving her these visions, if not Tildie? None of this made any sense, but she snatched onto the string of hope that she might soon see her friend again, alive, and compared to that nothing else mattered.

"Come on, we gotta go," said Emmet, reaching out to take her hand. "You were out for like five minutes. It's 5:46, your mom will be home at six, right?"

Justy let Emmet pull her to her feet, said goodbye to Mikayla, Mr. Haj, and Miss Kirby, then rushed out the door with Corrie and Emmet to Corrie's car.

They got to her house at three minutes until six. Thank God her mother's car wasn't in the driveway. Justy gave Emmet a quick peck on the lips and dashed into the house, leaving Corrie to take Emmet home.

Justy's mother arrived home less than five minutes later, giving her just enough time to remove her jacket and tennis shoes before grabbing a book and snuggling under a heavy wool blanket on the couch so she could pretend she'd been reading.

"Hey, Justy," said her mother, as she made her way into the living room, "how did today go?"

"Pretty good," she said, looking up. "Just tried to spend the day relaxing."

"No seizures?"

"No seizures." She hated lying to her mom, but she couldn't tell her the truth, not if she didn't want to be locked inside her room for the rest of her life.

"Good. You know, I've been thinking…maybe you should see Liz Hart again. Would you be up for that?"

Liz Hart was a therapist at Psychology Helps, a local mental health care clinic, whom she'd seen for about a year after her bout with anorexia. The woman had been helpful, to be sure, but Justy doubted she knew anything about ghosts and visions.

Still, she might be able to use this to her advantage. She hated lying to her mother, but it seemed necessary for now. She hadn't believed her about the visions before, and she doubted anything had changed in the last eight or so hours.

"It depends. If I do, will I get an early release from home prison for good behavior?"

Her mother laughed, which was always a good sign. "Justy, I'm sorry I grounded you, and I'm sorry I was so mean last night. I'm just…I'm worried about you. I was so scared when you vanished from the hospital. And if this isn't anorexia again…we need to figure out what's going on."

"I tried to tell you," Justy said, with a spark of anger, all thoughts of subterfuge forgotten, "but you wouldn't listen. I know you don't believe in the supernatural, but I'm telling you the truth. I had visions, and I'm not the only one."

"Oh? Who else? Your new friend Emmet? Or maybe Mikayla Danvers, who nearly killed you?"

Justy started to respond but stopped herself. Arguing right now would do absolutely no good and might even make things worse. Instead, she said, "Listen, Mom…I love you. I really do, and I know you love me, and you're just doing what you think is best, but I'm not lying, I'm not crazy, and I'm not anorexic. I'm telling you the truth. Why is that so hard to believe?"

Her mother stared at her for a second and then sighed. "I do love you, Justy, I just don't believe in this supernatural nonsense. If you do, that's just another reason for you to see Liz again."

"So anything *you* believe is true, and anything *I* believe is 'nonsense?' Is that what you're saying?"

"No, not at all. But this…everyone knows ghosts aren't real, and neither is psychic phenomenon, or any of those other things you mentioned."

"But how do you know that? How do you really know? There are so many things out there we just don't understand. Are there other civilizations out in space? Do our spirits really survive after we die? We have no idea, but that doesn't mean none of those things are real.

"You go to church. You're a Christian. You believe in God. But how is God any more believable than ghosts or spirits or aliens or anything else? Just because it was written down in a book that's been changed and rewritten a bajillion times in the last two thousand some odd years? Hell, even something like what happened in *Groundhog Day* could be real for all we know. Just because we don't believe in something doesn't mean it's not true."

Her mother's eyes went wide, and she didn't look like she knew what to say next. Justy had probably said too much, pushed things too far, but at the moment she just didn't care. She was sick and tired of her mother not believing her.

"Listen, Justine...I...I don't know, maybe you're right," she said, surprising Justy. "It just...it scares me, okay? I watched you go through anorexia, and it was terrifying. So very scary, I can't even tell you. You're all I have, and I thought I was going to lose you. Your father had just left us the year before, and...I felt like I was on the verge of losing everyone and everything I loved and cared about. And I feel that way again now, and it scares the hell out of me."

Justy stared at her mother. Her reaction, her making Justy stay home from school, not trusting Emmet, everything...it all made sense now. How could she not have seen it before? Her mother had gone through hell with her husband and then went through hell all over again watching her daughter recover from anorexia.

Her mom was sobbing now, crying into her hands, and Justy wrapped her arms around her, and then they were hugging, and Regina Friedman was crying into her shoulder, almost howling with grief.

"I get it now, Mom," she whispered, "I really do. But I promise, I'm not anorexic. I'm not taking drugs. I'm not doing anything bad. I'm just trying to save my best friend's life. And I'm not alone. Emmet is with me, and so is Mikayla, and Tildie's sister Corrie. Two teachers from my old school, Rogers West, are helping us. I trust all of them, and if you trust me, you'll have to trust them, too. We're going to bring Matilda Harper home again, and everything will be fine."

"I do trust you, honey," her mother said, tears still streaming down her cheeks. "It's the rest of the world I don't trust. But…okay. Okay. Do what you have to do, just promise me you'll be careful, and you'll ask me for help if you need to. Can you promise me that?"

She took her mother's face in her hands and tilted her head up, staring into her eyes. "Yes, I can promise you that. I do promise you that. I'll be safe, and my friends will help keep me safe, and I'll keep them safe, and we'll bring Tildie home. Thank you for trusting me. I'm going to school tomorrow, okay? And I'll text you and let you know if I have to go anywhere or do anything after school. Okay?"

"Okay," she said, with something between a sob and a laugh. "I almost feel like you're the adult now, and I'm the little girl. My big, strong Justy, all grown up."

Justy laughed. "Oh, I'm far from being a grown up. But with your love and support, I'm sure I'll get there eventually."

They hugged again for a good long while, before finally separating. After talking a little while longer, they decided to order pizza delivery from Ruskin's Pizzeria for supper, and once the pizza arrived spent the next couple of hours re-watching *Groundhog Day* for the umpteenth time and just enjoying each other's company.

It was a good night, and Justy promised her mother there would be many more good nights to come, hopefully some of them spent with Tildie watching movies and eating more pizza after she helped bring her best friend home.

16

Thursday

Emmet, Justy, and Mikayla sat at lunch together, happy to be halfway through the school day. After a long discussion on the Signal app last night, all three of them decided to just do their very best to enjoy school today and act like everything was normal while waiting to hear from Mr. Haj. If Emmet's plan worked, today might just be the day they found Tildie and brought her home.

He couldn't believe how much his life had changed in the last several days. He was falling for Justy (if he hadn't completely fallen for her already) and had made a new friend in Mikayla. Before finding Justy in the bathroom on Monday, he had absolutely no friends at all at this school, and little hope of finding any.

He'd been so depressed after Tildie disappeared, but now he had a glimmer of hope that not only was she still alive, but that they might be able to find her soon, maybe even today. On top of that, he'd finally learned to open up a little and try new things, to tell people how he felt, and to be himself.

Life really could change in a heartbeat.

"I sure hope everything goes according to plan at Rogers West," said Mikayla, in between bites of her meatloaf.

"Yeah, same," Justy said, also dining on meatloaf.

For the first time in a good long while, Emmet hadn't brought his lunch and had instead decided to try the cafeteria meatloaf. It wasn't bad but tasted considerably better once he covered it in catsup.

"I think it will," said Emmet, "once school is over and Mr. Haj has the chance—"

"What the heck is this?" interrupted Nick Sebastian, walking up to their table and staring down at Justy. "First you dump me, and now you're sitting with this tub of lard. What's going on?"

Emmet felt his cheeks burn. Why couldn't the assholes in this school just leave them alone? He started to say something, but Justy beat him to it.

"Nick, just go away," she said, rolling her eyes. "I didn't 'dump' you, because there wasn't anything to dump. We went on two whole dates like forever ago. As for Emmet, he's smarter, nicer, more handsome, and all around better than you'll ever be, so kindly fuck off."

Mikayla clapped, while Nick just looked on in shock.

"You little bitch," Nick said, slapping the back of Justy's head.

Justy winced and before he knew what he was doing, Emmet was out of his seat, marching up to Nick and pushing him backwards.

"If you ever touch her again," he said, "you'll regret it."

Nick started laughing. "Oh, really? What are you gonna do, fat boy?"

"Emmet, it's okay," Justy said, but he ignored her.

"Nick, I'm taller than you, I'm bigger than you, and I have a black belt in karate. Yeah, you didn't know that, did you? Fuck around and you'll find out exactly what I'm gonna do to your stupid, scrawny ass."

Nick stared at him, but Emmet held his gaze, refusing to look away. Finally Nick blinked, looked around the room, and slowly backed away.

"This isn't over, fatty," he said.

Emmet stepped forward and Nick flinched, jumping back, and he knew he'd won. "Oh, I think it is over," Emmet said, "unless you don't know what's good for you. Do you, Nick?"

Nick blinked again, turned around, and stomped away with his head down. Emmet let out a breath and looked around the room. Everyone was staring at him, eyes wide. He walked on shaky legs back to his lunch table and sat down.

"Holy shit, dude," said Mikayla, her eyes big.

"You didn't have to do that," Justy said, smiling, "but I'm glad you did. I really want to kiss you right now."

"Well, what's stopping you?"

She leaned in for a kiss, and as their lips met Emmet heard Mikayla clapping again. He was sure his face reddened a little at the attention, but for the first time in forever he just didn't care. He was done worrying about what other people thought of him.

He was going to bring Tildie home, enjoy his friendship with Mikayla, and explore what was happening between him and Justy as he felt himself falling in love with her a little more each and every single second he was around her.

He was going to allow himself to be happy.

Take that, Grandpa Roy.

"I had no idea you were into karate," Justy whispered, once the kiss was over.

"I'm not," he whispered back, "I've never taken a class in my life, it was just the first thing that popped into my head."

"You're brilliant," she said, giving him another quick kiss. "I still think you could kick his ass, though."

"Me, too," added Mikayla.

A few minutes later, a smirking Ashlie Bowman showed up at their table. "What's gotten into you, Justy? First you leave my table and hook up with old fatty here, and then you lure away Mikayla. That's not the Justy I know."

Tegan and Chrissie walked up behind her, looking nervous while still supporting their mob leader.

"Maybe you never knew the real me," said Justy, not even bothering to look at her. "And if you call my boyfriend another name, I'm going to kick your bitch ass. Got it?"

Boyfriend? Emmet couldn't help but smile. If he was Justy's boyfriend, that meant she was his girlfriend. He liked that thought. It felt right. This whole thing with Tildie had been a nightmare, but at least some good had come from it. Things would be even better once they finally got Tildie back.

"Tegan, Chrissie, and I are going to make your life a living hell. Don't you know that?"

"Leave us alone, Ashlie," said Emmet, staring into her eyes.

"Or what? What are you going to do if I don't, fatty?"

"If you don't," Mikayla said, rising from her chair, "*I'm* going to use my black belt in karate and kick your bitch ass, so Justy doesn't have to get her hands dirty."

Emmet held back a smile at Mikayla using the same karate bit he'd used with Nick. He was glad she'd switched sides, as it were. They'd come a long way in just a couple of days, the three of them.

Ashlie laughed. "Oh, little Mikayla finally speaks up, does she?"

"Let's just go sit back down," said Tegan, from behind Ashlie, "before we get in trouble."

"She's right," added Chrissie. "This isn't doing anyone any good."

Ashlie looked shocked. "What do you two think you're doing?"

"Justy and Mik are our friends, too," Tegan said. "Let's just stop already. If she doesn't want to sit with us, who can blame her?"

"I can fucking blame her!" Ashlie yelled. "And if you know what's good for you, you will, too."

"Or what?" asked Chrissie. "You'll call us names? Won't let us sit at *your* table?"

Ashlie looked stunned. "What did you say to me?"

Emmet cleared his throat, and they all turned to look at him. "Would you like to sit at our table, girls? Not you, Ashlie, just them."

Ashlie laughed. "Not in a million years."

Tegan shrugged and took the seat next to Justy, while Chrissie sat next to Mikayla. "I think I like this table better anyway," Chrissie said.

Ashlie looked like she was about to explode. She started to say something but instead turned around and stomped out of the cafeteria.

"Welcome to the good table," Justy said, "being an asshole is not required here, and is actually frowned upon. Do you think you can live with that?"

Chrissie smiled, and Tegan said, "You know what? I think we can."

A few seconds later, Joel DuBois walked over. "Is there room at the table for me?"

Joel was another one of the kids Ashlie's clique had harassed. "Sure thing," Emmet said, watching Joel take a seat.

Before too long, Allison Moxley, Harley Schmidt, and several other kids showed up, and soon their table, which had been empty when Emmet, Justy, and Mikayla claimed it, was filled to the max.

They had brought change to the hierarchy in AAFA's senior class, even if that change was small and may or may not last. It was still a win, a win against the bullies of the world, and that felt pretty damned good.

✳✳✳

Corrie hadn't received any GPS coordinates on her phone since they went to Bliss Café two days ago. She couldn't decide if that was a good sign or a bad sign but was trying to think positively so decided it must be a good sign because they were on the right track to finding her sister.

She'd just picked up the item Emmet had asked her to purchase from Best Buy and was on her way to take it to Mr. Haj and Miss Kirby at the Rogers West High School. It would be strange to visit the school after over three years away, especially knowing the person who might be responsible for Tildie's disappearance and potential death would be there, but she needed to get it to them before Cole left the school.

She wondered, not for the first time, why whoever or whatever had sent her GPS coordinates hadn't simply sent ones that would lead to this mysterious shed in the woods. Could it be because Tildie knew these coordinates for Mercy Hospital and Bliss Café by heart (for a while, there was a geocache spot right outside the hospital that they used to explore, and she'd probably looked up the coordinates for Bliss at some point since she worked there) but had no idea where she was being held? Maybe. It was all so confusing.

Corrie exited the highway, took a right onto West Walnut Street, and less than five minutes later pulled into the parking lot for Rogers West High School. She hadn't been back here in ages, but for a moment she almost felt like a teenager again, rushing to get to school before the final morning bell rang.

She drove around the side of the huge brick building, past the football stadium, and into the teacher's parking lot. And there was Miss Kirby, waiting for her as promised. She parked her car next to the woman and got out.

"Hey, Corrie," said Miss Kirby, walking over to greet her.

"Hey, yourself," Corrie said. "Miss Kirby…or should I call you Lela? It's weird seeing your teachers when you're no longer a teenager."

"You can definitely call me Lela, and yes, I'd imagine it is. C'mere."

Lela pulled her into a hug. Corrie faltered for a moment before hugging her back. "What was that for?"

"We didn't really get the chance to talk at Kevin's apartment. You were always one of my favorite students—I know we're not supposed to have favorites, but you were—and I'm so sorry about your sister's disappearance. Hopefully this will be the day we finally get her back."

Corrie felt tears well up in her eyes. "Thanks, Miss…Lela. I really appreciate that. I never told you, but your classes were what encouraged me to go to college in the first place. I've been majoring in psychology, and my plan is to eventually get my doctorate, though with the way my grades have been plummeting, I'm not sure that's going to happen."

"I'm so glad you got something good out of my classes, Corrie, and with Tildie's disappearance, it's no wonder your grades have suffered. I'm sure if you were to explain that to one of the counselors at the your university, they could help you figure out if you need to retake the classes. For the record, I think you'd be an amazing psychologist."

"Thanks, Lela. That means a lot to me. And I'll for sure talk to a counselor once we find my sister."

They stood facing one another for a second, neither of them sure what to say next, until Lela finally said, "So…you have something for me?"

"Oh! Yeah, I do." She opened the Best Buy bag she'd been carrying and pulled out the package. "Do you think you know how to do it?"

"I can figure it out. Between you and me, I'm not *that* old."

Corrie's face reddened. "Oh, I didn't mean it that way Miss Kirby, I just—"

"I know, I was just teasing you," she said, smiling. "And stop calling me Miss Kirby."

Corrie laughed. "Gotcha. Sorry, I'm just nervous…Lela. I hope this plan of Emmet's works."

"Me, too. I think it will." Lela ripped open the package Corrie had given her and scanned the instructions. "This seems easy enough. Keep an eye out for me for a few minutes, and I should have it done."

Ten minutes later, after Lela successfully installed the GPS tracking device onto Jared Cole's Toyota Prius, they were saying their goodbyes. Corrie initiated the hug this time, and Lela hugged her back in earnest. Then she climbed into her car and set out to AAFA high school to pick up Emmet, Justy, and Mikayla for the next part of their plan.

17

Kevin Haj stood outside in the teacher's parking lot, next to the exit from the gym, waiting for Jared Cole to walk to his car. Lela Kirby stood beside him, having just a moment earlier shared the login details for the Brickhouse Car Tracker app that they would use to track the GPS device currently hidden underneath Cole's car to the Signal chat so Corrie and the others could log into the app.

The bell had rung five minutes ago. Where was Cole? They had everything planned out but if he didn't show, none of it would work. Haj nodded at several teachers walking out to go to their cars, all of whom probably wondered why he and Miss Kirby were mulling around the parking lot.

"Okay, I'm going to go ask someone," said Lela, and walked away before Kevin could stop her.

They absolutely did not want to give Cole any reason at all to flee. If he did that, they may never find out where Tildie Harper was being held. He held his breath as he watched Lela talk to Jennifer Foley, one of the other PE coaches at the school.

"Well?" he asked, when Lela returned.

"I just said I needed to ask him something. She said he often goes to the teacher's lounge after school, to grab a snack. Beyond that, no idea."

"Well, hell. Okay, I'm going to go to the teacher's lounge, and you stay here. Okay? We'll have to wing it a little. If he's in there, I'll call you and we'll have our little 'discussion' over the phone. If he shows up here, then you call me and do the same thing. Sound good?"

She smiled. "Works for me. Just be careful, okay?"

"I will. You do the same."

"Roger that."

Kevin re-entered the school, passing by several more teachers and staff who were leaving for the day. He nodded and waved to a few but ignored Mr. Simonson, who seemed to want to have a conversation. He didn't have time for that.

He approached the lounge just as Cole was exiting. Shit. He quickly texted Lela to call him and then pretended to trip, bumping into Cole's shoulder.

"Oh, sorry," he said, doing his best to appear like he'd been distracted. "I wasn't watching where I was going."

"No worries," said Cole, with a smile. "It's almost the end of the week, we're all a little tired."

Cole was maybe six feet tall, muscular, and blond with green eyes. He was a handsome man, and Kevin could see students finding him attractive, but the fact that he used that to take advantage of Tildie was unconscionable.

"You got that right," Kevin said, just as his phone rang. He looked down at the screen and then said, "Oh, sorry, I need to get this," and answered the phone.

"Have a good night," Cole said, then started to walk away.

"Okay, I'm calling," said Lela's voice on the other end of his cell-phone.

"Someone spotted Matilda Harper?" he asked into the phone, turning partially away from Cole. "Seriously? Is she okay?"

Watching Cole out of the corner of his eye, he noticed him stop dead in his tracks to listen to Kevin's call.

"I sure hope she's okay," said Lela, into his ear.

"Are they sure it's her?" he asked.

"So, he's there listening?"

"Yes, that's amazing news. I'm sure her family will be thrilled. But she...what? They don't know where she went?"

"Oh, that's good! Make him wonder."

"Are they even sure it was her? She what? She ran away from them? Why?"

"Is he still there? You don't have to answer that, sorry. I just don't know what to say."

"So they're not 100% sure it was her?"

He surreptitiously shot a glance at Cole, just in time to see him quickly walking towards the exit.

"Okay," he whispered into the phone, "he's coming your way. I'll be out in a few minutes. Can you text Corrie?"

"Already on it. I'm in my car, by the way. I'll let you know as soon as he's in *his* car and has driven to the exit, and then you can come out and we can follow his ass."

"I'm ready."

"Here he comes," Lela said. "He looks panicked. Good. He's getting in his car now. Pulling out of his space, heading for the exit. He just turned the corner. The tracker app moved a little, so it's working. Okay, he's gone, you can come out now. Hurry, shake it like a Polaroid picture!"

"I'm shaking it. I'm outside now, almost to your car. And here I am."

They had planned on taking Kevin's car, but there wasn't time for that now. He opened the passenger side door and quickly got into her Ford Flex and buckled his seatbelt.

"Okay, we're going," she said, putting the car into reverse and backing out of the parking space. "Open up the app, Kevin, and let me know where he goes."

Kevin opened the app he'd installed just a little while ago and saw Cole's car moving down Walnut Street. He wondered where the track coach was going. There were only a few places in Rogers that they thought might match the woods Emmet had seen in his vision, and most of them were in the opposite direction.

"He's headed down Walnut, moving towards Bentonville. Did you text Corrie to let her know he's on the move?"

"Yep, right after I told you. So where's he going now?"

"He's...what?" Kevin stared at the app. "He's getting on I-49. I guess he's not keeping her in Rogers or Bentonville, like we thought."

"Which way is he going?" she asked, as they turned onto Walnut Street themselves.

"South."

"I'm shit with directions. Towards Fayetteville or Bella Vista?"

"Sorry. Fayetteville."

They reached the highway and followed the entry ramp onto I-49. They were too far back to see Cole's car, but the tracker app showed he was maybe half a mile ahead of them at most.

Both Lela's and Kevin's phones dinged, more than likely from a message sent via the Signal app. Kevin opened Signal. It was Emmet.

Emmet: *Where's he going?*

Kevin: *No idea. Springdale, maybe, or Fayetteville? Just keep following until we get there.*

Emmet: *We are. We're not too far behind you, I don't think.*

"Who was it?" asked Lela.

"Emmet. He wanted to know if we knew where Cole might be headed. Apparently Springdale," he said, as they took exit 72 to Highway 412, the first exit off the interstate to Springdale.

"Are there even forests in Springdale?"

"There are," Kevin said, "but they aren't very big, certainly not big enough to hide a shed."

They followed the tracker, and eventually it took them all the way through Springdale. The next thing he knew, the little blip on the app indicated they were headed towards Tontitown.

"I guess he's not going to Springdale, after all," Lela said.

Kevin nodded. At this point, he had absolutely no idea where Cole was going. They might be in for a long drive. He hoped Corrie had filled up her gas tank.

***

Emmet sat next to Corrie as she drove down highway I-49, not too far behind Mr. Haj and Miss Kirby…or rather, Kevin and Lela. That was going to take some getting used to, but according to Corrie, Miss Kirby said to call her Lela, and he imagined Mr. Haj would feel the same way.

They'd decided to drive separate cars in the unlikely event either vehicle broke down or had a flat tire. It was better to be safe than sorry. To that end, Corrie picked up Emmet, Justy, and Mikayla from AAFA maybe ten minutes ago and then drove to Rogers West, where they parked across the street from the high school and waited to hear from the teachers. Once they did, it was just a matter of following the blip on the GPS app.

"Where in the hell is this asshole going?" asked Corrie, as they followed the tracker through Springdale towards Tontitown. "I'm about to jitter apart."

"I'll be happy to drive," Emmet said, making the same offer he'd made when they were parked across from the high school.

"I'm good for now," Corrie muttered.

Emmet's phone dinged. It was a Signal message.

Kevin: *I think I know where he might be going. Before he moved here, he lived in Tulsa. Oklahoma has all kinds of forests. So it'll probably be another hour or so, if I'm right.*

"Well, hell," Emmet said out loud.

"What?" asked Justy, from the back seat. "What's going on?"

"Mr. Haj thinks Cole is headed to Tulsa. Apparently, he used to live there. That's, like what? Three hours away?"

"More like two," said Mikayla, who was sitting in the back next to Justy. "And we've already driven a good thirty minutes, so we should be there within an hour and a half."

"Good thing I filled this baby up this morning," Corrie said, patting the car's dashboard.

18

They arrived at the Sooner State Ancient Woods at just past six. The forest was a huge 1,380-acre nature preserve, according to Google. Their website boasted ancient cedars and oaks dating back over 500 years, all sorts of trails, and even tours. The park was open from 7am-6pm but only Friday through Sunday.

Justy could see why Cole had chosen this forest to hide Tildie. There must be deep parts of the woods nobody visited where she would never be found. She shuddered. This was bad, this was very bad.

"There's no way to track him," said Corrie, looking like she might cry, "and we have no idea where he might've gone."

As soon as they figured out where he was going they'd tried their best to catch up to him, but he still managed to get to the forest probably five minutes before they did. They could stand next to his car and wait for him to show back up again, but there were no guarantees they'd be able to force him to take them to Tildie.

"I didn't think about that," said Emmet, looking defeated. "I never imagined he was keeping her in a nature preserve or whatever the hell this place is."

"We're not giving up," Lela reassured them, while Kevin stared into the massive expanse of woodland.

"I think I have an idea," said Kevin. "I'm going to call him. We need to spread out, each of us go in different directions. When one of us hears his phone ringing, we notify the others and head that way."

"You have his number?" Emmet asked.

"Yes. I looked it up in the school directory before we left, just in case we needed it."

"What if he doesn't keep his ringer on?" asked Mikayla.

"We have to at least try."

"What are you going to say to him, assuming he answers?"

"I don't know. I'll wing it."

"We don't want to tip him off," Justy said.

Kevin nodded. "Don't worry, I won't."

Justy felt like she might throw up. To have gotten this close and then fail was unacceptable. They had to find Tildie, and this might be their one and only chance. She felt tears welling up in her eyes. Blinking, she did her best to turn off the waterworks. Now wasn't the time for this.

Before she knew it, they were all splitting up, going off in different directions, with their phones opened up to the Signal app. A few minutes later, she saw Kevin's message.

Kevin: *It's going straight to voicemail. He must have the ringer turned off. I've called three times. Anyone have any other ideas?*

Emmet: *FUCK!!!*

Mikayla: *It's okay, Em. We're not giving up.*

In an instant, Justy knew exactly what she needed to do. It was almost like a lightbulb went off in her head. It was dangerous, to be sure, but at this point, what other options did they have? She texted them.

Justy: *Run back as fast as you can to where we started. Hurry! I have an idea.*

Emmet: *What idea?*

Justy: *No time, just hurry!*

"Are you crazy?" asked Mikayla, when Justy explained her plan.

"No. No way," said Emmet. "I can't lose you, too."

"It actually makes sense," Kevin offered, "but only if you're sure."

"I won't do it!" yelled Mikayla. "I can't do it. What if—"

"What if it works?" Justy said, cutting her off. "Mik, I love you. You're a wonderful friend. Do this for me."

"Are you absolutely sure about this?" asked Emmet.

She pulled Emmet in for a quick kiss. "I'm absolutely sure. Now, Mik, slap me! Now!"

"I can't!"

"Please, Mik," she begged. "If you really love me, you need to do this. It's the only way."

"No!"

"Do it!"

"I love you," sobbed Mikayla, slapping her hard in the face, and Justy instantly tumbled to the ground.

Justy was somewhere else, surrounded in darkness. She turned in a slow circle but could see nothing at all. Was she dead?

"Help us find her," she screamed into the ether. "Help us save Tildie, before it's too late."

She heard a whisper in response, but it was so soft that she couldn't quite put together the words.

"I can't understand you."

"*Let…*"

"Let what? Please, help us. Help me help Tildie!"

"*…me…*"

"Let you do what?"

"*…in.*"

Let me in. She didn't understand exactly what that meant, but she supposed it didn't matter. It was now or never, and she had to save her best friend's life however she could.

"Okay," she finally said, "come on in."

And after that, everything changed.

She was having sex with Jared Cole, on a bed inside an apartment somewhere. He was on top of her, bucking his hips against hers, and it hurt and felt good at the same time. She stared up into his eyes.

"I love you, Sadie," he moaned. "Tell me you love me, too."

She heard herself say, "Yes, I love you Jared."

But did she really? This had all moved so fast. One moment she was trying out for the track team, the next she was winning races, and not long after that Jared was offering her rides home after practice.

The third time, however, he didn't take her home. They'd driven to his apartment, where he'd invited her inside. Just for a few minutes, he'd said, so they could discuss some upcoming races.

But they didn't talk about the races. Before she knew what was happening, he was telling her how beautiful she was, how any boy would be lucky to have her, and asking her if she'd ever had sex.

No, she told him, she'd never had sex. She was just sixteen, a sophomore in high school. Hell, she'd only dated a couple of guys, and neither one of them had made it past two dates. They'd both felt so immature and clumsy, nothing like Jared.

He took her home that night, less than thirty minutes after they'd stopped by his apartment. Two weeks later, on a Friday, they'd once again wound up in his apartment. She'd told her parents she was spending the night at a friend's house, but she knew where she'd be spending the night instead.

That was the first night they'd kissed, and before she knew what was happening, she was topless, and his hands were all over her as their kisses grew more and more frantic. He was so handsome, so fucking *hot*, and it felt so good, so right, as he pulled off her skirt and slowly slid her panties down her legs, and the next thing she knew he was inside her and they were making love on the couch.

He'd used a condom and had somehow gotten birth control for her to use, but three months later, two days before she turned seventeen, she'd missed her period. It had never come. She'd gotten pregnant.

Jared wanted her to abort the baby, but she refused. Sadie grew up in a Christian household and had been told all her life that abortion was *wrong*. Abortion was what sent you to hell. Her parents would disown her if they ever found out she got an abortion.

Of course, sex before marriage was also wrong, but she could let that one slide. She'd refused to get an abortion, and by that time she was starting to show a little, he'd seemingly relented and asked her to marry him, and of course she'd said yes. She was in love with this beautiful, charming man, this man who had seduced her when she was sixteen and taken away her virginity.

He had a surprise for her, he said, a present that would change her life forever, and he needed to give it to her before she revealed everything to her parents. They'd driven out to this huge nature preserve, Sooner State Ancient Woods, about twenty minutes outside of Tulsa, where they both lived.

Why was this surprise, this present, at some nature preserve? She wondered but didn't ask, because she trusted him completely. That was probably her hundredth mistake in a long line of many mistakes she'd made letting Jared Cole into her life, into her pants, but she was young and stupid, and desperate to be loved.

They began walking into the woods and kept walking for what seemed like forever. It was dark and the forest was more than a little scary. She heard the sound of a coyote howling in the distance and squeezed his hand, which she'd been holding for the last twenty minutes of their walk.

She was already regretting her decisions, regretting letting him take her into the woods, but it was far too late. She knew that even before he struck. She knew she was never going to see her parents again. She tried to deny the feeling, to push it away, but it wouldn't go away, and yet she kept on walking.

It was 7:18 at night when he killed her. He took her out to a lonely spot in the woods. He opened up a long duffel bag that he said contained part of the surprise he had for her and instead withdrew a shovel. She barely had time to say anything, even to think, before he swung the shovel at her stomach, knocking the air out of her, and she stumbled to the ground.

It hurt so much, and she was so confused. Why had he hit her? Where was her surprise? Didn't he love her?

"The birth control pills weren't real, you know," he said, standing over her, smiling, "and I cut holes in the condoms."

"But…why?" she managed to get out, her stomach on fire, as she gasped for air and struggled but failed to climb to her feet.

He shrugged. "Why not?"

Cole swung the shovel again, the sharp side hitting her in the side of the head. She collapsed to the ground and died pretty much instantly.

And that's where he buried her.

Justy climbed to her feet, somehow not Justy, not completely. Sadie was inside her, sharing her mind, sharing her body, which made no sense at all but at the same time completely made sense.

Emmet was by her side, helping her up. "Are you okay?"

"It didn't work, did it?" said Mikayla, "I hit you for nothing."

"Oh, it worked," said Justy/Sadie, smiling. "Follow me."

"But how? She slapped you and you got right up," Corrie asked.

Lela said, "I'm so confused right now."

"There's no time for that," Justy said. "I know where he's keeping Tildie. We have to hurry, before he kills her."

"But she's pregnant," said Kevin, "he won't kill her, at least not yet."

"Yes, he will," Justy said. "I was pregnant, too, when he murdered me."

Corrie stared at her, confusion written all over her face. She started to say something, but Emmet took her hand and squeezed it, and she remained silent.

"Follow me. And Corrie…Google the name 'Sadie Sawyer' and 'Tulsa' while we're moving. There has to be something online about me."

Justy took off in a run, moving past a huge cedar tree and into the woods, everyone following after.

✳✳✳

Emmet stared at Justy. What the hell was going on? And then they were jogging through the forest, struggling to keep up with her.

"Sadie Sawyer vanished from Tulsa five and a half years ago," Corrie said breathlessly. "She was sixteen, and according to the article I found, she's still missing."

Had Cole murdered this Sadie Sawyer? And was Justy even now channeling Sadie's spirit? He had so many questions, but right now all that mattered was getting to Tildie before it was too late.

Justy began to run faster, and Emmet and the rest struggled to keep up. How was she moving so fast? Unlike Tildie, she wasn't a track star.

Emmet nearly ran into another huge cedar tree, narrowly missing impaling his face on a branch. It was so dark in the woods. Kevin and Lela had brought flashlights, but they kept them off for now, because they didn't want to alert Jared Cole. None of that would matter, however, if they managed to break a leg or worse scrambling through the forest.

Kevin must have had the same thought, because he flicked on his flashlight. Justy was already a good ten feet ahead of them, and they needed to catch up as quickly as they could.

Justy stopped and held out her hand towards them, her palm up. "He's just past that little hill. We need to be quiet, and careful."

"Are you...who are you, now?" Emmet asked. "Are you Sadie now?"

"I am," she said, flashing him a crooked smile, "at least for a little while longer."

It was so dark in the woods, even though it was only about 6:30 in the evening. Enough light made it through the branches of the massive cedar and oak trees, however, to illuminate the little black shed in the middle of the forest.

The door to the shed was open, and from within the little building they could just make out voices.

"How would I escape?" screamed Tildie's voice from inside, "and if I did, why would I come back here?"

Emmet's heart was beating so fast it felt like it just might beat itself right out of his chest. Tildie was alive!

"Apparently Haj's source was wrong about that," said a man's voice, presumably Jared Cole, "but it doesn't matter. This is a little sooner than I'd planned but now seems as good a time as any to kill you."

Corrie started to run for the shed, but Justy put out her hand, as if to say, not yet.

"That's my sister!" she hissed, but Justy put a finger to Corrie's lips.

"We'll save her," Emmet whispered. "I think Justy...I mean Sadie. I think Sadie knows what she's doing."

"Kill me?" Tildie asked, her voice echoing through the forest. "I don't understand. I thought you wanted the baby? I thought the baby was the only thing keeping me alive?"

"I never gave a shit about the baby," Cole said. "Why would I want to raise a kid? I can't believe you were stupid enough to fall for that."

"Then why didn't you just kill me to begin with? Why bring me all the way out here just to torture me, wherever the hell we even are?"

"Why not?" he laughed. "It was fun to give you hope, to see how you'd react, but that hope is all over for you now. Given a little more time I'm sure I would have broken you, but *c'est la vie*. There's always next time."

Next time? He was already planning to do this again.

"We need to do something. Now," whispered Corrie.

"Together, I think Emmet and I can take him down," Kevin added.

"He has a gun," whispered Justy.

"How do you know that?" asked Corrie, but Emmet was sure she already knew the answer.

"Because I'm not Justy, at least not only Justy," whispered Sadie. "Just trust me. Justy will explain it all later, long after I'm gone."

"None of this makes any sense."

Sadie turned to her and smiled. "When has anything ever made sense?"

"Okay, tell us what to do."

"Emmet, Kevin," Sadie whispered, turning towards Emmet, "go stand on either side of the door. When he comes out, he'll have his gun. Kevin, hit his right hand with your flashlight. Emmet, tackle him."

How did she know all of this? But it didn't matter. He had to have faith that it would all work out, because what other choice did he have?

Emmet and Kevin slowly crept over to the shed, Kevin taking the left side of the door while Emmet took the right.

Sadie was saying something to Lela, Mikayla, and Corrie, but he couldn't make out what it was. He watched as Corrie and the two others hid behind trees on either side of the fence.

"Mister Coleeeee," called out Justy, in a sing-songy voice, "come out and playyyy."

"What the fuck?" screamed Cole from inside the shed. "Who's out there?"

"Help!" yelled Tildie. "He's going to kill me."

"Be quiet, you little bitch, before I shoot you in the head!"

"C'mon, Mr. Cole," Justy said, "forget about Tildie, let's go to your apartment and talk about the upcoming races. I know you'd never try to take advantage of a helpless, naive sixteen-year-old girl."

Shivers traveled up Emmet's spine. Is that what Cole had done to Sadie?

"Sadie?" asked Cole, still inside the shed. "You can't be her. You're dead!"

"Am I?" asked Justy. "Why don't you come out and see? Oh, and you can meet your little girl. She's so beautiful, Jared, the perfect combination of both of us."

"She's alive? How can she be alive?"

"Same as me, Jared. Why don't you come out and see?"

There was movement inside the shed as Cole tentatively stuck his head outside the door. "Where are you? I can't see you."

"Fuck you!" screamed Tildie, suddenly barreling at him from inside, hitting him hard and sending him stumbling through the doorway.

Kevin didn't hesitate. He swung the Coleman flashlight at the man's right arm, knocking the pistol from his hand. Just as Cole turned to stare at him, Emmet ran for all he was worth, tackling Tildie's kidnapper from behind, driving him to the ground.

Emmet, screaming and tears rolling down his cheeks, punched Cole in the back of the head over and over and over and didn't stop until Lela, Corrie, and Mikayla pulled him off the man.

"He's down, Em," said Mikayla, over and over, trying to calm him down. "It's over. We saved her. It's over."

"Emmet?" said a quivering voice. It was Tildie, standing on shaking legs within the doorway to the shed.

"It's me," he whispered, stretching to stare at her.

And then he was on his feet again, running towards his best friend, and they were both crying and hugging, and Emmet never wanted to ever again let her go.

"Oh my God," said Corrie, standing in front of them. "I never thought I'd see you again."

"Corrie?" asked Tildie, her eyes wet with tears.

They pulled Corrie into the hug as they all cried, and Emmet had never felt happier. Tildie was finally free, finally safe, and they were going to bring her home.

"Umm, guys," said Kevin, "we might need a little help here."

Emmet turned to see Justy standing over an unconscious Jared Cole, his gun in her hand. It was pointed at his head, and her hands were shaking.

"Sadie," said Emmet, stepping towards her, "you don't want to do this."

"Why not?" she asked, her whole body shaking now. "He killed me. I could have had a life, but he took it from me. He took me from my parents, from my friends, from everyone and everything. I could have gone to college, gone to the Olympics like I dreamed about, met a decent guy, fallen in love, and had a family. But instead, I didn't even get to graduate high school. He took it all away from me!"

"And if you kill him," Lela said, slowly walking towards them, "you'll be taking everything away from Justy."

Sadie's hands were shaking even more now. "It would be self-defense. He's a murderer. And a kidnapper. He kidnapped Tildie and would have killed her if not for me. He deserves to die!"

"He's unconscious," said Kevin. "It would be murder. You have to let this go, Sadie. You won. We saved Tildie."

"But nobody saved me!"

"Justy?" asked Tildie, blinking at her best friend from junior high. "What are you doing here, and why is everyone calling you 'Sadie?' I thought I made up Sadie in my head. I'm so confused."

"But you saved Tildie," said Emmet, for the moment ignoring his best friend. "We helped, but we couldn't have done any of that without you."

Tildie started to shake. "How could she not be Justy? I don't understand. Sadie is real, and he really killed her?"

"He really killed me," said Sadie.

"Then he does deserve to die," Tildie said.

"He definitely does," Corrie said, her eyes turned to steel as she stared at the unconscious track coach, "but maybe not this way."

"He probably does deserve to die," admitted Emmet, "but not tonight, and not by Justy's hands, especially when she's not currently in control of those hands at the moment."

"But he took everything from me," Sadie said. "Everything. I didn't get to have a life! He buried me in the woods and built a fucking shed over me. Like I was nothing. I didn't get to have a life!"

"Neither will he, now," said Kevin. "He's going to spend the rest of his life in prison, which is exactly what he deserves."

"It's not enough!"

"As much as I hate to say it, it's going to have to be enough," said Tildie, as she moved past Emmet, past Corrie, past Mikalya, Kevin, and Lela, and began slowly walking towards Sadie. "He took everything from you, but can you really justify using that to take everything away from Justy?"

"What are you doing?" asked Emmet, but Tildie turned to him and smiled, threw him and Corrie each a kiss, and kept walking.

"Sadie…you didn't get to have a life," she said, looking into Sadie's eyes, "but you saved mine, and I love you for that, but Emmet is right.

It isn't fair to take away Justy's choices, the way he took away ours. And I have an idea how you might get to have a life, after all."

"I'm listening," Sadie said, still pointing the gun at Cole's head.

Tildie got closer to Sadie and whispered something into her ear. They talked back and forth in whispers for a few more seconds and then Sadie smiled, nodded her head, handed Tildie the gun, and hugged her.

"I guess it's worth a shot," Sadie said, kissing Tildie on the cheek. "Thank you. I love you, too."

Emmet ran to them as Justy collapsed to the ground.

✳✳✳

Justy sat in the dirt next to Emmet and Tildie. She remembered everything that had happened once she let Sadie take over her body, and no part of her regretted a single thing. Sadie was gone now and even though they'd only been connected for a little while, she thought she was going to miss her.

Maybe, if she were very lucky, she'd see her again someday. Life was funny that way.

Kevin held the pistol on Cole, who was awake now, hands bound behind his back by some rope they'd found in the shed. He wouldn't stop screaming at them, so eventually they'd gagged him with Kevin's belt. Even if they couldn't kill him, he didn't deserve to be heard, not by anyone except maybe a judge, not ever again.

Kevin had telephoned 911 shortly after they found the shed, and eventually the police and paramedics, using Kevin's phone as a GPS, had managed to locate them.

The cops took everyone's initial statements while the paramedics tended to Tildie and Cole, who apparently had a concussion. Emmet wasn't the least bit sorry about that.

Eventually the cops had taken a handcuffed Cole back through the forest and into the back of a police car, while the paramedics carried

Tildie on a stretcher they'd brought and took her to Saint Francis Hospital in Tulsa.

Justy, Emmet, Corrie, Kevin, and Lela followed the police to the Tulsa Police Department, where they gave their official statements. According to the story they'd made up, Corrie had received an anonymous call telling her where her sister was being held. She wasn't sure if the story was real or not, and so she'd enlisted her friends and former teachers to drive to Tulsa with her.

It was a shaky story at best, but it would have to do. There was no way they would believe the truth. Hell, Justy had been there through all of it and barely believed it herself.

19

Justy, Emmet, Corrie, Mikayla, Kevin, and Lela sat in the waiting area of the emergency room at Saint Francis Hospital as the doctors examined Tildie, exhausted and silent.

"That was so weird," Justy finally said, and Emmet laughed.

"'Weird' is an understatement," he said. "So tell me, what did it feel like having your body taken over by a ghost?"

"Well, first of all, she didn't take over my body. I gave her temporary access to my body, thank you very much."

"Are you also going to give Emmet temporary access to your body?" asked Mikayla, waggling her eyebrows, "or has that happened already?"

Justy rolled her eyes at her friend, but inside she felt a deep, burning love for Emmet, so who knows? She didn't think that was going to happen any time soon, but maybe once they'd graduated high school and had both hit eighteen, maybe after they'd started college…yeah, maybe. Okay, probably. Almost definitely.

She knew teenage romance rarely worked out, but then again neither did trying to save your best friend from a serial killer. All she knew right now is that she felt amazingly happy and couldn't see sharing the rest of her life with anyone but Emmet.

"Sharing my body with Sadie was weird as hell," Justy said, ignoring Mik's question, "but…it also felt right. Some part of me is going to miss her, I think, even though we were only connected for…what, ten or fifteen minutes, maybe?"

"Something like that," Emmet said.

"She showed me so many of her memories. When she and Cole first met…it was all, like, 'you're so mature for your age, Sadie', shit like that. Grooming shit. It was disgusting, but she fell for it. Because why wouldn't she? She was sixteen. Jesus Christ, she was only sixteen."

"He told me similar things, when I was on the track team," Corrie said, "though I was a year older at the time. He told me I was 17 going on 30, crap like that. In hindsight it was so obvious what he was trying to do and thank God I didn't fall for it, but I also didn't report him. I should have reported him. I should have warned Tildie when she followed me into track, but I convinced myself it was all in my head. If I could go back and change it all, I would, in a heartbeat."

"None of this is your fault," said Justy.

"The shit that maniac put Sadie through was awful," said Emmet, "not to mention what he did to Tildie, but Justy is right. None of this is your fault, Corrie."

"I just hope he gets locked away for the rest of his life," Corrie said, anger flashing in her eyes.

"I think he probably will," said Kevin. "No one likes a pedophile, so it might even be worse than that, once he's sentenced to prison. I guess we'll see."

"Something I've been wondering about," said Emmet, "is how did Sadie see into the future, like Justy going to the hospital, so she could send Corrie there at the right time to find us?"

Justy shrugged. She had no idea, and Sadie didn't seem to know either. Maybe some things are just unknowable. However it happened, she was incredibly happy it had all worked out in the end.

"How long are they going to make us wait anyway?" asked Corrie, looking like she was on the verge of tears again. "I want to see my sister."

"We'll get to see her soon, I'm sure," Lela said, taking Corrie's hand. "It's hard being patient, especially after all this."

The moment they got into their cars to head to the police station, Corrie had called her and Tildie's parents. There'd been a lot of crying, and her parents had assured her they'd be at Tulsa's Saint Francis Hospital just as soon as the speed limit would allow.

Right after that, Justy called her mother and explained everything (well, except for the ghost part) that had just happened, and said she'd be home as soon as she could. She'd surprised Justy by telling her how proud she was of her, how much she loved her, and how she couldn't wait to see Tildie again. The conversation made them both cry.

"Hey, guys," said a young nurse with short brown hair. "We've moved Tildie to a room. She said she wants to see all of you, but first she wants to see," the nurse paused, looking down at a yellow Post-It Note. "Corrie, Emmet, and Justy?"

"That more than makes sense," said Lela. "We'll be fine out here."

Emmet and Justy, holding hands, followed by Corrie, followed the nurse to Tildie's room. Justy felt so nervous, more nervous perhaps even than when she'd let Sadie's spirit inside her. She was about to see her childhood friend after so many years apart. Could they be friends again, as almost-adults? She desperately hoped so.

The nurse knocked on the door to room 107, waited a few seconds, and then entered the room, Justy, Emmet, and Corrie close behind.

"If you need anything," said the nurse to Tildie, "just press the call button and I'll be here in a jiffy. Enjoy your time together, guys."

"I've missed you so much," said Justy, tears in her eyes again, the moment the nurse left.

Tildie looked so frail, lying in that big hospital bed, blankets pulled up to her chin. Frail, but happy, and more than a little dazed.

"I've missed you, too, Justy," Tildie said. "I've missed all three of you."

Emmet ran over and hugged his best friend, and for a moment Justy felt lost, no longer a part of anything, until Emmet gestured for her and Corrie to join them. A second later all three of them were awkwardly crowded on the hospital bed, hugging Tildie and crying.

"I never thought I'd see you again," whispered Corrie, kissing her little sister on the forehead, once the giant group hug ended.

"None of us did," Justy added.

"So Sadie really was real?" asked Tildie, staring up into Justy's eyes.

"She was real. She saved your life. How do you know about her?"

"I started dreaming about Sadie on my third night in that horrible little shed. She told me everything Jared had done to her, and about a week or so ago, she started showing up when I wasn't asleep, just floating there in front of my eyes, asking me all sorts of strange questions. She asked me for GPS coordinates. She asked me about Corrie, about you guys," she gestured towards Justy and Emmet, "and about Mr. Haj, who I mainly knew from fixing him coffees at Bliss Café. I had nothing else, so I went along with the fantasy, but in the back of my mind I knew I was going insane."

"Except you weren't," Justy said, reaching out to take her hand.

"Except apparently I wasn't," Tildie agreed. "That's still so fucking hard to believe."

They were silent for a while, until finally Corrie asked, "Is the baby still alive?"

"Oh, yeah," she said, touching her stomach. She was starting to show a little.

"Are you going to get an abortion?" Corrie asked. "I think there's still time, and if not I could probably get you a pill anyway."

"I hated this baby so hard while I was in that shed," said Tildie. "All I wanted was to get it out of my body, but Jared threatened to kill you and Emmet and Mom and Dad if the baby wasn't born, so I took the prenatal vitamins he gave me like a good little girl."

"I hope he goes to prison for a long, long time," Justy said, shaking her head. "That man is twisted and evil."

"No doubt about that. But the baby isn't. She deserves a chance at life, and I'm not going to be the one to take that away from her."

She? The baby was barely two months old. How could Tildie know it was a girl? But she didn't ask, instead just reassuring her that whatever decision she made, she'd be there for her, always.

Because that's what best friends do.

20

Six Months Later

Justy and Emmet walked into Mercy hospital, holding hands. It had only been a little over six months since they'd first kissed, and now they were dating and very much in love. Emmet surprised Justy in May by inviting her to prom at Arkansas Academy of Fine Arts, and they'd had an amazing time dancing and spending time together and with their friends from the "nerd table," as Ashlie now referred to it. Life was good.

They were both eighteen-year-old high school graduates now and intended to enroll in the University of Arkansas come fall. Justy had never been happier.

She and Tildie had spent a lot of time together getting to know each other again since her rescue, sometimes with Emmet, sometimes with the whole group, and sometimes just them. It was all wonderful.

"I'm happy Tildie's happy," said Emmet, as they made their way to her room, "but I still think it's a little weird that she decided to keep the baby."

"Maybe a little," Justy agreed, "but we need to support her decision."

"Yeah, I know. Tildie's our best friend."

Justy smiled. She couldn't believe how much her life had changed just in the last six months. She'd fallen in love with the boy she used to mock, reconnected with her best friend in the whole wide world, and was going to college soon. Life was strange, life was complicated, life could be awful at times, but…life was also good.

They reached Tildie's room and could hear voices coming from inside, more than likely Corrie and her parents. Justy pushed open the door and she'd been right about Corrie, but instead of Tildie's parents Kevin Haj was there.

"Emmet! Justy!" called out Tildie, lying in a bed, holding a swaddled little bundle of joy named Sadie.

They rushed over to her side and immediately saw Tildie was beaming with happiness. That was good enough for Justy and apparently for Emmet as well, who now wore a big smile.

"Wow, she's beautiful," Justy said, looking down at the baby.

"Isn't she?" Tildie smiled. "I never thought I'd have a baby at eighteen, but I really do love her."

"Hey, guys," said Kevin, standing next to Corrie. "It's good to see you two. Lela is coming by later, too."

"Good to see you too, Kevin," said Emmet, and Justy echoed the sentiment. "Are you still down for joining us for a game of D&D next weekend?"

"Wouldn't miss it for the world. Lela said she'll be there, too."

Corrie walked over and hugged Emmet and Justy. "I'm glad you guys came. Our parents were here earlier, and Mikayla said she was going to try to drop by later as well."

Mikayla would be going to the Urbana-Champaign university in Illinois, after receiving a last-minute biology scholarship offer. Justy was really going to miss her, but they vowed to see each other during breaks and vacations and to spend as much time together as possible.

Justy, Emmet, Tildie, Mikayla, Corrie, Kevin, and Lela. They were family now, all seven of them, and had enjoyed many dinners and spent much time together since the events in the woods six months ago. They'd witnessed together the unexplainable, the unfathomable, and the miraculous, and would always be there for each other whenever possible, always connected, always having each other's backs.

"Okay," Kevin said, "I really need to head out. Those math papers won't grade themselves. Tildie, I'm so happy I was able to stop by today."

"Me too, Kevin," said Tildie, and Justy could tell she really meant it. "I should be going home tomorrow, so don't be a stranger. You can stop by anytime."

"You can count on it. I'll see you soon."

"I'm gonna walk him out," Corrie said, "so you three can have some catching up time. I'll be back in a few minutes."

"Do you want to hold her?" Tildie asked Emmet, who looked a little scared, as soon as Kevin and Corrie left the room.

"But what if I drop her?"

Justy laughed. "You won't. But I'll let you off the hook just this one time. Can I hold her instead, Tildie?"

"Yeah, of course you can."

Justy took Sadie from Tildie's arms. The little girl really was beautiful. Having a baby at eighteen, especially one whose father had been convicted of multiple crimes and sentenced to two life terms in prison, was going to be rough for Tildie, but Justy was always down for babysitting duty.

She thought once again of the baby's namesake, Sadie Sawyer, and the connection they'd briefly shared. Sadie's parents had been notified after the authorities removed that horrible black shed and dug up her body. Justy met them at Sadie's posthumous funeral, and her heart broke for them. Sadie hadn't deserved such a fate, and Justy wished they could have somehow saved her just like Sadie's spirit had saved Tildie, but that just wasn't possible.

Or was it?

Until fairly recently in her life, she also hadn't thought seeing visions from a ghost was possible, nor sharing your body with one. So who really knew what was possible anymore?

"I have to ask," Justy said, rocking the baby back and forth, as a thought took shape inside her mind, "and please don't get mad, but why did you decide to name her Sadie?"

"Why do you think?" asked Tildie, smiling.

She looked down at little Sadie and their eyes met, and the hair on Justy's arms prickled as she felt an instant connection, saw a brief life lived, a life tragically ended way too soon, and against all odds that same life given a second chance, and finally understood.

Tom Cat

Alice Gardner loved her garden (it was even in her name, she liked to joke) though she wasn't so sure anymore that her garden loved her in return. It all started three weeks ago, when an enormous boom outside her house shook the walls and made half the plates in her China hutch fall and shatter on the hard wood floor below.

Murder, She Wrote was playing on her television that night as she worked on knitting a scarf, and she'd quickly switched the channel from Hallmark Mystery to CBS, half-expecting a breaking news announcement that some country or another we'd alienated had decided to bomb rural Illinois. Nothing. The world at large was safe, at least for now. Her China, not so much.

She spent a good ten or fifteen minutes cleaning up the shards and splinters of China and complaining to the imagined ghost of her dead husband before deciding to venture outside for a look. She lived ten miles outside of the tiny town of Hamilton, and her nearest neighbor was at least half a mile away. She didn't see anything or anyone and finally went back to her knitting and Jessica Fletcher before falling asleep on the couch.

It wasn't until the next morning that she realized whatever caused the noise had also ruined her garden. There was a huge hole right in the middle of her petunias and pansies. It was some damn teenager, she was sure of it, setting off an M-80 or something in her garden. Someone had knocked over her mailbox a couple of years back, so it was probably just more of the same nonsense.

She felt tears welling up but blinked them away. She'd shed enough tears over her 77 years on this planet and refused to waste any over some juvenile delinquent. Instead, she'd rebuild her garden, making it even better. Maybe she'd even put a fence around it, to help keep that damned black and white tomcat that seemed to haunt her yard from chewing up the leaves.

The next morning, Alice drove her Honda into town to Heyman's Nursery, where she picked up some flats of pansies and petunias, a bag of soil, and a bag of fertilizer. When she returned, that damned cat was digging into what was left of her garden.

"Oh no, you don't," she said, chasing the cat off with a broom she kept outside for that very purpose.

She'd thought about taking the cat in before, but just didn't have it in her. She'd lost Bruce nearly twenty years ago, and her beautiful middle daughter, May, passed away from cancer just over nine years later. Less than a year after that her Scottish Terrier, Oscar, had died of old age. Add to that the loss of her parents and both brothers and she just couldn't do it. She'd lost so much of her heart that she couldn't afford to give any more of it away.

Alice knelt beside her garden, pain flaring through her arthritic bones. She layered the garden with more dirt and fertilizer before painstakingly planting alternating rows of pansies and petunias exactly six inches apart.

That had been two weeks ago, and the results of her hard work weren't pretty. The plants had turned a sickly shade of blue and developed sharp, red thorns, and a thick green stem. She'd never before heard of either flower having thorns, nor of them turning blue. She'd dug up the plants (which was surprisingly hard to do; they had really taken root) and shoved them all in an old grocery bag before making a return trip to Heyman's Nursery and demanding a refund.

"Why, sure Alice, I'll replace these flowers for you," said Bill, the owner, "but I've never seen flowers do that. What fertilizer did you use?"

"The fertilizer I bought from you, Bill," she snapped, "the same fertilizer I've been using for years."

He'd ended up replacing the fertilizer and soil as well as the flats of petunias and pansies, and even offered to come help her plant them, to which she'd taken great offense. Alice had been gardening all her life, had even been born on a farm, how dare he think this was somehow her fault? The nerve of that man!

She'd walked away in a huff, driven straight home, put on her gardening gloves, gotten out her trowel, and replanted everything. That had been a week and a half ago, and the results were identical to the first planting. The flowers, seemingly healthy as she planted them, quickly changed color, and grew thorns.

Waving away an errant butterfly, Alice tried to yank the plants out of the soil, but try as she might, she couldn't do it. They had taken root even more so than last time. She began to dig at the base of one particularly huge pansy when she felt something sharp dig deep into the palm of her hand.

She dropped the trowel and fell back on her bottom, staring at her hand. One of those damned thorns had stabbed her, and the wound was deep. Cursing, she leaned against the house and managed to climb to her feet. Her hand was bleeding freely now and pulsing with pain.

Alice made her way back into the house, but not before kicking at the plant that had wounded her. She cleaned the wound as best she could with Peroxide and bandaged the palm of her hand. It still hurt, but the pain was lessening.

"Damn it, anyway," she said to the empty house, before trudging into her kitchen to start dinner.

That night, as she slept, she dreamt of the family she'd once had, of her beloved husband Bruce and their three beautiful daughters, April, May, and June. Inexplicably, all three girls were toddlers, though two years separated April and May while five years separated May and June.

It was summer, and they were barbecuing in the backyard. Bruce was grilling steaks and hotdogs, while Alice was playing on their little backyard swing set with the three girls. She pushed April, then June, and finally May.

April had been born in April, appropriately enough, though that wasn't the reason they'd picked the name, but when May came along in May, it seemed fitting to name her after her birth month. June was born in September, but by then the trend was set. She loved her girls with all her heart.

"Will I grow up to be big and strong like you and Daddy, Mommy?" asked May, feet stretched out to touch the sky as she swung.

"Of course you will, sweetie," she answered, though somewhere in her thoughts she knew this was merely a dream and May was long dead.

Alice pushed those thoughts away, enveloping herself in the fantasy. It was summer, her flowers were bright and blooming, the smell of sizzling steaks scented the air, and her three daughters were laughing. All was right with the world.

"Are you sure, Mommy?"

"I'm sure, sweetie. Big and strong, just like your Daddy."

"Alice, the meat's just about ready," said Bruce from the grill. "Can you go get the fixins'?"

"Sure, honey."

She turned to walk into the house when June began to scream. Alice's heart thumped hard in her chest as she turned back toward her daughters.

"Mommy," said June, now an adult, eyes filled with tears, "what happened to May?"

"What do you mean, darling, she's right here…" she said, turning to stare at the empty swing between April and June.

"Mommy," said April, who now appeared to be in her late fifties, "you didn't watch May close enough, and now she's gone."

"No, she must be here somewhere. Bruce, help…"

She turned toward the grill, where Bruce had been standing just a moment ago, but now he, too, had vanished. The steaks and hamburgers were burned to charcoal, and the grill was overgrown with weeds.

Alice turned around again, back to the swing set, and April and June were gone as well. The swing set, so sparkly and shiny just a few minutes ago, lay in ruins. One swing was missing, and the chains were rusted on the other two. Weeds had also claimed this backyard artifact, circling up around the poles.

She spun in circles, unable to breathe. Where had everyone gone? And then she noticed her garden, though it was normally on the other side of the house. The flowers were beautiful. The petunias were healthy and strong, a vibrant purple, and the red and yellow pansies looked magnificent.

"Come to us," a sweet voice whispered on the wind, *"be one with us."*

An aura of comfort seemed to emanate from the garden, a refuge from all she'd lost and a promise of life renewed. It was mesmerizing but also confusing. Her flowers had never spoken to her before.

"Bruce is here. May is here. So are your parents and brothers. April and June are coming soon. Join us."

She had a fleeting thought about Oscar, her little Scottish Terrier, who had died not long after May. Was he there, too? She asked the question into the wind, but the wind said nothing. She felt a moment of uncertainty, but then it was gone, replaced by something approaching bliss, promising blessed reunion.

Alice walked to the garden, no longer wondering how her flowers had learned to talk. It didn't matter anymore. She knelt on the ground beside her flowers, her knees no longer hurting as they usually did, and plunged her hands deep into the rich brown soil…

Alice woke up. She blinked, momentarily confused. Had she been dreaming? Something about her daughters and flowers... She glanced at her bedside clock. It was 4:07 in the morning. She rolled over and started to go back to sleep but let out a little yelp as she saw a pair of glowing eyes from outside her window.

It was that damned tom cat, just staring at her.

"Shoo!" she yelled from her bed, but the cat didn't move.

Still the cat stared. She rolled out of bed, her knees hurting the moment her feet touched the floor. Grumbling to herself, she walked over to the window that looked out into her backyard and banged her first against the glass.

"I said, shoo!"

The cat stood up, stretched, and hopped down from the windowsill. She watched his retreating tail as he disappeared into the dim early morning light.

"I'm up now, so I might as well stay up," she muttered under her breath, shaking her head. "Stupid cat."

Alice walked in her nightgown from the bedroom, down the hallway, though the living room, and into the kitchen before turning on a light. She'd lived in this house for over fifty years, she knew it like the back of her hand.

Speaking of her hand, it no longer hurt. She carefully undid the bandage and was amazed to see the wound had healed overnight. In fact, her hand looked exactly as it had before she'd stabbed herself on that thorn.

It must not have been as bad as she'd thought. That, or she was going senile. Maybe both.

"Getting old is for the birds," she whispered under her breath, as she reached into one of the cabinets to pull down a tin of Folger's coffee.

She walked over to the coffee maker, carefully filling the filter with two tablespoons of coffee crystals. She added tap water to the reservoir and hit the button. Two cups of coffee. If she had any more, she'd never get to sleep tonight, despite the hour she'd risen.

Five minutes later, the coffee was ready. Retrieving sugar and cream from the refrigerator, she flavored it to taste and took a sip. It tasted good, but somehow Bruce could always make a better cup of coffee than she could. God, she missed Bruce's coffee. She missed *Bruce*.

The rest of the day passed as it usually did, with Alice watching television and doing crossword puzzles. She even surfed the internet for a while, searching for but failing to find information on how pansies and petunias might change to what was currently growing in her garden.

She wasn't good with the Google, or with the Mac in general, honestly. The computer had been a gift from April a few Christmases ago, and she'd learned to use it, albeit begrudgingly, but she still wasn't sure she'd ever like it.

The phone rang once, but she let it go to the old answering machine she still used. It was June, her youngest daughter. She listened to the message. June was inviting her to come visit her and her husband Paul next month, but Alice just wasn't up to it.

She was never up to it and mostly ignored June and April's calls when she could and cut the calls short when she couldn't. She erased the message and went back to the *Law & Order* marathon she'd been watching off and on for the last two days.

"Mommy," said May, tugging at her hand, "you said you'd take me to visit Grandma and Grandpa."

Alice blinked. Was she dreaming again? She looked around. She was sitting on the couch, a book laying open in her lap. She must have fallen asleep.

"Come on, Mommy," said the little girl, tugging on her arm.

"Honey, Grandpa and Grandma passed away. You know that."

"No, they didn't. They were just here for my birthday!"

Was that right? Of course it was right. What was wrong with her?

"Okay, sweetie, let's go see Grandpa and Grandma. Do your sisters want to come?"

"Not yet," the little girl said cryptically, "but soon."

A shiver went down Alice's back. What did that mean?

"Come on!" she said, pulling Alice to her feet. "Daddy's there, too. So are Uncle Andrew and Uncle Robert."

Alice stood up, the book falling from her lap to land on the floor. She felt so good, so young. She looked at her hands. They weren't wrinkled, and there were no liver spots.

But why would there be? She wasn't even thirty yet. She shook her head at her own foolishness and followed May to the door. After they got back, maybe she'd drag Bruce into the bedroom and…

"What's that?" asked May, alarm in her voice.

They were outside now, though Alice didn't remember opening the door. She looked to where May was pointing. It was that damned black and white tom cat again.

"Oh, don't worry about him, honey, he's just a stray."

"Come on!" said May again, eyes darting between her and the cat.

The cat stood in front of them, hackles rising. He hissed as they took a step towards him.

"Kill him, Mommy," said May, an edge to her voice that made Alice nervous.

"Honey! We would never kill an animal. Why would you say such a thing?"

"Oh, all right. Come on, then."

Alice began walking toward the car, avoiding the tom cat, but May yanked her towards the garden. She looked down at her beautiful petunias and pansies, glowing in the sunlight. They smelled so nice. She almost wanted to lie down among them and take a nice, long nap.

The cat hissed again and swatted her leg.

"Kill him!" May growled. "If you don't, you're never going to see Daddy. You'll never be able to drag him into the bedroom and fuck him."

Alice stared at May, shocked at the little girl's words. Where had she learned language like that? She turned to face her daughter, but she was no longer there.

Panic rising in her throat, Alice turned to the left, to the right, and then she saw her. May was sitting in the garden, the beautiful garden with the gorgeous pansies and petunias, and they smelled so good.

She took one step toward the garden, and then another, and then one more.

Pain flared through her leg, and she screamed. She looked down. It was that damned cat, and he was biting her ankle! She tried to kick him off, but he held on fast.

"Kill him!" ordered May.

But she couldn't kill an animal, she just couldn't. She'd loved animals her entire life. Oscar had been her entire world after...

After what? Alice blinked, shook her head. This wasn't right. She bit down hard on her tongue and blinked again. It wasn't day, it was nighttime, and May wasn't sitting in the flowerbed.

She was.

Her arms were plunged deep into the soil, and the plants were moving, were sliding up her arms, thorny red tendrils reaching out for her face. She pulled back, but the plants wouldn't let go.

Dear Lord, what was happening?

"Come to us," whispered something in her brain. *"May is here, Bruce is here, they're all here, waiting for you."*

The cat finally let go of her ankle and darted up to the plant, swatting at the thorns that threatened to engulf her. The tendrils shot out toward the tom, but he was faster, avoiding every strike and giving two of his own in return.

"Kill it!" ordered the voice in her mind.

She wanted, needed to obey the voice, but instead she pulled back, away from the plants, shifting her arms out of the soil. But they wouldn't come out. She felt thorns digging into her skin, holding her tight.

The cat lunged, sinking his fangs into the thick stock of one of the petunias. She felt the grip on her hands loosen a bit, so she pulled with everything she had within her, harder than she'd ever pulled before.

She tumbled backwards, arms cut and bleeding but finally free. She stared at her hands. They were wrinkled and liver-spotted and covered in blood.

The cat howled, eyes wide with pain and desperation. The plant had finally managed to get hold of the tom and was pulling him into the dirt. The cat had saved her, and now she needed to save the cat.

On her hands and knees now, Alice reached out and snatched her trowel from beside the garden. She reared back and plunged it at the stalk of one of the plants holding the cat, nearly cutting the stalk in half.

"Mommy, you're hurting me!" shouted the voice in her head.

"Shut up!" she screamed, hacking and slashing at the plants. "Shut up, shut up, shut up!"

Finally, the cat was free, but she wasn't done yet. Pulling herself to her feet, she stumbled around the side of the house to the shed Bruce had built a lifetime ago and retrieved a shovel.

Walking on wobbly legs, she raced back to the garden and plunged the shovel deep into the soil of the garden, again and again, throwing mounds of plants and dirt behind her.

"Mommy, you're killing me!"

"You're already dead!" she yelled into the night, digging faster and faster.

"I'll kill April and June if you don't stop, you old bitch!"

She gritted her teeth, ignored her arthritic fingers, and kept digging. Finally, she uncovered a rock about the size of a softball. It was faintly glowing, a soft blue shimmer.

The cat meowed and looked up at her.

"Get back, you sweet old tom," she said, as she swung the blade of the shovel toward the rock.

She hit the rock again, and again, and again, and finally it cracked open, a blue *thing* tumbling out from within.

The creature was covered in slime and sported dozens of deep-red tendrils, almost like a spider if a spider had three times as many legs and was blue. Alice gasped as the creature scuttled out of the garden, watching it recoil as the cat lunged at it.

"Get back!" Alice warned, as she swung the shovel for all she was worth.

"Mommy!" screamed the thing inside her head, just before she cut it in half with the blade of the shovel.

The creature wiggled and then died. Just like that.

Alice shook her head. She didn't understand anything that had just happened, though some small part of her brain told her that the thing that had destroyed her garden nearly three weeks ago had been a meteorite.

She guessed there was life in space, after all, but it wasn't very nice.

The cat looked up at her quizzically and meowed.

"Come here, you," she said, bending on creaking knees to scoop the cat up into her arms.

It began purring immediately, cuddling her neck and biscuiting her arms.

Alice stared at her garden as she hugged the old tom. It was ruined, and she wasn't going to replant. That part of her life was over now, and at 77 she might not have that many years left, but she thought she just might have enough time to build another life from the remains of this one.

She took the cat inside. He'd saved her life, and she'd saved his. They were bonded now, and she loved him more than she could ever express. And April, and June, the two daughters she'd been ignoring ever since their middle sister's death, not to mention their children, Alice's grandchildren, and their children, her great-grandchildren. She loved them all.

Closing the door behind her, she sat the cat on the couch and went into the kitchen to open a can of tuna and put down a bowl of water. Tomorrow, she planned to drive to Hy-Vee in Keokuk to get cat food, a litter box, and some litter, but tonight Tom would dine on tuna and could shit anywhere he damned well pleased.

Tom ran into the kitchen, digging into his supper. Alice stared at him, and a smile slowly crept across her face. He was hers, and she was his. It almost felt like she was starting a new life, the way she'd felt ten years ago when she'd moved away from Carthage to this much smaller home outside of Hamilton.

She hadn't adopted anything but dogs since she and Bruce took in a beautiful little stray cat named Trixie back in the mid-80s. It would be lovely to once again have a feline companion.

Ignoring the pain in her knees, Alice left Tom to his tuna and made her way into the living room and towards the phone.

She had calls to make.

Next Time is Now

Peter lay on a queen-sized bed in a nondescript Super 8 motel room in Westbrook, Maine, strapped to an EKG monitor, trying to calm his nerves. This would work. It had to. He couldn't go through losing her all over again.

"It'll be okay, Peter," said Marnie Amari, squeezing his hand. "I still wish you'd let me do it, though."

They had argued about this for days. Marnie had a heart murmur. If her heart stopped, it might not start again. His would, or at least he hoped it would.

"I wouldn't be doing this if it were you," said Lillian, Marnie's older sister, who also happened to be a nurse at Westbrook Memorial Hospital. "And, for the record, I think you're both nuts. If we get caught, or the hospital notices the missing equipment, I'll lose my job and probably go to prison."

Marnie hugged her. "We won't get caught. It'll be fine, promise."

"But I'm not a doctor, and to stop someone's heart—"

"Let's just get this over with," Peter interrupted, trying to keep the fear out of his voice.

"I just met you," Lillian said, whirling to face Peter, "so don't tell me what to do, okay? Hell, *she* just met you. You two are insane."

"We know. You already said that."

"You'll be okay," Marnie whispered, ignoring her sister as she leaned down to brush her lips against Peter's. "I'm not gonna lose you again. I love you."

"I love you, too," he said, trying to smile, "with all my heart and soul. And if this doesn't work, well, there's always next time."

"It will work," she said, though he could hear doubt in her voice, "and then we'll live happily ever after."

"From your mouth to God's ears," he murmured.

"Are you ready?" Lillian asked, holding the defibrillator paddles she would use to stop Peter's heart. "Let's do this before I change my mind."

"Do it," he said, feeling the tension drain out of his body. What did he have to lose?

She placed the paddles against his chest. "Last chance, are you 100% sure you want to do this?"

"Do it," Peter said again.

"Just remember," said Lillian, "you asked for this."

"Remember, happily ever after," Marnie said.

He smiled at Marnie, and then felt a sudden, sharp jolt of pain flow through his chest and into the rest of his body, all his muscles tensing, and then…

He was floating over the bed, staring down at Marnie and Lillian and his own body. He looked dead. Well, of course he looked dead, because he *was* dead. It was a very strange feeling.

Peter could see Marnie talking but couldn't hear her words. He tried moving closer. It was almost like he was in water. He dog-paddled over to the love of his lives.

"Oh my God," whispered Lillian, staring at the flat line on the EKG machine, "he's dead. I murdered him."

"Calm down," said Marnie, reaching out to hold her sister's hand. "This is going to work. I know it will."

"Marnie, you've known this guy for three weeks. Why did I let you talk me into this?"

"I've known him a lot longer than three weeks. I've known him forever."

"So you keep saying," Lillian said. "I remember your dreams from when we were little. I understand why you feel the way you do. It's a nice fantasy and all, but this guy is conning you."

"Who would 'con' someone into stopping their heart?" snapped Marnie. "Just give it two minutes, pronounce him dead, and bring him back. It'll all be okay."

It was the same argument Marnie and her sister had been having for the last week. Peter tuned them out, letting the room once again grow silent.

He understood where Lillian was coming from. He could scarcely believe it himself when, just 21 days earlier, Marnie had bumped into him as he stood in line waiting for his Chai Latte at Starbucks.

She'd spilled her coffee on him, which burned like hell and instantly enraged him. He'd looked up, ready to tell her off, and then their eyes met, and first his anger and then the rest of the world fell away…

The first time he dreamt of her he was only five years old. He'd just watched The Wizard of Oz with his parents and his big sister, and that night he dreamed about what much later he'd come to know as the Salem witch trials.

Her name was Elizabeth then, and they'd just married after a very long courtship, neither of which was a concept his five-year-old mind could really understand. Hazel, a childhood friend of Elizabeth's who was upset because she wasn't invited to the wedding, began a whisper campaign that Elizabeth was a witch.

Word spread quickly, and before they even knew what was happening Elizabeth was jailed by the zealots that ruled Salem. Hazel, who'd never meant for things to go that far, confessed to making it all up. Her words fell on deaf ears, and soon she was sitting in jail beside her former friend.

The very next day, without benefit of anything approaching a real trial, they were both hanged. Peter (he could never remember what his name had been then) left the village and spent the rest of his life as a hermit, eventually dying of pneumonia when he was just 32.

The next time he dreamed of her, he was nine. He was a sheriff's deputy in Cody, Wyoming, and she was a schoolteacher. They met, instantly fell in love, and the very next day he was shot dead by a bandit while attempting to stop a bank robbery.

Sometimes their lives together were longer, but rarely for more than a year or two, and it always ended in one or both of their deaths. The longest they'd managed to stay alive after finding each other was three years.

Puberty brought even more dreams, and Peter was thirteen when he first dreamt about his life in ancient Egypt. He was a woman then, a priestess of sorts, in the court of the Pharaoh Khufu. She met Aten, a shopkeeper, while shopping for a new robe, and instantly fell in love.

Her family, of course, objected. She was a young priestess while he was merely a shopkeeper, and an old one at that. They were finally married, but Aten died of a heart attack less than a year later.

Peter made the mistake of telling his parents about this dream, which earned him a diagnosis of "something's wrong with him" from his mother and nine long months in therapy. The therapist diagnosed him with everything from dissociative identity disorder to body dysmorphia, and eventually he just went along with whatever she said, claiming he made up the dreams, and she pronounced him cured.

Just a year after the Egypt dream, in his freshman year of high school, Peter came down with the flu. He was sick for almost two weeks and had many vivid dreams about many different time periods, all with this same woman whose name as well as appearance changed with each dream.

She wasn't always a woman, and he wasn't always a man. Once they were even identical twin girls. During that life, he'd died from cancer at the age of 14, just after they had begun to remember their past lives.

The most vivid dream, however, was set in 1941, during World War II. This time, they were both men and met in Nazi Germany. He was an American solider who'd gotten separated from his unit during a skirmish in the Hürtgen forest.

Tired, hungry, and afraid, he wandered for hours before walking into a clearing containing six German soldiers. He tried to run, but they ran him down and captured him and immediately bound his hands behind his back. One of the soldiers, a hulking young man named Karl Gersdorff, volunteered to escort Peter back to their camp. His commanding officer was hesitant at first but finally agreed.

Almost a mile from the clearing, Karl brought Peter to a halt. He untied his hands and spun him around to stare into his eyes.

"You recognize me?" he asked, in broken English.

Peter stared into his eyes. He hadn't really got a good look at him back in the clearing, but now… His eyes went wide as he remembered. So many lives, so many faces, but he knew immediately that Karl, Elizabeth, Rashida, Audrey, Jonathan, and all the others were one and the same.

"You do, I knew you would," Karl said, pulling him close, kissing him on the lips.

Peter wrapped his arms around the German soldier, losing himself in the kiss. When they finally broke their embrace, Karl handed him his gun.

"What? I don't want this," said Peter, pushing the weapon away.

"I don't come back, they come for me. You got loose, attacked me, got my gun and shot me, and ran away. There's an old barn on the north end of town. I find you later, when it's safe."

"Shoot you?" he asked, staring at the gun. "I'm not going to shoot you, I just found you."

"Shoot me in the leg. It's the only way," Karl insisted, waving the gun at Peter.

A shot rang out and Peter gasped as a small hole appeared in Karl's forehead. He watched in confusion as the big German fell to the ground. Peter was at his side in an instant, dropping to his knees in the cold, wet grass, but Karl was already dead.

He turned to stare at Bobby Sparrow, his best friend in the unit, and the rest of his fellow soldiers. Bobby held a smoking pistol in his hand, and was saying something…

Peter waved away that memory. He didn't like remembering that one. He stared down at Marnie and Lillian, wondering how much time had passed. He concentrated and could once again hear them talking.

"…cursed. I don't remember it, but he does. This could fix everything, at least for this life," Marnie was telling her sister.

"Do you realize how crazy you sound?"

They were still arguing. He wondered how much time it'd been. There was a clock on the stand beside the bed, and it read 1:18 in the afternoon, but he didn't know when they'd stopped his heart. He wished he'd paid attention.

Of course, if he'd paid better attention at the very beginning, this might not be happening.

His oldest memory, one he'd first dreamt of as a sophomore in college, was of growing up in what he later deduced must have been some hidden part of Africa. He was part of a tribe that practiced something like Voodoo. Hell, maybe it *was* Voodoo. He'd never been able to figure it out and supposed it didn't really matter.

He was one of the three main hunters for his tribe, and she was Abena, the daughter of the village's high priestess. They were in love, and she was pregnant with his child, never dreaming tragedy was about to strike.

Peter and one of his hunt-brothers, Hamundi, were tasked with a very special quest: to bring down an old and particularly elusive lion that had just a few days earlier attacked and nearly killed one of the children in the village. King Enzokuhle, Abena's father, who had once been the greatest hunter in all the land, went with them on this special hunt.

The lion's trail took them far from home, and after a while it began to storm. Peter and Hamundi suggested they return to the village and hunt another day, but the king insisted they continue to track the lion.

They had just cornered what they thought was the lion hiding behind a huge clump of shrubs. A loud crack of thunder rang through the jungle, and a giant wildebeest burst forth from the bushes. Hamundi jumped out of the way, but the beast struck Peter in the side, goring him with one of its horn and sending him flying into King Enzokuhle.

The two fell into the long, wet grass together, and as Peter struggled to his feet, he realized King Enzokuhle wasn't moving. Peter's spear had impaled the king in the throat, killing him instantly.

Wounded and grieving, Peter suggested to Hamundi that they give up the hunt. Hamundi agreed, and together they dragged Enzokuhle's body back to their village.

The high priestess was enraged when she saw the dead king's body, demanding to know what had killed him. Scared and afraid, Hamundi immediately pointed at Peter, claiming it was his carelessness that had cost King Enzokuhle his life.

Abena, grieving for her father, nevertheless defended Peter, telling her mother that she knew he wasn't a careless hunter. Peter tried to tell the high priestess about the wildebeest, tried to show her his own wound, but she wouldn't listen.

The high priestess' anger only grew as Abena continued to defend him, shouting at them both. Finally, she called forth from some other realm this huge orange and green lion-like creature covered with scales and with seven tentacles for arms. Peter had never seen anything more frightening in any of the many lives he'd since lived and prayed he never would.

The priestess referred to the monster as *Xhahgoth,* and using magic it somehow gave her, she cursed Peter and Abena to be together forever, throughout all their lives, but for one of them to always die just as they found each other. It was a powerful curse, and the villagers gasped all around them, then turned away, shunning them.

He remembered stumbling away from the village with Abena in humiliation, but what happened after that, he had no idea. He and Abena had reincarnated over and over, always finding each other, and always losing each other soon thereafter.

He'd been shot and killed when the police raided the speakeasy they both worked at in New York in the mid-1920's.

She'd been lost to the great fire of London in 1666, run over by a horse galloping away from the flames.

He'd suffered a stroke at the age of sixteen. She'd died in childbirth. They'd both drowned when the pirate ship they'd hitched a ride on went down to the British Royal Navy's cannon fire.

It was then, on that pirate ship, as the great boat was sinking, that they'd come up with the mantra they'd always say when one or both of them was about to die. "There's always next time."

He—

Something was happening. Peter could see a bright light in the distance, and it was all he could do to force himself to turn away. No, he wouldn't lose her this time. He looked down, and Lillian was shocking his chest with the paddles, again and again.

"Why isn't it working?" Marnie cried, staring at Peter's body.

"Because I'm not a doctor!" shouted Lillian, dropping the paddles to the floor. "I'm so sorry, Marnie, but we have to get out of here. I am not going to jail."

Marnie stared at her sister in disbelief. "I'm not going anywhere without him."

I'm here, Peter shouted, but of course they couldn't hear him. They had been foolish to think they could escape the old woman's curse by circumventing the rules.

Peter swam through the air toward Marnie, but it was like swimming through a swamp. One stroke forward, and then he was sliding backwards again, towards that light.

"Dammit, Peter," Marnie sobbed, slamming her fists into his chest over and over. "Wake up. Wake up! I am not going to lose you again!"

He was slipping away. The light was dragging him in.

I love you, Marnie, he mouthed, just as his feet touched the light.

He reached towards her one last time, and then—

Peter gasped, eyes opening, staring up at Marnie. He had never seen such a beautiful sight in all his lives. He blinked, looked around, and then the pain came. His entire body hurt, and it felt like his ribs were broken.

"Oh my God, you're alive," Marnie whispered, Lillian standing beside her staring wide-eyed. "You're fucking alive, Peter. We did it!"

"I love you, Marnie," he managed to get out, for real this time, before he passed out from the pain.

Peter woke up just an hour later, in the hospital but very much alive and happy. Lillian didn't lose her job and Peter and Marnie lived happily ever after, just like Marnie said they would.

Online Undead

My name is Charlie (no relation to Leroy) Jenkins, and I think I'm being haunted. But I'm getting ahead of myself, and it's not so much haunted as...well, I suppose I should start at the beginning.

Nathan and I had been best friends since second grade, when his family moved here from Dallas eight years ago. His parents didn't allow him to socialize outside of school at first, but we'd found other ways to connect. We did everything together online we could, really, but mostly what we did was play video games. We spent so much time paired up in the digital world, it was almost impossible to believe that I'd never see him again not only physically but also digitally.

Around fifth grade, Nathan's parents loosened up a bit and we'd begun hanging out more in person, but the pattern had already been set. The digital world was our domain, and we spent most of our time together there, battling dragons of all different shapes, sorts, and sizes.

We started with Disney's Toontown Online, quickly progressed to Pirates of the Caribbean, and then to City of Heroes, and when NCSoft stupidly shut down CoH, moved on to Secret World: Legends and World of Warcraft. Lately, however, we'd been going the nostalgia route, playing Toontown Rewritten (a fan-made server created after Disney shut down the original) while our phones were almost completely dedicated to Pokémon Go.

We'd both reached level 38 in Pokémon Go, just a few days before Nathan died. In fact, his Dragonite still sat in the Poké gym on Maple Street, alongside my shiny Tyranitar.

We were proudly team Mystic, and I was dreading the day when a yellow or red team would come along and knock us out of the gym. That gym was one of the last connections I had with my best friend. I fed both our Pokémon golden razz berries every day, along with four other Pokémon in the gym, to keep them strong. If I couldn't have my best friend in the real world, at least I'd still have a small part of him in the digital.

It was Friday, but I wasn't in school. Instead I lay on my bed, reading *Termite Girl,* a new comic book from Anomaly Studios, while absent-mindedly transferring Pokémon I'd caught over the last few days. Mom and Dad had half-heartedly encouraged me to go to school but ended up relenting and letting me stay home another day.

Nathan's funeral had been yesterday, less than a week after he'd killed himself. He jumped off the top of his two-story house, landed headfirst in the rose garden below, and broke his neck. He died almost instantly, according to what the police told his parents.

But why had he killed himself? His parents claimed he'd been suffering from depression, but if that were the case, he'd certainly never told me. He'd seemed upset about something the last time I'd chatted with him, but not sad. If anything, he was angry. When I asked him what was going on, he'd blown it off and said he'd explain it later, in person. That had been just hours before his death.

We'd made plans to participate in the upcoming Pokémon Go community day that weekend. In a rare truce in the ongoing sibling wars, my older sister Taryn had even agreed to drive us downtown for the event. Nathan had crushed on Taryn for years and was super excited about that. He never would have killed himself, not in a million years, at least not before seeing Taryn.

Except that he did.

I shook my head, trying to keep myself from crying. Part of me hated Nathan for doing this, and the other part of me just wanted to curl up and sleep and do my best to forget all about him.

A knock sounded at my door, startling me. I dropped the comic book onto my little bedside table, then stood up from the bed.

"What?" I answered, a little more tersely than I'd intended.

"You doing okay, Charlie?" asked my mother's voice, though the door.

"Not really," I admitted.

"Can I come in?"

"Sure, I guess so."

We talked for about thirty minutes, with her reassuring me about a million times that Nathan's death had nothing to do with me, how none of it was my fault, and that eventually I'd come to accept it but would feel "down" for a while.

Gee, Mom, no shit? Your best friend kills himself, are you supposed to celebrate? Eventually she left, and I got out my laptop and booted up Toontown Rewritten for the first time since Nathan's death.

Toontown, both the original and revived version, was based entirely in a cartoon world. The familiar opening screen of a cartoon monkey in a lab coat greeted me, and I typed in my name and password. I selected my most powerful toon, a blue bear by the name of Master Presto Fiddlesticks, and logged in.

My friend Miss Grouchy was online, the game told me as I zoned into the snowy territory known as the Brrrgh, as well as two of my other online friends, Weird Billy Slimeyfoot and Captain Spaceman. We'd been playing with Miss Grouchy on and off for a couple of years, while the other two were recent acquaintances.

Hey there, Presto, Miss Grouchy said to me, through an in-game whisper, **haven't seen you for a bit. What's up?**

I paused before typing. How much should I tell her? Miss Grouchy was a middle-aged woman who lived in Kentucky. She didn't really know me in real life, though we'd interacted in several of the Toontown Facebook groups and even exchanged a few emails.

Not much, I started to type but then erased it. There was no way I could pretend nothing was wrong. Okay, here goes. **I'm sorry to have to tell you this, but Pierre died.**

I waited for a reply, immediately wondering if I was doing the right thing.

You're joking, right? I just saw him online about ten minutes ago. I was gonna ask him to do a boss with me, but he logged off almost immediately.

My heart caught in my throat. What the hell? Had someone stolen his account? I couldn't see his parents logging into Toontown with his or anyone else's account, and Nathan was an only child, so there was no one else who would have access or even opportunity.

There could be more than one Sir Pierre Sparklewicket on Toontown Rewritten, of course, so maybe she'd simply seen someone else. He'd picked the name from a name generator, just like I'd done with my own character. In the two years we'd been playing, however, we'd never seen another toon with the same name as either of our characters.

Hey, can you help me take over a 4-story or higher Cashbot building? she whispered. **I need three of them for one of my tasks.**

I didn't answer, but instead just stared at the screen. Surely, she was mistaken. Probably someone with a similar name. I started to ask her if she was 100% sure it'd been Pierre when a message popped up on the screen.

Sir Pierre Sparklewicket is coming online!

A jolt of hope coursed through my body which was quickly replaced by anger. Nathan was dead, and he wasn't coming back. Someone had indeed duplicated his name or stolen his account. Nathan had always been careful with his passwords. How was this possible?

Who is this? I demanded. No answer.

Pierre is dead. Who are you? No answer.

I slammed my hand against the bed in frustration, causing the laptop to bounce and nearly tumble to the floor. I quickly caught the computer, secured it on my lap, and checked to make sure the pretender was still online.

I can only use Speedchat, Pierre whispered to me.

On Toontown, there was chat, speedchat, and whisper. Speedchat had all sorts of pre-written phrases one could use to communicate with the other players in the game. In chat, you could type whatever you wanted, but certain words were censored and would translate into nonsense words depending on your animal species. Whisper could use either chat or Speedchat, but it was private and could be sent no matter where the recipient was in the game.

I hit F9, the keyboard command to take a screenshot of the game. I would screenshot everything he said, if necessary, so I'd be able to show it to one of the game masters and get this imposter thrown out of the game.

Why are you using my friend's account? How did you get his account?

Sorry!

Who are you? I tried again.

That was fun!

A chill ran down my spine. **Please, stop. This is freaking me out.**

Speak of the devil, I see Pierre is on! Miss Grouchy whispered to me. **Want to help me with a 4 story Cashbot building? I just need 2 now.**

Can't right now, I quickly typed to her in response. Then to Pretend Pierre: **Look, *growl*, this isn't cool.** I'd typed "asshole," but TTR's word censor didn't like that, and replaced the word with "growl."

OK.

Okay, what?

Let's all go for the same cog, Pretender Pierre messaged.

This guy was just screwing with me. As I stared at the screen, trying to think of what I should do next, he sent me another message.

Easy does it.

Easy does what? I responded.

No.

No what? I was done talking. I had to see if this Pierre was the same neon green cat that Nathan had played. I immediately teleported to him, and that's when the game crashed.

"God damnit!" I yelled out loud, as I quickly relogged.

By the time I zoned in, he was gone.

Still upset about Toontown, I decided to get out of the house and ride my bicycle down to the park. Mom half-heartedly objected, because it was still school hours, but she eventually relented and let me go after I mumbled something about Nathan. I knew I could only use the "dead friend" card for so long, but I didn't care.

One of the Poké gyms that Nathan and I still held was just a few blocks from my house, at the park. I spun a Pokéstop on the way to the park and got three red Pokéballs and a Razz Berry. I deleted the balls but held on to the berry, because they helped you catch Pokémon.

All of this was virtual, of course. Neither Pokéstops nor Poké gyms existed in the real world. Instead, they were just within the game but were tied to real world locations. The one I was heading towards was located inside Canterburry park, a place Nathan and I used to hang out at a lot when we were younger.

I leaned the bike against a tree and dropped down to the bench beside it. My shiny Tyranitar was still in the gym, along with Nathan's Dragonite, a Rhyperior, a Gyrados, an Espeon, and a Machamp. I fed them all Golden Razz Berries, to strengthen them in case the gym was attacked by one of the other teams.

I caught a couple of wild Pokémon—a Teddiursa and a Croagunk—and was just about ready to bicycle home when a trainer battle invitation popped up on my screen.

NateTheGreat wants to battle!

I stared at the screen, blinked twice, and then slowly scanned the park. What the hell was going on? Nathan and I had achieved "Best Friends" status in the game, so we didn't have to be close to one another to do battle, but nevertheless I had a feeling I was being watched.

I turned on the video recorder on my phone before clicking "let's do it!" Whoever was impersonating Nathan had challenged me to a Master League battle, which meant there was no limit on the combat power of the three Pokémon I could choose for the fight.

I chose Tyranitar, Gyarados, and Ho-Oh, and the battle began. The imposter's Dragonite managed to defeat my Tyranitar in a very close fight. My Gyarados, however, quickly vanquished his Dragonite and destroyed his Articuno.

His final Pokémon, another Dragonite, appeared on the screen and took out my Gyarados. My final Pokémon, Ho-Oh, appeared on the screen, and the battle was on. Normally, a Dragonite would probably defeat Ho-Oh, but this Dragonite didn't have many hit points left at all and quickly succumbed to my "brave bird" attack.

I won.

"Okay, you've had your fun," I said out loud, "now tell me who you are."

No answers were forthcoming, however, and I was instead greeted with another battle invitation. I accepted, and this time he chose Kyogre, Infernape, and Lugia, all of which I easily defeated.

Once again, I received a battle challenge, and once again I accepted. My Tyranitar easily disposed of his Latios and Machamp but lost to his Espeon. My Gyarados, however, mopped the floor with his Espeon, winning the battle.

Whoever had taken over Nathan's account certainly wasn't as good as Nathan. We'd always been closely matched, and I didn't think I'd ever beaten him three games in a row.

I stared at my phone, waiting for a fourth challenge that never came. Apparently, the imposter had given up. I got on my bike, shaking with anger, and headed home.

That night, I logged into City of Heroes Homecoming and World of Warcraft, but Nathan's characters never appeared. I logged back into TTR, but nothing there either.

Had the pretender already grown tired of this silly and hurtful game? Part of me hoped so, but another, smaller part that I didn't want to think about wanted it to continue so I could catch the bastard and make him pay.

I lay in my bed, unable to sleep. What could have gone so wrong in Nathan's life that he'd decided to kill himself, and why hadn't he talked to me first? We were best friends, weren't we?

That last thought shamed me. Of course, we were best friends. *Had* been best friends. As much as I wanted to believe otherwise, I'd probably never know the answer.

I thought back to all we'd shared over the years, the games we'd played, the sleepovers, and how it all started in second grade, when he was new, sending messages written in secret code back and forth in Mrs. Greenberg's class...

Wait a second. I jumped up from bed, grabbed my laptop, and booted it up. I went into the screenshot folder and looked at the screenshots of the conversation I'd had with Pierre earlier today. Then I opened my phone and watched the recording of the battle I'd had this afternoon.

It took me a while to understand it, but when I did, I felt a shiver run down my spine. I shook with anger as tears streamed down my face.

This was real. This was all real. Nathan had reached out to me from beyond the grave, and I was the only one who could make this right, the only one who could avenge Nathan.

I had to come up with a plan, one that wouldn't have me join Nathan in death. As just such a plan began to come to fruition, I downloaded a certain app I'd need for tomorrow onto my phone.

Nathan had been murdered, and I intended to prove it.

I woke up the next morning, doubting everything. Did teenagers really come back from the dead, just to send their best friend messages through Toontown Rewritten and Pokemon Go? Was any of this possible? Was I sure? Because if I wasn't sure, I could unnecessarily hurt a lot of people, as well as get myself into a world of trouble.

I looked at my clock. It was just a few minutes after nine. I'd fallen asleep around 3:30 in the morning, so I had gotten at most five and a half hours of sleep. It would have to do.

I booted up Toontown Rewritten, and Pierre was there waiting for me. I was almost certain he would be. I teleported to him immediately and arrived in a glitched area that we'd always referred to as "the ether." Of course he'd be in the ether.

I spun around through the blackness and could see cartoon buildings off in the distance. I couldn't immediately tell what street we were on, but I knew we were in Donald's Dreamland, so I thought it was probably Lullaby Lane.

I can only use speedchat, he said.

I know, I typed. **I'm starting to understand.**

He jumped up and down, and then said: **That's going to leave a mark!**

I started to type the letters into my phone, but as it turned out, there was no need. The message was short and to the point.

Easy does it.

166 | J o e   D e R o u e n

Later!

Later!

You can stop now, I typed. **I get it, and I'll do it. I'll tell every-** one.

Thanks! Pierre said.

I miss you, I responded.

Using the Sad emotion, Pierre's monkey face looked tearful for a few seconds.

Sorry!

I know you are. This is going to be the last time I see you, isn't it?

Yes.

No.

Which way?

I think he was trying to tell me he didn't know.

I need to go soon.

I wiped my face with the back of my hand, and realized I was crying. I blinked back the tears, half-afraid that Nathan would vanish while I wasn't looking at the screen, but he was still there.

Let's go to my house! Nathan's toon said.

That's the plan, I responded. **But you already know that, don't** you?

Yes.

Okay, I typed, **I'm gonna do this.**

Good luck!

Thanks, buddy, I typed, **I'm going to need it.**

He whispered **Bye!** and logged out.

I few seconds later, hands shaking, I did the same.

I stood outside Nathan's house, trying to find the courage to ring the doorbell. There was still police tape around the rose garden, where Nathan had landed. I tried not to look at it. Finally, my finger stabbed the ringer.

"Charlie," said Nathan's father, as he opened the door, "what are you doing here?"

"We need to talk," I said, and he stood aside to let me into the house.

"Come on in. Nathan's mother…Mrs. Chandler and I were just eating breakfast, you're welcome to join us."

I followed him through the living room and into the dining room, where Nathan's mother was already waiting. A plate of half-eaten scrambled eggs, bacon, and toast sat before Mrs. Chandler, along with a half-full wine glass and an empty wine bottle.

"Hello, Charlie," she said, her voice flat.

Amanda Chandler was short and petite, with red hair, pale skin, and freckles. David Chandler was taller, had dark hair, a long nose, and his head always looked a little big for his neck. Nathan looked nothing like either of them, and now I knew why.

"Charlie's going to join us for breakfast," Mr. Chandler said. "How do you like your eggs, Charlie?"

"I know what you did," I said, ignoring his question. "I know you killed Nathan."

He looked away for a second and then quickly looked back, a snarl on his face. "That's an awful thing to say, Charlie. I know you're grieving, but we're grieving too, and I think it'd be best—"

"What are you talking about?" asked Mrs. Chandler, rising from the table.

"You stole him," I said, thinking back to what Nathan had told me yesterday the first time he'd logged into TTR. "You stole Nathan from his real parents."

Mr. Chandler's face went white. "But how could you…I mean…"

"Nathan told me everything," I lied. "He wrote me an email right before you murdered him."

"Oh, my God," whispered Mrs. Chandler, staring first at me and then at her husband. "David, what did you do?"

Mr. Chandler looked at his wife, then at me, then at his wife again. "I didn't...I didn't murder him. It was an accident. He found out, Amanda. He found out."

"Found out what?"

"You know what!"

I stared at Mrs. Chandler. She had to know, didn't she?

"You'd just miscarried for the second time and were so depressed," Mr. Chandler continued. "You wouldn't get out of bed. I had to do something."

"You said we adopted him."

"You knew it wasn't true."

"I believed you!"

"Then you believed me because you wanted to believe me! You never asked for the papers, you never asked anything. You knew. You knew!"

"I didn't know!"

"How did Nathan find out?" I asked, interrupting them. "He didn't say in the email."

"I'd kept...some of his things. A blanket with his initials on it. I hid them in the attic, and he was up there looking for something, one of those stupid board games you two used to play."

I suddenly remembered Nathan saying he wanted us to play Pandemic again. Pandemic was a clever board game where the players worked together to eradicate four different diseases, and we'd played the shit out of it when we were ten. If I hadn't agreed to give it another go, maybe he'd still be alive. I shook my head. There was no time for self-recrimination.

"Who did you take him from?" Mrs. Chandler asked, her voice rising. "Who else did you put through the same hell I'm going through right now?"

"Amanda, it wasn't like—"

"Who, God damn you, who?"

"I was in Houston, on a business trip. They were a young couple. He was in a stroller, and they weren't even paying attention to him. They didn't care about him, but I knew you would."

"What was his name?"

"It doesn't matter—"

"What was his fucking name?"

"Milo. Milo Daughtry."

My best friend's real name was Milo Daughtry.

"Why did you kill him?" I asked.

Mr. Chandler whirled to face me. "I didn't kill my son!"

"He wasn't your son," I countered.

Mr. Chandler buried his face in his hands. "He...confronted me, wanted to know about the blanket. The initials. M.D. I told him it was a mistake, something we'd ordered that was wrong, but he didn't believe me."

"What did you do to him, David?" asked Mrs. Chandler, between sobs.

"He also found something else," Mr. Chandler whispered. "A newspaper article I'd kept about the...incident. He looked it up on the internet. He knew, Amanda. He knew. I tried to talk to him, tried to reason with him, but he was so angry."

"You killed Nathan," Mrs. Chandler said, more a statement than a question.

"No! I loved him, just like you did. But he...he didn't understand, he said he was going to the police. I couldn't let that happen. We struggled, and he...he fell down, broke his neck. He...died."

I stood there, just staring at the couple I'd known for nearly eight years as my best friend's parents. Mrs. Chandler really hadn't known about Nathan's true origins.

When I thought about it, it was always Nathan's dad that didn't want him visiting friends, Nathan's dad who claimed Nathan was depressed. It might have been a willful ignorance, but Nathan's mom really didn't know any of it.

"And you made it look like a suicide," I said, my hand slowly sliding into my pocket.

"I had to! I can't go to prison. I didn't do anything wrong! And you...you can't tell anyone. You won't tell anyone."

He was on me in a second, arm across my throat, pressing me hard against the wall. "Promise me you won't tell anyone, and I'll let you go. Promise me!"

I couldn't breathe, and stars danced before my eyes. I fumbled in my pocket, hoping with everything I had inside me the automation app I'd set up worked, but couldn't quite grasp the phone. My vision was going dark. Maybe I'd see Nathan again sooner than I'd thought.

"Get off him!" Mrs. Chandler yelled, pulling at his arm, scratching his face.

Mr. Chandler elbowed her in the face, breaking her nose. There was blood everywhere as she stumbled back against the dining table.

He let up on my throat just enough that I was able to breathe again. I kicked him hard between the legs and he went sprawling to the ground.

Yanking the phone out of my pocket, I began to dial 911 but saw that the phone was already connected to the emergency service and that the recording I'd made earlier of Mr. Chandler's confession had been sent to the police. I stared at the phone. How was that possible?

I heard sirens in the distance. The calvary was coming, but would they get here in time?

"You little shit," Mr. Chandler gasped, struggling to his feet. "You did this, you pushed Nathan from the window, and then came here to kill us, too, but I killed you first. That's what I'll tell the police, and they'll believe it."

"No, they won't," I said, backing away from him. "I recorded everything. They already know the truth."

"You're lying," he screamed, charging at me.

Mrs. Chandler appeared behind him, smashing the empty wine bottle over her husband's head. Glass flew everywhere, some of it sticking to my clothing. Mr. Chandler slumped to the floor in front of me, unconscious or worse.

"I'm so, so sorry," said Mrs. Chandler, tears streaming from her eyes and her face covered in blood. "I didn't know. It was stupid not to ask. Maybe I just didn't *want* to know."

She took me in her arms and together we grieved for Nathan. The police found us that way just a few minutes later, when they showed up at Nathan's house.

My parents were scared out of their minds, of course, when the cops called them from the police station, told them what had happened, and asked them to come down as soon as possible so they could be with me while Detective Johnson took my statement.

Mr. Chandler, very much alive and in county jail, was being charged with kidnapping, murder, and two counts of attempted murder. His confession existed both on my phone and on the recording of the 911 call I'd made. He was going to prison, Detective Johnson assured me, for a very long time.

But had I really called 911? If I had, it must have been by accident, and there was no way I could have played the recording for them. Had

Nathan somehow dialed the number and routed the recording through the phone? Those were questions I'd likely never have answers for, and that was okay. I'd like to think that Nathan was looking out for me one last time, and maybe he was.

That was three days ago, and Nathan hasn't visited me since. Things finally settled down in the Jenkins household, and Taryn had even started being nice to me.

Mrs. Chandler—Amanda, she insisted I call her now—had come by earlier today. I was her last connection to Nathan, and she was mine. She had also saved my life. My parents told her she was always welcome at our house, and I hoped she would take them up on the offer.

So how had I figured out that Nathan's dad had stolen him as a child and then murdered him? There had been no email, of course, though I'd told both Amanda and the police there had been but that I'd deleted it out of fear. They'd never believe the truth. Hell, I barely believed the truth myself.

I thought back to my first ghostly Toontown conversation with Nathan, and the phrases he'd said to me:

I can only use Speedchat.

Sorry!

That was fun!

OK.

Let's all go for the same cog.

Easy does it.

No.

If you took the first letter of the first letter in each phrase and put them together, it spelled "I stolen." That was the only way using Speedchat that Nathan could tell me he'd been kidnapped as a baby.

With the Pokémon Go battle, it was the same thing, only with the Pokémon he chose.

Dragonite

Articuno

Dragonite

Kyogre

Infernape

Lugia

Latios

Machamp

Epseon

Using the first letter in each Pokémon's name spelled out dadkillme. Dad kill me. Thinking about it now gave me shivers.

Now that he'd received justice, Nathan was probably gone for good. I knew this, but I couldn't help but hope that he'd show back up again for one last adventure in Toontown Rewritten, Pokémon Go, or one of the other countless games we played together.

I logged into Toontown Rewritten to find out.

A Match Made in...Somewhere

Veronica swiped through Matchstick, the newest matchmaking app, trying to find a date. She hadn't been out with a man other than Stephen in over seven years, and it'd been eighteen months since he'd passed. It was time to get back in the saddle again, as it were.

She'd set up her profile last night and already had three messages. She was surprised, especially because she had no profile picture, just a photo of a portrait a friend had painted for her ages ago.

"Hey, Veronica," read the first message, from someone named Aaron, "you sound great, and I love the painting. Very unconventional. I'd love to get together, maybe for coffee Sunday, sometime after church. What do you think?"

Veronica laughed. That wasn't going to happen. She looked at the guy's photo. Tall, handsome enough, with black hair and a beard to match. Ah, well. She deleted the message unanswered.

"Why hide behind a painting?" read the next one, from Will. That's all it said. *Fuck you, Will,* she thought, as she deleted his message and blocked him from ever again seeing her profile.

The third message was from a douchebag named Chad. In her mind, all Chads were douchebags, simply because they were named Chad, but she opened the message anyway.

"Hey, Ronnie," said the message from douchebag Chad, "you sound fun."

There was more, but she deleted the message without reading the rest. She hated the nickname "Ronnie." Chad was indeed a douchebag. Theory proven.

She was about to close the app when a new message came in, from someone named James. She warily thumbed open the message, expecting more douchebaggery, but was pleasantly surprised.

"Dear Veronica," the message began, "your portrait is gorgeous, your profile enchanting, and I'd love to take you to dinner. Would Saturday evening work? You sound like an amazing woman, and I eagerly look forward to learning more about you. Best wishes, James."

She was intrigued. James had no photo, but so what? It didn't really matter what he looked like, and she could hardly throw stones, since her profile pic was a painting. Dinner on Saturday night sounded lovely. Still, she scanned the rest of his profile. A girl couldn't be too careful.

He was a night owl with a thirst for life who enjoyed collecting art, attending concerts, and studying history. He was looking for someone who enjoyed candlelit dinners and moonlit walks. He wasn't a fan of spicy food, which was good, because she wasn't either.

"Dear James," she spoke into her phone, letting voice-to-text do her typing for her, "I've enjoyed reading your profile, and I'd love dinner Saturday night. When and where? Let me know. I'm including my phone number, so feel free to text or call. Sincerely, Veronica."

She glanced at her watch. It was 9:30 p.m. He said he was a night owl, so she was curious if he'd respond right away. She was soon rewarded with a trill from her cellphone.

"Hello," Veronica said, as she thumbed the answer button.

"Veronica, this is James. I decided since you just messaged me, it would probably be okay to call. If I've been too bold and you're busy or about to head to bed, let me know and we can talk another time."

He had a British accent, which for some reason surprised her. It was sexy as hell, though. She'd lived in London for a while many years ago and absolutely loved the accent.

"Hello, James," she said, smiling, though of course he couldn't see her. "This is a perfect time. I'm not busy, and I'm a bit of a night owl myself."

"Well, then. We're a match made in…well, somewhere."

She laughed. "Indeed, we are. So, James, tell me about yourself."

"Well," he said, drawing out the word, "what would you like to know that my profile didn't already cover?"

"Whatever you want to tell me. I'm not the least bit sleepy, so I have time if you do."

She stretched out on the large couch that took up almost the entire south wall of her study, getting comfortable. She was already enjoying the conversation and looked forward to where it might lead.

"Where do I begin?" he said. "At the beginning, I suppose. I was born in the United Kingdom, as you probably guessed by my accent, in a small town named Bristol. That was…well, longer ago than I'd care to admit."

He laughed, and she laughed with him.

"What do you do for a living, if you don't mind me asking?"

"Not at all. I deal in antiquities. Mostly paintings from the 17th and 18th centuries. I think that's partly why I was so intrigued with your profile. Your portrait is beautiful. If you don't mind me asking, who did it?"

"An old friend," she said, "long since passed away."

"I'm so sorry to hear that."

"It's okay. At least I have the painting to remember him by."

"So, what do *you* do for a living, if I may be so bold as to ask?"

"I suppose I was bold for asking you," she said, laughing, "so you can be bold as well. I'm a hematologist. That's a—"

"A blood doctor," he finished for her. "Unfortunately, I have an iron deficiency, so I'm all too familiar with blood."

"I'm sorry to hear that," she said, and she meant it. "I hope you're not scared of hematologists."

He laughed, which was the response she was hoping for. "Maybe a little, but I suspect you'll be worth the risk."

They talked all night, until just before dawn. They talked about their childhoods, their former romantic partners, their regrets about the past, their hopes and dreams for the future, and everything else in between.

The next night, after she'd had dinner, she called him. It was Thursday, just two days before their date. They once again talked into the wee hours of the morning before saying their goodbyes.

Friday night, it was his turn to call her again. That's when things got really interesting.

"I have to admit, James," she whispered into the phone, "I find you incredibly intriguing, and we haven't even met yet. I haven't felt this way about a man in a long time."

"I feel exactly the same way," he said, sending shivers up her spine. "I wish it were Saturday night already."

"Mm-hmm. You and me both. And I'm already pretty sure I'm going to invite you back to my place after dinner. If that isn't too forward of a thing for a girl to say."

"If I'm not being too forward myself, I certainly hope that you do."

She had an idea. "If you were here right now…what would you do?"

"Well," he said, "I am a gentleman, so what I'd want to do may well be different from what I'd actually do, at least on a first date."

"Pretend you're not a gentleman," Veronica said, slowly sliding her hand under her skirt and past her panties, "at least for tonight."

"I'd love to kiss you," he said, as her fingers found their destination, "your lips, and then your neck. I'd spend so much time nibbling on your neck."

"That sounds incredible, and I know I couldn't help myself from reciprocating."

"And then I'd lead you to the bedroom…"

Friday night was amazing, twice over. When they finally hung up, she was sure she'd found exactly who she'd been looking for. This really could be a match made in…somewhere, as he'd said.

She fell asleep satiated for the moment but desiring more. Tomorrow couldn't come fast enough.

Veronica pulled up to the *La Grenouille* at just past nine o'clock at night, tossing the keys to her candy apple red Jaguar to the valet. She was dressed to kill in a tight black top, a red miniskirt, and black stiletto heels.

Walking into the fancy French restaurant, she scanned the bar area for James. He'd told her he was tall, had short black hair, and would be wearing a black pinstripe suit. And there he was!

"James, I presume," she said, walking up to him.

He turned to look at her with piercing blue eyes, which took her breath away. Yes, he was almost definitely the one.

"Veronica. You look amazing, even more beautiful than your portrait."

They shared a brief hug and a kiss on the cheek. He ordered them a bottle of *Château Margaux*, a red wine that she absolutely adored, and they sat at the bar and talked while waiting for their table.

"Is it weird," she asked, as her fingers brushed across his hand, "seeing me in person, after our…conversation last night?"

"If by 'weird' you mean exciting and utterly wonderful," James said, "then yes, it's incredibly weird."

They talked for a while, sipping their wine, and then their table was ready. James pulled out the chair for her, and she lowered herself into the seat. A true gentleman.

"Have you been here before?" he asked, after he was seated.

"I have not, but I've always wanted to. This is the perfect place for a first date. The wine is delicious, and the company even better."

"The first date of what I hope is many," he said, as he picked up a menu and began to read.

"I'll have *le Bass a l'Huile de Truffe et Foie Gras, Soba et Enokis*, please," Veronica said, when the waiter came to take their order, which was Chilean sea bass with white truffle oil with noodles and mushrooms. "*Merci beaucoup.*"

"And I'll have *le Canard au Bok Choy et Raisins, Couscous Israelien Citrone*," said James, which was roasted duck with Bok choy, candied raisins, and Israeli couscous.

After the waiter was gone, James said, "*Votre français est magnifique. Je ne savais pas que tu parlais français.*"

Her French was beautiful, he hadn't known she spoke the language.

"*J'imagine qu'il y a beaucoup de choses que tu ne sais pas encore sur moi,*" she replied, "*mais j'ai hâte de vous donner la tournée complète.*"

I'd imagine there's a great deal you don't yet know about me, but I look forward to giving you the full tour.

He laughed. "My dear, you are full of surprises. Your French is so much better than my own."

"I'm not sure that's the case, but I'm nevertheless flattered. I'm amazed I remember as much as I do, it's been years since I lived in France."

He smiled at her. "New York, London, France…is there any place you haven't been?"

In your bed, she wanted to say, but she didn't. She wasn't quite that brazen, at least not yet. Instead, she said, "Life is far too short not to see the world. I've been many places, but there are still many, many more that I wish to visit."

"My thoughts exactly," he said, and then the food arrived.

The sea bass was exquisite, though she wasn't exactly hungry for fish. In fact, they both seemed to do more pushing the food around their plates than eating.

When they were done, James paid the bill and left a more than generous tip. As they left the restaurant, Veronica reached out to take his hand, and his fingers squeezed hers.

"At the risk of being forward," James said, looking into her eyes, "would you like to come back to my place?"

"I was about to ask you the same thing," said Veronica, laughing. "We're quite the pair, aren't we?"

"Indeed," he said.

In the end, they settled on his place. She followed him to his home, which was just about half an hour from the restaurant. He lived in a beautiful condominium in the West Village area of the city, on Washington Street.

He led her through the entryway and into the darkened living room and then made his way to the coffee table and lit a trio of candles.

"Might I get us some wine?" he asked, as he blew out the match.

The room was gorgeous. A long black leather couch filled the north wall of the room, while a huge flat screen television took up a good portion of the south wall. A beautiful marble fireplace occupied part of the west wall of the room. Vibrant paintings depicting scenes from all over the world adorned the walls, interspersed with bookshelves holding what looked like hundreds of books.

"I am thirsty," she said, pulling him towards her, "but not for wine."

They kissed deeply and with passion, lost in the moment. Finally, he pulled back.

"Have you ever wanted to live forever?" he asked, looking into her eyes.

"Sometimes I feel like I have. But yes, that's one of my greatest desires. How about you?"

"Very much so. The world is huge, and there's so much to do. But what is forever without a companion to share it with?" He took her hand and led her to the couch.

She sat beside him, her hand in his. She'd always miss Stephen, but it really was time for a new love to walk with through this crazy adventure called life.

"Life is certainly better when you have someone who shares their heart with you," she said, "and with whom you can share yours."

"I agree completely. Imagine the things we might do together, the places we might go, the sights we might see."

She kissed him again, long and hard. "You had me at 'I agree completely.'" She said, when they came up for air.

"Before we go any further, Veronica," James said, "I have something to confess. I'm a lot older than I might at first appear. Several hundred years older, in fact. I know that sounds insane, but—"

She silenced him with a finger to his lips. "I knew it! I should have guessed your secret earlier, when you didn't have a profile picture, but I finally figured it out in the restaurant."

"Figured what out?"

"That you're a vampire, silly."

"You know?" he asked, eyes big, "and you're not scared?"

"I do know, and I'm not the least bit scared. In fact, I think I just might be falling in love with you."

He smiled, bearing his fangs. "As I am with you. Would you join me, then, Veronica? Allow me to turn you, so we can rule the night together?"

"James," she said, bearing her own fangs, "I'm 342 years old myself, and I was just about to ask you the exact same question, before I realized that I didn't have to."

"I should have guessed! Your portrait…Nattier, correct?"

She smiled. "Correct. He was a dear friend."

His eyes grew large, and then he laughed. "I guess we really are a match made in…somewhere."

"You know what?" Veronica inquired. "I'm starving. Since neither one of us really ate much of our suppers, how about we go out and find ourselves a little snack and then come back here and see what happens?"

"I thought you'd never ask," James responded, as he quickly shed his clothing and turned into a bat.

Veronica followed suit, transforming. They flew up the chimney and out into the night, to hunt, and to see what their future together might bring.

Haunted

"Daddy's killing Mommy," I said, shortly before my father snatched the phone from my four-year-old hands and yanked it out of the wall.

That's one of my earliest memories. Not knowing what else to do, I'd called my grandmother from the telephone in the kitchen, while my father strangled my mother in their bedroom.

Grandma called the police, and before long there were two units at our house on Gravel Drive in the small town of Keokuk, Iowa. My father answered the door, all smiles, jokes, and 'How ya doin', Randy? Sorry you had to come out,' in that Texas drawl of his.

My mother said she was fine, like she always did, and that Grandma misunderstood me. Of course, that didn't explain the marks on her neck, nor her black eye, all of which the officers studiously ignored.

After all, my father was one of them. He was a deputy with the Lee County Sheriff's Department. He could, and often did, get away with anything.

The officers apologized to my father, who by that time was starting to sober up from all the Budweisers he'd downed with one of his girl-friends at Pony's Tavern earlier in the evening.

"Don't ever do that again," he said to me, as soon as the cops had gone. "Mom and me, we argue, that's all. Isn't that right, Manda?"

"Right as rain," my mother said, trying her best to smile.

"Okay, Daddy," I mumbled, staring at the green carpet that covered the living room floor.

"Now, come here," he said, taking off his belt.

"Frank, can't you let this one go? This one time? Please? He was just scared. He won't do it again."

My father looked like he might hit her. Instead, he took a deep breath and balled his hands into fists, squeezing so hard that his knuckles turned white. He slowly counted to ten, nodding his head. "Okay, but just this once. If it happens again, Georgie, you'll get double the swats. Is that understood?"

"Yes, Daddy," I agreed, before making my way to the false comfort of my bedroom.

That night, I dreamt my father tried to kill me. He was chasing me through a huge house, carrying that damned belt of his, calling my name. It was a dream that would haunt me for years to come.

I sat on a brown leather couch in the spacious office of Dr. Diane Thornton, my latest psychiatrist in a long string of many, telling her my life story. I started with childhood. It wasn't pretty.

My father died when I was 12, and until recently I thought I'd put him behind me. I'd had nightmares about him for years, but the last decade or so had been mainly Frank-free. I was here now because they'd started up again, with a vengeance.

"Did he ever seek help?" Thornton asked, one leg folded over the other, peering at me through her black-rimmed glasses.

"For his drinking? No, not really. I mean, he swore off drinking all the time, and would maybe stay sober for a couple of weeks at most, and then something would set him off and he'd be back in the bar again."

"You mentioned him drinking with his girlfriend."

"He always had a girlfriend on the side, I think. He was 19 years older than my mother, and she just...put up with it, even though she knew. She was his third wife, and I was his eighth kid."

Thornton sat up straight in her chair. "His eighth? Oh, my. What was that like?"

"It was like nothing, really, because I rarely saw my half-brothers and sisters. They all lived in Texas, with their mothers, and they were all a lot older than me. Essentially, I was an only child with a shitload of siblings I rarely if ever saw."

"And you're married, correct?"

"I am," I said. "Her name is Angela, and we'll have been married 20 years this coming April."

"Children?" she asked.

"Two. Our daughter, Sierra, and our son, Benjamin. Ben is 15 and a Sophomore in high school, and Sierra is 19 and just started college at the University of Arkansas."

I am 48 years old and a moderately successful writer. I live in Bentonville, Arkansas, a good ten hours from where I grew up. I've been blessed with a beautiful wife, an amazing daughter, and the best son a man could ever ask for, and I love them with all my heart. I don't drink (I've never even tasted alcohol) or cheat on my wife, and I've never once struck either of my kids or my wife.

When I was unsure of my ability to parent, I'd just do whatever my father failed to do or not do whatever he did. It's worked out pretty well so far.

"And do they know about your past?"

"Angie knows everything, and the kids know bits and pieces."

"Why do you think he was the way he was?"

That question stopped me. I'd never really thought about why he did the things he did, said the things he said, and I admitted as such.

"Do you have any other memories of your father?"

"Oh yeah, Doc. We're just getting started."

In second grade, my father came to my school drunk, demanding to know where I was. My mother had arrived at the school just five minutes earlier, and my teacher, Mrs. Gilpin, and the school's principal, Mr. Neill, had hidden us inside a storage closet.

I didn't know it at the time, wouldn't know it for forty years until a friend on Facebook who I'd gone to school with told me, but Mrs. Gilpin had all the other kids hide under their desk. Like a nuclear attack, I suppose. Stop, drop, and roll, or something like that.

"Why did he come to school, Mommy?" I whispered into the dark, but she shushed me as she slid a hand around my mouth.

I listened to my father's angry voice demanding to know where I was, as Mr. Neill tried to calm him down. A few minutes later, he left, and the principal opened the door.

I thought it was my father and began to cry.

"It's just me, George," said Mr. Neill, as he reached down to pat my shoulder. "Everything is fine."

"Do you want to come back to class, George?" asked Mrs. Gilpin, appearing from behind Mr. Neill.

I looked up at my mother. "Do I have to?"

"You do," she said, "because I have to get back to work at the shoe store. The bus will bring you home, just like usual."

"Why did Dad come to school?" I repeated the question I'd asked earlier.

"We'll talk about it later," she whispered into my ear, as she crouched down to hug me. "Now scoot."

We didn't talk about it later, and I never found out why my father showed up drunk at my school.

"It was around that time, I think, that I started to count," I said absentmindedly, staring at the diplomas and certificates that littered the walls of her office. "First the tiles on the ceiling in that closet, then my stuffed animals, the Cheerios in my bowl, anything and everything. Counting relaxed me, somehow, made me feel better."

"Obsessive compulsive disorder," said Dr. Thornton, typing something on her laptop. "A pretty common way of dealing with stress, and you had a lot of stress to deal with, George."

"OCD, PTSD, and depression. I have all three, at least according to the other therapists and psychiatrists I've seen."

"With your background, I wouldn't doubt it. Tell me, do you have any good memories of your father?"

That question always threw me.

"Just one," I admitted, "at least that I can remember. Him helping me put together a Mego Hall of Justice playset when I was maybe 4 or 5 years old. I couldn't get the viewscreens to snap into place, so he helped me. Took all of five minutes, and that's it."

"The bad is much easier to remember than the good," Dr. Thornton said, and I had to agree. "Now how old did you say you were when your father...passed?"

"He didn't 'pass,'" I said, irritated by the phrase, "he killed himself three weeks after my twelfth birthday."

"I see. Would you like to tell me about that?"

"My mother, my uncle Andy, my grandmother, and me, we were coming back from Des Moines, where we'd gone to visit my great aunt. It was about nine in the evening and suddenly there were red lights and a siren behind us. It was a police car, but we weren't speeding or doing anything wrong.

"My mother pulled the car over and my father came up to the window, in uniform, drunk. He had his service revolver and shoved the gun in my mother's face and said he was going to kill her."

"That must have been terrifying."

"Honestly, by then I was used to it. That wasn't the first time he'd threatened us with a gun, though it was the first time he'd done it in uniform, and it was definitely the last."

"What happened?" asked the doctor, on the edge of her seat.

"My uncle—my mother's brother—got out of the car, told my father that he just wanted to talk to him. Uncle Andy was nineteen then, had just graduated high school the year before. He had also recently earned his black belt in Karate.

"I couldn't really see what happened next, but Uncle Andy essentially kicked my father's ass. Next thing I knew, my father was lying on his back on the side of the road, and we were quickly driving away.

"The next day, he was all apologies, and the thing is I think he really was sorry. He was in tears and yet again swore off alcohol, asking me and my mother to forgive him, but by that point, it was too late. My mother had finally—finally—had enough. She and I moved in with my grandmother that evening, and dear old dad was suspended from the Sheriff's Department a day or two after that."

"And how long was it after that incident before he committed suicide?"

"Less than a week. He'd asked me to go to the movies with him, and I'd refused. I wouldn't even talk to him. I was scared he was going to kill me. The very next day, we got the call that he'd shot himself with an old shotgun he'd had in our garage."

"And how did that make you feel?"

"How do you think it made me feel?" I snapped. "I felt guilty, I felt sad, and I felt blessed relief. I was almost ashamed at the relief I felt, but I was glad he wasn't around to torment me anymore, but mostly what I felt was anger."

"Anger?"

"I'd always thought that when I got 'big,' when I became an adult, I guess, I'd kill him myself. Or at least beat the living hell out of him, or something, but he cheated me out of that, took that away from me like he'd taken so many other things from me. The bastard went and killed himself before I ever had the chance."

"I see," she said. "Are you close to your mother now?"

"Not at all. My mother was almost as bad as my father, in her own special way. Her father was also a violent alcoholic, so she'd essentially married her old man. Thought she could 'fix' him, and all that. She repeated that pattern twice more after my father, but I'm not even going to get into my good-for-nothing stepdads that came after dear old dad killed himself. We'd be here all day.

"And she lied all the time about shit that didn't even matter. She liked to pretend that her life had been perfect. She'd clam up anytime I tried to talk to her about my childhood, so I finally gave up. I haven't seen her in at least five years, and we haven't talked on the phone for about a year. She called me on my last birthday, we had a five-minute conversation, and that was that."

Dr. Thornton had no response, and neither of us spoke for a moment, until finally:

"According to the intake notes, you're currently taking—" she started to ask, typing on her laptop again.

"I take 300 milligrams of Wellbutrin," I interrupted, "as well as 200 of Zoloft. Together, they've made me a more or less functioning adult."

She stopped typing and looked at me. "If you're already taking meds and are getting along well, why did you come to Psychology Helps? We have many fine therapists you might benefit from seeing. Liz Hart in particular seems well suited for your needs."

"My father," I said, finally coming to the moment in the conversation I'd been dreading, "is haunting me."

"That's perfectly understandable, George," Thornton said, adjusting her black-framed glasses. "Your father's actions were very traumatic for you. I'd be surprised if memories of him *weren't* haunting you."

"No, no. You don't understand. It's not just the memories. He's actually haunting me, and I think he's trying to kill me."

Dr. Thornton didn't believe me, of course. She said my dreams were just that: dreams. That's what I'd always believed as well, until evidence of my father's…visitations started showing up in my waking hours.

It all started a little over a month ago, the day after I'd finalized my trip to Cologne, Germany. I'm a travel writer, you see, and my dream destination was Cologne, where my mother's side of the family originally immigrated from. I've wanted to visit Cologne practically all my life. I finally got the gig and was happier than I'd been in years.

That same night, I dreamt of my father for the first time in a decade. It was like my psyche couldn't handle me being content for any length of time and decided to punish me. In the dream, I discovered my father was still alive and had somehow faked his suicide. Then he was at the front door, shouting, "Let me in, Georgie! Let me in!"

I chanced a look out the peephole, and yes, it was him, all right. It was really him, and he was carrying that stupid black leather belt of his in one hand and looking pissed. He kept slamming his fists against the door, demanding to be let inside, and that's when I woke up.

I found myself in the same dream the next night, and the night after, and the night after that. "Let me in!" he demanded, over and over, but I never did. In fact, I started barricading the door. In one of the dreams, I even hid in a basement that doesn't even exist. Anything to avoid confronting the man who'd made my childhood a living hell.

It wasn't until the fifth night that I began to believe this might be something more than nightmares.

I'd always showered right before bed. That night I turned the water as hot as I could stand it, so hot that my skin turned red. It relaxed me, though, and I was feeling better until I stepped out of the shower.

The steam had clouded the mirror above the sink, and in the condensation, someone had written "king." I stared at it, confused, and then remembered something I hadn't thought about in over forty years. As a very young child, my father's nickname for me had been "King Georgie."

I shivered despite the heat trapped in the bathroom, and for a moment thought I might be going insane. I closed my eyes and steadied myself against the shower door, and when I opened them again the word was gone.

That night, Angie told me I screamed in my sleep and when she tried to wake me, I grew violent and nearly hit her. That sobered me. There was no way in hell I was going to hit my wife, accident or not. One way or the other, the dreams needed to go. That's when I began looking for psychiatrists.

If I couldn't stop the dreams on my own, and it became frighteningly clear that I couldn't, perhaps I could medicate them away instead. But Dr. Thornton refused to give me the sleeping pills I requested, instead wanting to admit me to Springwoods, a "behavioral health hospital" (aka looney bin) in Fayetteville.

No, thank you.

Instead, I started taking Benadryl an hour before I went to sleep each night. The allergy medicine knocked me on my ass and provided dreamless sleep for several nights in a row until the bottle went missing. I never found it, and I'm ashamed to admit that I even accused Angie of hiding the medicine.

Three days before my trip, something happened. I couldn't find my passport. It had been on my desk before I'd walked into the kitchen to make myself a sandwich but was gone when I came back. Angie was at work, Sierra and Ben were at their respective schools, so that left our two cats as the only suspects. The thing was, though, Clink was asleep on Ben's bed, and Clank was busy chasing imaginary butterflies in the living room.

I felt gooseflesh prickle my arms but ignored it, instead getting down on my hands and knees to search under and then behind my desk. It wasn't in either of those places, but I did find it twenty minutes later, shoved between two books on one of the three bookshelves that adorned my little home office.

How had it gotten there?

My mind flashed back to the word "king" written on the bathroom mirror, and I felt like I was going to throw up. This was not happening. Ghosts weren't real, and my father was long dead, buried in his shithole of a hometown, Vidor, Texas.

But who had written on the mirror? Who had hidden my passport?

"Fuck you, Dad," I said out loud, then screamed it. "Fuck you, you piece of shit! Leave me alone and get the hell out of my head!"

I'd kept very few things that belonged to my father. His wallet, an old pocketknife, and a silver cross on a necklace. These three items I kept in a box deep in my closet, and in fact hadn't even looked at them in years.

I felt compelled to check on them, and they were still there, untouched, in the back of my closet, behind some old DVDs and an even-older bowling trophy.

I held the wallet in my hand, opened it, and flipped through it. His driver's license, social security card, some photos of me as a child, photos of his other kids, a grocery list, a phone number I'd never had the nerve to call written on a crumpled piece of paper—everything was there, just as it was the day he took his life.

Was his spirit somehow tied to his belongings? I cringed at how stupid that sounded. I'd had these items since he killed himself 36 years ago. If ghosts were real and his spirit really was tied to his wallet, or his pocketknife, or the necklace, why had he waited so long to manifest himself?

I rolled my eyes at my own foolishness and put the wallet back in the box and shoved the box back behind the DVDs and the bowling trophy, where they belonged.

The morning I was supposed to go on the trip started out as a nightmare and quickly descended into madness. At first, I was feeling great. I was getting ready to go to a country I've always wanted to visit. What could possibly go wrong?

Answer: everything. I was packed and ready to go. I'd said my good-byes to the kids, and Angie was ready to take me to the airport. Problem was, her car keys weren't hanging on the hook, where they normally were. They also weren't in her purse, the kitchen, or anywhere else she might have left them.

I began to panic. We couldn't find my car keys, either. It felt like my heart skipped a beat. This was not happening. This was *not* happening. They weren't on my desk, in the bedroom, between the couch cushions, or in the pair of pants I'd been wearing yesterday.

"What're you looking for?" asked Ben, as he walked into the bedroom.

"My Goddamned keys!" I snapped, instantly regretting it as I saw the look of hurt and alarm on Ben's face. "Sorry. I'm just…the plane boards in an hour and a half, and neither one of us can find our keys, and—"

"Maybe call Sierra?" he said, interrupting me. "I mean, it's less than thirty minutes from her dorm to the house, and she doesn't have any classes since it's Saturday."

"That's a great idea," I said. "Thank you, thank you, thank you."

I pulled out my cellphone, only to discover it was dead. I pressed the power button, but it wouldn't turn on. That panic feeling again, and a sudden rage, the kind I was normally able to repress. I curbed my desire to throw the Samsung against the wall and instead asked Ben to call.

"She's leaving her dorm now and will be here as soon as she can," Ben said, as soon as the call was finished. "See? Crisis averted."

I pulled my son into a sudden, fierce hug, surprising him. He returned the hug, and I felt hot wetness on my cheeks. I was crying.

"What was that for, Dad?" my mini-me asked, as I quickly wiped away the tears.

He looked just like me at that age, minus the haunted eyes my mother always claimed I'd had, and hopefully minus the depression and anxiety that were always with me as well. If nothing else, I'd been a better father to Ben than my father had ever been to me.

"Just for being you," I said. "You're the best son in the world."

Fifteen minutes later, Sierra was driving me to the airport in her hand-me-down Kia Soul. She had the windows down, and her long black hair kept blowing into her eyes. I feared we might get into an accident and said as much.

"Fix my AC for me?" she asked, grinning, as she tied her hair back into a ponytail. "Better?"

"Better," I agreed. "And I'll cover half of that air conditioning repair if you can cover the other half. Deal?"

"Deal," she said, laughing. "Thanks, Dad."

We arrived at the airport with thirty minutes to spare. It wasn't ideal, but it was what it was. I hugged Sierra goodbye and ran into the airport, luggage in hand.

"Running late," I said as I jogged up to the United Kiosk, "Sorry."

"No problem, sir. May I see your ticket?"

I reached into my pocket for the ticket, but it wasn't there. I felt bile rise in my throat. I checked my other pocket, then began to sort through my luggage.

"If you purchased online, your ticket should be in your email," the clerk said. "Open it and I can scan the barcode."

I glanced at the clerk. Her nametag read "Courtney."

"My phone didn't charge last night, and it's dead. Any other options?"

The plane was probably boarding now. The clock on the wall said 8:32, and flight 5420 was set to depart at 8:45.

"If you have the credit card you purchased it with, I should be able to bring it up."

"I'm a travel writer, and the magazine I'm writing for bought the ticket. 'Amazing Travel.' My name is George Winters. Can you look it up that way?"

"I'm afraid not, sir. If you don't have your ticket, we'll need the credit card it was purchased with."

My heart began to thud in my chest. "I already said, I don't have it!"

"Sir, you don't need to take that tone. I'm trying to help."

"I know you are," I yelled, "but the plane leaves in—" I glanced up at the clock. "Jesus Christ. It leaves in three minutes, and I have to get on that plane."

"We all have planes to board," said an old, balding man behind me, "and, unlike you, we all have our tickets."

I glared at him over my shoulder. "Just give me a few more minutes, and—"

"Is there a problem over here, Courtney?" asked a big, burly security guard walking towards me.

"Mike, this gentleman—"

"There's no problem," I yelled, feeling like I was having a heart attack. "Just let me get on my Goddamned flight."

"Sir," said the guard, "I'm with airport security. I think you'd better come with me."

"No! I have to get on that plane."

Mike with airport security grabbed me by my shoulder and pulled me out of line. "If you leave now and don't make a scene, I won't have to report this. If you don't, you might end up going to jail."

"Mike," I said, "I have to get on that plane. If I don't, then he's won."

"He?" asked Mike, looking puzzled.

I started to say 'my father' as a huge explosion rocked the airport. All eyes turned towards the sound, and a little boy looked like he might cry.

"What was that?" I asked.

Mike pulled a walkie-talkie off his belt. "Central, this is Mike. What the hell was that?"

No response.

"Central, I repeat, what happened?"

"The plane," came a woman's voice. "Take off looked fine, it was gaining altitude, then nosedived straight into the ground. This is awful, Mike. There couldn't have been any survivors."

"What flight?" I asked numbly, though I thought I already knew the answer.

Mike repeated the question into his walkie.

"Flight 5420 headed to Dallas. Mike, you'd better get down here. We're going to need all the help we can get."

Because of all the emergency vehicles and general chaos, it took me over three hours to find a cab and get home. My family had seen the news report on television and thought me dead, so imagine their surprise when I walked into the living room, alive and whole.

Flight 5420 would have connected to another plane in Dallas and that plane would have taken me and a whole lot of other people to Germany. But that wasn't going to happen now, because the plane's engine had malfunctioned. All those people, dead, and I could have been one of them.

I sat alone now in my bedroom with my eyes closed, and whispered, "come in, Dad."

I opened my eyes, and my father stood there, looking down at me. I rose to my feet, immediately taken aback by the fact that he was a good four inches shorter than me. He had always seemed like a giant when I was a child, but was of average height, at best.

"Hello, Georgie," he said, though I didn't really hear the words so much as they echoed in my head.

"I thought you wanted to kill me," I said, thinking about the dreams, "not save me."

He'd hidden my passport, two sets of car keys, and my plane ticket, all of which we'd found piled on my desk after I'd returned home. If I'd gotten on that plane, I'd be dead, along with the other 73 souls who had perished when the engine malfunctioned and downed the aircraft.

"I never, ever wanted to hurt you."

"But why were you so violent, in my dreams? Slamming your fists against the door, demanding to be let in."

"I wasn't," he said. "That was all you, Georgie. You remembered the man I was, and so that's what you saw."

I'd always despised the name 'Georgie,' but held my tongue. "How is this even possible?"

"Hell if I know," he said, and we both laughed. "I've always watched over you, as best I could. I needed to make up for the awful father I'd been to you, the father who hurt you so much."

"Why did you hate me?"

Ghostly tears began to trail down my father's cheeks. "I never hated you. I loved you so much, just like you love Ben and Sierra. I just...there was something wrong with me, Georgie.

"I was so sad all the time, and so damned angry, and scared, and then sometimes everything fell away, and I was so excited over some little thing or another, usually a woman, that nothing made sense anymore. I drank to keep my own demons at bay, never realizing until it was too late that I was becoming a demon myself."

A light flickered on in my brain. "You had bipolar disorder," I said, "or something like that, and back then you probably wouldn't have even known what that was, let alone how to seek help."

My father shrugged. "How long ago was that, Georgie? I can't tell anymore."

I told him that he had killed himself 36 years ago this past April. He looked surprised.

"How did you know?" I asked. "About the plane, I mean."

Another shrug. "I just did."

I guess I had no choice but to accept that answer, because he was starting to fade away.

"Why did you kill yourself?" I asked quickly, a question I'd never even realized I cared about until now.

"Because if I didn't, it was only going to get worse. I refused to allow myself to hurt you and your mother any longer."

This time, it was my eyes that began to brim with tears. "I'm sorry you had to make that decision."

"Georgie, I don't have much time left. Do you think you can forgive me for the father I was?"

I wanted to, lord knows I wanted to, but I wasn't sure I could and told him that. There was just so much rage I felt, so much anger at what he'd put me through.

"Don't forgive me for me, son, forgive me for yourself. Let the rage and the anger go with me and live your life."

I knew he was right, but it was so damned hard. But what thing worth doing wasn't hard? I needed to forgive him, not just for myself but for Angie, Ben, and Sierra as well.

I hadn't always been the perfect father or husband I liked to pretend I was. That anger and hurt from my childhood had always been there, festering, taking up residence in the back of my mind. It came out in little ways, such as snapping at Sierra to let me work, being overly competitive at video games with Ben, being cold to Angie.

He was almost translucent now. "I have to go, George. I love you, and I'm so proud of the man you've become."

"I love you, too, Dad," I said, startled even as the words left my lips. I realized it was true and suddenly remembered all the good times that had been so hard to dredge up just a week earlier.

Mom and Dad taking turns reading to me when I was a toddler. Dad teaching me how to ride a bike and comforting me after I'd fallen and scraped my knee. Him and me watching professional wrestling together every Sunday morning, cheering for our favorites.

The bad had swallowed the good, to be sure, had outweighed it by a huge amount, but that didn't make the good any less important, or any less valid.

And in that moment, I forgave him.

Hidden Rooms

Have you ever had a dream where you find a forgotten or perhaps an altogether previously unknown room in your house? Of course you have. Everyone has these dreams. Maybe the room is filled with items you lost over the years, maybe it's empty, or perhaps it's something completely different.

You might get to it through your closet, or through an attic hatch you never noticed in the ceiling. No matter how you come across this room, it's almost always both a surprise and at the same time just as familiar to you as your left hand.

My name is Alanton Quincy, and my hidden room has always been filled with books. Books I'd never known existed, sometimes by my favorite authors, people like Coral Hennessey or Herm Finshaw, but mostly by people who weren't even real outside of dreamland.

Names like Christopher Golden, Douglas Adams, Robin Raven, Mercedes M. Yardley, Mary Robinette Kowal, Patricia Rose, and CJ Rutherford. They didn't exist in the real world, but these authors and their books damn well sure existed in my dreams.

I'd spend hours (at least it felt like hours to me, inside the dream) trying to read these books, with the words constantly swimming around both the pages and in my head. Sometimes I'd be able to read a coherent sentence or two, but more often than not, I'd just *know* what the book was about despite not having successfully read any of the words inside the book. I was never, however, privy to the endings. These dreams frustrated me to no end, because I never found out how any of these phantom books with their intricate plots wrapped up.

The rooms themselves were always different. Sometimes a hidden elevator somewhere in my house would take me to the room, other times a doorway might simply appear in the hallway between the bedroom and the living room. Sometimes the entire house was different, and once or twice I found the hidden room inside a department store that was somehow connected to an apartment I'd lived in fifteen years earlier.

Dreams are crazy like that.

For years growing up, I would have these dreams maybe once or twice a month, and they always fascinated me. I "read" books such as *Moonheart, Replay, The Time Traveler's Wife, The Outsider, Memories of a Ghost, Treaters,* and more. All these books were fascinating in the dream world but made absolutely no sense whatsoever the moment I awoke. Most of the time I couldn't even remember the plots, let alone the endings.

I kept these hidden room dreams to myself, convinced that people would think I was crazy. After all, I was the only one who had dreams like this…or so I thought.

Everything changed about a year and a half ago, when I found an online group on MyFace dedicated to these hidden dream rooms. That's how I learned pretty much everyone has had the hidden room dreams at one time or another, and it's also how I met Samshe Havendore, the woman who would change my life forever.

"My hidden room dreams are usually about clothing and shoes," Samshe told me, in one of our first all-night chats. "New blouses, skirts, bowling boots, you name it. Stuff waaaay better than the ratty clothing I had growing up, even better than the stuff I have now. Much more stylish. I know that sounds foofoo, but there you have it."

Samshe was a 26-year-old psychology doctoral student, I later found out, living in Shackleford, Illinois, just about two hours from where I lived in Austinville. She was anything but foofoo.

"Mine are almost always about books," I told her, though she already knew that from reading my many posts on the subject. "Mostly books that don't even exist, written by authors who also don't exist, authors with names such as Stephen King, Ken Grimwood, and Joe DeRouen."

"Those are funny names," she responded, and I had to agree. "Are the books any good?"

"That's the thing. They're amazing, at least until I wake up. There's this one book, *Memories of a Ghost*, that I've read countless times. Claire Summers is the protagonist, and the book is set in this made-up place called Arkansas. I read that one over and over growing up, all in my dreams, of course, but I can't tell you what happens after Claire meets this man named Jimmy at a park, because what little I remember doesn't make any sense. But I know I've read the book almost all the way through before and loved it, I just can't remember what happened. It's maddening."

Shoes and skirts, thankfully, didn't have plots, so Sam's dreams didn't frustrate her nearly as much as mine frustrated me. Still, though, she really coveted those fancy bowling boots.

Some members of the group dreamt about rooms filled with dolls and action figures, rooms containing strange music on small, flat silver circles, rooms that were identical to other rooms in their house but entirely mirrored, or rooms with tunnels to other houses, and some dreamers dreamt of rooms that were entirely empty save for their favorite, long-lost toy from childhood. Everyone's rooms seemed different, with no rhyme or reason as to the room's contents.

Long story somewhat shorter, Samshe and I grew close and quickly fell in love. We eventually met in person, and that love grew stronger. I'm 33, so at first it felt strange to be dating someone that much younger than me, but we got over that pretty quickly. I moved to Shackleford, and we bought a house together and got married later that same year.

We never forgot how we met, and our obsessions with the hidden rooms grew even stronger. One day Jimson Kale, one of the moderators of the dream group, shared an article from an independent media site called the New York Times about a doctor attempting to prove that people could share dreams.

According to the article, the doctor claimed he had successfully shared dreams with three of his test subjects. They'd used a new drug created to help Epilepsy patients, Luhsepheria, to relax the doctor and his subjects and make them more susceptible to the seemingly impossible.

Each subject had memorized a 6-digit number and shared that number with the doctor inside their dreams. Upon waking, the doctor immediately wrote down those numbers and had been right all three times.

Samshe found the idea of sharing dreams fascinating, almost as much as she had the hidden rooms. She wanted to get the drug (with her connections at the university hospital, that would be relatively easy) and use it in an attempt for us to share a dream, meet up in dreamland, and explore each other's rooms.

Share my books? I don't know why, but the idea troubled me. *The Shining*, for example, had some pretty gruesome scenes. I didn't want her thinking I was a psychopath.

"If this works," she said, "and I can actually go into your hidden room, you can find a book you've read but not told me about. If I read it and it's about what you remember it being about, that would prove we shared the dream. I could even do my doctoral thesis on that."

I flashed on Joe DeRouen's short story collection, *Odds and Endings: Fiction Short and Otherwise*. There was a story in there called *The Kitten Tree* that had really freaked me out and left me feeling unsettled for days. I could never remember the plot in the morning, though, other than that it was about a cat named Cherry and a little boy named Joey. That might work.

"Just think about it," she said, "and if I can get the drug, maybe we can try it."

A week and three days later, at 10:00 on a Saturday night, I found myself lying next to Samshe in the bed we shared, getting ready to take the drug.

"Are you sure this is safe?" I asked the love of my life, for probably the 1,000[th] time, as she drew exactly 10 milligrams of Luhsepheria from the little blue vial.

"As sure as I can possibly be," she said, laying the injector on the bed beside me. "You can still back out, though. I don't want you to do anything you don't want to do."

That was the thing, though. I did want to do it. I was so deeply in love with Samshe that I would have done anything for her, but I actually did want to do this.

Just not for the reasons Samshe did.

In addition to allowing two people to share dreams, the drug was also supposed to increase lucidity. Hersheffield Kamelwood, the doctor in the article, claimed to have been able to successfully read the back of a cereal box in one of his dreams.

I just wanted to finally read and hopefully remember the entire *The Kitten Tree* story. And if that worked, I could read *The Shining, Moonheart, Small Things, Darling, Hospital of Haunts, Practical Demonkeeping,* and all the other thousands of books inside my hidden room, and this time hopefully remember the stories.

"Yes," I finally said, looking into Samshe's beautiful peridot eyes, "I want to do this."

We took our injections and lay down next to one another, our fingers intertwined as we tried to fall asleep. After fifteen or twenty minutes, I managed to drift off.

I was in my childhood home in Chenoa, Dakota, where I'd lived when I first dreamed of the hidden room. There was the brown leather couch, the old television, the cherry-wood floors, the altar, everything. I knew instantly I was dreaming, but it all felt incredibly real.

"Alanton?" said a voice behind me. Samshe!

I whirled around to stare at her. She was dressed in a beautiful, flowing red gown, the same gown she'd been wearing when we got married. She was crying.

"Are you okay?" I asked, instantly going to her side.

"These are happy tears. We did it. We dracking did it!"

I kissed away her tears, held her tight, and then together we began to search for my hidden room.

We never found it.

"I don't understand," I said. "It's always so easy to find. If the dream takes places in this house, it's usually in the closet in my old bedroom. If it's not there, then it's through the laundry room."

"Maybe it's because we're lucid?" she asked. "I'm never lucid when I find mine, the lucidity always comes afterwards."

I shrugged. I guess that made sense. The drug provided instant lucidity as well as the sharing, however, so there wasn't a whole lot we could do about it. Apparently, we could share a dream while lucid or visit our hidden rooms, but not both.

Samshe remembered everything the next morning, and so did I, which was almost frustrating. I wanted to read *The Kitten Tree*, damn it. Sharing my childhood home with my wife was fun, but that wasn't exactly the point of the experiment.

We tried five more times after that, with similar results. Once we were in her old apartment, twice we were in the house we shared, and the other two times we were in a hotel that neither of us recognized.

We had never been able to access our hidden rooms.

The experiments weren't a total failure. Samshe and I had what we agreed was the best dream sex ever on that second try, when we appeared in that mystery hotel. But we hadn't accomplished what we were hoping to accomplish, which frustrated us both.

What's worse was that we were no longer able to access the hidden rooms in our regular dreams, either. It was like they were just...gone. Closed off to us forever. She missed her fancy clothing, and I missed my books.

"Maybe if we up the dosage some more?" I suggested one evening.

"It's just not safe," she countered. "We already went from 10 to 20, which is well beyond what they give to Epilepsy patients, for Hera's sake. Any higher and...well, we might not wake up."

"I almost wish we'd never done it in the first place."

Samshe glared at me, hurt passing across her face. "You blame me for this, don't you? For losing your hidden room?"

"No, that's not what I meant," I said quickly, but part of me did blame her. I'd lost my books. No more King. No more Volley. No more DeRouen, and no more *The Kitten Tree*.

Reaching across the table, she took my hand in hers. "We shared dreams, though. That's amazing, isn't it?"

"It sure is," I agreed, all the while wondering about Danny Torrance, Jeff Winston, and Cherry the cat.

I finally did it on a Fryday night, when Samshe was out with friends. I'd feigned sickness, but insisted she keep our plans and enjoy herself.

"Are you sure?" she asked, pulling on her green *Trekker Wars* t-shirt over her bra.

We were supposed to go bowling with Olathe and Tersia, two of her doctoral candidate friends from the university, just like we did the third Fryday of every month.

I was sure, I told her, and she was out the door. She was probably relieved, in a way, because I hadn't been very pleasant to be around for the last few months, ever since my hidden room disappeared. She deserved a night out without having to deal with my doom and gloom.

Standing in the bathroom, I drew 50 milligrams from the vial of Luhsepheria I'd hidden behind the toilet. Walking into the bedroom, I sat on the side of the bed, wondering if this would work.

This was more than double the highest dosage we'd taken before. I knew full well this much of the drug could potentially kill me, but at this point I just didn't care. I was going crazy without my books. Samshe wouldn't be happy, but if it worked and I could find my hidden room, and if I didn't die in the process, I'd more than make it up to her later.

I injected the serum before I could talk myself out of it, lay down on the bed, and almost immediately passed out.

I know how *The Kitten Tree* ends now. Cherry the cat was never actually in the story, but her death spawned the kitten tree and all the horror that came after.

Danny Torrance had come out of things okay, all things considered, though his father hadn't been quite as lucky.

Jeff Winston eventually caught up to the present and stopped replaying his life over and over again.

I'd immediately zoned into the hidden room the moment I'd fallen asleep. The problem was, I couldn't get out. There just weren't any exits, and I never awoke. Had it been a day since I've injected the Luhsepheria? A week, a month, a year? A decade? Was I lying in a coma somewhere, or was I dead? I had no idea, but I'd read every one of the 5,042 books in the library. Twice.

"How can I help?" asked Joe DeRouen, the author of *Small Things*, *Memories of a Ghost*, and so many other books I loved.

"I don't think you can," I said, shrugging.

Joe first appeared in my hidden room 1,672 books ago, and then again about every 200 books or so. This was his seventh visit. He told me he never remembered our interactions when he awoke the next morning, but that they always came back to him every time we shared a dream.

"The thing I've always wondered," he asked, "is how did you get trapped in my hidden room?"

I shrugged again. His hidden room, my hidden room, what difference did it really make anymore? Maybe Joe was a figment of my imagination, a dream companion to stave off the loneliness I felt so acutely. Maybe he was real, and I'd managed to enter his dreams. Maybe I was a character from one of his books or short stories. Maybe we shared this hidden room from across two different universes. I had absolutely no dracking idea, and neither did he.

Joe had never heard of Luhsepheria, nor of Austinville, Illinois, or even the United States of the North American Union, the country in which I lived. In his waking world, he said, it was simply called the United States of America, Arkansas was a real state, and there were two Dakotas.

He also said he'd never met anyone named Alanton or Samshe, and that the names sounded made up.

Me, I'd never heard of anyone named Joe, except in my dreams.

"There has to be something I can do to help you."

I waved off the offer. "When did you first dream about me?"

"Maybe three years ago," he said, "maybe a little longer."

Had I really been unconscious that long? Then again, it could be three minutes, or a thousand years. And then I had an idea.

"Actually, there is something you can do for me," I said, thinking.

"Anything."

"Write a new book. I've read everything in here so many times now."

Joe smiled. "Oh, that's easy. I already have."

He handed me a book he hadn't previously been holding in his hands, but at the same time had always been there. Dreams are weird and confusing.

I took the book from his hands. There was a spooky looking butterfly on the cover, surrounded by plants and darkness.

The book was titled *Eventual Beginnings: Stories Short and Longer.*

The moment Joe left the hidden room, I flipped the book over and read the blurb on the back. There were sixteen stories in the collection, and the one titled *Connections,* about a girl named Justy who was apparently possessed by a ghost, sounded especially intriguing. I couldn't wait to delve into it. I missed Samshe with all my heart, but perhaps the characters in this assortment of short stories would help keep me company, at least for a little while.

I opened the book and began to read.

The Magical Book

Erica Mosley stood next to the Little Free Library in her front yard, looking through the newest books people had donated, including a cookbook, some children's books, a book about genealogy, and a handful of novels. She absolutely loved owning her own little library, and she loved her husband even more for building it for her.

"Erica's Book Nook," the name she'd registered the library under, had only been up for about four months but was already getting a lot of traffic. It rarely went more than a few days at most without getting new donations, and she loved going through and stamping the books.

It was getting hot outside, and she felt a little wave of dizziness hit her. She really needed to drink more water. Erica cradled the books in her arms, walked past a startled butterfly, and hauled the armful of new additions into the house.

She walked into the kitchen and deposited the books onto the little island counter in the middle of the room, where she kept a pink ceramic bowl full of stickers with her library's registration number and location printed on it as well as an ink stamp with the same information. She downed a quick glass of water and then began sorting through the books.

Erica had read in the Little Free Library Stewards group on Facebook that stamping or putting stickers on the books was a good idea, as it kept the books from being sold in used bookstores, helping ensure they would eventually circulate through other Little Free Libraries. It also made her smile to think of people seeing her identifier and thinking about her little library on Canal Street in Rogers, Arkansas.

"Okay, I just might read that one," she said to herself, setting aside a book called *More Genealogy Tip of the Day* by Michael John Neill.

She'd always been interested in genealogy, especially since she was adopted and knew next to nothing about her birth family, and besides the book looked interesting. She stamped or stickered the other books and was about to take them back out to the library when she noticed another, smaller book that had somehow escaped her notice. It was multi-colored—orange, green, red, pink, purple, yellow, and black swirls that somehow seemed to move the longer she stared at it. It didn't have a title or an author on the cover, which was strange.

Suddenly intrigued, Erica put down the books she'd been about to take out to the LFL and picked up this book instead. She began to read.

Suddenly intrigued, Erica put down the books she'd been about to take out to the LFL and picked up this book instead. She began to read.

Her eyes got big as she stared at the words on the page. What were the odds that this book would not only have a character with her name, but that this fictional Erica would also be in a kitchen and have a Little Free Library? She shook her head and began reading again.

Her eyes got big as she stared at the words on the page. What were the odds that this book would not only have a character with her name, but that this fictional Erica would also be in a kitchen and have a Little Free Library? She shook her head and began reading again.

Erica quickly shut the book and, with trembling fingers, dropped it on the counter beside the other books. Was this a joke? It almost had to be a joke, but who had created the book and how had they known everything she was going to do before she did it? For that matter, who would play such a joke on her, even if they somehow could?

Or maybe she was dreaming. That was the only logical answer. She pinched her left arm, then pinched it harder, but nothing changed. Then again, she'd pinched herself in dreams before and it rarely if ever worked, so what did that even mean?

Maybe it meant she was going insane. She wished Dustin were here so she could show him the book, but of course he was at work. The only reason she wasn't at work herself today was because she had an appointment for kidney dialysis. Which meant she'd have twice as much to do tomorrow at Psychology Helps, where she worked as an administrative assistant.

She glanced at the clock. It was almost ten in the morning, and her appointment was at 10:30. She decided to do her best to put this strange book out of her mind for now and get ready to go to the kidney center. Her dialysis usually took at least four hours and if she wasn't on time there was a good chance she'd lose her spot.

Despite that, Erica almost picked up the book again but forced herself to leave it on the counter. There'd be time for reading later. If she wanted to stay alive until a kidney was found that could be transplanted into her apparently unique body, she needed to stay healthy, and that meant dialysis.

She walked into the garage, climbed into her green Kia Niro, and took off for the Henderson Dialysis Facility, the entire time thinking about that strange book. She got to the facility just before 10:30.

Sandra, one of the nurses at the facility, hooked her up to a dialysis machine and then moved onto other patients. Erica had been having dialysis for almost five years now. At first it was once a week but now it was twice a week, once on Monday and then on Friday.

She was only 34 years old but had apparently been born with dysfunctional kidneys. Dr. Ritter, her nephrologist at the Mercy hospital, told her she needed a kidney transplant almost three years ago, but they had yet to find a match for her. It was frustrating, especially as it continued to get worse.

Needless to say, she spent a lot of time getting dialysis. All told, it was at least eight hours a week, sometimes more. The one bright spot was that she had a lot of time to do things on her phone, and so for almost the entire time she sat there with her left arm attached to a CVC line she scoured the internet for information on the book.

"We're almost done," said Sandra, interrupting her train of thought.

"Thanks, Sandra," she replied, immediately switching her attention back to her phone.

She'd spent almost four hours Googling and had yet to find any mention of a book like she'd found in her Little Free Library. She'd fallen down a few rabbit holes, to be sure, but nothing panned out. There was an AI service where you could make a book about someone (why do that when you could write it yourself, she thought) but even that couldn't predict what someone was going to do before they did it.

Before she knew it, Erica finished dialysis and was driving home. She was surprised to see Dustin's SUV in the driveway. What was he doing home early on a Monday? And then she remembered he told her he'd get off at two today, for some reason or another. She really needed to start writing these things down.

She walked into the house and straight to the kitchen. All the books, including the one she'd begun thinking of as "the magical book," were gone. What the hell? She looked in the cabinets beneath the counter, even though she knew they couldn't possibly be there. Neither were they in any of the drawers. Had Dustin moved them?

"Hey, babe," Dustin said, walking into the kitchen. "How was dialysis?"

"What happened to the books that were here?" she asked, ignoring his question.

"Oh, I took them out to the library. Thought I'd save you the trouble."

"No!"

He looked at her with wide eyes, his mouth opening to respond, but she was already turning away from him, running out the door. Surely no one had come by already and snatched that book. Surely.

She rushed to the library, opened the door, and began to shift through the books. There was the genealogy book from this morning as well as the cookbook, the novels, and all the books that'd already been there, but no magical book. Where was the magical book?

"Erica, what's wrong?" asked Dustin, walking up to her. "Were those books not supposed to go in the library?"

"No, they fucking weren't!" she yelled, immediately regretting it.

"I'm sorry, hon," he said, looking around the neighborhood, his face flush with embarrassment. "I had no idea. I was just trying to help."

Erica took a deep breath before allowing herself to respond. She felt an irrational surge of anger and tamped it down. None of this was Dustin's fault. If anything, it was her fault for leaving the damned book on the counter and forgetting he was coming home early today.

"No, I'm sorry. It's not your fault, but there was this book with all these colors on the cover, and I...I wanted to read it." She felt like she was going to cry. "All the other books are still here, but that one...that one's gone."

He cocked an eyebrow. "I don't remember seeing a book that looked like that. Are you sure it was in the kitchen?"

"I'm sure."

"Well, if you really wanted to read it, we could always go look for it at a bookstore or order it off Amazon or something."

She wanted to scream again. Instead, she took another deep breath. "It didn't have the title or author listed on the cover, and I didn't have the chance to look inside to see those things because I had to get to dialysis."

"Well, shit."

"It's okay," she said, trying to regain her composure. "Maybe whoever took it will bring it back."

She knew that wasn't likely. The magical book was gone forever, taken from her before she even had the chance to really read it. Sighing, she grabbed the genealogy book and followed Dustin back into the house.

Still forlorn, Erica dragged herself through the rest of the day. They'd driven to some of the other little free libraries in the area, on the off chance someone had taken it and dropped it off at one of those, but of course they didn't find anything. She knew they wouldn't, but Dustin had offered, and she wanted to make him feel better. Still, it was a waste of time.

"So, how did dialysis go?" Dustin asked as they were eating dinner.

"Oh, it went fine," she said, then took a bite of the spaghetti he'd made them.

It was delicious. About three years ago, when she'd just gotten out of the hospital, he'd taken over cooking and had slowly learned to be an amazing chef. She still missed cooking sometimes, but certainly didn't miss the cleaning up process afterwards.

"When's your next appointment with Dr. Ritter?"

"Friday morning at nine," said Erica. "Dialysis is scheduled two hours after that, so it's going to be a busy day."

"I wish we could find you a kidney replacement."

"Oh, me too. But that doesn't seem like it's going to happen any time soon."

Erica had AB- blood, which was extremely rare. On top of that, she had an even more rare combination of Human Leukocyte Antigens, which made finding a kidney donor just about impossible, especially since she was adopted.

She'd sent her DNA to both Ancestry and 23andme in hopes of somehow finding a relative whose HLA might be compatible and who was also willing to donate a kidney, but so far no luck. She'd found absolutely no one related to her, let alone anyone who matched her antigens.

After supper they watched a little television and then it was bedtime. Erica brushed her teeth, slipped on her nightgown, and walked over to her side of the bed. After all the excitement with the missing book, not to mention dialysis, she was exhausted and wanted nothing more than a good night's sleep.

As she sat down on the bed she noticed the drawer on her nightstand was slightly open. Curious, she pulled it all the way open and was stunned to see the book inside. What the heck was going on?

"Dustin, come here for a second," she called out through the bedroom door.

"Yeah?" he asked, as he entered the room.

"Did you put this in my nightstand?"

She held up the book with the colorful cover.

"Umm, no, I sure didn't. Is that the book we were looking for?" he asked, raising his eyebrows.

"Yes, this is most definitely the book we were looking for."

"Well, I didn't put it there. Is there any chance *you* did and forgot?"

She stared at him, biting back an angry retort. Of course she hadn't put it there. But if she didn't and he didn't, then who did? She supposed it didn't matter, so long as she had the book. What mattered was ending this silly argument so she could start reading.

"Maybe I did put it there," she said, lying. "I suppose it's possible. I was in a rush this morning."

"Well, then, mystery solved," said Dustin. "So what's this book about anyway?"

That stopped her. She had absolutely no idea what the book was about. Then she had an idea.

"Here, why don't you tell me?" said Erica, passing him the book.

"Huh," he said, flipping through the first few pages. "It's about British history. This is boring as shit. I didn't know you cared about that. To each their own, though."

He laid the book on the bed beside her and then wandered off to another room in the house. She immediately snatched up the book, flipped it open, and began to read. The words she'd read before had changed, and now the book started anew with everything she'd just done.

He laid the book on the bed beside her and then wandered off to another room in the house. She immediately snatched up the book, flipped it open, and began to read. The words she'd read before had changed, and now the book started anew with everything she'd just done.

She blinked. It wasn't about British history at all. Had the book somehow masqueraded itself as something he wouldn't like? That didn't make any sense, but none of this made sense. She continued to read, this time not taking her eyes away from the pages.

She blinked. It wasn't about British history at all. Had the book somehow masqueraded itself as something he wouldn't like? That didn't make any sense, but none of this made sense. She continued to read, this time not taking her eyes away from the pages.

Erica thought maybe she was beginning to understand the book, at least a little. This book was powerful, and at least for now for her eyes only. If she kept reading, she could only learn more.

Unfortunately, she was getting sleepy, so sleepy that she could barely keep her eyes open. In fact, she felt exhausted. She yawned, struggling not to fall asleep, but it was useless. The next thing she knew…

Erica opened her eyes. Light shone through the blinds of her bedroom window. It was morning. What had happened? The last thing she remembered was reading that book, and—where was the book?

She sat up in bed, looking all around. And there it was. It had fallen on the floor. She rolled over to grab the book, at the same time glancing at the clock on her nightstand. It was just after seven in the morning, and she didn't have to be to work until nine, so she had a little time to spend reading.

She flipped open the book and everything from last night had vanished. That seemed impossible, but so was a book that told you what was currently happening in your life. She watched in amazement as new words appeared on the blank page.

She flipped open the book and everything from last night had vanished. That seemed impossible, but so was a book that told you what was currently happening in your life. She watched in amazement as new words appeared on the blank page.

Erica instantly trusted the book, knowing deep in her heart that whatever it did was for her own best interests, even if that meant lulling her to sleep. The book would never hurt her and would only help her.

She had a feeling she should call in sick to work today. They'd been very understanding about her doctor's appointments and other health-related concerns, they'd be understanding about today, too, but the sooner the better.

Should she call in sick to work? Even after a good night's sleep, she still felt exhausted. Her office could get by without her for one more day, she decided. She'd work extra hard on Wednesday and Thursday.

Erica picked up her phone, called her boss, and left a message. "Hey, Carmen. I'm really sorry, but I don't think I'll be able to make it into the office today. Dialysis was rough yesterday and I'm not feeling great. Thanks for your understanding."

She thumbed off the phone, for a moment feeling guilty that she was skipping work, but the feeling quickly passed. Her health had to come first. Once she had a new kidney, if that ever happened, there'd be plenty of time to spend at the office.

Besides, the book seemed to want her to stay home. Maybe by reading more than a little snippet at a time, she could finally figure out what was going on.

"Hey, you're up early," said Dustin as he walked into the bedroom.

Dustin was a foreman for Heiselberg Construction and was used to getting up early and working long hours, but he knew she didn't usually get up until around eight on weekdays.

"Got up and didn't feel great," she said. "I called in sick to work. Hopefully I'll feel better tomorrow."

"Do you need me to stay home with you, maybe take you to the doctor?"

"No," she said, perhaps a little too quickly. "I think I'll feel better by the end of the day, and I should be fine for work tomorrow. I think dialysis just wore me out."

They said their goodbyes, his more reluctant than hers, and then he was off to work. She had until at least six tonight, when he'd come home, to read the book. Hopefully she'd be able to figure out what its purpose was, because she definitely believed the book had a purpose. Why else had it come back to her, safely hidden in her nightstand drawer?

She picked up the book and began to read.

She picked up the book and began to read.

Erica knew she didn't have much longer to live. She didn't know how she knew, but nevertheless, she knew. Maybe another year or two, tops, before her kidneys failed completely.

What? She slammed the book shut, her heart pounding in her chest. Was this true? Was she really going to die within the next two years? She had a feeling deep in her gut that it was true and that the book wanted to warn her.

Dr. Ritter hadn't told her anything of the sort, of course. She was always optimistic, assuring her they'd find a match "eventually," but she knew that wasn't going to happen, at least not through conventional means.

Were her parents, whoever they were, still alive? Did she have siblings or half-siblings? Cousins? Grandparents? She'd wondered about this all her life, even when she was a young girl, but had never been able to find any answers.

Was there, perhaps, another way to find the answers she sought? She watched the book as more words appeared on its bright white pages, knowing, but unsure how she knew, that the answers were somewhere within.

And then she had an idea. Just a little while ago, the book had essentially told her to call in sick today. Or had it? Perhaps instead it had given her a glimpse of the future, had somehow known she was going to call in sick even before she did?

She hoped with everything within her that what she was about to try would work. She wasn't ready to die yet, to leave Dustin behind. She picked up the book and once again began to read.

She hoped with everything within her that what she was about to try would work. She wasn't ready to die yet, to leave Dustin behind. She picked up the book and once again began to read.

Erica flipped ten pages ahead in the book, reading about her and Dustin going out for dinner on their 12th anniversary. Scanning the pages, not yet finding what she was looking for, she skipped another ten pages, and then twenty, and then thirty, and then sixty, and then finally, at the end of the book, there it was.

Erica flipped ten pages deeper into the book, and then ten more, then twenty, thirty, and finally sixty. There were two pages left in the book. She took a deep breath and watched as words appeared on the pages.

Two years almost to the day that Erica first found the book, she died from kidney failure. Her funeral was beautiful, with Dustin giving a moving speech and her adoptive parents weeping in the first row, but of course Erica wasn't there to see any of it.

Erica Elaine Mosley, 36, passed away peacefully on Thursday, July 27th, at Mercy Hospital in Bentonville. She is survived by her husband, Dustin Mosley, and her adopted parents Leif and Lauren Karr. Family, friends, and other people whose lives Erica touched are invited to the Derringer Funeral Home, 2702 Serling Street,

Rogers, from 4 p.m.-7 p.m., on Tuesday, August 3rd, to reminisce, grieve, support each other, and celebrate Erica's life.

On the day of the service, a stranger showed up to offer her condolences to Dustin and Erica's parents. Her name was Delilah Jones and she was, she explained to them, Erica's biological mother. She had Erica when she was sixteen and her parents had forced her to put the child up for adoption. She'd never known Erica's whereabouts or even her name, and her parents only shared that information with her after they came across Erica's obituary in the Northwest Arkansas Democrat Gazette.

When Dustin explained that Erica died of kidney failure, Delilah broke down in tears. She had the same blood type as Erica and may well have the same strange Human Leukocyte Antigens. If she had only known, she would have gotten tested and, if she matched, gladly donated a kidney.

Erica closed the book with shaking hands, her vision clouded with tears. She had two years to live, but now she knew the name of her biological mother. Could her future be changed? Could she not only live a longer, healthier life, but also meet her birth mother and whatever other relatives she might have?

She was about to find out.

Four months later

The last four months had been a whirlwind of emotion. When she'd first contacted Delilah, the woman had been skeptical, but Delilah's parents had quickly been able to confirm Erica was telling the truth.

They exchanged emails and talked on the phone for about a week before meeting in person, and that same day met with Dr. Ritter. The doctor ran a multitude of tests, confirming that Delilah did indeed have the same HLA as Erica and would be the perfect candidate to donate a kidney to her. A month and three weeks later, it was done. According to Dr. Ritter, the surgery had gone perfectly, and Erica's body had no problem at all accepting her mother's kidney.

Delilah was able to leave the hospital three days after donating her left kidney but visited Erica every single day as she recovered. On day ten, Erica finally got the okay to head home.

"How're you feeling, babe?" asked Dustin, as they walked out of the hospital together, hand in hand.

"Great," Erica said, "better than I have in years."

"I'm so glad," said Delilah, walking on her other side.

"All thanks to you," she said, "Mom."

Erica told both Dustin and Delilah about the book and at first they'd seemed skeptical but eventually believed her, driven by the fact that when Dustin read it the book still told him facts about British history, while to Delilah it was a book about math, a subject for which she had absolutely no interest.

As soon as they got home, Erica excused herself and went into the bedroom, retrieving the book from her nightstand drawer. She flipped it open, but it was still blank, just as it had been ever since it told Erica her mother's name.

She looked at it again now, perhaps sensing that something had changed, flipping to the very end of the book. She gasped as she read the final page.

Erica knew the book had served her well, and that it was time for her to let it go so someone else in need might benefit from its gifts. A part of her wanted to keep it, to learn more about her future, but another, bigger part of her knew that wasn't necessary. The future was a gift, and the best gifts were often surprises.

Besides, she knew all she needed to know about her future now. The final line of her story read "and she lived happily ever after."

Her eyes filled with tears of joy as she took the book outside to the Little Free Library. She kissed the book, silently thanking it for not only extending her life in the form of a healthy kidney but also introducing her to her birth mother, who had quickly become an integral part of her life.

She placed the magical book into the library and closed the door, trusting it to wind up in the right hands. She didn't turn back once as she walked back into the house.

It was time to live her happily ever after.

The Urn

The urn was forged in the year 1392, or so the little leaflet claimed. How could they really tell, anyway? Was the date stamped on the bottom of the urn, or had they figured that out with carbon dating? Josh Drake didn't know; in fact, all he did know was that he was going to win that urn, even if he had to sell his house to do it.

He'd dreamt about nothing but the urn for the last week. In the first dream, he'd been exploring an old cave when he'd stumbled upon the urn hidden in a crevice. In the second, he'd found it buried under a mountain. The dreams went on and on, with Josh finding the urn in different places.

Finally, just yesterday, he dreamed of coming to this auction in Joplin, Missouri, where he knew the urn would soon be sold. He'd woken up, Googled auctions in Joplin, and sure enough found the urn.

It would be the eighteenth item of the day to go up for auction, according to the schedule they'd posted on the website. He'd immediately driven to the bank, taken out his and his wife's entire life savings, hopped into the car, and drove six hours to Joplin. He arrived just in time for the thirteenth item, a weird painting of a giant orange and green scaly cat-like creature with seven tentacle-like arms.

According to the leaflet they'd given him when he walked through the door, all the items in today's auction were from the collection of Dr. Samuel Newport, a world-renowned archaeologist and collector of curiosities who had died earlier this year.

The strange painting of the green and orange, multi-armed creature went for $2,300. Well, hell. He'd withdrawn $5,892 from the bank. Even if the urn went for twice as much as the painting had, he would still have enough. He was golden.

He hoped it didn't go for nearly that much, however, because he was already in the doghouse with Faith, his wife of seven years. She'd been amused when he first told her about the dreams, and then increasingly alarmed as he seemingly became obsessed with them.

She had been calling him nonstop for the last four hours. She'd found out, he imagined, that not only had he failed to show up for his job, probably costing himself his position as a history teacher at Carthage High School, but had also drained their bank accounts.

He didn't know if she'd actually found any of this out, however, as he'd avoided her calls and eventually just muted his phone. He'd deal with Faith later. What other choice did he have?

"Well, that's a strange one," said an old man dressed in a crisp blue suit sitting beside him, bringing his thoughts back to the present.

Josh blinked, mumbled something, and then looked up, staring at the fourteenth item on the auction block.

It was a necklace made of different-sized teeth. According to the auctioneer, the necklace contained teeth from twenty different species, including humans. It was found in Romania by Dr. Newport, during an archaeological dig he led in 1978.

The necklace ended up going for $4,100.

"I thought it might go for more," whispered the old man who'd spoken to him earlier. "It's rumored to have belonged to Vlad the Impaler."

"That's interesting," mumbled Josh, though he really wasn't interested at all in the necklace, nor in the man sitting beside him.

He felt his phone vibrate. It was a text message from Faith. *Where are you? You're scaring me. The school said you didn't show up for work, and you won't answer your phone. Call me! Please!*

He pressed the power button on his iPhone, turning it off. He'd respond to Faith after the auction. At least she didn't know about the money. Not yet, at any rate.

"What're you here for?" asked the old man. "I'm Franklin, by the way. Franklin Comey."

"Joshua Drake, and I'm not really sure," Josh said, lying, wishing this guy would just stop talking.

"Oh, well, that's okay. I'm here for the urn. Supposed to be from 18,000 BC, maybe earlier. Lots of crazy rumors about it. I'm here on behalf of the Rutledge Museum of History in Chicago."

18,000 BC? Clearly, Comey didn't know what he was talking about. The leaflet said it was from 1392. But what if Comey were right? If so, it would probably go for a lot of money. Josh's breath caught in his throat. Museums have deep pockets. How could he possibly compete with a museum?

The next item, the fifteenth up for auction, came and went, with a woman two rows behind Josh winning the prize. He didn't even know what the antiquity had been, just that it sold for over $10,000. He was out of his league here. He prayed that the urn didn't go for more than $5,892.

The sixteenth item, a damaged silver flute from 500 BC, went for a mere $840. That gave Josh hope. The next item, however, took that hope and dashed it to the ground.

The seventeenth item on the auction block was a stone carving of a strange little creature that looked remarkably like Groot from one of those Marvel movies. It was over 15,000 years old and had been discovered centuries earlier in Africa. It went for $57,980.

"Wow," said Comey. "We almost bid on that. I'm glad we didn't. Well, the urn is next. Wish me luck."

"Good luck," Josh said numbly.

The urn, the auctioneer explained, was first discovered in a cave in Greece in 1392. Josh blinked. It was just like in his dream. The urn was lost and rediscovered many times over the next 600 years, most recently by the deceased Dr. Samuel Newport.

Josh had read the leaflet wrong. Comey was right. The urn wasn't actually from 1392, only first discovered then. According to the auctioneer, it was carbon dated to be nearly 20,000 years old.

"The bidding starts at $1,000. Do I hear $1,000?" asked the auctioneer.

Comey immediately raised his paddle.

"We have $1,000, do I hear $1,500?"

Josh raised his paddle. Comey looked at him, raised an eyebrow, and smiled. "'Not really sure,' my foot."

"We have $1,500, do I hear $2,000?" The auctioneer pointed to the back at someone Josh couldn't see. "We have $2,000, do I hear $2,500?"

Josh started to raise his paddle, but Comey beat him to the punch.

"We have $2,500, do I hear $3,000?"

"$5,892!" Josh heard himself shout, as he frantically waved his paddle in the air.

He felt like he was going to pass out. What had he done? That was their entire life savings. Faith would divorce him. He'd probably already lost his job. All for this stupid urn.

"We have $5,892, do I hear $6,500. Going once—"

"$6,500," said Comey, raising his paddle in the air.

Josh felt like someone had kicked him in the balls. He couldn't believe this bastard had outbid him. The whatever museum in Chicago didn't need the urn. He needed the urn!

"$8,000," came a voice from a few chairs in front of him.

"$10,000," Comey said, raising his paddle in the air, glancing at Josh.

Their little house on Buchanan Street in Carthage was worth around $70,000. Could he take out a second mortgage online? He snatched his phone out of his pocket, forgetting he'd turned it off earlier. He pressed the power button, but it was taking too long.

"$15,000!" said a voice from behind him.

"We have $15,000, do I hear $20,000?" asked the auctioneer.

"$20,000," said Comey, once again raising his paddle in the air.

"Fuuuuck!" screamed Josh, as he fumbled with his phone.

Everyone, including Comey, turned to stare at him. "Are you okay, Mr. Drake?" Comey asked.

"No, I'm definitely not okay," yelled Josh. "I've lost my job and my wife, all for that fucking urn I'm not even going to win!"

"Sir," said a voice suddenly beside him, "you need to calm down. Let's step outside for a few minutes."

Josh stared up into the face of one of the security guards he'd seen earlier when he first walked into the building. The next thing Josh knew, the guard and another one like him were hauling him kicking and screaming out of the building.

"You need to leave the premises," said the first guard. "Where's your car?"

"I'll be good," promised Josh. "Just let me go back in, okay? Maybe it's not too late."

"Sir," said the second guard, "do we need to call the police?"

He stared defiantly at the two security guards for a moment or two and then turned around and stomped off towards his green Dodge Dart. He climbed into the vehicle and sped off down the road, only to turn around a few minutes later.

He slowly drove past the building where the auction was being held. Good, the guards had gone back inside. There was a Murphy gas station on Rangeline Road, right across from the building.

He parked off to the side of the gas station, waiting until the path was clear, and crossed the road back to the auction house. He ducked behind a car just as he saw Comey walking out the front. He was holding the urn!

Comey walked straight to his car, a brand new, shiny silver Ford Explorer. The bastard was probably rich, maybe even owned that museum in Chicago where he claimed to work. Or, hell, maybe that was all a lie, and he wanted the urn for himself.

Looking back and forth for guards, not seeing any, Josh jogged up to the man just as he was putting the urn in a Styrofoam container in the back of his SUV. He turned, keys in hand, eyes widening as he saw Josh.

"You!" said Comey. "Look, I don't want any trouble."

Josh held his hand out. "I just came over to apologize. I've had an awful week, but that was no reason to act the way I did. I'm sorry."

"That's very kind of you," said Comey, not taking his hand, "but I really need to get going. It's a long drive back to Chicago."

"Of course. I just wanted to ask—what did it go for?"

Comey looked at him warily, but finally said, "$186,000."

"Well, congratulations," Josh said, still holding out his hand. "That's way more than I had anyway. No hard feelings, Mr. Comey?"

"No, of course not, Mr. Drake," said Comey, finally reaching out to shake Josh's hand.

"I'm sorry," Josh said, as he grabbed the man's arm, twisted it around his back, and pushed his head repeatedly into the still-open back of the explorer.

Comey gasped once before collapsing to the ground. Josh loaded the man into the back of the vehicle, beside the Styrofoam case that held the urn, and closed the door.

"Is that blood?" said a female voice from behind him.

Josh startled, spinning around to come face-to-face with a blonde woman wearing a long green dress. He looked at the concrete ground; it was covered with blood, as was the back of the car. He even had blood on his shoes.

"That *is* blood!" she yelled, backing away from him. "You're that crazy guy from the auction."

Shit. Josh looked around, unsure of what to do. The parking lot was full now, and everyone was staring at him.

"David, call 911," he heard a voice say.

"That's definitely the guy from the auction," another voice said.

Backing away from the woman in the green dress, he stepped on something. Looking down, he could see it was Comey's keys. He must have dropped them. He picked them up and climbed into Comey's car. He'd have to come back for his own car later.

"Hey, you! Stop!" a voice called out. One of the security guards.

Comey's Ford Explorer was keyless. He pressed the ignition button, but it wouldn't start. Why wouldn't it start?

The security guard was at the car window now, demanding to know where the blood had come from. The door automatically locked the moment he got inside, thank goodness. He ignored the guard, tried to start the car again, but nothing.

Press the brake before pushing the button, whispered a voice.

Josh turned left, then right, but there was no one there other than the security guard. Who had said that? Comey? But even if Comey were awake, why would he help him?

He stomped down hard on the brake and pressed the button and was rewarded with the sound of the Explorer roaring to life. Thank God. He backed out of the parking space, immediately slamming into something.

Screams echoed through the parking lot, and for a second the car wouldn't move. Then it was rumbling over something, the car shaking, and he heard more screams. Had he run over someone?

He finished backing out and saw that he had indeed run over some-one. The girl in the green dress lay sprawled across the pavement, her arms and legs twisted in odd angles, blood everywhere.

Josh closed his eyes, shook his head, then opened them again. The guard was pounding on his window. He stomped down hard on the ac-celerator, nearly hit someone else, then zoomed out of the parking lot.

Where could he go? They could figure out his name from the bidding registration he'd filled out before the auction started. It probably wasn't safe to go back to his car, but where else could he go?

He realized he was speeding. He forced himself to slow down. It wouldn't do to get pulled over by a cop or get into a wreck, it wouldn't do at all, especially after having run over someone.

His phone beeped, startling him. He remembered turning it back on in the auction house but hadn't looked at it since. He risked a glance at the phone. It was a text from Faith.

Please, Josh, said the text, *let me know where you are. I'm worried as hell about you. Just let me know where you are.*

He almost laughed. She was worried? She wasn't the one who'd just assaulted someone and stolen his car, then ran over someone else. All for that damned urn. That urn that he'd dreamed about over and over and over this whole last week.

What the hell was wrong with him?

Find a hotel, that voice whispered again.

"Comey, is that you?" he yelled into the back of the SUV, all the while knowing it wasn't.

A Drury Inn & Suites appeared on his left. Without even thinking, he yanked the wheel and rolled into the parking lot. He parked off to the side, backing into the parking space so hopefully no one would see the blood on the rear end of the SUV.

He opened the back of the explorer to find Comey staring up at him. The man wasn't dead, thank God, but he was badly injured. There was a huge gash across his forehead, and he was covered in blood.

"Jesus Christ, I'm so sorry," Josh said.

"Just…help me up," the old man whispered. "You can have the car."

"I don't want your car," he said, "just the urn."

"You don't…you don't want the urn. It's—"

He never heard the rest of what Comey was trying to say, because at that moment the voice, the voice he now knew was in his head, screamed at him.

Franklin Comey wants to rape Faith and then kill her. Kill him, before it's too late.

"You…you want to rape and kill Faith?" asked Josh, staring down at the man's outstretched hand.

"What are you talking about? Who's Faith?" Comey asked. "You attacked me."

"You won't hurt my wife!"

Josh was on Comey in a second, his hands around the man's neck, squeezing, digging his thumbs into his skin, squeezing so hard it made his fingers hurt. It was done in just a moment. Comey's eyes rolled back in his head and his chest stopped rising and falling.

He was dead.

Wild-eyed, Josh scanned the parking lot. No one had seen him kill this monster. Good. He just had to get inside, rent a room, and—

No, said the voice in his head. *There's no time for that. Room 216, she'll be stepping out of the room by the time you get there. Take her.*

Josh grabbed the Styrofoam crate from the back of the Explorer, avoiding touching Comey, and then closed the back. He walked into the hotel, nodded at the clerk, and went to the elevator. He took the elevator to the second floor and reached room 216 just as the door opened.

A twenty-something brunette dressed in skinny jeans and a white blouse stepped out of the room, then yelped as she saw him. "I didn't order anything."

He pushed her back into the room and closed the door behind him. Dropping the Styrofoam case to the floor, he was on her in a second, his hands around her throat, just like he'd done to Comey.

She immediately brought her knee up into his crotch, and an almost-unbearable pain coursed through his body. He started to fold into himself, but that voice, that damned voice, told him to ignore the pain.

"Help me! I'm being attacked, in room 216," he heard her yelling into the telephone on the bedside table.

He leaped across the room, wrapping his arms around her throat, twisting her neck, twisting it hard, hearing it pop. Her body went limp, and she collapsed to the floor, the phone tumbling from her hand.

"Hello? Miss Armstrong? I'm calling the police right now," said a voice from the phone. "Miss Armstrong?"

Josh hung up the handset, walked over to the Styrofoam crate, and snatched it from the floor.

Hurry, said that voice inside his head, *before they get here*.

He knew what he had to do now. He ripped open the crate, pulled the urn out, and stared at it. He could see it up close now and noticed that there were rows of that weird cat-like creature from the painting engraved in the pottery, circling the entire urn.

Josh heard knocking on the door, and then a click, as the door began to open.

Do it, said the voice. *Now. Now!*

He was never going to see Faith again. He knew that now. He'd never teach at the high school again, either. He'd never do anything, ever again. His life was over. But that was okay because *his* life was just beginning again.

He threw the urn to the ground, shattering it. Green and purple smoke began to pour from the remains of the urn, more than the urn could possibly have contained, and then *Xhahgoth* stood before him.

He looked just like he did in his painting; an eight-foot-tall green and orange cat-like being with seven tentacles, dripping purple and blue ichor all over the room's gray carpeting.

There were screams from behind him, but Josh ignored them, because they didn't matter anymore. Nothing mattered anymore.

The creature opened its mouth, and after that, the world changed.

Alternate Life

October 3rd, 1985

Zachary Wright sat hunched over his Commodore 64 computer, staring at the screen on his television, playing Attack of the Killer Slugs. It was a stupid game, he decided, but it was something to do. Despite his best efforts, the slugs kept killing him, forcing him to start over.

"Stupid slugs!" he yelled before exiting the game, ripping the cartridge from the port on the back of the computer, and hurling it across the room.

He wanted to punch something, or better yet, someone, and just keep on punching. Some days, it was all he could do not to take one of his stepfather's hunting rifles from the garage and put a bullet into his own brain.

No one would miss him anyway.

He hated his life.

Zachary was fifteen years old, a Sophomore at Carthage High School. He'd been bullied mercilessly ever since the middle of second grade, when they'd first moved to the little Illinois town from across the river in Iowa a few months after his father died.

He was the chubby kid who didn't want to play football, the kid who loved comic books and dreamed of someday writing them, the kid who aced all the tests but still had shitty grades because he didn't turn in his homework, the kid who "didn't live up to his potential." The kid who no girl would even look at or talk to, much less date. The kid everyone wanted to bully, and no one wanted to be friends with. He was a nerd, through and through, and no one had time for nerds.

Before yesterday, he had exactly one friend: a shy, skinny kid by the name of Eric Brass, who he'd always suspected had become friends with him only because he was almost as unpopular as Zachary was, and they both loved comics. Earlier today, that theory had been proven correct.

School bullies Kurt Farley and Todd Jones were making fun of Zachary, as usual, while he was in line for the cafeteria during lunch. They were chanting "Fatty, fatty, two by four, couldn't fit through the lunchroom door" at him, over and over and over again

He remained stoic, staring ahead, waiting for his turn in line, all the while imagining them dead. That usually would have been it, but Eric happened to come up behind them in line.

"Hey, Brass," said Farley, stopping the chant for a moment. "Why do you hang out with this fat ass anyway?"

Eric looked startled, then swiveled his head from Zachary to Farley. "Umm, because we're friends?"

Jones laughed. "Why would you want to be friends with this tub of lard?"

"Leave him alone," Zachary whispered.

"What did you say, fat ass?"

"I said, leave him alone," Zachary repeated, louder this time.

Farley reared back to punch him, but then Eric began to chant: "Fatty, fatty, two by four, couldn't fit through the lunchroom door."

Farley began to laugh and was soon joined by Jones and most of the other kids in the cafeteria.

Something broke in Zachary. He felt tears pushing at his eyes, threatening to roll down his cheeks. He turned away. He wouldn't let them see him cry. He wouldn't.

"What're you kids doing?" asked Tillie Young, the head cook in the cafeteria, stepping out from the kitchen. "Stop it, before I call Mr. Twaddle down here."

Zachary pushed past Farley and Jones, through the laughing throng of kids, and out the side door of the cafeteria into a cold October afternoon. Fuck this shit. He was done.

After he left school, he roamed around the town square for a while, eventually winding up at Newsland, the little newspaper store that served Carthage. He looked through the comics that had come in on Wednesday, making a mental note of which ones he wanted to buy when he got his meager allowance on Friday, before finally walking the mile and a half home.

He'd left his house key in his bag in his locker at school, so ended up having to get the ladder out of the garage, scale the side of the house, and let himself in through his second-story bedroom window. He was thankful he always left it unlocked, or he might still be stuck outside in the cold.

Lightning flashed outside, startling him out of his memories. The lightning was followed a few seconds later by a huge clap of thunder, and then it began to rain. Well, at least that would be an excuse to ignore his stepdad's usual "get off that damned computer and go outside for a while" demands once he got home from the factory.

His mother, a nurse at Carthage Memorial Hospital, met Bobby two years after she and Zachary moved to Carthage. He'd gotten hurt at the factory and wound up at the hospital, needing his arm stitched up. It had been "love at first sight," according to Mom.

He still thought it was the biggest mistake she'd ever made and told her so often. Bobby was a cranky asshole who never tired of riding Zachary's ass about getting more exercise, losing weight, and working on his grades at school.

Zachary's real father had been an alcoholic who died way too young from cirrhosis of the liver, which was essentially what you got if you drank too much booze for too long. He wasn't a kind man, but he was a better man than Bobby. Then again, who wasn't?

In addition to losing his best friend, he'd lost his cat three weeks ago. His mother insisted on keeping Trixie outside, which Zachary had always hated. She'd come home beaten-up multiple times and even lost the tip of her tail in a fight with a dog.

It was only a matter of time, he argued, before she didn't come home at all. There was no getting around it, his mother said, because stupid dumbass Bobby was allergic to cats. Trixie could only come inside when Bobby wasn't home, and even then, he had to vacuum the carpet after.

Three weeks ago, she vanished. Her outside food and water bowls remained untouched. Was she dead? Had someone stolen her, or had she just gotten lost? He would probably never know for sure, which bugged the hell out of him.

Sighing, pushing memories of his dead father and his more-than-likely-dead cat out of his mind, Zachary opened the terminal program on his Commodore 64, which was used to connect to CompuServe. After that, he plugged his 300 baud modem into the back of the computer and dialed CompuServe's phone number. He unplugged the cord from the phone as soon as he heard the screechy noise that meant he'd connected and quickly plugged it into the back of the modem.

A few minutes later, it asked him for his CompuServe ID number and password. He dutifully typed in his ID number ("72689,598") and password ("drowssap," which was "password" spelled backwards) and finished the login process.

He had to call long distance to Chicago to reach CompuServe. Mom and Bobby would be pissed, but he didn't care. He wouldn't stay on long; just long enough to navigate to the video game forum and hopefully get some help with Attack of the Killer Slugs, so he could finally defeat the shiny green slug guarding the entrance to level 17.

Hopefully, the charge would be so small that Bobby wouldn't even notice. Though when it came to money, he seemed to notice just about everything. At least he'd have something new to bitch about other than the price of cat food.

Another flash of lightning, followed by a huge thunderclap. Zachary looked out his bedroom window. It was really coming down now. Raining cats and dogs, as his mother sometimes said. Maybe Carthage would flood, and he wouldn't have to go to school tomorrow. Wishful thinking.

Just as he'd finally found his way to the video game forum, there was a third flash of lightning followed almost immediately by a huge clap of thunder, and then the lights flickered, and the house went black.

"Aw, no!" Zachary screamed into the darkness.

He hoped with all his heart that his Commodore 64 wasn't fried. That would be his luck. He'd spent almost all last summer painting fences, mowing lawns, and shucking corn in order to earn enough money to buy the damned thing. If it were ruined, he'd be royally screwed.

He hated school. Hell, he hated life. Comic books and his computer were his only escapes. If he lost his C64, one of the few good things he had in his life, he wasn't sure what he'd do. Maybe he'd take the rifle to the school, kill Farley and Jones, and then shove the barrel in his mouth and kill himself.

Zachary balled his hand into a fist and was about to slam it into the little desk that sat in front of his bed when the lights came back on. Off one second, and then back on the next, just like that. He shook his head, staring at the TV screen, which just showed static.

It must have been a brownout, rather than a full-on blackout, or else the TV would be off. His C64 was likewise still running, which was confusing, given the static on the television screen.

He blinked. The static was gone, replaced by a white screen with words on it. It looked nothing like the CompuServe he was used to visiting. He read the words "Welcome to the Attack of the Killer Slugs group" superimposed over a graphic of a slug from the game. Beneath that were the words "Attack of the Killer Slugs" and beneath that it said "private group. 5.4k members."

There appeared to be posts from various people, but the format didn't look like anything he'd ever seen on CompuServe. What the heck was going on?

Using the cursor keys, he scrolled down the posts. One, from someone named Scott Sterling, talked about loving the game as a kid. Was this guy nuts? The game had only been out for maybe six months.

He continued to scroll down, then froze. There was a post from someone with the name Zachary Wright. His name. He read the post, feeling a shiver travel down his spine.

I played this game all the time in high school. Never did complete it, though. I was in an awful mood one day and threw the cartridge across the room and broke it. Tried to find another copy but they were all sold out by the time I got together the money to pay for it.

What the hell? He got up from the desk, walked across the room, and retrieved the game. It had a long crack in the case and the metal part that plugged into the C64 was loose. Shit!

How in the hell did this asshole who was using his name know about something that just happened five minutes ago?

He walked back to his desk and sat down. The post this other "Zachary Wright" made had a blue button beneath it that kind of looked like a thumb with the number 17 beside it.

There was a little graphic beside his name. He clicked on it, and it brought up another screen, this time with a bigger version of that same graphic (he thought it was a person but wasn't sure, the image looked all jumbled) with the name Zachary Wright—*his* name—beneath the picture.

On the right side of the screen were two buttons, one labelled "add friend" and the other labelled "message." There were three little dots to the right of the message button, which he ignored. He clicked the message button, and a little window appeared at the bottom of the screen that said, "You're not friends on Facebook."

No shit, Sherlock, thought Zach, *I don't even know what Facebook is.*

He typed "Who are you?" into the little box and pressed Enter on his keyboard.

A few seconds later, a message popped up. It said: *Who are YOU? You don't even have a name, just numbers. Why are you writing me? Are you a Nigerian prince or something?*

Zachary stared at the screen. Nigerian prince? What did that mean? He decided it didn't matter. This was confusing enough as it was.

72689,598: *I'm Zachary Wright. Why are you using my name?*

Zachary: *Your name? Look, I don't know what kind of scam you're running, but I don't have time for this shit. Consider yourself blocked.*

72689,598: *What do you mean, blocked?*

Zachary: *Okay, this is strange. Why can't I block you? Is it because you don't have a name? How are you doing this?*

72689,598: *I told you, my name is Zachary Wright.*

Zachary: *You don't have a profile either. WTF?*

72689,598: *What does WTF mean?*

Zachary: *You're kidding, right? What the fuck?*

72689,598: *I don't think you're supposed to use that kind of language on Com-puServe.*

Zachary: *CompuServe? Is that even still around?*

Another clap of thunder startled Zach, and he jumped, nearly falling from his chair. The rain against the windows was even louder now. It sounded like it was getting really bad outside.

He turned back to the TV screen, half-expecting it to be blank, but the chat window was still there. He began to type again.

72689,598: *CompuServe is new, at least to me.*

Zachary: *I just Googled it. I was thinking Amazon bought CompuServe, but it was AOL. They bought it in 1998, and Verizon bought AOL in 2015. It's still around, kind of, but no one uses it anymore. I'm surprised Amazon didn't buy it, since they buy everything.*

Zachary stared at the words, not comprehending. It was 1985. How would this guy know what would happen 13 years from now, let alone in 2015? He felt a powerful urge to turn off the computer and forget about everything that had just happened but couldn't quite bring himself to do that.

72689,598: *It's 1985. My name is Zachary Jonathan Wright, and I'm really confused right now.*

Zachary: *It isn't 1985, and how did you know my middle name?*

72689,598: *That's your middle name, too?*

Zachary: *This isn't funny. Okay, wise guy. If you're going to pretend to be me, what's my birthday?*

72689,598: *I don't know what your birthday is, but mine is December 4th, 1970. I'll be sixteen in two months.*

Zachary: *You could have Googled my birthday. Let's try something a little more difficult. What was my sophomore English teacher's name?*

72689,598: *You keep saying you "Googled" something. What does that mean?*

Zachary: *Answer my question and I'll answer yours.*

72689,598: *Fine. I don't know who your sophomore English teacher was, but mine's Miss Lang. Audrey's her first name, I think. Audrey Lang.*

Zachary: *Red hair, beautiful blue eyes, and the prettiest face?*

72689,598: *How did you know that?*

Zachary: *Because she was my teacher when I was in high school. One morning, I got to school early for some reason and walked into her room. What happened?*

72689,598: *How could you know about that?*

Zachary: *What happened?*

72689,598: *Okay. It was near the start of the school year. For some reason, she was changing clothes. I think she thought the door was locked, but it wasn't, and I saw her left boob. I ran out of the room. I know she saw me, but she never said anything, and I never told anyone. Until today.*

Zachary: *I never told anyone either, not a single soul. This is crazy.*

Another boom from outside. He half-expected the lights to go off again, and part of him wished they would. That way he wouldn't have to deal with whatever the hell was happening. Could this "Zachary Wright" somehow really be him from the future?

72689,598: *Now that we've got that out of the way, what's Google?*

Zachary: *Google is a search engine. You can find anything on the web using Google.*

72689,598: *What's the web? What's a search engine?*

Zachary: *The web is the World Wide Web. The internet. And a search engine is something you use to search the internet.*

72689,598: *I have no idea what the internet is, but I guess that doesn't matter. What's today's date?*

Zachary: *It's October 3rd, 2027. What's the date wherever you are?*

Zachary took a deep breath. 2027 was 42 years from now, which would make this Zachary 57 years old. How was this possible?

It's October 3rd, 1985, he finally typed. *There's a storm happening here right now, and I think it messed with my computer.*

Zachary: *It's storming here in Missouri, too. And guess what? I remember your storm. That was the day I ruined my copy of Attack of the Killer Slugs.*

72689,598: *You live in Missouri?*

Zachary: *I do, in a town called Joplin. Anyway, that was also the day I left school early and got in trouble for skipping.*

72689,598: *Bobby?*

Zachary: *Yes, good old Bobby the dumbass. Lol*

72689,598: *lol?*

Zachary: *Sorry. It means "laughing out loud." Don't worry too much about Bobby, though. He's mostly all bark and no bite. Did you know his dad killed himself when he was 10? I think that's probably why he was such an asshole.*

72689,598: *His dad killed himself?*

Zachary: *He did. I found about it years later, long after Mom divorced him.*

72689,598: *She divorces him?*

Zachary: *That's right. Your Mom dumps his ass not long after…oh, shit!*

72689,598: *What?*

Zachary: *Eric, your best friend, that's what. I hadn't thought about this in such a long time. What happened…or what's about to happen, in your case…changed my life forever. I'm not sure how to tell you this, young me, I'm really not.*

"Zach, get your ass downstairs," shouted a voice, as if on cue. It was Bobby Moore, Zach's stepfather. "Now."

Zachary jumped, nearly falling out of his seat. What was Bobby doing home? "I'll be right there."

"I said now, you little asshole."

He wanted to ask Future Zachary what he was talking about, but there was no time. Besides, he and Eric were no longer friends. Eric betraying him had already changed his life forever. Maybe Future Zachary had just gotten the date wrong.

"Coming," yelled Zachary, getting up out of the chair and walking out his bedroom door.

Bobby was soaking wet, standing in the middle of the little kitchen of the house they rented at the edge of Carthage. He was still wearing his work clothes from Methode Electric, a factory that produced car parts. He didn't look happy.

"The school called me," said Bobby. "They said you ran out of school during lunch. Said you were fighting."

"I wasn't fighting," Zachary said.

"They tried to call your mom, but they couldn't get hold of her at the hospital, so they called me. I had to leave work because of your fat ass."

Zachary felt rage flooding his body and it was all he could do not to punch Bobby in the face. He hated Bobby almost as much as he did the kids from school, if not more. Zach's real father had died when he was seven, and it wasn't long after when Bobby swooped in to save the day.

Bobby was a real asshole.

"Don't call me that," Zachary said, staring at Bobby.

"What?"

"I said, don't call me that. Don't call me a 'fat ass.'"

"I wouldn't have to call you anything if you didn't skip school. No wonder your grades are so bad. All you do is lie around and watch TV or play on that stupid computer thing. Why your mom let you get that is beyond me."

Most things are beyond you, Bobby, he thought, *because you're a dumbass,* but he didn't say the words. Instead, he said, "Some kids attacked me. I didn't want to get in trouble for fighting, so I came home. I only missed half a day."

Thunder shook the house and both Zachary and Bobby jumped. The lights flickered again but didn't go out.

"It's almost three," said Bobby, looking at the big clock above the refrigerator, "so there's no point in going back now. But tomorrow if these kids want to fight, then fight. A bloody nose or a black eye will make them leave you alone. And no more television for the rest of the night. Understand?"

"I understand," Zachary said, relieved that Bobby hadn't tried to take away his computer.

"And I want those dishes washed and trash taken out by the time I get home at six, or no computer for a week," Bobby said, as if reading his mind.

Zachary winced and said, "Okay," then got to work.

It took Zachary less than 45 minutes to wash and dry the dishes and to take out the trash, which left him absolutely soaked, but it felt like the longest 45 minutes of his life. He hoped future Zachary, as he'd taken to thinking of him, was still logged into CompuServe or Facebook or whatever it was.

Oh shit! He'd left himself logged in all this time. The phone bill was going to be enormous. Zachary raced upstairs, but the lights went out halfway up. This time, they didn't turn back on.

Morning came, and the electricity was working again. Both the storm and the outage had lasted long into the night, and Zachary had a hard time falling asleep. He yawned, stretched, and then remembered yesterday.

He quickly rolled out of bed, ran to his desk, and flicked the power button on the side of his computer. He closed his eyes, praying to whatever cosmic being might be listening out there that he hadn't lost his connection to the future.

Zachary felt the bottom fall out of his stomach as his Commodore 64 loaded to the regular "READY" screen. He only had one shot left.

He navigated to the terminal software and dialed CompuServe, waited for the call to connect, and plugged the cable into the modem currently inserted into the back of his computer.

After what seemed like an eternity, the CompuServe welcome screen loaded, making no mention of Facebook. He navigated to the video game forums, but nothing there either.

The connection was gone.

Zachary had feigned being sick, hoping to stay home, but his mother was having none of it.

"You're going to school, Zachary, and that's final. In fact, you're lucky we didn't ground you after what you did yesterday," she said, as they sat around the table for breakfast. "I would have, you know, but Bobby is much nicer than me."

Bobby winked at him, and he thought he might throw up. Bobby was an absolute asshole to him 99% of the time, and if his mother didn't know that, well, she just wasn't paying attention.

Zachary got dressed and waited outside for the bus. The yard was muddy, and the tree across the street in Mr. Gordon's yard had lost nearly all its branches, but other than that Carthage seemed to have pretty much survived the storm.

He sighed as the school bus pulled up to the curb, with Mr. Farley, Kurt Farley's father, driving. Thank God today was Friday, because he had a feeling this was going to be one hell of a long day.

The first half of Zachary's day passed in a long blur. He had English class that morning with Miss Lang, followed by math, history, and art. Eric was in his art class and tried to talk to him, but Zachary ignored him, so Eric went back to his drawing.

He was currently working on a portrait of Spider-Man, which Zachary had to admit was very good. Too bad Eric was a no-good traitor.

They'd planned on pursuing their dreams of creating comics—Zachary writing and Eric drawing—after college, but Zachary would just have to find someone else.

During the last few minutes of art, he'd been summoned to the principal's office. Mr. Twaddle was kind once Zachary explained what happened yesterday in the cafeteria. He'd let him off with a warning but let him know that, if he was caught skipping school again, he'd get a week's worth of after-school detention.

Zachary brought his lunch today so he could avoid the lunch line and hopefully Kurt Farley and Todd Jones. A bologna and cheese sandwich, a bag of chips, and a Snickers bar. Eric tried to talk to him again while he was retrieving his lunch box from his locker, but Zachary wasn't in the mood to listen.

"I'm sorry," Eric said. "I just—"

"You just what?" yelled Zachary in his former friend's face. "You hate me just like the rest of them do. Fuck off and die, man."

"But—" Eric said, but Zachary would never know the rest of what he was going to say, because he pushed Eric into the lockers and then marched off to the lunchroom.

Zachary sat alone in the cafeteria, at the far end of the table from Julie Moss, Jill Anderson, and Tammy Hawkins. Sure, none of the girls would give him the time of day, but at least they wouldn't try to pick fights with him. He could eat his bologna and cheese sandwich in peace. He saw Farley and Jones staring at him a couple of times, but when he turned to look at them, they just laughed and looked away.

"How come you're not sitting with Eric?" asked Julie, startling him. "You always sit with Eric."

He looked up from his sandwich, straight into her beautiful green eyes. He held the gaze for just a second and then looked back down at his sandwich, like he always did.

He'd had a crush on Julie since 4th grade but had never said anything. She'd always been friendly enough, but he knew that's as far as things would ever go.

Sometimes girls would pretend to be interested in him, but it always turned out to be a prank. He thought his heart might break if Julie did that to him, so he avoided her whenever possible.

He finally dared a second glance. The other two girls were staring at Julie, looking shocked that their friend would stoop so low as to talk to Zachary Wright. He hung his head once more, as if studying his half-eaten sandwich.

"We're not friends anymore," he finally mumbled.

"Because of what happened yesterday?"

He winced. Of course she knew about it. Everyone probably knew about it by now, even the kids who weren't in the lunchroom at the time. Heck, the whole town probably knew about it by now.

"Yeah, because of what happened yesterday."

"I'm sorry," she said, and he thought she probably meant it, but couldn't think of how to respond.

Mercifully, the bell rang, and it was off to science class. Just two more classes after that one and school was done for the week. Then he could get home and try to figure out how to make his Commodore 64 connect to 2027 again.

He'd turned his computer on and off while connected to CompuServe at least a dozen times now, but it was still stuck in 1985. He was putting off the inevitable, he knew, but he also knew it was incredibly dangerous, and he wasn't exactly ready to die, at least not before he read whatever Future Zachary had been about to tell him yesterday afternoon.

It had been something about Eric, but what? Eric had already betrayed him and joined with his enemies, so what else could possibly go wrong? If he and Eric got into a fight, Zachary was pretty sure he could take his former best friend, even though he hadn't been in an actual fight since 5th grade. So what was it?

It was now or never. Zachary stood up from his computer and followed the cord that connected it to the wall, knelt beside it, and slowly wiggled the plug maybe a quarter of the way out of the socket. Not enough to depower the C64, just enough to expose the plug. This was either going to work or he was going to electrocute himself and destroy his computer.

He'd searched the garage earlier and found items he thought could help him create a power surge: an old car battery, a set of jumper cables, a flat-head screwdriver, and a pair of rubber gloves.

Slipping on the gloves, hoping they'd protect him from the electrical shock that he was sure would come, he carefully connected the jumper cables to the battery. He hoped the thing still had at least a little juice. He attached the other end of the cables to the screwdriver. Everything was ready.

Thinking only of Future Zachary and Facebook, Zachary touched the screwdriver to the exposed plug and…

October 3rd, 2027

Zachary Wright stared at his laptop, willing his younger self to come back. What happened? He was there one moment and gone the next. And then he figured it out. That's when Bobby had come home and reamed him out for cutting school. It had all been so long ago and he had blocked out so much of what happened from his memories, but it was slowly coming back to him.

He was 57 years old, soon to be 58. He lived in a shitty little apartment in Joplin, where he worked for Wal-Mart as a janitor. He'd never been married, and drank himself to sleep almost every night, just like his father had done before he died. He had Type 2 Diabetes and lately had been having problems with his liver and kidneys.

Zachary didn't have any friends to speak of and only a few acquaintances. He'd never let himself get close to anyone ever again, not after what happened with his best friend Eric in high school.

At first, he'd thought Mr. 72689,598 was a troll or a catfisher, or something else equally scammy, but then he'd remembered that number. That had been his CompuServe ID number all those years ago. When he asked him about seeing Miss Lang's left boob, he knew he really was talking to himself.

He had no idea whatsoever how this connection between the present and the past had been forged, and half thought himself lying in a coma somewhere, dreaming all of this. Maybe he'd finally shot himself in the brain, like he'd been working up the courage to do for as long as he could remember, but fucked that up, too.

Life had gotten even worse after Eric died. All the kids blamed him for Eric's death, and he blamed himself, as well. He ended up dropping out of school and getting his GED, and eventually he moved away to live with his aunt Sue in Hannibal, Missouri.

He checked his 7-year-old laptop again. Damn it. Where had Zachary gone? And then he saw words appear and knew what he had to do.

October 4ᵗʰ, 1985

72689,598: *Are you still there?*

Zachary: *I am! What happened?*

72689,598: *I'm sorry I disappeared yesterday. I got in trouble with Bobby and had to do chores, and then we lost power. I thought I'd lost this connection for good, but I managed to get it back.*

Zachary: *What do you mean, yesterday? You've only been gone for about ten minutes.*

72689,598: *That's weird. It's been a little over a day for me.*

Zachary: *What's the date?*

72689,598: *October 4, 1985. It's Friday.*

Zachary: *Oh fuck! Listen, you need to get to Eric's house as fast as you can.*

72689,598: *Why? So he can call me names again?*

Zachary: *He didn't want Farley to hit you. He thought if he joined in the teasing, they'd stop. And they did, didn't they? He never meant any of that, never meant to hurt you. You were the only friend he had. He explained all of that in the note he left.*

72689,598: *What note?*

Zachary: *He left a note after he…did what he did. He really was trying to save you. Save us.*

72689,598: *If that's true, why didn't he just tell me that?*

Zachary: *He tried! He tried twice that day, but we wouldn't listen. We pushed him into a locker and that's the last time we ever saw him.*

72689,598: *What do you mean? Did he move?*

Zachary: *No, he didn't move. He killed himself!*

72689,598: *But why? This doesn't make any sense.*

Zachary: *Because of us, that's why. He left a note saying he was sorry for making fun of you, that you were his only friend, and he'd let you down and didn't deserve to live.*

Zachary stared at the television screen, not comprehending. Why would Eric kill himself over their friendship? But then he remembered Eric had a bitch for a mother and an asshole for a father, his older brother picked on him nonstop, and he was bullied in school just as much as Zachary was. All of that was the real reason they bonded. Their love of comic books was just a bonus.

He'd been so wrapped up in his own problems that he'd forgotten all about Eric's. He and Eric had been there for each other since they first met in third grade, but now Zachary had abandoned him without even letting him explain why he'd done what he'd done.

72689,598: *When does he kill himself?*

Zachary: *I don't know. He might have done it already.*

72689,598: *What do you mean, you don't know? How can you not know?*

Zachary: *They found his body out by the lake, in a little wooded area by the dam. He hung himself from a tree. His parents didn't report him missing for two days, and then it took another day for the police to find him. They said he probably killed himself on October 4ᵗʰ…which is your today. You have to stop it, Zachary.*

72689,598: *But how? This is my fault. My fault!*

Zachary: *Talk to him. Forgive him. Forgive yourself. Tell him you love him. You can do this. You have to do this.*

It was almost six, and if he had any chance at all of stopping Eric, he had to move fast. He ran down the stairs and into the living room, where his mother and Bobby were watching a rerun of *Knight Rider*.

"Mom, I need you to take me to the lake," said Zachary.

He'd decided against going to Eric's house, because he didn't want to miss him. If he could get to the lake before Eric did, he could stop him from killing himself.

"Not this late, you don't," said Bobby before his mother could even speak. "Besides, what's at the lake?"

"Eric is at the lake."

"That friend of yours?" asked Bobby. "You'll see him on Monday at school, as long as you don't skip again."

Zachary sighed, took a deep breath, and said, "My best friend is about to kill himself. I need to get to the lake."

Both his mother and Bobby stared at him. Finally, his mother asked, "Why would he do that?"

"It doesn't fucking matter why, I have to stop it!"

"Okay, that's it," said Bobby, rising from the couch where he sat with Zachary's mom. "Apologize for speaking to your mother that way and then get your ass up to your room, or you'll wish you had."

"Bobby—"

"No, Carol. We've let him get away with this kind of shit for far too long, and now he's making up stories."

Zachary didn't have time for this. He spun on his heels, ran into the kitchen, and pulled his mother's keys off the hook beside the door. He would drive himself if he had to, license or not. He was through the door and almost to the car when a hand grabbed his shoulder.

"Give me those keys, Zachary," Bobby said, anger in his eyes.

"Look, I know you don't believe me, but Eric is going to kill himself. I know your father killed himself, which is probably why you're such a miserable asshole. Now leave me alone!"

Bobby clenched his fists and for a second Zachary thought he might hit him, but a moment later he unclenched his fists and asked, "How did you know about that?"

"I overheard you and Mom talking one night," he said, lying. "I'm sorry he did that, I really am. But if I don't get there in time, Eric is going to kill himself, too. Let me go."

Bobby took a deep breath, and then another, before saying, "I can't let you—"

"I can't believe this shit!" shouted Zachary. "My best friend is going to die, all because you won't—"

"You didn't let me finish. I was going to say, I can't let you go alone. We'll take my car, Zachary. It's faster. Now, let's go!"

It took them less than five minutes to get across town, drive down North County Road 1820, and to the Carthage Lake dam. There were two light poles there, one on either side of the road, but one was burned out and it was difficult to see.

"Take this," said Bobby, pulling a red flashlight out of the glovebox of his 1979 powder blue Ford Mustang.

"Okay," Zachary said, grabbing the flashlight as he climbed out of the car.

"I'll search the south part of the woods, and you go north. If you find him, yell."

"Got it."

"And be careful."

"Bobby," Zachary said, "thank you."

Bobby nodded once, then turned and disappeared into the trees.

Zachary took off running past the dam and into the north side of the woods. Future Zachary hadn't seemed to know exactly where they found Eric, or even when he died, and he prayed he wasn't too late.

He heard a noise deeper into the woods. Pushing past a tall black oak tree, he broke into a clearing and there was Eric, trying to throw a rope over the branches of another huge oak tree just a few yards from where he now stood.

"Eric!" yelled Zachary, skidding to a halt beside his startled friend.

Eric jumped, quickly turning around. "Zachary? What are you doing here?"

"Trying to stop you from hurting yourself."

"But...I thought you hated me. You told me to fuck off and die."

Zachary blanched. He remembered saying the words to Eric, but even as angry as he'd been, he hadn't really meant them. He could never mean them.

"I'm so sorry," Zachary said, voice shaking. "I know you were just trying to help me. I never should have said those things to you. You're my best friend, Eric. I'd never, ever want you dead. Never."

Eric stared at him. "You're all I have, man. I just…I screwed up. I'm sorry."

Zachary took the rope from Eric's hands, threw it to the ground, and pulled his best friend into a hug. They'd never hugged before—straight boys didn't hug, all the kids said—but it felt good, it felt right. Eric was his best friend, the brother he never had, and he loved him. Fuck what the other kids thought.

"You saved me from getting my ass kicked by Kurt Farley," he said, feeling tears trailing down his cheeks. "Who could ask for a better friend than that?"

Zachary called out to Bobby a few minutes later, and his stepfather was beside him in under a minute. He smiled and squeezed Zachary's shoulder, and for the first time ever Zachary felt like maybe Bobby could fit into his life, after all.

Bobby drove them back to Zachary's house, and Eric spent the night. He called his parents to let them know where he was, but they hadn't even missed him.

Zachary told Eric all about Future Zachary, though he never once said the word "suicide." Eric knew that he knew, but there was no point in mentioning it. Eric ripped up and burned the suicide note he'd written. Hopefully, he would never again consider such a rash and permanent solution, but if he did, Zachary would be there to talk him out of it.

He booted up his C64 (amazingly, it still worked) and logged into CompuServe, but of course the connection to the mysterious service known as Facebook had been severed. It had served its purpose, after all. Just as he was about to log off, however, he noticed someone had sent him a letter. He never had letters in CompuServe.

He opened the letter and began to read:

Dear me,

Not sure if you'll get this, but it's worth a try. I hope you saved Eric. If you did, I suspect I'll cease to exist and will be replaced by a new and better me. In other words, you.

Anyway, one last thing I wanted to tell you. I went to my 20th high school reunion, even though I ended up not graduating in Carthage. Julie Moss was there, though she was now Julie Howard. She had a crush on me back in the day, she said. Who knew? She was always hoping I'd ask her out, but of course I never did. She thought I didn't even like her. Talk about missed opportunities. For me, maybe, but not for you, huh? Do with this knowledge what you will.

Some advice, from an old man:

Do good, whenever possible.

Live your life on your own terms.

Forgive yourself and forgive others.

Don't be afraid to tell people how you feel.

Be the person I wasn't able to be.

Ask the Gordons about Trixie.

Stay away from alcohol. It was your birth father's undoing, and it could be yours, too.

Love,

Me

Zachary closed the letter and ended his session on CompuServe. He smiled, thinking about Julie and her beautiful green eyes. Julie, the girl who'd always been nothing but sweet to him. He'd always been terrified to talk to her, but now...

If he could change Eric's fate, maybe he could change himself, too. Maybe he could do his homework, exercise more, and stand up to bullies rather than running away from them.

Tomorrow, first thing, he would walk over to Mr. and Mrs. Gordon's house and ask about his missing cat, and then Monday maybe he could ask Julie out on a date.

The future wasn't set in stone, after all. The possibilities were endless.

October 3rd, 2027

Zachary Wright closed his laptop. He'd just sent the message to himself that he remembered reading all those years ago, the message that would give him hope for a better life.

He'd rented a room at a hotel in Joplin, Missouri, a place he'd never actually been before in this version of his life. It was storming outside, just like Future Zachary had told him it was all those years ago. He had to get things exactly right.

It had worked, too. Eric was still alive, and the two were still best friends. They both lived in Chicago now and saw each other nearly every day and their families even vacationed together.

He still remembered Trixie, and how happy he'd been to find that the Gordons had taken her in. They hadn't realized Trixie was his cat, they said, and offered to give her back, but he wanted her to have a home where she could be a permanent inside cat, so he'd let them keep her. He had visited her every day, until he went off to college, and even then, he spent time hanging out with the Gordons and Trixie on the weekends.

And Julie, his beautiful Julie. He'd asked her out the Monday after Eric's near suicide attempt and to his surprise she said yes, ignoring the laughter of her girlfriends. They'd dated throughout high school, broken up over something stupid just before college, and got back together during their sophomore year at Western Illinois University in Macomb.

They'd been together ever since. They married a year after graduating college, her with a degree in history and him with a degree in creative writing. Eric had been his best man at the wedding. Two years later, Julie gave birth to their son Robert. They'd named him after his stepdad Bobby, who his mother hadn't dumped, after all.

He and Bobby had gotten close after they'd saved Eric's life, and Zachary finally had a father again, a better father than his own biological father had ever been. Bobby seemed to find a redemption of sorts in helping to save Eric's life when he couldn't save his own father's life, and that helped make him a better man.

They'd been there for each other when Zachary's mother died from breast cancer ten years ago, and he and Julie still drove to Carthage twice a year to visit him. Bobby doted on Robert and Robert's sister Rachel, who had been born just three years after Robert.

Robert was married now and had a child of his own on the way. Zachary couldn't wait to meet his grandson and introduce him to Bobby, Eric, and everyone else who mattered in his and Julie's lives.

For a while, the further he got from the events of October 1985, he almost thought he dreamed everything and had maybe even written that letter to himself. When he read about a little website called Amazon that sold books, however, something Future Zachary had mentioned briefly in their initial conversation, he knew for certain it was all true.

That night, Zachary told Julie everything about his experiences with Future Zachary and Eric's close brush with death. She believed him but was a little annoyed that he hadn't told her sooner. When he told her what he had planned for the future, however, she forgave him.

When Amazon went public in 1997, they were ready. They'd been saving their pennies since he first read about Amazon, and he invested heavily in the initial public offering of $18 a share. The worth of the stock quickly ballooned, and today it was worth nearly $3,000 a share.

He'd been writing comic books for Image then, but in 2002 he quit and started his own comic book company, Anomaly Studios, and Eric, who'd turned out to be an amazing comic book artist, joined him as an equal partner in the company.

When Google went public in 2004, they sold half of the remaining shares they had in Amazon and bought 2,000 shares of Google. Today, the shares were worth $2,600 each, and his and Julie's net worth was around $10 million.

When Council Tree Productions approached them to pitch turning some of their comics into TV shows, they were more than ready. They'd written three long running series so far, including the hit sci-fi drama *The Mandela Effect*.

For her part, Julie had gone back to college and earned a master's degree in history as well as a teaching license and currently taught history at Harry S Truman Community College. She made sure to never change clothes in the classroom.

He'd never forgotten what Future Zachary wrote in the note. Do good, whenever possible. Forgive others, forgive yourself, be honest with people, live your life on your own terms, and stay away from alcohol. He'd made mistakes along the way, to be sure, and hadn't always followed those tenets, but he did make sure to stay away from alcohol.

Even though the digital note was long gone, lost in the dust that was once CompuServe, he'd managed to print it out on a dot matrix printer in 1987. He'd copied it word for word when sending his younger self the message.

He'd done his best to live life according to the first item on Future Zachary's advice list: Do good, whenever possible. To that end, Zachary and his company supported a multitude of charities, and had created Alternate Life, a non-profit company that provided, among other things, a suicide prevention hotline, online and in-person courses, and free psychiatric and therapeutic care and medicine to those who needed it, no questions asked.

It was the least he could do.

He stood up from the hotel bed, slipped the yellowing and brittle note into the file folder where he usually kept it, grabbed his suitcase, and headed out the door to check out of the hotel.

It was time to go home to Julie.

It was a good life.

What If

Sarah Patton wasn't a stupid woman. She didn't believe in magic or miracles, psychics or premonitions, but something was happening to her that she didn't understand.

She was standing in line behind three other people inside a Value-Mart when it happened. She wasn't in any great hurry but waiting for her turn to check out was so boring that she started to daydream. *What if,* she thought, *that tiny old woman with the 50-pound bag of dog food dropped the bag and it split open, covering the floor in Purina kibble?*

It was such an absurd thought, the product of a bored mind, and she never expected it to actually happen—never really even wanted it to happen—but happen it did. All over the floor.

"I'm sorry, I'm so sorry," said the woman, as she watched the dog food go everywhere.

"Well, shit," said the man between them, as he angrily pulled his cart out of line and went in search of another cashier.

Sarah stared at the chaos, shaking her head, eyes wide.

"I'm so sorry," said the woman, staring at the dog food.

"It's okay," Sarah said.

"Clean up on register 3," said the cashier into her phone. Then, to the woman, "Don't worry about it. Things happen."

A few minutes later, two men with brooms and dustpans showed up and began to clean the floor. By that time, Sarah was in the line next to the line with the spill, watching as they cleaned up the mess.

It was so weird. One moment she was imagining the dog food bag splitting open, and the next it did just that. She shook her head. If she had magical powers to make things happen, she sure wouldn't waste them pranking some poor lady's dog food.

"Ma'am, there are other people in line," said the cashier, a sour-looking man of maybe fifty.

"Oh, sorry," she said, realizing he was waiting for her to put her purchase on the conveyer belt thingy.

One by one, she removed the items from her cart. It was mostly frozen food, some fresh produce, a new hairbrush, a catnip mouse for Charlie, two cases of Dasani 16-ounce bottles of water, and a bottle of smart water bearing an image of a butterfly in the middle of an orange and yellow infinity symbol.

"Ma'am, this is 15 items or less," the cashier said, "and you have 16 items."

"Do I?" She counted everything. He was right. She had sixteen items. "I'm so sorry. Several are duplicates, I thought it was individual items."

"Well, it's not."

She stared at him. "Should I go to another lane?"

He sighed before saying, "No, it's okay. Just be more careful next time, will you?"

She smiled her best smile. "Sir, I promise, I'll do my very best."

"Sarcastic bitch," he mumbled under his breath.

Well, screw you, too, she thought, as she pulled a $50 bill out of her purse. $47.96. Groceries were so expensive these days.

What if he accidentally gives her too much change, and then gets fired when his cash drawer isn't correct at the end of the night? A silly, vindictive thought, to be sure, but she didn't exactly deserve to be called a bitch, either. Plus, money is tight these days.

"$52.04 is your change," he said, handing her the fifty back, in addition to two one-dollar bills and four pennies. "Thanks for shopping at Value-Mart, have a nice day."

She stared at the money in her hand. He must have gotten confused and mistook the fifty for a hundred.

"Oh, come on," said the shopper behind her.

Sarah felt the world began to close in around her. She stuffed the money in her purse, grabbed her bags, and hurriedly left the store. Outside, she took several deep breaths, finally allowing herself to calm down.

Had she somehow become psychic and could sense things before they happened? She thought about that as she walked to her car, an old Chrysler Pacifica minivan.

She concentrated, trying to sense what song would be playing on the radio when she turned on the van. Tom Petty, she decided. Maybe *I won't Back Down* or *Free Fallin'*. But it wasn't either of those songs, it was a song called *Human*, by someone named Dodie, at least according to the readout on her SiriusXM radio.

"Well, so much for that," mumbled Sarah to herself, as she drove out of the parking lot.

She wasn't looking forward to going home. The kids would get out of school in just a couple of hours, and Brad would be home from work just two hours after that. She loved her family, she truly did, but, between them and her job at the hospital, she rarely if ever got any alone time.

Plus, Brad had been an absolute jerk lately. He'd been passed over for another promotion and had been taking out his disappointment by being grumpy with her and the kids. She hated to admit it, but sometimes she wished she'd pursued her dream of acting. Maybe she would have met some charming, hunky actor like Chris Evans or Pedro Pascal, fallen in love, and lived happily ever after.

Instead, she wound up never leaving Arkansas, married a man who complained about everything, and gave birth to two kids who took her for granted, avoided doing their homework whenever possible, and constantly hogged the Xbox.

She pulled into her driveway, unloaded the groceries, and beelined her way inside. Just an hour before the kids got home. If she hurried, she could take a nice, relaxing bath, all by her lonesome.

"Hey, Charlie," she said, pausing putting away the groceries long enough to pet the pretty Siamese cat who twirled his way between her ankles.

He purred. At least she'd always have Charlie.

Sarah closed the door behind her, turned a bubble bath, and stripped out of her nurse uniform. "Alexa," she said to the Amazon Echo sitting on her sink, "shuffle my favorite songs."

She dipped a toe into the bathwater as Amy Shark sang about unrequited love in her song *Everybody Rise*. Perfection; both the temperature of the water and the song. She slowly lowered herself into the bath, enjoying the heat as it enveloped her.

She glanced at the clock after the song changed to *Victoria's Secret* by Jax. She had 40 more minutes before the kids got home. She took a deep breath, held it, and let it out, letting her mind wander as the music played in the background.

Her thoughts flitted back to Chris Evans as she allowed herself to close her eyes. *Wouldn't it be funny if my life was a dream*, she thought, *and I was really married to Chris Evans all along?*

Somewhere in the distance, she heard ringing. She tried to ignore it, but it seemed to get louder. She opened her eyes. *Shit.* She'd fallen asleep, and the kids would be home in less than ten minutes. Worse yet, her phone was ringing. No one ever called her unless they were trying to get her to cover someone's shift at the hospital or sell her something.

Sighing, she forced herself out of the tub, wrapped a fluffy orange towel around her body, and padded into the bedroom. She picked up her phone. The call wasn't from the hospital, however. It was from a 323 area code, a number she didn't recognize. Probably a bill collector, and they'd left a message to boot. She thumbed the voicemail button and held the phone up to her ear.

"Hey, Sarah, this is Marty," said an unfamiliar voice through the cellphone. "Colbert wants you on his show again. Gimme a call when you can."

Sarah stared at the phone. What show, and who in the hell was Marty? And Colbert...Stephen Colbert, host of *The Late Show* on CBS? Was she still asleep and dreaming? She pinched herself but didn't wake up.

But she *was* dreaming, wasn't she? She realized the entire bedroom was different. It was twice as large as her real bedroom, for one thing, and had a huge widescreen television hanging from the wall for another. There were other differences, too.

The door to the bedroom opened and she let out a little yelp. Did school let out early? She blinked as Chris Evans walked into the room, unable to believe her eyes.

"Sorry, babe, didn't mean to startle you."

She stared at him. It was Chris Evans. In her bedroom. In Arkansas. Okay, she was definitely still asleep and dreaming.

"That's okay," she said, walking over to him as she let the towel slip from her naked form. May as well enjoy the dream while she could. "Make it up to me?"

She kissed him, long and hard, and when they finally came up for air, he said, "I thought you'd never ask."

Sarah opened her eyes, grinning to herself. That had been an amazing dream, three times over. Chris Evans, in her bed. Who could ask for anything more?

She glanced at the clock on her bedside table. It was 6:17. Shit. The kids were definitely home now, as was Brad. Why hadn't anyone woken her? She needed to get supper started.

"Getting up?" said a voice beside her.

She startled, turning towards the voice. "What?"

Chris Evans smiled at her, sleep in his eyes. "I said, are you getting up? I thought we might order in tonight. Maybe pizza?"

She stared into his deep blue eyes. She must still be dreaming. That was the only explanation. "Umm, sure."

"Are you okay?" he asked, holding his hand up to her cheek.

"You wore me out," she said, laughing. "It isn't every day you get to have sex with Chris Evans."

"We've been married for six years, silly," he said. "You can have sex with 'Chris Evans' whenever you want, just like I get to have sex with Sarah Goodrich-Evans."

Sarah sat in the bathroom, trying to stave off a panic attack. According to Chris (who seemed like he was just a hair away from having her committed) they'd met ten years ago on the set of one of the Avengers movies, where she, instead of Scarlett Johansson, had played the role of Black Widow.

They'd fallen in love three years later, during the filming of the second Avengers film, and married that same year. She'd lived in Hollywood since her first big break, at the tender age of 22, when she won the role of December on the popular sci-fi drama *The Mandela Effect*.

She'd never met Brad while working as a barista at Bliss Café, never had kids, never gone to college, never got a nursing degree, and never even adopted Charlie. Was she going insane? Sure, she'd gotten to have sex with Chris Evans, but never in a million years would she give up her kids, her husband, or even her cat for her celebrity free pass crush.

Sometimes fantasies were meant to stay fantasies.

She thought back to when all this started, when the dog food split open and covered the floor at Value-Mart. She'd thought it a strange coincidence that she'd had that exact thought just seconds before, but what if it were more than that?

"Honey," came Chris's voice through the door. "Are you all right?"

"I'm okay," she replied, "just a weird dream, that's all. I'll be out in a few minutes."

There was a pause. "All right, if you say so. I still think we should call the doctor, though."

"Just let me finish going to the bathroom."

She wasn't going crazy. She had married Brad Patton right after graduating college. They'd had twins Martina and Matthew two years after that and adopted Charlie from the local animal shelter just a few years ago.

She'd taken all of them for granted and essentially wished them away, but could she wish them back? Did she really want to?

What if my phone rang right now, she thought, as a sort of test, *and it was Brad?*

The phone rang. She answered it. It was Brad. He apologized, said he'd accidentally dialed the wrong number, and terminated the call. She recognized the caller ID number as his cellphone number, the one she'd memorized years ago.

"Sarah, it's been long enough. If you don't come out right now, I'm calling 911," said Chris, on the other side of the bathroom door.

What if Chris walked over to the bed, laid down, and fell asleep?

"Chris?" she asked. Nothing.

She left the bathroom to find Chris sound asleep in bed.

What if, what if, what if? There were just so many possibilities. She could keep this life of fame and fortune, could win an Oscar, write a book; the possibilities were endless.

But what was fame and fortune without Brad and the twins? What was an Oscar without Charlie? What was her life without all the memories she'd made over the years, the good and the bad ones, the happy and the sad ones?

Could she be happy married to Chris Evans while also being a big-time movie star in her own right? Of course, she could. It was hers for the taking. But…it felt hollow, somehow. She genuinely loved Brad, despite all his flaws, and he loved her despite all of hers. They'd built a family, a life. They'd given a cat in need a home.

A fantasy life with Chris Evans versus her real life with Brad. In the end, it wasn't even a contest.

This crazy magical ability she had somehow developed or been given was dangerous. What if she imagined an alien invasion, or a nuclear war, or, heaven forbid, zombies? Like everyone, countless strange thoughts flitted throughout her head every day. That didn't mean she wanted them to come true.

She made up her mind.

Kissing Chris Evans on the forehead, she said goodbye to him, to fame and fortune, to Stephen Colbert, to her Hollywood home, and everything that came with it.

She thought a lot about what she actually wanted in life, and then imagined herself back in the bathtub, waking up…

Sarah woke up in the bathtub. Her bathtub, not Sarah Goodrich-Evans' bathtub. She stood up, got dressed, and walked into her bedroom. There was no $10,000 television hanging on the wall, and her bedroom was more shabby chic than Hollywood elite, and that was okay with her.

"Sarah," said Brad, walking into the bedroom with wide eyes and a smile as big as the sun. "You'll never believe what just happened."

"Well, you're home early. Why don't you tell me about it?" she said, meeting his smile with one of her own.

She'd wished to be home, and she'd wished her power away. It was just too dangerous. However, she'd also made a few upgrades along the way.

Sarah followed Brad into the living room, listening as he told her about not only getting a promotion at work but also winning $647,000,000 on the multi-state Lotto. Would he stay with the job or retire? That was entirely up to Brad, and she was fine with whatever choice he made. She was pretty sure, however, that she was done with nursing. Maybe she'd join the local community theater. That might be fun.

That night, once Brad and the twins had finally gone to sleep, she looked for the little black book she'd imagined hidden inside an old cardboard box in the back of her closet right before she made her final "what if." The little book that would grant her carefully written out wishes, was indestructible, and would only work for her.

And there it was. It held exactly 100 pages, and she'd forbidden herself from ever using it to wish for more pages. Once she'd used up the 100 pages (both the front and back of the paper, so really it was 200 pages) that was it.

It was plenty.

After all, Sarah Patton wasn't a stupid woman.

Beautiful Monster

Happy Together, an old song by The Turtles, played on the Amazon Echo while Jack used a hacksaw to disassemble Miranda's body. It was ironic, he thought, because they had indeed been very happy together, for many long years, but that had all changed less than 24 hours ago.

Finally, he sawed through the ankle bone. That was a tough one. Jack tossed the foot into the Hefty black trash bag he had purposed for the task at hand and then began working on the other foot.

"Alexa, next," he said, and the 1960s playlist skipped ahead to the next song, *Yesterday* by The Beatles.

Yesterday, all their troubles seemed so far away…

Jack had been looking for something to watch on Netflix when the knocking started. He set the remote aside and, using his cane, levered himself up from the golden couch that occupied most of the west wall of the living room.

"I'm coming, I'm coming," he mumbled to no one in particular, as the knocking reverberated through the house.

At 77, Jack no longer walked as well as he used to walk, peed as well as he used to pee, or thought as clearly as he used to think. It'd been a good life, though, all things considered, so he wasn't complaining. He just wished people had a little more patience these days.

"Package delivery," yelled a woman's voice from the door.

"I'm coming," he repeated, a little louder now, as the knocking turned to pounding.

Package delivery? On a Sunday? He hadn't ordered anything, but maybe Miranda had. It seemed like she was always getting packages from Amazon: herbs and charms and whatnot.

"Alexa, what time is it?" he asked the device that sat on the coffee table.

"The time is 5:34 p.m.," the Amazon Echo responded.

Police sirens screamed in the distance, and they were getting closer. He wondered what was going on outside, then decided he probably didn't want to know.

"I have a package for you," the voice on the other side of the door called again. Though he could barely hear her over the sirens, she sounded almost frantic.

"All right," he said, finally reaching the door.

He unchained the door and pulled it open, and the next thing he knew he was lying flat on his back, staring up at the ceiling. His hips hurt, and his vision was blurry. He must have lost his glasses.

"Sorry about that, old man," said a male voice from somewhere, and then strong arms were surrounding him, hoisting him up from the floor.

"I don't think they're going to find us here," said a woman's voice, the package delivery girl, "but we can't take any chances."

"What's happening?" Jack asked, rubbing his head. "I can't see any-thing."

He was sitting on the couch now. Someone shoved his glasses onto his face, and he blinked, staring up into the dark blue eyes of a man some fifty years his junior. The man wore jeans and a ripped leather jacket. He had black hair, a jutting chin, and a small scar on his left cheek.

"Listen, grandpa," the man said, "I don't want to hurt you, but I will if I have to. Me and my lady here, we're in trouble, and we're gonna be needing whatever cash you have and your car. Okay?"

"Oh, my," said Jack, blinking. "I think I have maybe $50 in my wallet, and you can have that, but my wife has the car and won't be back for hours."

"Well, shit," said the woman, a tall redhead with porcelain skin who looked a little like Miranda had half a lifetime ago. "Want to try next door?"

"I guess we're gonna have to," the man said, pulling a gun out of his leather jacket, levelling it at Jack's head.

"Wait!" yelled Jack. "Please don't kill me."

"Give us one good reason why we shouldn't," asked the woman, looking down at him.

Where was his cane? If he only had his cane, maybe he could knock the gun out of the intruder's hand and call 911. He peered around the man but didn't see the cane anywhere.

"My bank card," he finally said. "I can get you money. We have nearly $5,000 in checking, and probably $25,000 in savings. With that, you could buy a brand-new car. Take my wallet."

He offered up his wallet with trembling fingers, and the woman snatched it away. She pocketed the cash and the debit card, then tossed the wallet onto the coffee table that sat before the couch.

"Brandon, with that money we could buy a car and—"

"Damn it, *Cassidy*, now he knows our names," Brandon said, interrupting her, "so we really do need to kill him now."

"I have a bad memory. I forget things easily. I won't tell."

"Besides which," Brandon continued, ignoring Jack and looking at Cassidy, "we could have all the money in the world, but we'd still need IDs to buy a car. Everyone's gonna be looking for us."

Cassidy ignored him, instead concentrating on some of the artwork that hung above the television. "What's this ugly ass thing?" she asked, pointing at a painting of Miranda.

"Who cares?" asked Brandon, before Jack could respond. "I'm gonna kill him, okay?"

"Yeah, that's fair," she said, shrugging her shoulders as she turned away from the painting. "Kill him."

"Wait! I lied. Miranda just went to the store. She'll be back in probably 30 minutes. You can have the money, the car, everything, just please don't kill me."

Cassidy looked at him with something like disgust. "Wow, old man. You know you just killed your wife, right?"

"No, you don't have to kill us. Just take the money and the car."

"Actually, we do," said Brandon, waving the gun in his direction. "But I'll tell you what. Tell me the PIN number for your card, and I promise to make it quick."

"You still have time to stop this. You don't have to become killers."

"Become killers?" asked Cassidy, laughing. "We're already killers. Why do you think they're after us? Now, what's the PIN?"

Jack rattled off a four-digit number.

"Good boy," said Cassidy, throwing him a kiss.

There! His cane was on the floor, over by the door. If he could just get to it… Oh, who was he fooling? They'd just kill him all the faster. Even fifteen years ago, that might have been a different story, but he was old, his body was failing, and before too long—

"Tell you what," said Brandon, interrupting his thoughts, "we'll kill you both together. That way, you'll get to say goodbye to your old lady. We're not monsters, after all."

Cassidy smiled at him. "You're so romantic."

"When we get out of this town, baby, we'll—"

Brandon stopped talking midsentence, and they all turned as one to stare at the front door as the knob turned. Miranda was home. Jack held his breath as the door swung inward, and in walked his beautiful Miranda, carrying a paper grocery bag from Whole Foods.

"We have company?" she asked, staring at the home invaders.

Miranda was 68 but still looked as beautiful as she had the day they met. Her red hair had long since turned to gray, but other than that she really hadn't changed that much.

"Sit down by your husband," Brandon commanded, waving the gun at her.

"Thanks to hubby here, you're gonna die," said Cassidy, stretching out the word die.

Jack winked at her, suppressing a grin.

"Oh, my dear Jackson, this is another fine mess you've gotten us into," she said, ignoring Brandon and Cassidy.

"Hey," said Cassidy, "he said sit down. I suggest you do what he says."

"Or what?" Miranda asked, moving her gaze to Cassidy. "You'll kill me? Aren't you going to do that anyway?"

"Yes, but—"

"But what?" Miranda interrupted.

"Hey! I can kill your old man now. Would you like that?" Brandon turned the gun towards Jack.

Miranda pointed at the gun, and it flew out of Brandon's hand, crashing into the grandfather clock that stood beside the couch.

Brandon's face turned white. "How—"

"What the fuck?" yelled Cassidy.

Miranda turned to Jack. "These two will do, I guess. It's probably about time, anyway, don't you think?"

"Past time, at least for me," Jack said.

"What're you talking about?" Cassidy asked, turning from Miranda to stare at Jack.

"You picked the wrong house," said Jack.

"Let's just get out of here," Brandon said, taking hold of Cassidy's hand. "We'll find another car."

Miranda laughed, a laugh that made Jack's heart soar. And then she changed, revealing her true form, the form Jack had fallen in love with all those many long years ago.

She stood nearly eight feet tall, had seven long tentacle arms, was covered in glowing pink and blue scales, and yet strangely resembled a giant cat. Jack had never seen anything so beautiful in his entire life.

Brandon and Cassidy were screaming then, backing up against the wall, begging for their lives. Miranda snaked out a tentacle, tenderly caressing Cassidy's cheek.

In an instant, Miranda was human again, just a 68-year-old woman. She let out a little "oh" and collapsed to the floor.

Brandon stared at her, closed his eyes, then opened them again. "It was all just an illusion, that's what it was. It had to be. She hypnotized us or something, and then the old bitch had a heart attack."

"Did she?" asked Cassidy, a smile slowly creeping over her lips. "Are you so sure?"

"What are you talking about? C'mon, let's just kill the old man and get out of here."

"Come here, my love," said Cassidy, gesturing to Jack.

Jack stood up, crossed the room, and took her hand.

"What the fuck?" said Brandon, staring at her like she was crazy.

"And now you," Cassidy said, grabbing Brandon by the wrist.

Brandon began to scream just as Jack slumped over. Everything went dark, and the next thing he knew he was staring at his own body from across the room.

"Are you okay?" asked Miranda, from inside Cassidy's body. "I wasn't expecting to do this today, but the Gods always provide."

"My wife, the beautiful monster," said Jack, from Brandon's lips. "It's been, what? Three thousand years? I'll never get used to that. But, yeah, I'm just fine."

Miranda smiled. "3,382 years since we first met, but who's counting?"

Jack laughed, reaching out to take his wife's hand. "And we've yet to take an innocent."

"And we never will."

"Wow. No more aches and pains. And…just wow. I feel good. I forgot what this feels like."

"All that energy, almost overflowing," said Miranda, a gleam in her eye.

"So much energy."

"Shall we adjourn to the bedroom, then?" Miranda asked, pulling him after her, not waiting for an answer. "Let's release a little of that 'energy.' We'll get rid of our old bodies in the morning and then figure out where we go from here. After all, we have plenty of—"

"Time," he finished for her, as they reached the bedroom door. "We have all the time in the world."

Jack followed her into the bedroom. He was looking forward to getting to know all the curves and crevices of Miranda's new body.

"Alexa," said Miranda, to the Amazon Echo they kept in the bedroom, "shuffle 1960s playlist."

Happy Together began to play as they tumbled into bed.

Forks

"When a fork appears in the road, how do you know which path to take? And when you finally do choose a direction, possibly at random, and another fork appears, how do you make that decision?" Adam Wheeler asked the audience of nearly 250 who sat before him. "How do you know which path leads to the most desirable result?"

Wheeler stood on a small stage in the private courtyard of Wheeler Dynamics, the technology company he'd spent the last thirty years building, surrounded by employees, investors, and a handful of reporters.

"Sure, there are educated guesses," he continued, enjoying the feel of the spring sun on his skin and the gentle breeze brushing against his graying hair, "but even the most educated of guesses can fall short. Should I have made a right instead of turning left? Should I have said yes instead of saying no? Should I have asked for that pretty girl's phone number?"

That line earned him a laugh from the crowd.

"Of course, most of those things are easily correctable. A 'no' can turn into a 'yes.' Three lefts can make a right. You can ask for the girl's phone number the next time you see her. But what about those mistakes that aren't so easily corrected? What about, for instance, the nuclear plant that exploded in Russellville, Arkansas in 2047, killing thousands of people, all because of an improperly installed circuit?"

Someone in the crowd gasped, and Wheeler smiled. A doctorate in physics, another in engineering, and countless hours spent finding investors, creating this company, and hiring only the best and brightest minds, all for this moment. He intended to put on a show they'd never forget.

"It's senseless tragedies like Russellville that Wheeler Dynamics wants to…circumvent," he continued. "Russellville already happened. Dr. Christina Stewart, one of the most brilliant physicists in our lifetime, died in the explosion. We can't change that tragedy…or can we?"

"Yes, ladies and gentlemen, we're talking about time travel," Wheeler finally said, smiling at the incredulous faces in the audience, "but not changing the past. That would be incredibly dangerous, and perhaps impossible. It might even create an alternate reality. We just don't know. But what if we could go back in time and secretly evacuate that nuclear power plant before the meltdown occurred? Bring all those lost souls forward in time, Dr. Stewart included, to the present, to continue their lives?"

His own tragedy happened when, at the age of five, he lost his parents and sister in a car accident in St. Louis. Sadly, there was no way to change that one, at least not without risking reality. He shook his head, doing his best to put thoughts of his dead family out of his mind.

"The timeline would still be intact, but without the loss of life. And while we've yet to send a human back in time, this isn't just hypothetical, my friends. We've done it! We've invented time travel. And what's more, we have proof. Alice?"

Alice Fletcher, Wheeler's long-time assistant, wheeled a gleaming metal machine the size of a small closet onto the stage. Connected to the machine was a monitor and a keyboard. She stood beside the contraption, awaiting further instructions.

"It may not look like much," Wheeler said, "but don't judge a book by its cover. It's what's inside that counts.

"Now, I need a volunteer from the audience, someone who isn't an employee of WD. Okay, you," Wheeler said, pointing towards a young woman with short blonde hair who raised her hand. "What's your name?"

"Hello, Dr. Wheeler. I'm Katie Flynn, from MSCNN News. If I volunteer, may I ask a question?"

Wheeler smiled. "After the demonstration, Ms. Flynn, you'll be the first reporter I call on. Fair enough?"

"Fair enough," she agreed, smiling, while a male reporter who stood beside her rolled his eyes.

"Wheeler Dynamics always rewards initiative," Wheeler said, gesturing for the young woman to come on stage.

"Okay, what do I do?"

"Give me a personal item, something small, one that is easily identifiable and indisputably yours."

She looked at him, a smile in her eyes, before removing the holographic press pass that hung around her neck.

"Will this do?"

"This will do quite nicely, Ms. Flynn, with one addition." He pulled a block of Post-It Notes from his pocket along with an ink pen. He peeled a sheet from the Post-Its, affixed it to Flynn's press pass, and handed her the pen. "Sign and date this, will you?"

She arched an eyebrow before doing as he requested. "Signed and dated, Mr. Wheeler."

Flynn tried to hand the press pass to Wheeler, but he refused. "I want you to be the one to place it into the machine, Ms. Flynn. Alice, if you will?"

Alice escorted the reporter to the machine she'd wheeled out just minutes earlier. She pressed a button on the contraption and a door whirred up into the body of the machine, revealing a 2'x2' opening. Inside the opening was a small metal box.

"Ms. Flynn," said Wheeler, walking over to stand beside her, "would you please remove the box?"

Flynn removed the box. She tried to open it, but it was locked.

"You'll need this," said Wheeler, producing a key, handing it to Flynn. "Why don't you show us what's inside?"

Flynn unlocked the metal box, peered inside, then presented the box to Wheeler and the audience. "It's empty."

"Quite right," he said. "Please put your press pass inside the box, lock it, and put the box back inside the machine."

She did so, and after tried to hand the key back to Wheeler. Just like he'd done with her press pass, he refused to accept it.

"Keep the key, Ms. Flynn. You'll need it later."

"Now what?" asked Flynn.

"You're about to find out," he said, walking over to the machine.

Wheeler typed a few commands into the keyboard, and the door holding the metal box closed. The machine began to hum. A few seconds later the hum vanished, the door slid open, and the box was gone.

"Where did it go?" Flynn asked, eyes wide.

"About twenty years into the past. Not only can we control what time the box travels to, we can also control where it goes. In this case, we've teleported the box about two feet beneath the ground."

"You know, my boss will kill me if I don't get that press pass back," Flynn said, generating a laugh from the crowd.

"Have no fear, Ms. Flynn, you'll get your press pass back, and the story of a lifetime to go with it. Did you notice a red chair in the audience?"

"Umm, no," she said, looking confused.

"Hey, I'm sitting on a red chair," said a man from the audience.

It was David Chester, one of the billionaires he hoped would invest in this project. His seating was no accident.

"So you are," said Wheeler, smiling. "Would you mind moving, Mr. Chester? Just for a moment?"

The billionaire looked confused but stood up as instructed. Two Wheeler Dynamics employees appeared from behind the stage, carrying shovels.

"These fine gentlemen are Joel Ransom and Gregory Dunn. They're about to help us make history."

Ransom removed the red chair, and the two began to dig. A few minutes later Ransom shouted, "Eureka!" just as Wheeler had instructed. Dunn reached into the hole they'd made and pulled out a small, rusted metal box, the very box Katie Flynn had placed in the time machine just five minutes earlier.

"Gregory, will you please bring the box on stage?"

"It would be my pleasure," Gregory said, making his way on stage to hand the box to Wheeler.

"It's locked," Wheeler said, before passing the box to Flynn.

"Ms. Flynn, would you do the honors?"

Flynn looked skeptical but inserted the key into the rusted box. She had to wiggle the key a few times, but the box opened.

"Oh, my," she said, eyes growing big as she stared down into the box.

She pulled out her press pass, the Post-it Note still attached. She held it up for everyone to see. The ink had faded a little, but the date and the name "Katie Flynn" was still very legible.

The crowd gasped and then began to applaud. Once the applause died down, Wheeler pointed at the hole in the ground and said, "Twenty-five years ago we picked out that spot and made sure it was never disturbed. All for this moment. I think it was worth it. Don't you?"

The crowd laughed and began to clap again, and Adam Wheeler knew he had changed the world.

All of that happened over twenty years ago. Wheeler, now in his late seventies, still remembered the on-air interview he had with Katie Flynn, and how not long after that his face was on every television station on the planet. He'd become famous overnight. He'd golfed with presidents, dined with kings and queens, and had become a billionaire several times over.

Eventually the hoopla settled down, and it was back to work. Progress was slow, and it took years before they could send anything back in time larger than that damned metal box. Finally, they cracked the size issue. Unfortunately, other problems proved harder to solve.

Adam Wheeler stood alone in the lab with the time machine, staring at the contraption he'd spent a lifetime creating. It'd come a long way since that demonstration, though it wasn't by any means perfect.

The first time they tried to send a living creature into the past—a turtle named Frank—it exploded. It was like someone had shoved a hand grenade into poor Frank's shell. It was quite a while before the lab smelled normal after that.

A year and a half later, they finally succeeded in sending a small dog back in time ten minutes. The dog developed a brain tumor the size of a golf ball and died three months later, but at least she'd lived for a time.

There were other issues as well. Try as they might, pinpointing the destination with a living creature was much more difficult than it was with an inanimate object. With Frank, they missed the mark by three miles and ten days. The dog, Sparky, had been more on target, but still not perfect.

They had yet to successfully send a human being back in time and had never succeeded in bringing anyone forward in time or sending anything to a future date. Despite that, he had few reservations about what he was about to do.

And why would he? The world had grown tired of Wheeler Dynamics and their time machine. According to a recent poll, 67% of Americans now thought sending Katie Flynn's press pass into the past had been an elaborate hoax. Investors pulled out of the company, and they were barely staying afloat. In fact, had he not poured nearly all his own money back into the company, they would have gone bankrupt years ago.

Truly, he had nothing left to lose.

"It's now or never," Wheeler whispered to himself, as he adjusted the time machine.

There! The coordinates were set. This was a one-way trip, and for a moment he felt some trepidation. He stepped into the time machine and prepared to press the button that would propel him into the past.

His hand shook as it hovered above the button, fear momentarily getting the best of him. This was the right decision, wasn't it?

Wheeler had lived a long, albeit lonely, life. He'd never married, never had children. Because he'd lost his entire family at such a young age, he couldn't bear the thought of ever again losing anyone else. He'd made sure never to let anyone into his life who he could possibly care about, much less love.

He thought back to that trip to St. Louis so very long ago that had ended in tragedy. Adam Wheeler and his father, mother, and sister were en route to Six flags when, according to police reports he'd later obtained, an old man darted out into the middle of the road. His father apparently swerved to avoid hitting him but hit him anyway, and the next thing Adam knew, he was waking up on the side of the road, beside the dying man, surrounded by paramedics.

After hitting the man, their Kia Sedona minivan had run straight into a truck hauling furniture destined for sale in various Wal-Marts across Missouri. The minivan didn't stand a chance.

Adam's father was killed instantly, said the medical report he'd eventually read years later, as was his ten-year-old sister Greer. Adam's mother wasn't so lucky. She'd lived until just a few minutes after the ambulance arrived, her brains slowly leaking out her left ear and onto the pavement on the side of the road.

Adam was thrown clear, somehow, a broken right arm and a bump on the head his only injuries. He didn't remember much else from that day, but he'd seen all the police reports. It wasn't pretty.

He remembered staring into the old man's eyes as he died. Oh, how he hated that man! Police had never identified him. He'd carried no ID, and his fingerprints matched none on record. Wheeler had wanted to find and somehow punish the man's family for what he'd done, and it always gnawed at him that he'd never even been able to find out the man's name.

He pulled himself out of his reverie, forcing his thoughts to the present. Adam knew this was a one-way trip, and that he'd probably die within a month of using the time machine. He'd also decided that dying from a brain tumor would be a small price to pay for saving his family. Besides, if this worked, there was a good chance he'd cease to exist anyway. It had never been about saving Dr. Stewart or any of the others who'd died throughout history, just his own family.

For years, he'd fooled himself into thinking otherwise. He'd even convinced himself that changing the past was dangerous, if not outright impossible. His conscious mind, however, had finally come around to what his subconsciousness had known all along. All his work, all the fund-raising, all the preparation…it all came down to this one moment, everything else be damned.

If it worked, he would never have invented time travel, and he'd have his family back.

Was he being selfish? Probably. But he didn't care.

He pushed the button and…

Adam Wheeler blinked. He was standing beside a road somewhere, and his head hurt like hell. And why was it so bright? He stared up at the sun, momentarily blinding himself. He blinked again, stumbling onto the pavement. Where was he?

He heard the screech of tires, and then pain, unbearable pain, as he was thrown to the side of the road. He watched with fading vision as the Kia Sedona minivan that had just hit him swerved to slam into a furniture truck, and a small body was thrown from the collision.

He met his own eyes for a moment, tried to speak, to tell himself how sorry he was, how he'd chosen the wrong fork. The words wouldn't come, and everything faded to black.

Identity Crisis

John Donavon awoke in a small, windowless room, unable to see. It felt like it was morning, though there was no way he could be sure. Time didn't have much meaning for him anymore. He clapped his hands, and the 20-watt light bulb hanging over his bed came to life, filling the sparse room with a yellowish light. It had taken him a good three or four hours to figure out the bulb was attached to a clapper, but by now he was almost used to it.

This room had been his life for nearly a week. The bed, the light bulb, a metal toilet in the corner, a sink beside it, and a door with a keypad that, no matter how many different number combinations he tried, wouldn't open.

The same thing, morning after morning, for six days. Only this morning, something was different. He was startled by a scratching noise coming from somewhere inside the wall to the right of his bed. This was new. He rolled out of bed and dropped to his knees beside the wall, pressing his ear to the sheetrock. The noise seemed to be getting louder. Scritch, scratch, scritch.

And then it stopped. He waited a moment, but nothing. Frustrated, he punched the wall, sending a jolt of pain through his knuckles.

"Shit!"

Cradling his throbbing hand, John slumped against the foot of the bed and began to cry. The last thing he remembered before waking up in this dark and lonely room was going into McNulty's, a little hipster bar on Walker Street, on a business trip to New York City. After that, it was all blank. Try as he might, he couldn't dredge up even a glimpse of what might have come after.

He was supposed to be gone for two nights, and it had been at least six, so surely his wife had reported him missing by now. He wondered for the thousandth, maybe millionth, time about his wife and daughter, what they were doing, what hell they were going through. Mackenzie was only six years old. Did she think her father had abandoned her? He couldn't stomach that thought. And Maureen. What did Maureen think?

They'd had problems last year, after he'd had a brief fling with someone at the office, but she'd forgiven him, and he'd vowed to make it up to her and had made good on his promise. He hadn't cheated since. But what if Maureen thought he'd run off with his new secretary or something? Would she even contact the police?

That thought terrified him. He got up and began to pace the room, something he'd been doing a lot of lately, as he felt the walls begin to close in on him. He was not going to die here. There had to be a way out of this and back to Maureen and Mackenzie, but how?

His captor came into his cell every night when John was sleeping and left a tray of food on the floor at the foot of his bed. It was always scrambled eggs, bacon, toast, and orange juice, and a two-liter bottle of water that would last him through the day, and this morning was no different. Every night, he fell asleep vowing to see his captor's face, but every morning woke up after he'd already come and gone.

He knelt to retrieve the tray, and there it was again. That noise coming from inside the wall. Ignoring the food, he dropped to his knees again and pressed his ear against the plaster, listening, immediately tumbling backwards as something hard and sharp bit into his cheek. He backed away from the wall, holding his face as blood ran between his fingers. He bit down on his lips, keeping inside the scream he felt fighting its way up his throat.

John's gaze fell back down to the wall, where he saw what looked like the tip of a flathead screwdriver disappearing, leaving a small hole in its wake. Dust floated from the hole to gather on the concrete floor of his cell.

"Hello?" said a tentative, female voice from the other side of the hole. "Is anyone there? Please tell me someone's there. Please."

He said nothing for a minute, afraid it was some cruel trick devised by his unknown captor. After all, the monster had toyed with him before. Just yesterday, he had left a wadded-up piece of paper on the floor that contained eight numbers that John had hoped were the combination for the lock that held him in his cell. It wasn't, of course. It was just another way to torture him, and it worked.

"Please, answer me, I know I heard someone there," pleaded the voice on the other side of the wall. "Please!"

"Hello," he finally answered, still pressing his hand against his cheek. "Who is this?"

"Thank God!" said the voice. "He told me I was all alone, but I had to hope."

"Who is this?" He repeated. "And why did you stab me with that screwdriver?"

"I'm…I'm so sorry, I didn't mean to hurt you! My name's Kenzie Graham. I've been locked in this room for a while now. Five or six days, I think. What's your name?"

The name "Kenzie" reminded him of his daughter, and he thought for a moment his heart might break. He swallowed, held his breath for a second, and bit back his despair. He debated revealing his name, then decided it didn't matter. His captor undoubtedly already knew his identity from his missing wallet.

"My name's John Donovan," he finally said. "Are you a prisoner, too?"

"Yes. I was kidnapped, John."

"How?"

"I met a guy on Matchstick, one of those Internet matchmaking sites, and we decided to meet in person at a bar, but he never showed. Some other guy offered to buy me a drink, and I stupidly accepted, and he must have roofied me. Next thing I know, I'm waking up here, in this room." Her words came out in a rush, tumbling hurriedly after one another, leaving her gasping for breath.

"What did he look like?" he asked automatically.

"He was tall, maybe six feet or so. Dark hair, maybe blue eyes. Lean. He was wearing a suit, I think. Everything from that night is still so fuzzy, and I can barely remember even talking to him before I woke up here."

He shivered. She could almost be describing him.

"Did he…did he do anything to you?"

"He didn't rape me, if that's what you're asking."

"What did he do?"

"He didn't hurt me at all," Kenzie whispered, "at least as far as I know. But I think he's going to kill me. Last night, he brought me up-stairs and handcuffed me to a chair and let me eat. It was the first food I'd had since that night in the bar. Before that, all he'd given me was water. It was almost like a final meal."

No food? If she wasn't being fed, why was he?

"How did you get the screwdriver?"

"He was about to bring me back downstairs when the phone rang. The screwdriver was on the kitchen counter, right by the door. He looked away for a second to answer the phone, and I didn't even think. I just grabbed it and shoved it down my shirt."

"Smart."

"I was so afraid he'd notice it missing and kill me, but that was prob-ably ten hours ago and I'm still alive."

"Does your room have a keypad in the door?"

"It does. Does yours?"

"It does. Have you tried prying it out of the wall? Maybe, I don't know—"

"First thing I tried," she said, cutting him off. "It's set really flat into the door. All I managed to do was scratch it up a lot, and I'm scared to death he'll notice."

"Maybe if you just keep digging through the wall."

She poked the screwdriver through the hole again, wiggling it, making the hole just a bit wider.

"It took me two hours just to make that tiny hole. I don't think we have enough time, and my hands ache so much. Fuck, John. Why did I ever go to that stupid bar?"

"What was the name of the bar?" he asked, suddenly sure he knew the answer.

"McNulty's. Why?"

"I was there, too," he whispered.

"What? I can't hear you."

"I was there, too. Six nights ago. That's where I was taken, I think. At McNulty's."

"Oh my God. That could have been the same night."

John almost didn't want to know, but he had to ask. "Was it Friday night?"

"Yes! Around nine at night. I was wearing—am still wearing—a yellow floral print skirt and a blue top. Do you remember seeing me?"

An image came unbidden to his mind, a beautiful young woman of maybe 25 wearing the clothing Kenzie had just described. She had long flowing hair that was dyed blue, and she carried a small purse. He remembered her smiling randomly in his direction as she entered the bar.

"What color is your hair?"

"Well, it's normally blonde, but right now it's—"

"Blue," he finished for her.

"You *did* see me!"

"I think so."

"What do you look like?"

"I'm 6'2" and have brown hair."

"What color are your eyes?" she asked, a hint of suspicion in her voice.

"Green," he said quickly. It was a lie. His eyes were blue, the same as her abductor's. He didn't want to scare her but immediately felt guilty for lying.

"Okay. What were you wearing?"

"Business clothes. I'd just gotten off work. But he took my clothes. The first morning I woke up here, there was a plain white t-shirt and a pair of blue jeans waiting for me at the foot of the bed."

"That's weird," she said.

"Yeah."

"What happened to you in the bar, John?"

"That's the thing. I don't remember. I only remember walking into the bar, sitting down to order a drink, and then nothing."

"Nothing at all," she asked, "besides seeing me?"

"Nothing at all," he agreed, "besides maybe seeing you."

"So, tell me about yourself, John. What's a nice guy like you doing in a place like this?"

He chuckled and heard her laugh in response and in just a few seconds they were both laughing, howling like there was no tomorrow. He laughed so hard he had tears in his eyes.

"Thanks," he said, once they'd both stopped laughing. "I think I needed that."

"What do you do for a living?"

"Pharmaceuticals. I'm director of sales at Serling MediCorp."

"Nice. So, you live in New York?"

"Ohio, actually. I was here on a business trip. What do you do?"

"I go to school. Getting my master's in art education. Oh, and I work at a Starbuck's. How lame is that?"

"It's not lame," he said. "You're working towards a better future."

"Not much of a future if we don't get out of here."

"We will."

"Are you married?" she asked.

"I am, with a daughter. You?"

She laughed. "Nope. Still haven't found Mr. Right."

"Don't worry, you will," he reassured her. "Eventually."

"Soooo," she said, stretching out the word, "how are we getting out of here, John?"

"I don't know."

"He had to have made a mistake. Something we can use against him. I've tried every number combination I can think of, and that damned keypad won't open, so—"

"Wait a minute," he said, remembering the discarded paper he'd found yesterday.

He'd torn the paper into tiny bits in anger, but he still remembered them. At least, he hoped he did. 12-04-00-27. He said the numbers out loud.

"Huh?"

"I found that number on a crumpled piece of paper in my cell yesterday. I tried it on the keypad, but it didn't work. Maybe it's for yours?"

"Say the numbers again," she said.

He repeated the numbers.

"That's my fucking birthday, John, and the last part is my age! December 4th, 2000. How do you know that? Are you working with him?"

"What? No!" he shouted. "It was on a piece of paper he dropped in my cell. Jesus Christ. Could it really be that simple?"

"What do you mean?"

"Enter the numbers in your keypad. 12-04-00-27."

He stood up, not waiting for an answer, and entered his own birthday and age into the keypad. The lock disengaged, and he opened the door. The area outside the room was pitch black.

"It worked," said Kenzie's voice, just a few feet away. "I can't believe it worked!"

"Shit. I just walked into a wall. I can't see."

"Follow my voice," she said. "Come to me and let's get the hell out of here."

He walked away from the door and through the darkness, nearly jumping when her hand found his in the darkness.

"John? Please, tell me that's you."

"It's me, Kenzie," he whispered.

She threw herself into his arms, hugging him so hard he could barely breathe.

"Thank goodness," she murmured, her voice quavering.

"Let's be quiet, now. Do you still have the screwdriver?"

"I do," she whispered. "Do you want it?"

"I do," he said, and she pressed it into his hand.

"Okay. The stairs are just a few feet from my room, I think. Here! I wish there were a fucking light switch somewhere. I don't want to clap."

"Let me go first," he whispered, maneuvering himself in front of her, as they began to climb the stairs.

There were ten steps in total, and John cringed at every footfall, at every squeak. Finally, they reached the top. The door was locked. He found the keyhole by touch and slipped the screwdriver inside, but it wouldn't budge. He hammered at the plastic end of the tool until his hands ached, but still nothing.

"I can't spring the lock, so I'm going to try to break the door," he whispered to Kenzie. "If anything happens to me, just get past me and run for help. Okay?"

"Okay, John," she whispered into his ear. "I'll get help and come back for you. Be careful."

He slammed his shoulder against the door, but it wouldn't budge. He hit it again and again, alternating shoulders, until finally it began to buckle. Though his arms were on fire, he kept crashing into the door until finally, mercifully, it splintered open. John fell through the doorway into a kitchen, landing on yellow linoleum, staring up into blessed light, light so bright it hurt his eyes.

Kenzie scrambled over him, tripped, landing on top of him. She looked down at him and their eyes locked, and that's when she started screaming.

"Be quiet! Jesus Christ. What's wrong?"

"Please don't kill me, please don't kill me," she yelled, scooting frantically away from him across the linoleum. "I'm sorry I took the screwdriver, okay?"

John stared at her blankly.

"Kenzie, I don't understand."

"This is all some sick and twisted game, isn't it? God, I'm so stupid!"

"Stop screaming!" he yelled, feeling awful as she shrank away from him. "Kenzie, I'm not going to hurt you."

"It was you in the bar that night," she whispered, her hand over her mouth. "I am so fucking stupid."

"What do you mean? Do you remember seeing me in the bar?"

"You bought me a drink, and when I told you my name, you said it reminded you of your daughter."

John's heart caught in his throat. "I…I did not. It wasn't me, Kenzie. I swear to God, it wasn't me." But how did she know his daughter was named Mackenzie?

"We drank for a while, and then you asked me if I wanted to go back to your hotel with you," she whispered. "You didn't even bother taking off your wedding ring."

"I wouldn't!"

"You did! And stupid me, I said yes. I remember getting in your car. A red Nissan Maxima. A rental."

The kitchen spun before John, and he had to fight not to throw up. His rental was indeed a red Nissan Maxima. He felt the world closing in on him. He lurched to his feet, leaning against the large oak dining table that took up half the kitchen.

"The last thing I remember," she said, tears streaming down her cheeks, "is you leaning across the seat to kiss me."

"Kenzie, I swear to God, it wasn't me. It couldn't have been me."

"Then who was it?" she demanded, staring at him so hard that he had to look away.

"I…I don't know. But why would I lock you up? Why would I lock myself up?"

"To fuck with me! To give me hope before you murdered me. I poured my heart out to you down there, John, and it was all a game."

"No!"

"Yes," she said, hands on her hips.

He started to move towards her, and she backed away. "Are you going to kill me now?"

He looked down at the screwdriver in his hand and felt himself go numb. He opened his fingers, letting it clatter to the floor.

"It wasn't me. It couldn't have been me. Wouldn't I remember it?"

"What if…" she stared at him, falling silent.

"What? What if, what?"

"What if you have a split personality, and don't know you're doing these things?"

"That doesn't make any sense!"

"Doesn't it? Maybe that's why you lock yourself in that room at night."

That stuff only happened in the movies and in books, didn't it? Sure, he knew there were documented cases of people with multiple personalities, but something this extreme?

"Get out of here," he said, making a decision.

"What do you mean?"

"I mean, get out of here. Go! Run to the neighbors, whatever. Call the police. They can sort this out."

She edged away from him. "You're just going to let me go?"

"I didn't kidnap you! Now go!"

She stared at him for a moment before turning and darting through the door that led from the kitchen into another part of the house.

John looked around the kitchen, for the first time really taking it in. A stainless-steel refrigerator stood to the right, beside a glass top stove. A laptop computer sat in the middle of the kitchen table. It was just an ordinary kitchen, not the kitchen of a murderer. Then again, what does a murderer's kitchen look like?

Wordlessly, he sat down and opened the laptop. The screen brightened, and he was rewarded with a screen full of folders with various women's names on them, including one titled "Mackenzie Graham." Almost without thinking, he opened the folder. It contained seven photos. He clicked one at random, and it was Kenzie, asleep in bed. What the hell? He clicked on the next photo, and it was a passed-out Kenzie inside a car. Inside his rental. Her shirt was pulled up and her bra was pulled down, and a man's hand—please, dear Jesus, let it not be his hand—was fondling one of her breasts.

He backed out of the folder and found another, titled "Victoria Rogers," and opened it. There were seventeen photos in this one, all showing a dark-haired young woman either asleep or bound and gagged. John felt sick but continued to click on the photos.

"You sick son of a bitch!"

He jumped, nearly falling out of the chair. Kenzie stood above him, a pistol in her hand.

"Kenzie! Why are you still here?"

"The doors are all locked. I can't get out. But I found this." She waved the gun in his direction.

"Are you going to shoot me?"

"If you don't let me out of this house, I will."

He ignored her. "Look, it's his laptop."

"Don't you mean *your* laptop?"

"No, dammit. I didn't do this. I didn't do any of this!"

She circled around the table to stare at the screen. "Then what's that, John?"

He turned his attention back to the laptop. A man sat beside a dark-haired woman, his arm around her shoulder. Her eyes were open, but her throat was slit. She was dead, and the man sitting beside her was him. He screamed, flinging the laptop from the table, throwing himself backwards, tumbling out of the chair.

"Oh no, dear God, please, no," he screamed, scuttling across the linoleum.

"Is that what you were planning to do to me, John?"

"No! Oh Jesus, no, Kenzie. What's wrong with me?"

"The other you, John. Maybe he calls himself Jonathan or Johnny, or some other name entirely, I don't know. He doesn't like women. In fact, he hates women. He kills women."

"I don't remember that! I didn't do those things. I couldn't have done those things."

"You didn't, John, but *he* did," she said, walking towards him. "He kidnapped me, and he was going to rape and kill me. But guess what?"

He looked up into her eyes. "What?"

"You can save me. You can stop him."

"How?"

She knelt beside him and pressed the pistol into his hands.

He pushed himself backwards, only to feel the wall at his back. "I don't want that!"

"Stop him, John! Don't let him kill me. Don't let him hurt Maureen, or little Mackenzie. It's the only way."

Tears clouded his vision. "I'd never hurt Maureen, or my daughter."

"Just me?"

"No! I'd never hurt you. I'd never hurt anyone."

"Maybe *you* wouldn't, but *he* would. I'm your daughter, John, and he wants to hurt me. He wants to fuck me, and then kill me, and then fuck me all over again. Don't let him win."

His body trembling, he pressed the barrel of the pistol to his temple but couldn't bring himself to pull the trigger.

"I can't," he sobbed.

"Do it, John."

"I can't!"

"Do it for Mackenzie, before he finally gets what he wants and hurts her, too. Do it!"

"All right!"

"Do it now, John."

"Forgive me," he whispered, as he pulled the trigger.

***

Janie Saunders smiled, pulling the blue-haired wig from her head and shaking out her raven-black locks. It was using his daughter's name that did it, that finally pushed him over the edge. He was too far gone at that point to recognize that it was her in the "Victoria Rogers" folder wearing makeup to make it appear that her neck had been slit, or that his eyes were closed in the photo.

She pulled a small digital camera from her back pocket and snapped a photo of John Donovan's corpse, gun still clutched in his hand. One more trophy for her scrapbook.

He really had invited her back to his hotel after a few drinks, only he hadn't drugged her, she'd drugged him. Up until that point, he was going to live. She'd given him a chance.

Cheaters. What can ya do?

FORB1DD3N FRUIT

Gable Simmons carefully put on his brand new SecondChance bodysuit, preparing to interact with his wife Willow for the first time since her death. He always thought he'd be the one to go first, but at 71 he was still going strong while Willow, three years younger than him, had died a month earlier from pancreatic cancer.

Thankfully, SecondChance had just come online, and he'd been able to have her consciousness uploaded into their system. If she'd died even a week earlier, he would have lost her forever. He couldn't imagine how he'd feel if Willow had been taken from him for good.

He shook his head. It was silly to ponder such thoughts. He should just be happy that such an awful thing didn't happen and leave it at that. Willow would now live forever inside the virtual world and, when it was Gable's time to shake off that proverbial mortal coil, he'd happily join her.

"It says to put on the helmet, lie down, close your eyes, and let the machinery do its magic," said Gable's daughter Juniper, reading the instruction manual that came with the suit.

"Tell her we love her, Dad," chimed in Rowan, her twin sister, "and we miss her."

"And we'll see her soon," added Juniper, brushing her long black hair back out of her eyes as she continued to read the manual.

Gable promised he would relay their messages and told the girls he loved them. Slipping the sleek metallic helmet over his head, he laid back on the cot the technicians had installed in his home just a few hours ago. Closing his eyes, he prepared to enter the world of SecondChance to spend some time with the love of his life.

Gable blinked. He was standing inside the home he'd shared with Willow for nearly fifty years, exactly where he'd been before he donned the bodysuit. But one thing was different: his wonderful, amazingly beautiful Willow was there, lounging on the couch with a book in her hand, smiling up at him.

Something else was different as well. Willow had been 68 when she passed, but the woman before him was much, much younger.

"I look just like I did on our wedding day," she said, setting the book aside and rising from the couch to throw herself into his arms. "What do you think?"

That made perfect sense. He could picture her now, standing next to him on the altar in that beautiful, flowing white dress. That was one of the best days of his life.

"You were always beautiful no matter what age you were," he said, eyes filling with tears. "I've missed you so much, Will."

"How long has it been?" she asked, in a whisper. "I remember being in the hospital and then…nothing."

"You…passed 27 days ago. It's been awful. I didn't think I could survive it, but here we are. Thank goodness for SecondChance."

He pulled back to stare into her beautiful emerald eyes. She looked absolutely gorgeous, but she'd always been gorgeous to him, from the moment he'd first laid eyes on her during his senior year of college.

"Thank goodness for *you*," she said, kissing him. "The love of my life, my amazingly brilliant and handsome husband who wouldn't even let death separate us."

Gable laughed. "I'm not exactly handsome anymore, but I do appreciate the sentiment."

"I've always thought you were incredibly handsome no matter what, but you do know in here anything is possible, don't you? You just concentrate and, poof. You are whatever age you want to be, and you look however you want to look. That's the beauty of SecondChance, according to the speech the Wheeler Dynamics 'facilitator' gave me when I woke up here."

Gable looked down at his wrinkled, liver-spotted hands. He closed his eyes, concentrated, opened them, and the spots were gone. He walked over to the mirror they had put up beside the front door some thirty odd years ago and stared at himself. He was 25 again, with a full head of ginger hair and bright blue eyes. The transformation almost made his head spin.

"This is amazing," he said, walking back over to Willow. "I'll almost be sad to go back to my real body."

"You're not leaving yet, are you?" she asked, biting her lip. "We have some lost time to make up for, don't you think?"

"You're absolutely right," said Gable, pulling her close and kissing her deeply.

When the kiss finally ended, she said, "You were always such a great kisser. I hope I am as well."

"Oh, my darling, you're the best."

Gable and Willow lay in their king-sized bed, wrapped in each other's arms, spent. They'd made love three times, something they'd never been able to accomplish once he'd hit thirty-five. He felt like a new man, and with a start he realized he was. This version of him existed only within Wheeler Dynamics' SecondChance network.

"What're you thinking about?" she asked him, tracing the tip of her finger along his chest.

"You, what else? Us, our life together, this whole thing. It's amazing."

"Isn't it?" she said, snuggling closer. "Now we can be together again. And when you pass, which I hope isn't for many, many years, you can join me permanently in here."

"It's perfect," said Gable, gazing into her eyes. "Just perfect."

"And whenever we get hungry, there's unlimited food here. Whatever we want, we just stand in front of the stove and think about it, and voilà, we have it. No more cooking!"

"But it isn't real food, is it?"

"Define 'real,'" she said, with a lopsided smile. "It tastes real, and isn't that all that matters? I think, therefore I am, and all that jazz. The food in this house is as real as the house itself, or us for that matter."

He supposed that was true and slowly nodded his head in agreement. It would take him a little time to get used to this, having whatever he wanted at his fingertips.

"Something I've been wanting to ask…how did Juniper and Rowan handle my passing?"

He remembered how devastated the girls had been right after their mother died. It wasn't a good time, and he admitted as much.

"But they're so happy that they're going to get to see you again. SecondChance will install their units tomorrow, and I'm sure they'll be here right after that."

"That's great! I'll be so happy to see them. But for now, I think I've worked up an appetite. Want to try that illusionary food I told you about?"

Gable laughed. "Sure, why not?"

Willow stood up from the bed and stretched, and Gable felt that familiar feeling of love mixed with the lust she'd always brought out in him. He watched as she slipped into the clothes she'd been wearing before they so eagerly undressed each other.

"God, Willow. You really do look just like you looked the night we first made love."

She smiled. "I remember it like it was yesterday. I still can't believe we managed to wait until our wedding night."

Gable stared at her. What was she talking about? They'd had sex the third week they'd been dating, in her dorm room at the college. How could she have forgotten that?

And then he realized she was joking, making a reference to a little white lie she'd told their daughters when they were eight years old. Spurred on by something they'd seen on StreamVid, they surprised their mother by asking when she and their father had first "been intimate." Stunned and embarrassed, she'd quickly said, "on our wedding night, of course," and had never bothered to correct the lie.

"I almost forgot about that," he said, laughing.

She turned to him. "What do you mean?"

"That you told Juniper and Rowan that our 'first time' was on our wedding night."

"Well, wasn't it?"

She looked confused, and Gable's heart sank. How could she possibly not remember?

"We had sex in your room at college," Gable said, "right after we got back from that Chappell Roan concert. Your favorite song was 'Pink Pony Club.' When we got back to your room, you practically ripped off my clothes. You really don't remember?"

She stared at him for a second, her eyes going blank, and then a little smirk crossed her mouth, and she started laughing. "I got you. Of course I remember! That was one of the best nights of my life. It was amazing."

Gable smiled, laughing along with her, but inside he felt shaken. Willow had never been one for practical jokes, especially not about their history and their love for each other. Had something gone wrong with the transfer? He shook his head. The technology was new, but the technicians assured him everything had gone perfectly. Could they have been wrong?

Seemingly sensing his confusion, Willow walked up to him, said, "C'mere, you," and pulled him into a deep kiss. Before he knew it, they were in bed again, making love for the fourth time since her death, all thoughts of the technology having gone astray forgotten.

Gable lay in bed, lost in thought while Willow showered. Why did she need to shower in a virtual world? Why did she need to eat, for that matter? He supposed it helped perpetuate the illusion that she was still alive, which wasn't necessarily a bad thing.

There were already thousands of people within the digital walls of SecondChance, according to the press releases, and apparently you could visit other people who had passed within a community center of sorts. The idea of meeting people after death that you'd never met while alive both fascinated him and made him nervous.

He felt his stomach grumble. Enough philosophizing. He was getting hungry, and he doubted virtual food would do the trick. Gable wasn't sure how long he'd been within the walls of SecondChance, but it would probably be time to leave soon and check in with his daughters, not to mention eat some real food. But all of that could wait for a little while longer.

He got up to do a little exploring of this virtual version of the house he'd lived in for so long. Everything was more or less identical to his real home, though certainly tidier.

Walking into the living room, he noticed the book Willow had been reading when he'd first entered SecondChance still lying on the couch. It was *Replay* by Ken Grimwood, a fascinating tale about a man who lives his life over and over again. It had been Willow's favorite novel for as long as he could remember. She'd probably read it at least twenty times over the course of their long marriage, and he'd even read it a few times himself.

Picking up the book, Gable flipped to the start of the novel. He remembered the opening line as something like "Jeff Winston was talking to his wife when he died," but what he saw now was just gobbledygook, random lines of letters, numbers, and nonsense characters. He blinked, but the book remained unchanged.

X09W QR#^59@ 8632410 KF$ LVS)* P\@d S(S J!*3 63^X19JD!

"Reading my book, huh?" said Willow's voice from behind him, making him jump. "Oh, I'm sorry, I didn't mean to startle you."

"It's okay," he said, still staring at the book. "But I can't read this. It's just nonsense."

"What do you mean? I thought you liked *Replay*."

"I did. I mean, I do. It's a wonderful book, but I literally can't read this. It's like some weird computer code or something. Is this how all books look in here?"

She stared at him. "What are you talking about?"

"Here," he said, handing her the book. "Just look at it."

Willow took the book from his hands, flipped to the start of the novel, and read out loud, "'Jeff Winston was on the phone with his wife when he died. 'We need,' she said, and he never heard her say what they needed, because something heavy seemed to slam into his chest, crushing the breath out of him.'"

What the hell? He grabbed the book back from her, flipped to the opening line, and there it was, just as she'd read. The weird characters and symbols were gone, replaced by actual words.

"I don't understand," he said, as he let the book drop to the couch.

"Don't understand what?"

"Why the words looked so strange to me. It was just lines of nonsense the first time I looked at it, but now it's back to normal."

Willow stared at him, not saying a word.

"Willow?"

No answer.

"Willow!"

"Oh," she said, blinking. "Sorry. I was just trying to remember something the facilitator said. I think he mentioned how it might take human brains a moment or two to acclimate to this virtual world. That's probably what happened."

"Why didn't they tell me that? They didn't say anything about not being able to read."

Willow shrugged. "I don't know, my darling, but let's not worry about that for now."

She reached out to take his hand, pulled him close, kissing him deeply. Her kisses felt amazing, and before he knew it, she was pulling him back into the bedroom, hungrily nibbling on his neck.

Something wasn't right. It almost seemed like she was trying to distract him. He pulled away just as she lowered herself onto the bed.

"What?" she asked, hurt flashing across her face. "Don't you want me anymore?"

"You know I do. You're all I ever wanted, and it was so awful when you died. A few years after your death the girls tried to get me to date again, but—"

His mind was reeling. What was he talking about, a few years after her death? She'd been dead less than a month. He shook his head. What was going on? Did he have virtual reality induced dementia? Was that even a thing?

"But what?" Willow asked, looking up at him with those beautiful green eyes.

"I think something's wrong with me," he whispered.

"There's nothing wrong with you, Gable. You're just not used to this virtual life. The facilitator told me—"

"But why didn't they tell *me*?" he asked, interrupting her.

She had no answer, and instead reached up to him, wanting him to join her in bed for yet another round of lovemaking. He almost did, too. It was so tempting. *She* was so tempting.

Instead he said he'd be back, quickly spoke the exit phrase, and the next thing he knew he was lying atop the cot in the real world, in his real house, staring up at his daughters.

"Something's wrong," he said, the moment he slipped the helmet off his head.

Rowan and Juniper looked at each other, and Juniper sighed.

"What?" he asked.

"Do you think we'll ever get this right?" asked Rowan, looking at her sister.

Juniper shrugged. "No clue, but all we can do is keep trying."

"What are you girls talking about?" Gable asked, standing up from the cot and letting the helmet fall from his fingers. "Get what right?"

"Her," said Rowan. "You. Everything."

"Your mother…that's not really her, is it?"

The pieces were starting to come together. Willow not remembering the first time they made love. Her long, blank stares. That wasn't really Willow, just some poorly created facsimile. But if that were true, where was she?

Juniper shook her head, staring at the floor. "It's as close as we could get. We gave them all your notes, everything, combined with what we knew, so if it's not accurate, well, that's on you, not us. No one ever told us that your first night of…being together…wasn't on your wedding day, and you didn't include it in your notes. That's not our fault."

Gable felt a shiver trail up his spine and the room almost seemed to spin before his eyes. Was this all a dream? A nightmare?

"It's always something, though, isn't it?" asked Rowan. "Last time it was the first meal you shared together. The time before, it was the fact that she wasn't supposed to like your favorite movie, *Ink*. Why didn't you tell us these things?"

"I don't understand what you're talking about!"

This time it was Rowan who sighed. "Dad…this is getting old. We can't be expected to know everything, especially about your sex life, of all things. Please don't put us through that again."

He felt like he was going insane. That flash of a memory about dating after Willow died. She died less than a month ago, he'd never dated anyone. Had he?

"Mom died almost ten years ago," said Juniper, "three years before SecondChance existed, so of course she couldn't be downloaded. She's gone. This is just an AI simulation of her. Two years ago, you read an article about SecondChance and got this idea in your head."

"An idea you just couldn't let go," added Rowan, "no matter how much we begged and pleaded. You obsessed about it and ended up writing nearly a thousand pages of notes about Mom, and then…"

"And then what?" Gable asked, his heart beating hard in his chest.

"You killed yourself, you son of a bitch," yelled Juniper. "You killed yourself and left behind all the pieces for us to put back together again."

Gable stumbled against the cot, reaching out a hand to steady himself. He'd committed suicide? But that was impossible. Wasn't it? Was he not real, either? He loved Willow with all his heart, but would he really kill himself over her?

"Oh, you're real, all right," Juniper said, as if reading his thoughts, "and you definitely killed yourself. It's legal to commit suicide now, if you're over a certain age or terminally ill, and hooked up to their fucking stupid machines. Your body is long gone, but your consciousness exists inside SecondChance, where it will reside until the end of time. Or something like that."

"Dad, you did this to yourself," said Rowan. "Losing Mom was so hard on all of us, but you became miserable, said you couldn't live without her, and so you sold the house, used every last dime to set up that contract with SecondChance, conned us into borrowing what you couldn't cover, and then killed yourself."

"That's not fair," Gable said, getting angry. "You don't know what it was like for me. That's not fair at all."

He felt like everything was spiraling out of control. He remembered it all now. After Willow died, he'd become bitter. He had missed her so damn much, so he did what he had to do to be with her again, at least as close as he was ever going to get. Why couldn't his daughters understand that?

He supposed Willow was his forbidden fruit, gone before she could be downloaded into SecondChance. But that fruit tasted so good, and he couldn't live without it. Without *her*. What choice did he have but to replicate the love of his life?

"I can't take even one more second of this, you selfish prick," said Juniper, tears rolling down her cheeks. "Computer, 76 Horatio melon 421 cinnamon onions 42, end simulation."

Gable looked around in horror as the house began to change, to fold away into nothingness. And then his hands vanished, followed by his arms, the girls, everything around him, and then—

✳✳✳

Rowan sat up from the cot, removing the helmet that connected her to SecondChance from her head. "You could have told me you were going to shut it down, you know. Now I'm going to have a massive headache."

They were in the tiny studio apartment they shared in New York City, the only thing they could afford after selling everything so Dad could live his dream.

"I'm sorry," said Juniper, sitting up beside her. "I just had to get out of there. How many more times are we going to go through this?"

"As many times as it takes to get it right. As much as a 'selfish prick' as he was, you know Mom would have wanted this for him."

Rowan was right. They'd run through this scenario five times so far, though, and each time Dad had figured out what was going on. She wished he'd been this smart in the real world.

"I'll message the Wheeler Dynamics tech and tell him about their nasty little sexcapade in her college dorm room," Juniper said. "You'd think with all those notes he took, Dad would have thought about that."

"And don't forget to tell them to fix the reading problem. I think that was the main thing that clued him in this time. I guess despite their promises, they haven't worked out all the kinks of a simulation within a simulation yet."

Juniper sighed and began writing the email.

Disconnections

Keelin Clarke had been through more than a few tornado warnings in her 23 years growing up in Northwest Arkansas and they'd never amounted to much of anything, so after a while she started ignoring them and just doing as she pleased. She hadn't expected this one to amount to anything, either, but in hindsight she should have realized she'd be wrong eventually.

She'd been walking the trail around Lake Atalanta in Rogers at just past four on a warm Spring afternoon when the tornado struck. One minute everything was fine, and the next it was drizzling rain, and then a moment after that the wind picked up dramatically and branches were being ripped off trees and slamming into the ground all around her.

"Oh, shit," she yelled, as she began to run for the parking lot.

A huge bolt of lightning hit a Bradford Pear tree right next to her, and for a second the entire sky lit up and she saw stars. Then the tree was collapsing, and she had to throw herself out of the way to avoid getting squashed. It landed on the trail she'd been walking just a few seconds before. The ground seemed to shake as the tree slammed into the dirt, and Keelin felt a branch slap into her back, nearly knocking her over.

Sirens sounded in the distance, warning the town of the tornado just in case there were any other idiots like her out here running for their cars. She finally reached the parking lot, and her car was the only car there, whereas an hour earlier there were at least five others.

She pressed the open button on her key fob, expecting the usual honk from her powder blue Kia Soul as it unlocked, but nothing happened. Still running, she pressed it again, and still no honk.

Keelin finally reached the car just as the rain began to pour down from the heavens. She pulled on the handle, and it was unlocked, so the key fob must have worked after all. The tornado and the clamor of thunder were nearly deafening, so maybe she just hadn't heard it. She opened the door and threw herself into the car, hurriedly put on her seatbelt, and pushed the key into the ignition, turning it, except it wouldn't turn. What the hell?

She glanced around the car. Something was wrong. Where was her light blue Stanley mug she always kept filled up with water, the one that almost exactly matched the color of her Soul? And where was the little blue cat plushie she always kept on the dashboard?

Had someone broken into her car and stolen those things? And why was there a Jack in the Box wrapper on the passenger seat? Rogers didn't even have a Jack in the Box. She'd never eaten anything from that restaurant or even stepped foot inside one. In fact, the closest Jack in the Box she knew about was in Tulsa, Oklahoma, which was probably at least a hundred miles away.

The car rocked and for a second she thought someone had crashed into her, but it was just the wind from the tornado. Jesus, it must be getting closer. She tried turning on the engine again, but nothing happened. Was she going to die here, at Lake Atalanta, trapped in her car, all because she'd ignored the weather forecast?

"Hey, what are you doing in my car?" yelled a man's voice from outside, startling her. "Get out of my car!"

She turned to see a blond-haired man probably about her age drenched in rain, staring through the window, his hands balled into fists as he pounded on the window.

His car? What was he talking about?

"This is my car!" she screamed, as she once again failed to start the engine.

"Jesus Christ, this is *my* car and there's a tornado out here, and I'm getting soaked! At least let me into my own damned car. Please!"

She stared into his eyes. Was this his car? Maybe that's why none of her stuff was in here, and the car wouldn't start with her key. If so, where was *her* blue Kia Soul?

She tried turning the key one more time but of course it didn't start. Making a decision, she hit the lock switch and unlocked the car. The man scurried around to the other side and jumped in.

"Here," he said, passing her a set of keys. "Let's move!"

She took the key and inserted it into the ignition, turned it, and was shocked when the car's engine came to life. What the hell was happening? She hurriedly backed up from the parking spot, eyes going wide when, a second later, an electric pole crashed into the area where the car had been just a few seconds ago.

"Shit, shit, shit, shit, shit!" she screamed, her heart racing.

"Drive!" screamed the man.

She quickly backed away from the broken pole, swerving around it, racing out of the parking lot, and turning onto North Lake Atalanta Road. There were downed tree limbs everywhere. She avoided what she could and just drove over what she couldn't, praying it wouldn't cause them to wreck.

"I'm sorry," she finally said. "Your car looks identical to mine. I wasn't trying to steal it, I swear, but apparently someone stole *my* car. I really don't understand what's going on."

"It's okay," he said, yelling over the tornado sirens, "just get us out of here. I'm Jeff, by the way. Jeff Clarke."

"Seriously? Clarke is also my last name. Keelin Clarke, and I'm confused as fuck right now."

"You and me both, Keelin."

The tornado sirens were starting to give her a headache, or maybe it was the howling wind all around her, doing its best to push her off the road. She stared straight ahead, focusing only on what was in front of her, ignoring everything else.

"So…where are we going?"

"Well, I live in Bentonville. How about you?"

"Rogers, in the Junction apartments off Walnut, kind of by Arby's. Can I drive myself there and then you can have your car back?"

"Sounds good to me."

"So, if you don't mind me asking," she said, a few minutes later, "why do you have a Jack in the Box wrapper in your car? There isn't a Jack in the Box around here I don't know about, is there?"

Jeff let out a nervous laugh. "I wish. I love their burgers. But no, I was in Tulsa last weekend visiting my sister. They have several Jack in the Boxes there."

Well, that was one mystery solved. At least she wasn't going completely batshit crazy.

Their car was the only car on the road, so at least she could drive fast. Before she knew it, she was on West Walnut Street, almost home. She roared past Arby's, turned on 45th street, and there it was—The Junction in Rogers—the apartment building where she lived with her big sister Melissa.

She'd made it home alive!

Keelin pulled into the parking lot, turned left, and…someone in a red SUV had stolen her assigned parking spot. Cursing, she drove over to the "visitors" section and parked there instead.

"Sorry again for the mix up," Keelin said, her hand on the door handle, "I really think someone must have stolen my car. That's the only thing that makes sense. Thanks for letting me use yours, and I hope you make it home in one piece."

"Oh, wow. I hope you're able to get it back. Anyway, it's not a problem, and I think I'll be fine. Be safe!"

She jumped out of Jeff's car and ran up the stairs, her hand never once leaving the railing, headed for her second-story apartment. The wind around her was howling now, or maybe that was the tornado sirens, she could no longer be sure.

Pulling her keys from her purse, she jammed them into the keyhole on the door, but just like her car keys earlier, they wouldn't turn. What was going on? She started slamming her fists against the door, praying Melissa was home, shouting, "let me in! Let me in!"

She felt a sudden gust of wind behind her, pushing her hard against the door, and she banged her forehead against the wood. For a moment she saw stars, and then the door was opening, and she stumbled into the apartment, falling to her knees.

"Goodness. Are you okay?" asked a voice she didn't recognize.

Keelin looked up into the faded blue eyes of a gray-haired old woman probably in her late sixties or early seventies. The woman maneuvered around her, shouldering the door closed against the pervasive winds.

"Who…who are you?" Keelin asked.

"Funny, I was about to ask you the same thing," said the woman, reaching her hand down towards Keelin.

Taking the woman's hand, she pulled herself to her feet. She glanced around the apartment. Everything was different. Gone were the paintings she and Melissa had created together at a craft workshop a year or so ago, replaced by a shelf filled with books and knickknacks. A couch still occupied the east wall, but it was gray instead of blue, and the television across from it looked smaller.

"This…this isn't my apartment, is it?"

"I'm afraid not," the old woman said, as the winds shrieked over their voices. "But I couldn't leave you out in that mess, could I? Now, come on. We need to get into the bathroom."

Keelin numbly followed the woman into the bathroom, the same bathroom where she'd taken a shower last night, but now it looked different. The shower curtain was a faded pink instead of the "Hello Kitty" one Melissa had insisted they use, and the rug in front of the toilet was pink instead of white.

"I don't understand," Keelin said, in a half-whisper. "This is apartment number 242, right?"

The old woman nodded. "It is indeed. I've lived here for three years, ever since the apartments were built."

Keelin thought she was going to cry. "I'm so confused. Melissa…she's my sister…we've lived here for a year and a half now."

"I don't know anyone named Melissa," the old woman said, shaking her head. "What's your name? I'm Audrey."

"I'm Keelin Clarke. This is the Junction in Rogers apartment complex, right? I didn't go to the wrong apartment building, did I?"

"Nice to meet you, Keelin. And yes, this is the Junction in Rogers apartment complex. Did you maybe hit your head and are a little dazed right now?"

Keelin blinked. She did indeed hit her head, but that was only after she got to the door of the apartment. Was she forgetting something? She didn't think so, but something was clearly wrong.

"I…I don't know," she said, starting to cry. "Someone stole my car, and now my apartment is no longer my apartment. I don't understand what's happening."

It was then that the lights went out.

"Oh, dear," said Audrey, through the darkness. "Electricity's gone. I figured that would happen sooner or later, but what awful timing."

Keelin laughed through her tears. "Timing is everything, isn't it?"

"It can be," Audrey said.

"Here," said Keelin, rooting around in her little purse for her phone. "Let me turn the flashlight on…oh no!"

"What is it?"

"My phone is dead. The battery must have died. I don't understand, it was at like over 60% less than an hour ago."

"That's okay," said Audrey, "I know my way around my own bathroom. Just hold tight."

A door creaked open, and then a moment later Audrey was pressing a handful of cloth into Keelin's hands.

"What's this?"

"I figure we can make little beds from these towels," said Audrey's voice through the darkness. "It looks like it might be a long night."

Stifling her tears as best she could, Keelin dropped to her knees and used the towels to create a makeshift pillow. Maybe this was all a bad dream and going to sleep would actually cause her to wake up and everything would be normal again.

She curled up into a ball and used her one remaining towel to cover herself, lying her head on the "pillow," knowing there was no way in hell she'd be able to fall asleep with all this anxiety swarming through her brain. She began to count backwards from one hundred, a trick Melissa taught her when they were both teenagers and Keelin was nervous about auditioning for a school play, and the next thing she knew she was drifting off to dreamland.

Keelin was in a house she'd never seen before, looking for her phone. Where had she put the darned thing? She wandered into a bedroom that wasn't hers, and…

"Wake up," said a far-off voice. "I think the tornado's over."

She opened her eyes, and an old woman was staring down at her. Audrey. So it hadn't been a dream, after all. The lights were back on in the bathroom, so the electricity must have come back on as well. Keelin scrambled to her feet, ignoring her aching neck and back.

She stared at herself in the huge bathroom mirror on the wall above the sink. Her long blonde hair was tangled, and her forehead had a huge, ugly bruise, probably from her headbutting the door while trying to get into the apartment.

"How long was I asleep?" Keelin asked, as she ran water into the sink and splashed it into her face.

"Maybe three hours," Audrey said, looking at a clock on the wall. "It's ten o'clock now. Darby said the tornados are gone, thank goodness."

"Darby?"

"You know, Darby Bybee, the 40/29 meteorologist guy."

Keelin wasn't a big TV watcher, instead choosing to spend most of her free time on the internet, but the name did sound familiar.

"And you said 'tornados?' There were more than one?"

"There were seven."

"Seven tornados? Jesus Christ. I'm amazed any of us are still alive."

"They're all gone now, though," Audrey said, "but Darby said the city is in ruins."

"Well, I'm glad they're gone, at least," said Keelin, her mind reeling. Seven tornados? It almost sounded like a horror movie.

"Now we just need to figure out where you need to be."

"Thanks so much for letting me stay here," Keelin said. "I'm sorry again for just showing up like that."

She followed Audrey out of the bathroom, down the hall, and into the living room. This all looked so familiar, other than the different furniture and decor. She shook her head. Could there be two "the Junction in Rogers" apartment buildings, both on 45th Street? It seemed implausible, to say the least, but that almost had to be the truth. Didn't it?

"I'm famished," Audrey said. "I have some leftover pizza from last night I could heat up. Would you like some?"

Keelin's stomach growled at the mere mention of food, so of course she said yes. Thirty minutes later, after they devoured the leftover Canadian bacon, mushrooms, and extra cheese pizza, Keelin once again thanked her for all she'd done for her.

"It was no trouble at all, and…you're welcome to stay the night, if you want. I do have a spare bedroom."

"Oh, no, I couldn't ask that."

"Nonsense, dear. You're not asking, I'm offering," said Audrey.

"Well, thank you, but I really need to get home to make sure my sister's all right. I do appreciate the offer, though."

"But how are you going to get home? You said someone stole your car."

"Walk, I guess," Keelin said. She hadn't really thought about that.

"Tell you what," Audrey said slowly, "you can borrow my car for the night if you promise to bring it back first thing in the morning."

Keelin stared at her. "Audrey, you don't even know me. Heck, I just realized I don't even know your last name. Are you sure you want to let me borrow your car?"

"It's Lang. Audrey Lang. And you just had your car stolen—you really need to report that, by the way. Anyway, I don't expect you'd steal my car after yours was just stolen, and if I'm somehow wrong about that, I'll just call the police. What's the worst that could happen?"

Keelin hugged the old woman, startling her. "Thank you! I promise you, I won't steal your car, and I'll bring it back first thing in the morning. I swear."

Audrey smiled and passed her a set of keys. "It's a big red Dodge Durango. Just press the key thingy and it'll beep so you'll know where it is. Be careful out there. We have no idea what condition the roads are in. Keep my car safe, but more importantly, keep yourself safe."

Keelin thanked the woman again, promised her she'd be back in the morning, and then scampered out the door, anxious to get home. She walked down the stairs and for the first time since she'd driven here this afternoon she took the time to look around.

Everything looked identical to her apartment building, right down to that stupid orange truck with the Punisher logo on the bumper that was always in the corner parking spot. What are the odds that there would be two of those trucks parked in the same space at different but identical apartments?

She shook her head and clicked Audrey's key fob, and the SUV in her parking spot beeped. Well, why not? They assigned the spots based on the apartment numbers, so it only makes sense that Audrey's assigned parking space would mirror her own.

She unlocked the SUV and slid into the driver's seat. This was so much larger than her Kia Soul that it was kind of intimidating. She shrugged, pressing the dashboard button to turn on the car and slowly backing out of the parking spot to drive to the apartment complex's exit.

There were branches everywhere, and one house just across the road from her had lost half its roof. Keelin shuddered. She wasn't looking forward to seeing whatever other damage Rogers had suffered, but she really needed to get home. Melissa must be worried sick.

She paused to retrieve her phone along with the USB-C charging cable she always kept in her purse and plugged it into the USB receptacle beneath the radio before turning onto 45th Street. And there was the Belk department store Melissa always shopped at, and just down the road the little Scottsdale shopping center that contained the Akin's Natural Foods store that they sometimes walked to.

What the hell? She knew there weren't any other Akins in Rogers, not to mention the Pet Smart or Staples that were on either side of the grocery store.

Come to think of it, as she'd driven out of the apartment complex she was pretty sure she'd seen the Reagan Elementary school down the road to the left, though it hadn't really registered at the time.

She felt like she might throw up. She pulled over into the parking lot beside Pet Smart, her heart nearly beating out of her chest. What was going on? Was she going insane, after all?

Keelin checked her phone. It was at 5%. Surely it would be okay to power it on. She hit the power button with shaking fingers, waiting for it to boot up, and then tried calling her sister. The call wouldn't go through, wouldn't even ring. The phone flashed the words "no service" at her.

She clicked the Facebook icon, but of course it didn't work either. She wasn't connected to anything. The tornados must have knocked over one of the cell towers or something. Well, hell.

Turning around in the parking lot, she headed back to the apartment building. Maybe she'd simply walked to the wrong apartment and Audrey had misheard her when she'd asked if she was in apartment 242. Yeah, that must be what happened. That was the most logical answer. Nothing else made sense. But that didn't explain why Audrey had her parking space.

Keelin parked the SUV, got out, and ran up the stairs to the apartment that in any logical universe was hers. It definitely said "242" on the door. She tried her house key again, and of course it didn't work. Keelin felt like she was losing her shit. She wished her damned phone worked. She desperately needed to hear Melissa's voice, to prove to herself that she was real and not someone who'd escaped from the looney bin or something.

The door to the apartment opened and she jumped back, her heart beating even faster now. It was Audrey.

"Well, this is a surprise," the old woman said. "Come on in."

"I don't understand what's going on," Keelin whispered, as she followed Audrey back into the apartment.

"What do you mean?"

"I mean, this is where I live. This very apartment. I walk to Akin's all the time. I live across from Reagan Elementary. You're even parked in my parking space."

"Are you sure you have the right building? You did hit your head, after all, and…well, maybe you're just confused?"

Keelin wanted to scream. Instead she grabbed her wallet from her purse and opened it to her driver's license. Her license said Keelin Rose Clarke and listed her address as the apartment in which they were currently standing. She showed the license to Audrey, and the old woman's eyes grew large.

"Oh, my. You definitely aren't confused, are you? This doesn't make any sense whatsoever and I wouldn't believe it if I didn't see it with my very own eyes. Can I maybe call someone for you? Your sister? She might know what's going on."

"I tried to call her earlier, but my phone wouldn't work. I think the service is out."

"And that's one of the reasons I kept my landline," Audrey said, smiling. "You can never trust new technology, not completely."

Keelin wanted to hug the old woman again. Audrey had a landline! She followed her over to a corner of the living room, which contained an end table upon which sat a clunky, old-fashioned phone. She rattled off Melissa's phone number and Audrey dialed the digits on the phone and held it up to her ear.

"I'm sorry for calling so late," Audrey said, "but I have your sister here. What? Is this Melissa? Well, can I speak to Melissa then? Oh, okay, I'm sorry for bothering you. Have a nice rest of your night."

Keelin felt faint. What was going on? "Are you sure you dialed the right number?"

"I'm pretty sure I did," she said, handing her the phone, "but you can try for yourself, just to make sure."

With the tiniest sliver of hope in her heart, she carefully dialed the number again. Someone picked it up on the first ring, but of course it wasn't Melissa.

"What's your problem, lady?" yelled a woman's voice on the other end. "I told you; there's no Melissa here."

"Who...who are you?" asked Keelin, her voice quavering.

"It doesn't matter who I am. Now stop calling me!"

The woman on the other end of the phone hung up, and Keelin began to cry. What was happening to her? Where was Melissa?

"It's okay, Keelin," Audrey said, reaching out to take her hand, pulling her into a hug. "Why don't you try to get some sleep, and we'll tackle this again in the morning?"

"I...are you sure you want some crazy girl in your apartment?" she asked, into Audrey's shoulder.

Audrey laughed. "I was a high school teacher at a little school in a tiny town in Illinois for nearly 25 years, and I saw a lot of crazy. I know crazy, and that's not you, sweetie. Besides, your driver's license is just like you said. But we'll figure all of this out in the morning. It's almost ten, well past my usual bedtime, and I bet you could also use some sleep."

"Okay. I mean, thank you. Thank you so much."

Keelin numbly followed Audrey into her guest bedroom, the same bedroom where Keelin usually slept, though of course none of her things were there. This was all so strange.

"I keep my little Dell laptop in here, over on that desk by the wall," Audrey said, pointing out a little brown desk. "Feel free to use it, maybe you can contact your sister on the Facebook or something."

She felt the urge to laugh at "the Facebook" but kept the laughter inside. "That's a good idea. Thanks."

"Oh, the pin number to get into the laptop is 4321," said the old woman, as she walked to the door. "Goodnight, Keelin."

"Goodnight to you, too, Audrey. And thanks again. I really do appreciate this."

Audrey nodded, closing the door on her way out. A few seconds later, after plugging in her phone to charge for the night, Keelin walked over to the desk, sat down, and powered on the laptop. After waiting for what felt like an eternity (but was probably less than two minutes) the login screen finally popped up. She entered the PIN, then searched for Google Chrome. Not finding it, she begrudgingly opened Microsoft Edge instead.

A few seconds later, she was on Facebook. She entered her email address and password, but it told her the email address she'd entered wasn't correct. She tried three more times with the same results.

Trying not to panic, she opened another tab and went to Gmail, but it also wouldn't recognize her credentials. She wanted to cry. Instead she created a new email—keelinclarke2001@gmail.com—and used that to sign up for a new Facebook account.

Once she'd verified her email, she searched for herself. Six or seven "Keelin Clarke" profiles showed up, but none of them were hers. Desperate, she searched for Melissa's account, breathing in a huge sigh of relief when it came up.

Except it listed her name as "Melissa Clarke Childs." What the absolute hell was going on? Had Melissa got married in the sixteen or so hours since she last saw her? Of course she hadn't, she wasn't even dating anyone, but the profile picture was definitely her sister.

She couldn't hold it in any longer. Tears began to stream down Keelin's face and the room seemed to spin before her. She was having a panic attack. She closed her eyes, took a deep breath, let it out and took another, and then three more, before telling herself that when she opened her eyes she'd be home and that all of this would have been a bad dream.

Keelin opened her eyes, and the Facebook profile of Melissa Clarke Childs was still there. What was happening to her? Did she no longer exist? She took another deep breath and clicked on Melissa's "about" info. It claimed she lived in Tulsa, Oklahoma, and was married to someone named Quincy Childs.

Someone or something seemed to be erasing her from reality. She decided to go to Amazon, because she was curious about something. She didn't seem to exist there either, so she had to make a brand-new account. She found a book of short stories she'd been wanting to read, *Hospital of Haunts*, and entered her Amazon Prime Visa card when checking out, but it said it wasn't a valid card. She tried her debit card and Discover card but got the same results.

She had a little over $30 in her wallet, but after that she'd be broke with no way to access the $1500 or so she had in the bank. She was immensely grateful that Audrey had taken her in tonight, but she doubted the woman would extend her stay. She was truly screwed.

Navigating back to Facebook, trying not to think about money, she typed in "Bliss Café," where she worked as an assistant manager, and held her breath. The page thankfully seemed to still exist. She let out her breath, and, scrolling through the posts, allowed herself a brief smile when she came across a photo of Matilda "Matty" Harper, a former employee who'd gone missing last year but had thankfully been found alive.

There were, however, no photos of Keelin. She saw almost all the employees she knew, and a few who somehow she didn't, and one who looked vaguely familiar, but nothing of her. Suddenly enraged, she slammed the laptop closed, not even bothering to turn it off.

Fuck this. She yanked off her shoes, her blue jeans, and her shirt, and then got into bed and under the covers. Keelin's shift at Bliss started tomorrow morning at ten—assuming the tornado hadn't destroyed the café, that is, and assuming she actually existed—and she fully intended to grab an Uber or ask Audrey to drop her off at Bliss so she could find out what the hell was happening.

She noticed an old-fashioned alarm clock on the bedstand table and set it for nine, just in case she didn't wake up earlier. Then she turned out the lights and began her usual backwards countdown from one hundred, doing her very best to force herself to go to sleep and hopefully awake tomorrow fully out of this nightmare.

Keelin was at Rosewood Cemetery, where her grandfather was buried. What was she doing here? She glanced around, and there was Melissa, their parents, some cousins, aunts and uncles, and Kya, her old college roommate.

"I miss her so much," Melissa said to Mom, who hugged her tight.

"What do you mean?" asked their father. "Miss who?"

Melissa looked confused. "I have no idea."

"What are we even doing here?" asked her mother. "Come on, let's go."

"No! Don't leave me!" screamed Keelin, but they either ignored her or couldn't see or hear her.

Keelin frantically looked around the cemetery. Her cousins, her aunts and uncles, and Kya were all gone. One by one, her parents and then her sister vanished as well, leaving only Keelin.

She dropped to the dirt and began to cry.

What was that awful sound? Keelin burrowed deeper under the covers, trying to cover her ears with her pillow, but she could still hear that obnoxious noise.

Her eyes snapped open. It was that damned ancient alarm clock. She reached blindly towards the nightstand, finally found the clock, and pressed the button on the top. Mercifully, it fell silent.

She had a bad dream last night, something about her not existing, but she couldn't quite remember it. Which was for the best, she instantly decided. She had enough weird shit going on without adding nightmares into the mix.

"Oh, my head," Keelin mumbled to herself, flinching with pain as she pressed the palm of her hand to the bruise on her forehead.

She shook her head and stretched, considered for a moment falling back to sleep, but then forced herself to sit up. Keelin looked around the room. Last night as she'd fallen asleep she half-expected to wake up in the morning back in her real room with everything having been a crazy dream, but of course that hadn't happened.

Keelin should have known better than to even hope for such a scenario. She was still in Audrey's house, in her guest room, and she still had no car nor, apparently, a sister.

Rolling out of bed, she quickly got into her jeans, put on her shirt, and slipped into her shoes. It was 9:04 in the morning. She had to be at work in less than an hour. She wasn't in the best shape, and was wearing the same clothes as yesterday, but they would have to do.

She snatched her phone from the bedstand, still plugged in. Pressing her fingerprint on the screen, she unlocked her phone and tried once again to navigate to Facebook, but AT&T's service was still out.

Walking over to the desk, she opened Audrey's laptop and used Microsoft Edge to once again go to Facebook so she could check out Bliss. There was a new post, which read, *Yes, we're open! Miraculously, the tornado missed us. Come on in and grab a small coffee, on the house!*

Keelin realized she'd half been hoping they were closed. She wasn't looking forward to going to work this morning, especially after everything that happened last night. Also, she still needed to contact the police to report her car as stolen.

She heard a little knock at the door, followed by Audrey saying, "Can I come in? Are you decent?"

Laughing to herself, Keelin walked to the door, opened it, and gestured for Audrey to enter. "I'm about as 'decent' as I'm going to get. Good morning."

"Good morning to you. I hope the bed was comfortable enough."

"It was great," said Keelin. "I was out like a light pretty much the moment by head hit the pillow. Thank you again for letting me stay here, by the way."

"It was no problem at all."

"I have one more favor to ask you," Keelin said, biting her lip. "I work at Bliss Café in downtown Rogers, and my shift starts at ten. If it isn't too much trouble, could you please drop me off at work? I promise I'll be out of your hair after that."

Audrey smiled. "Tell you what, why don't you just take the car again? I wasn't really planning on using it today anyway."

"Are you sure? I've already put you out so much."

"Nonsense. I trust you."

"Well, thank you."

"You're welcome. If you'd like, I can cook us up a little breakfast."

This woman was so sweet, but Keelin turned her down, saying she'd just grab something at the café. She wanted to get there early to deal with whatever craziness she might find.

It took forever to get through all the traffic and barricades as the city worked to repair what they could and move what they couldn't. She'd still be at Bliss early, but not as early as she would have liked.

The devastation from the tornado was awful. The Popeyes restaurant had been destroyed and the little shopping strip with the antique mall across the street had been all but obliterated. There was devastation all down Walnut Street, and Keelin realized how lucky she'd been getting out of Lake Atalanta alive.

Bliss Café had apparently been just as lucky. While the little bakery across the street was now missing its roof, Bliss had remained un-touched.

Keelin parked Audrey's car, pocketed the keys, and walked into the café. She was ten minutes early, but didn't care. She craved a little normalcy after last night. She'd been working at the coffee shop for almost two years, and if that didn't qualify as "normal" she wasn't sure what did.

Maggie Brass, the owner of Bliss Café, was standing behind the counter when Keelin walked in. Keelin smiled and waved at her, and Maggie smiled back.

There were maybe ten or eleven people in the café, mostly all sitting at a large table together. Sydney Mortimer, a girl who Keelin had met in college, was handing out small coffees from a rolling cart.

"I'm so glad Bliss survived the tornado," Keelin said, as she walked up to Maggie.

"You and me both," said Maggie, smiling. "Would you like a coffee?"

"No, thanks, at least not yet," Keelin said, maneuvering around her boss so she could head to the back to go grab one of the generic badges they kept there for the employees who'd misplaced or forgotten theirs along with one of the extra aprons.

"Excuse me, customers aren't allowed back there," said Maggie, stepping in front of her.

"What do you mean? I just need to get my stuff."

"What stuff?"

"I…forgot my badge and my apron. Sorry. It won't happen again."

"Are you okay?" Maggie asked, her eyes travelling to Keelin's forehead.

"Yeah, it's just a bruise, Mags. I'll be just fine."

Maggie stared at her. "Mags? Very few people call me 'Mags,' and I don't know you. How did you know that was my nickname?"

Chills traveled down Keelin's spine. "Don't know me? I've worked here for two years. Of course you know me."

"Is everything okay here?" asked Sydney, joining them at the register.

"Syd, you know me, right?" asked Keelin, tears blurring her vision.

"I'm afraid I don't, ma'am."

"I got you this job! How do you not know me?"

Every instinct in her told Keelin to run, to run fast and far away from here, but she forced herself to stand her ground. This was all just some elaborate prank. It had to be. Nothing else made sense.

"How could you have gotten me this job when I don't even know you?" asked Sydney, looking genuinely confused.

Keelin grabbed her by the shoulders and stared into her eyes. "What's wrong with me? Why don't you know me?"

"Get off her," yelled Maggie, grabbing Keelin by the arm and pulling her off Sydney. "You need to get out of here, now, before we have to call the police."

The entire café seemed to spin before Keelin's eyes. Was she dreaming? Was she dead, and this was some absurd form of hell? None of this made any sense. Her car had vanished, someone else lived in her apartment, her sister was married and living in Oklahoma, and her boss and co-worker didn't even know her.

"Please," whispered Keelin, staring into Maggie's eyes, "remember me. You have to remember me!"

All the customers at the large table were standing now, staring at her, and a couple of them had their phones out, probably preparing to take pictures to post on social media or maybe to call 911. She felt like she might pass out. This was all just some horrible nightmare. It had to be. Nothing else made sense.

"Keelin," said a man's voice off to the side, "what are you doing here?"

She spun on her heels, staring at Jeff Clarke, the man whose car she'd driven last night. He was wearing an apron and a badge that said, 'Hi, I'm Jeff, asst. manager at Bliss Café.'

"You know this woman?" asked Maggie.

"Well, 'know' is a stretch, but I met her at Lake Atalanta last night."

"She claims she works here."

Keelin was breathing hard, gasping for breath, her heart slamming against her ribcage. She was just a figment of everyone's imagination. She didn't exist. She'd never existed, and her entire life was a lie.

She pulled away from Maggie, ran past a startled Jeff, and out through the front door, sprinting past the little green bench that sat beside the entrance to the café. She slipped and nearly fell, but someone grabbed her, kept her from falling.

"Keelin, it's okay," whispered Jeff, turning her around to face him. He must have followed her outside. "We'll figure this out."

"I'm dead," she sobbed, "that must be it. I'm dead, and this is hell."

Jeff guided her over to the bench and helped her sit down. "You're not dead, and this isn't hell, though the tornados certainly made this town look that way. Now tell me what's going on."

She couldn't stop crying. Jeff pulled her into a hug, and she sobbed into his shoulder. "I don't seem to exist anymore," she said, when the tears finally subsided.

"Well, that's not true," he said, smiling. "You're sitting here right in front of me."

"My car is gone, my apartment is gone, my sister is married and doesn't live here anymore, and no one at the place I've worked at for almost two years knows who the hell I am. If that's existing, then maybe I don't want to exist anymore."

"Are you sure you don't, like, have amnesia or something like that, and think you're someone else?"

She wanted to scream. Instead, she fumbled in her purse and pulled out her wallet, like she'd done with Audrey, flipping it open to her driver's license. She took it out and handed it to him.

"I'm Keelin Rose Clarke, just like it says on my license. See? I live in apartment 242 at the Junction in Rogers. Except that apparently none of that is true."

Jeff stared at the license for a moment before handing it back to her. "You're definitely who you say you are, and your address matches up. Weird thing, though. In addition to having the same last name, we share the same birthday. September 23rd, 2003."

"That is weird. Same day, and the same year."

"Yeah. We're both 23."

"You know, I visited the Bliss page on Facebook last night," she said, "and I didn't realize it at the time, but I'm pretty sure I saw you."

"That would make sense, I've been working here for two years," he said, smiling.

On top of all the other weird shit going on in her life, she shared the same last name and birthday as this man she'd never met before. The same hair color, too, and the same shade of blue eyes. She wondered if they were related, somehow. This was all so confusing.

His first name also seemed familiar. And then she remembered her grandfather, who'd passed when she was a little girl, had been named Jeff. The hairs on her arms prickled. Her brain was trying to put all this together but wasn't quite there yet.

"My grandfather was also named Jeff," she said. "On my mother's side. Jeff Conroy."

His eyes grew wide. "That was my grandfather's name."

"And you have a sister named Melissa, don't you?"

"I do. How did you know that, though? We don't really even know each other."

"And if you'd been born a girl, they were going to name you Sarah, your father's mother's name. Right?"

"Yes, that's what they've said. Again, how do you know that?"

"Because if I'd been a boy, they were going to name me Jeffrey," Keelin said, finally starting to put it all together. "And I was almost Sarah, but an old friend of our parents, Keelin Masters, died in a car accident a month before I was born, and they decided to name me after her instead."

"You said 'our' parents. You think we're related, don't you? What, were we twins separated at birth or something? Our parents gave you up for adoption but kept me?"

She ignored his questions and instead asked one of her own. "Yesterday, at Lake Atalanta…you like to go wander the trails after work, don't you? To relax and de-stress. That's why you were out there."

"Yes, but how could you possibly know that? That makes absolutely no sense. Hell, none of this makes any sense."

"Welcome to my world," she said, laughing. "Though I guess you're the one who should be welcoming me to yours."

Her missing car, the apartment, her phone and credit cards not working, no one knowing her. It all made sense now, as much as any of this could possibly ever make sense.

"Welcoming you to my what?" Jeff asked, looking perplexed.

"Your world, silly. We're the same person, and I'm not supposed to be here."

Keelin and Jeff sat on the couch in Audrey's apartment, along with Audrey, eating ham and cheese sandwiches the old woman had made them for an early lunch. Jeff ended up claiming he'd gotten sick and skipping work (Maggie wasn't happy about that) and met her at Audrey's apartment. He seemed to believe her, mostly, but was just as dumbfounded by the whole thing as she was. Audrey, however, apparently had no problem with any of this.

"It actually all makes sense," she said, once they'd explained everything. "Somehow one of the tornados picked you up and brought you to our reality."

"Except it didn't," Keelin said.

She went through everything that happened at Lake Atalanta in ex-cruciating detail, going over it again and again until she thought her head would explode. The tornados had come nowhere near her, nor had she been struck by lightning, wandered through a glowing portal, or any of the other usual sci-fi tropes.

"There was something you said," Jeff said, "about lightning hitting a tree, and you thought you saw stars for a moment. I think that's when it happened."

She thought back to yesterday afternoon. She remembered the sky lighting up around her, and then for a second it was like she was staring up into the heavens even though she was definitely looking straight in front of her. All she could see for a moment were these little sparkles of light, which she thought of as stars, but what if they weren't stars at all? What if she really had stumbled through some sort of interdimensional doorway and wound up in a world where she'd been born a boy, and her sister was married to some guy in Tulsa?

Score one for the sci-fi tropes, after all.

"I think you might be right," she said slowly. "Everything was really bright for a second. I assumed it was the lightning, but…"

"Maybe it wasn't," Audrey finished for her.

"Yeah, maybe it wasn't."

"The real question," said Jeff, "is how do we get you back to your reality?"

"I think we need to go to Lake Atalanta," Audrey said, and Jeff nod-ded. "If there's a way, that's where we'll find it."

"If I do get home, somehow, everyone will think I'm crazy. I wonder if I'll manage to convince myself I hallucinated all of this and made the two of you up in my head? Because certainly no one will believe me. Hell, I barely believe it myself."

"You're definitely not crazy," said Jeff. "Either that, or Audrey and I are crazy, too."

"I'm sorry I roped you two into this."

"Are you kidding?" asked Jeff. "How could I *not* help you? You're essentially me. Well, with lady parts, but still."

Audrey snort-laughed at that, while Keelin just rolled her eyes and smiled.

"As for me," Audrey added, "this is the most interesting thing that's happened to me since I moved to Arkansas fifteen years ago. Keelin, if we can get you back to where you belong, we're going to do it."

Keelin felt like crying. If she could somehow get back to her own reality, and that was a huge "if," she was really going to miss these two. But she had to do it. This wasn't her life, and she missed Melissa, her parents, and everyone else she knew, even her boss Maggie.

She needed to go home.

They stood in the parking lot at Lake Atalanta, where less than 24 hours ago the tornados had struck. There were branches and debris everywhere, not to mention electrical posts. It was a huge mess.

"This whole thing makes so me sad," said Audrey, as she and Jeff followed Keelin through the parking lot towards the trails.

"Tell me about it," Jeff said. "It'll take years to get things back to how they were before the tornados, and we'll never get everything back, not fully. That little antique store on Walnut, for example. It's just gone."

Keelin wondered how her reality had fared. Probably not much better, and possibly worse. She hoped she would get the chance to find out.

"Okay, here's the start of the trail I was on," she said, walking past a huge clump of tree roots that had been ripped up from the ground, ducking to avoid a lone yellow butterfly flying past her head. "And over there, through that broken bunch of trees, is where I think—I *think*—I was when the Bradford Pear tree almost fell on me. Close to where the lightning struck, and I saw stars."

"I don't see anything," said Jeff, walking over towards the felled Bradford Pear. "I was kind of expecting to find some shimmering portal or something. I'm not sure why I thought it would be so easy."

Keelin felt like crying again, but she was out of tears. She was never going to see her sister again, nor her parents, or anyone else she'd known and loved in her home reality. She had no money and no place to live and no way to even get a new job, not without a valid driver's license or social security card or any of the other things that had been taken away from her.

"You can stay with me as long as you need to," said Audrey, surprising her. "We'll get this figured out."

"Thank you. I may just have to take you up on that," she said, turning to smile at her, touched by the woman's generosity.

"I think—" said Jeff.

"Think what?" Keelin asked, turning back around, but Jeff was no longer there.

"Oh my God," said Audrey. "He just…he was there one second, and then he just…he just up and vanished."

"What?"

"He was standing over next to that downed Bradford Pear tree, and then…he was gone. Just…gone."

"Like walked deeper into the woods or something?"

"No, Keelin. He just vanished, right in front of my eyes. There one moment and gone the next."

Keelin's heart was racing. Had he been shuttled off into her universe somehow? She ran over to where he'd been standing, waving her hands in the air, searching for him as if he were somehow still there but invisible, but nothing happened. He was gone.

"Oh, Jeff," she said, tears running down her cheeks. "I'm so sorry."

And then she felt something, a sort of pull in her chest, but nothing was touching her. She waved her hands in the air again, and now she felt the tug in her fingers, then her arms, and finally her whole body.

"Keelin?" asked Audrey, walking up to her. "What's happening?"

"I don't know," she said, the pull almost unbearable now, "but I think I might be going home."

She took a step forward, and...

Jeff was there, staring at her, but Audrey was gone.

"Holy shit," said Jeff, his face white as a sheet.

"Yeah, holy shit. I think I'm home now. But you're here," Keelin said, breathless

"I don't think for much longer," he said, moving towards her. "I think there's something here, something where you're standing. It almost feels like a little crackling cloud of static electricity, and it's pulling at me, just like it did before it zapped me here."

"That same pull I felt just a few seconds ago," she said. "I think whatever this is grabbed the wrong person, and now it's trying to make things right."

"I'm so glad I got to meet you, Keelin," Jeff said, reaching out for her hand. "My twin sister, of sorts."

"Complete with lady parts," she said, and they both laughed. "I'm so glad I got to meet you too, Jeff. The brother I never had. I'll miss you."

"I'll miss you, too," Jeff said, pressing something into her hand before pulling her in for one final hug, "Don't forget me, okay?"

"I never could. And who knows? Maybe we'll see each other again someday."

They were holding each other tight, and the next moment he was gone. There one second and gone the next. Just like that.

She opened her hand. It was his work badge. 'Hi, I'm Jeff, asst. manager at Bliss Café.' His way of making sure she didn't convince herself that none of this had really happened. She smiled and slipped the badge into her purse.

Keelin walked away from the downed tree, stepping over broken branches towards the parking lot. And there it was. Her beautiful little powder blue Kia Soul, cleaved nearly in half by the electrical pole that narrowly missed her in that other reality.

She pulled out her phone, already knowing what she'd find. She was right. The phone was once again at 0% battery. Whatever force had shuttled her back and forth between realities had also drained her phone.

"I don't want to believe she's gone, but…oh my God!" said a voice from behind her.

She turned around. It was Melissa, along with her parents, and they were staring at her like they'd seen a ghost. And then Melissa was running towards her, throwing her arms around her, hugging her so tight it almost hurt.

"It's okay," she said, hugging her back, "I'm here now, and I'm safe."

Her parents joined them, hugging her, crying tears of joy, and then she was crying, too. She was back with her family again, the family who she'd grown up with and who truly knew her, and she thought her heart would burst with joy.

"With your car like that, we thought…we thought you were dead," sobbed Keelin's mother.

"We're so happy you're okay," said her father.

"Where have you been?" asked Melissa, staring into her little sister's eyes. "How did you escape the tornados?"

"You're not gonna believe me at first," said Keelin, smiling, as she reached into her purse to retrieve Jeff's name badge, "but, boy oh boy, do I have a story for you."

Bliss

CAFÉ

484 SERLING ST.
ROGERS, AR

Afterword

All of the preceding stories are connected to at least one other story in the collection in some way or another. Some are obvious (Connections and Disconnections, for example) but others much less so. Can you find the connections? Please write me at joe@joederouen.com when you find them! (or, heck, even if you don't find them)

Be sure to sign up for my newsletter! bit.ly/3DB6MES

About the Author

Joe was born in Carthage, Illinois, and currently lives in Rogers, Arkansas with his wife Andee, their son Fletcher, and their cats Archer, Biscuit, Frosty, Weiss, Grilled Cheese, and Eclipse. In addition to being an award-winning author, Joe is a substitute teacher and website designer. He collects all sorts of things, including Mego action figures, books, and Bicycle playing cards. When not writing, you can probably find Joe playing City of Heroes: Homecoming on his PC or Stardew Valley and Pokemon Go on his phone. Connect with Joe at JoeDeRouen.com.